To the Great Army

To the Great Army

N. L. Collier

Copyright © 2020 N. L. Collier
The moral right of the author has been asserted.

Apart from any fair dealing for the purposes of research or private study, or criticism or review, as permitted under the Copyright, Designs and Patents Act 1988, this publication may only be reproduced, stored or transmitted, in any form or by any means, with the prior permission in writing of the publishers, or in the case of reprographic reproduction in accordance with the terms of licences issued by the Copyright Licensing Agency. Enquiries concerning reproduction outside those terms should be sent to the publishers.

This is a work of fiction. Names, characters, businesses, places, events and incidents are either the products of the author's imagination or used in a fictitious manner. Any resemblance to actual persons, living or dead, or actual events is purely coincidental.

Matador
9 Priory Business Park,
Wistow Road, Kibworth Beauchamp,
Leicestershire. LE8 0RX
Tel: 0116 279 2299
Email: books@troubador.co.uk
Web: www.troubador.co.uk/matador
Twitter: @matadorbooks

ISBN 978 1838594 541

British Library Cataloguing in Publication Data.
A catalogue record for this book is available from the British Library.

Printed and bound in Great Britain by 4edge Limited
Typeset in 11.5pt Aldine401 BT by Troubador Publishing Ltd, Leicester, UK

Matador is an imprint of Troubador Publishing Ltd

"For all flesh is as grass, and all the glory of man is as the flowers of the grass…" (Brahms, A German Requiem)
To the fallen of the Great War

„Denn alles Fleisch es ist wie Gras, und alle Herrlichkeit des Menschen wie des Grases Blumen…" (Brahms, Ein deutsches Requiem)
Den Gefallenen des Großen Krieges

I

The LVG and I pottered westwards, past Hannover and on over a peaceful, wintry Germany. From up there you could forget that the country was being slowly strangled, that so many of its young men were lying in the earth.

It's as well I set off early – six hours' flying plus a stop for fuel will take most of the daylight. If the headwind's not too strong I can make it all the way to our airfield, but I don't want the setting sun in my eyes for the last few kilometres. I'll be very near the Front by then, and if I get jumped by a flight of Camels I'm dead. The LVG's a lumbering donkey compared to my Fokker Triplane.

That reminded me just how vulnerable two-seaters were – and my haversack was hardly a replacement for good old Burkhardt and a Parabellum.

It's ages since I even thought about Burkhardt. I saw him dying again, held his hand as I tried to work out what he wanted to say. *If only I could have got him on the ground sooner.*

You can't bring the dead back to life, Franz. Just make sure you don't join them – and stop daydreaming and think about the flight…

The direct route from Berlin to Belgium lay over neutral Holland, and I was very tempted to take it.

If I have engine failure over Holland, I'll be interned and my war will be over. I don't even have to have a real problem. I could just land, and I'd never have to fight again.

I knew it wasn't the right answer. It would save my life – or rather, postpone my death – but I wouldn't be able to look in the mirror. *Karl wouldn't do it. I'd never be able to look him in the eye again. And what about Otto and Horstmann and the Chief? They have to continue fighting – and so do I.*

I'll go via Cologne. That'll remove the temptation, and it'll save me having to land there if I have a genuine problem. I don't actually want to be interned anyway. I'll finish the war whole, or in hospital, or in a box, not in some bloody Dutch prison.

The slow journey gave me far too much time to think. I had to pay some attention to navigation, but once I'd got the correct drift applied and seen how the time was working out, that wasn't complicated. It was only too easy to start having gloomy thoughts, never seeing Karl again being the worst one.

I want to see your face, hear your voice, and lie in your arms again, just one more time before I die.

Tomorrow I'll be back in the sky over the trenches. Tomorrow the killing starts again. I wonder if my fear will show. The morning's not the problem – everyone's scared then. Everyone looks pale as the eastern sky turns violet. The problem's the quiet times, when I just start shaking.

My right foot juddered on the rudder bar. *I'm frozen,* I thought, as indeed I was after three hours of winter flying – but it was the usual cold from deep inside, that came with nausea, sweating, and a racing pulse.

Please God, don't let me end up like Widemayer. I could see him cowering against the wall, muttering. That was worse than burned bodies, worse than Karl lying on the stretcher with his dazed eyes and bloody mouth…

Stop. You must stop, or you'll go mad. But I couldn't. I wanted to forget, to not care, but I knew that if I ever did I would have lost my humanity.

A hot meal and a few cigarettes at Cologne sent my blood trudging round again. My feet ached as the circulation returned, and I wanted to stay on the ground long enough to get warm again, but I had to get going. The sun was already past its zenith.

I left Aachen just on my right, flying south of the town and setting course over Belgium. *How we all cheered in '14 as we crossed the German border, on our way to war. Of the five of us who volunteered together, I'm the only one still unharmed. Kurt and Anton are dead, Otto and Karl have both been wounded, Karl twice, and only Franz Becker still has a whole skin – if not a whole mind.*

I wonder how many of the young men on that train are still alive. So many were dead before the end of '14. They didn't realise, when they volunteered in those heady August days, that they had so little life remaining. And if they had realised they would still have gone, believing that a hero's death was the most beautiful of all.

I'd believed that too, until I saw Anton by the light of the flare, and asked myself what was beautiful about being mutilated and screaming for hour after hour, until exhaustion put an end to it.

I didn't want to imagine what that must feel like.

The last half-hour of the flight was torture. I was so cold I could hardly think, and I was well within the range of enemy patrols. *If they see me, I'm dead. It's as simple as that.*

I saw the sugar factory and our airfield with immense relief. The LVG tried to swing after landing and my numb feet were crude and awkward on the rudder bar, but I managed to keep more or less straight. As I neared the hangars, Zaffke and Braun came out with chocks. The silence when I shut the engine down was colossal, and my ears rang. There was no sign of Uhlig, but then he wouldn't have known it was me.

I was so frozen I could hardly get out.

"Welcome back, sir," said Braun. "Didn't realise it was you!"

"Incognito! Just as well the crosses are nice and large, or you'd both have been on the machine gun!"

"Of course, sir," Zaffke replied with a grin.

"Leutnant von Leussow sends his regards," I said to him, "and he signed the portrait and sent it to your home."

"Oh – that was most kind of him. May I ask how he is, sir?"

"Not well at all – but then he's lucky to be alive."

"Can we expect him back?" asked Braun.

I shook my head. "I very much doubt it."

"Well, sir, if you ask me he's earned a rest," said Zaffke.

"I agree."

The squadron was flying. The only aircraft in the hangar was Horstmann's Triplane, and Schiffer and Kessler were patching holes in the lower wing. *Far too many. Bugger's getting careless.*

"Leutnant Horstmann borrowed your aircraft, sir," said Braun.

"Fair enough."

I unpacked with a profound feeling of depression, which the room did nothing to lift. It was so spartanly functional that it made Karl's house look luxurious. I gazed gloomily at the wooden walls, decorated only with photographs of naked women.

It'll be better when they come back. But of course I didn't know who would come back. The lovely Susanne waited patiently on Horstmann's bedside table, and I hoped she wouldn't be disappointed.

Be good to have a photograph on my table – but of whom? I've still got Maria's picture in my wallet, but God knows why I bother. I'm never likely to hear from her again. I'd feel so much better with Karl's calm eyes looking at me – but that's stupid. No one puts his best mate's photo by his bed.

Stop moping, Franz. Go to the main hut and say hello to Fellmann – and have a stiff drink. The light's starting to fade and they'll be back soon.

"Welcome back, sir," said Möller as I entered the Ops Office.

"Thanks."

Fellmann looked up. "Becker! Just in time to help me with the spares order!"

"Cheers, bastard! I'm not doing that without a brandy – I'm still bloody frozen."

He gave me a puzzled look. "How did you… ah, that was you in the two-seater!"

"That's right – we've got it as a runabout."

"Good idea – pity Claudette's doesn't have a landing strip! Möller, get us three brandies, would you?"

"Yes, sir."

While he was out of the room, Fellmann said quietly, "So how's Karl?"

"Pretty bad still – I mean, he's healed up but he's – well… rather frail."

Fellmann's face wrinkled in sympathy. "Not a word I'd ever associate with him."

"No, quite."

Möller came back, and Bleif followed with the brandies.

"Right, let's get this done and then you can tell me all about the aircraft trials," said Fellmann.

Five minutes later we heard engines and went to the window. Nine Triplanes broke formation overhead the field.

I looked at Fellmann.

"Brockmann crashed last week," he said. "Spun off his final turn. His replacement should be here tomorrow."

"Ah."

Bastard to have survived the trenches and then crash – but then he wasn't very experienced. At least it was quick.

We finished the spares order and headed for the mess. Boots rang on the wooden steps, accompanied by voices and laughter.

The door flew open.

"Hey, it's Becker! Back from rogering every woman in Berlin!" Horstmann was in high spirits. "While you've been away, I've been catching you up! Just got number six! So watch out!"

"You won't catch me," I said cheerfully. "I'm miles ahead of you, and I'm back now. Did you bring my Triplane back in one piece, or is she a flying colander like your own?"

"She took a couple of hits, but they'll be patched by tomorrow. You can have your favourite steed back."

"Oh, good." *I hope that sounded convincing…*

Otto limped in. "Franz! Back from careless copulation in the capital? From frolics and fornication in the fleshpots? From dipping your wick in delicious women?"

I was laughing. We all were.

"Well, did you give them all one for all of us?" Horstmann demanded.

"Not for *all* of you. I was only there a week, for Christ's sake."

Horstmann shook his head. "Fellow's got no stamina. Terribly sad, really."

"I did all right, thank you."

"You did get a bit, then," said Bretti. "I was worried for a moment there."

"Am I smiling?"

One of the faces is new – of course, Böhle got shot down just before my leave. Bad of me to have forgotten.

The new fellow looked horribly young, and was staring at me.

"Aren't you going to introduce us?" I said to Horstmann.

"Sorry – forgot you hadn't met. This is Langer, who's been with us just over a fortnight."

We shook hands. *No need to be quite so starry-eyed*, I thought, feeling about a century old.

"Bleif! Champagne!" shouted Horstmann. Then he gave me a suddenly serious look. "I suppose your being back means I have to hand over command."

"'Fraid so. Shall we get it done now while we're sober?"

We headed for the Chief's office. It was rather colder than the mess.

"Not much point having the stove going when I've not been in here much," he said.

"So how have you enjoyed it?"

"More than I thought I would. I didn't realise how much paperwork there is, though – thank God Fellmann knows his way around all that."

"Yes – amazing how much technical stuff he knows as well."

Horstmann laughed. "That's for sure – it's been an education! Anyway, as you may have heard, we lost Brockmann, which is a right bastard as he was a good bloke, and Bretti's doing very well. Beilke and Teuffel have got one more each. And that's about it, really. Everything's in the squadron diary."

"Quiet three weeks, then!"

He gazed at his hands for a moment, and when he looked up the twitch was there at the corner of his eye. "I just hope they've come up with a decent aircraft, because frankly I don't know how the rest of us are still here."

"They just might have done. Look, let's go back into the mess and I'll tell everyone at the same time."

"Certainly, Squadron Commander, sir!"

"Piss-taking bastard!"

The mess was quite warm, and, with another brandy and a fag, I started to thaw out a bit.

"So tell us about the aircraft trials," said Benner.

"Well, keep your fingers crossed, because Fokker have come up with something rather good." I told them about the V11.

"So will it stay in one piece?" asked Beilke.

"Does anything?" said Otto with a sigh.

"We all turned the thing inside out," I said, "and there were no signs of any problems."

"I'll believe that when I see it," said Teuffel.

"Ye of little faith," retorted Fellmann. "Any aircraft will break if you stress it hard enough."

"True… but I'd like something that'll hold together when we meet the Tommies," Eichner said.

"Did you say in-line engine?" asked Benner.

"Yes."

"Won't that give us a problem against those fucking Camels?" said Beilke.

"It's fast," I said, "and it's got a good rate of climb and good high-altitude performance. We can't have everything."

"In-lines will be easier to maintain, and more reliable," said Fellmann.

"Yes, but we're just going to get out-turned again, like in the Albatros," Horstmann grumbled.

"If it's fast then we can hit and scarper, and those Camel bastards won't have time to turn," said Bretti.

The debate continued after dinner. I left them to it for a few minutes, went to my room and fetched the cigars.

"These are a present from Karl," I said, putting them on the dining table. "They belonged to his father."

"That's bloody decent of him," said Horstmann, sniffing one with appreciation.

"Well, he can't smoke them himself," I replied.

"What – Karl's not smoking? That's unimaginable!" Otto said.

I laughed. "Yes, it was rather strange."

"So how is he?" asked Bretti.

"As well as a fellow's likely to be after that." I really didn't want to say any more, and only half of them knew him anyway.

"What happened to him?" asked Benner.

"Got shot through the chest," I said.

"Fucking hell – how'd he manage to land?"

"Badly!" Fellmann said cheerfully. "We've still got some of the spares."

"And what the fuck use are Albatros spares?" demanded Horstmann.

"You never know…"

I kept drinking in the hope that I would sleep. Yes, I'd feel like crap in the dawn, but then I would anyway.

Late in the evening, Otto came and sat beside me. "So how is Karl really?" he asked.

I took a long drag on my cigarette. "Well, he won't be coming back. He can hardly climb the stairs. I thought he'd be a lot better than that and it was quite a shock."

"So that's one of us who'll make it through."

"Given up on 'after the war', have you, then?"

He laughed, but before he could reply Bretti joined us.

"Becker, thank you so much for letting me have Christmas," he said. "I didn't know until after you'd gone."

"No problem – the Chief wanted to send me to Adlershof and I wanted to see Karl."

"How is he?"

"Out of the war, I reckon."

"Good."

And then Eichner asked me, and when we got to our room Horstmann said, "So how's Karl?"

Pitifully thin, gets so out of breath just walking slowly, and the house feels so empty and haunted…

I didn't want to talk about him any more, and I just repeated what I'd said to Bretti.

"Good thing, too," said Horstmann. "He's done more than enough."

I lay staring at the ceiling in the darkness, wishing I could sleep and, most of all, that I were still with Karl in Brandenburg.

Ten seconds later, Schiffer knocked with the shaving water. My stomach turned over with a horrible jolt as I woke fully and realised where I was.

I forced myself out of bed. *I really don't want to do this...* My hands shook so much that I cut myself shaving, and then almost spilled my coffee.

The whole squadron was going up with Horstmann leading, at my suggestion. Three weeks away was a long time.

My nerves vanished as the wheels left the ground, only to return tenfold when Eichner spotted a flight of SE5s. I was certain I could smell petrol, and my breakfast rose in my throat.

Stupid bastard. There's no way you can smell anything through a balaclava and a scarf. It's all in your mind. And half the reason you're shaking is because it's so fucking cold.

Yes, and the other half is because I'm so fucking scared.

What matters is how you behave when you're scared...

We had the advantage of height. Horstmann signalled to me to attack with Langer, Teuffel and Schulte.

As I half-rolled into the dive the fear evaporated, and I was suddenly completely calm and focussed. They scattered to meet us and I was on their leader's tail in a flash. He was sharp but I had the better rate of turn – but three weeks *was* a long time away and although the tracer went into his fuselage I couldn't manage to hit him, and after a couple of bursts I had to break off because a flight of Camels had joined the fray, along with the rest of the Jasta.

Bretti hurtled past my nose, pursued by an SE5, and I turned in behind it. The stupid sod didn't look round, and I got in nice and close – and once again couldn't hit anything that mattered. And of course one of his friends was trying to get on my tail.

A Camel left the fight in haste, trailing smoke, and Langer went spinning down. I couldn't watch to see if he pulled out – I was far too busy trying to fend off two Camels at once – then Horstmann joined me and the four of us had a merry dance.

Suddenly we were on our own. The Camels headed west and we chased them, while the SE5s buggered off to the south. After a few minutes we let the Camels go and turned east. I was suddenly aware of the frigid air pouring into the cockpit, chilling me to the bone.

We had another hot fight that left me soaked with sweat, and by the time we got back to the airfield I was so cold I thought I'd never be warm again. The temperature on the ground was below freezing, and the grass crunched under my boots as I shivered my way towards the huts.

"Poor little Langer," Teuffel said. "Only been here five minutes."

That's always the way.

"Since you were leading, would you like to debrief?" I said to Horstmann.

"Thanks."

He kept it short, thank God. I was in dire need of dry underwear and a dry shirt.

Our room was freezing and we changed hurriedly.

"Amazing how much we sweat when it's so fucking cold," Horstmann said. "I just hope this lot's dry when I need to wear it again."

"You and me both."

After second breakfast, I borrowed Zaffke's rifle and went to practise my circles. Bretti came with me.

"Loser buys the winner a bottle of fizz?" he suggested.

"You're on."

Ten minutes later I wished I hadn't taken the bet.

"Not bad," I said. What I meant was 'bloody good', but I wasn't about to say that. Not to Bretti.

"Karl gave me a few tips," he said with a grin.

He did me as well, but to lesser effect. "Point is, you were able to act on them. Fizz is clearly on me!"

The next day it snowed, and I lay in bed postponing the evil moment of getting up for as long as I could.

"If I weren't so bloody hungry I'd stay here all day," Horstmann said.

"You and me both. That was quite a wake."

He sighed. "Let's hope his replacement lasts a bit longer."

Bleif had got the mess stove belting out heat, and it was actually quite pleasant in there. By lunchtime it was obvious that flying was off, and our lazy day was interrupted only by the arrival of a lanky fellow called Sobek, who had tarnished epaulettes and a dented pilot's badge.

"How the fuck did you get here in this weather?" asked Teuffel.

"Got a lift – artillery wagon dropped me near the sugar factory."

"Do excuse our comrade's lack of manners, and welcome to the Jasta," I said, and made the introductions.

"Another new room-mate," Benner said. "You don't want to share with me – none of them's lasted five minutes!"

"Death is better than listening to your snoring!" said Schulte.

"That bad?" Sobek said. "You should have heard my old observer – used to make the windows rattle!"

"How long were you on two-seaters?" asked Bretti.

"Too fucking long."

He turned out to be a cheerful, friendly fellow with a good hard head. By midnight no one was feeling any pain at all, and it was a shock to see the stars when we finally headed for bed.

"Tell me I'm seeing things," said Otto.

"'Fraid not," Beilke slurred. "Thash O… Orion."

"Fuck Orion," said Teuffel.

Otto laughed. "Like to see you try!"

I didn't need to put schnapps in my coffee before the dawn flight – I was still quite well awash.

The appalling cold at altitude blew the last of the booze clean into Holland. *Maybe we should market this as a hangover cure… Not sure anyone would buy it, though.*

My duff luck continued – by the time the Chief was due back I still hadn't added to my score, to my intense frustration. Bretti managed to get a two-seater, and Teuffel was certain he'd sent a Camel down out of control, but Fellmann couldn't get anyone to confirm it.

"World's going to the dogs," Teuffel grumbled. "A gentleman's word should be good enough."

"Agreed," said Horstmann, "but we don't have time to watch them all the way down, do we?"

"Suppose not."

Fellmann put his head round the door. "I'm just off to the station to fetch the Chief, so by the time you all get back he should be here."

If we all get back, I thought as we suited up. Sobek had done well in his mock combats the day before and he was to fly on my right wing.

He did far better than I'd expected. I was actually quite impressed, but was careful not to say so. He knew it hadn't gone badly, though. *Tricky, isn't it – you need just the right amount of confidence. Too much is even more dangerous than too little.*

"Don't forget there are plenty like the Chief on the other side," I said to him.

"Don't worry, sir – I know what you mean."

"Talking of the Chief, where is he?" asked Beilke.

"Good question. They must have been held up somewhere."

They still hadn't arrived by dinner time.

"Excuse me, sir," Bleif asked me, "but should I serve dinner?"

"Yes, do. We don't know how much longer they'll be."

We were on the pudding when we heard the car draw up. Two minutes later we all stood as the Chief and Fellmann entered the mess, accompanied by a youth dressed as a pilot.

"Welcome home, sir," I said, echoed by the others.

"Thank you," said the boss with a warm smile. "This is War Volunteer Weber, joining us from the Fighter Pilot School at Valenciennes."

Christ.

"Better get him to Claudette's tomorrow," Otto muttered in my ear.

The boy was obviously ravenous and cleaned his plate in no time.

"Would you like some more?" Fellmann offered.

"If there is some, yes, please." He gave Fellmann a cautious smile. I daren't catch Horstmann's eye.

"Did anything else come out of the trials, sir?" I asked the Chief.

"Yes. In fact I've got a couple of announcements to make." He stood up and rapped on the table. "Gentlemen, I have some news for you. I take it Becker told you about the Fokker V11?"

There was a murmur of assent.

"Well, Fokker's got the contract to build them, with the improvements that we all recommended, and it'll be designated the DVII. The first ones will go to Richthofen's outfit, of course, but we're optimistic about getting a couple fairly soon. It's a damned good aircraft and I'm sure you'll all like it. The second piece of news is that we're to be issued with parachutes."

It took me a moment to realise what he'd said. *Parachutes. He really said 'parachutes'. I don't have to burn, or crash if I'm too badly hit to fly.* A huge weight lifted off me, and I suddenly realised how heavy it had been.

The faces round the table showed the same profound relief. We'd been given a chance of avoiding a horrible death.

Horstmann was the first to recover the power of speech. "When... er, when will they be here?"

The Chief smiled. "They already are. That's why we were so late – we made a detour and collected one for each of us."

My hands started shaking uncontrollably, and quite absurdly.

"So we can use them tomorrow?" asked Beilke.

"That's right."

"Jesus fucking Christ," said Teuffel.

Benner gave the only adequate response. "Bleif! Champagne for us all, on me!"

"On the Kaiser," said the Chief.

You're just as relieved as we are. I remembered the flicker of fear in his eyes, the day I'd got soaked in petrol – and then I remembered that his wife was pregnant.

"That's the best excuse for a party we've had in a long while," Bretti said later. We were all well lubricated by then, and Weber was looking rather green. Five minutes later he rushed out into the night, pursued by cheers from us all. It was a while before we realised he hadn't come back.

"I expect he's gone to bed," said Schulte. "That's what I did the first time you bastards got me pissed!"

"Not that you took much persuading," Bretti retorted. "I think I'll just go and check."

"Very conscientious, young Leutnant Bretti," said Beilke.

Eichner put the Liesl song on the gramophone, and we were in the middle of the verse where Liesl was... never mind what, when Bretti burst in with a gust of cold air.

"Come and give me a hand, you boozy lot!" he shouted.

"What for?" demanded Otto. "Liesl's just about to—"

"Sod Liesl," Bretti said impatiently. "I need a hand with Weber."

"Oh, we all want to sod Liesl!" Eichner said with a laugh, and took the needle off the record.

"Isn't he in bed, then?" asked Schulte.

"Only if you call the mud 'bed'."

"We did in the infantry," said Otto.

"Much you know about that!" Horstmann retorted.

"Will you bloody lot come and help or not?!" Bretti almost shouted.

"All right, all right! We're coming," I said, and heaved myself out of my chair with a ridiculous effort.

The cold night air hit my face and I almost slipped on the duckboards. They were covered with a layer of snow and frozen mud, and very hard to stand up on – that's my excuse, and I wasn't alone. Teuffel almost fell off, and so did Benner.

And there was Weber, lying face up to one side of the boards, fast asleep.

"Shame to disturb him," said Otto.

"He'll freeze to death if we leave him there," Bretti replied, "and I can't move him – my feet just slide."

It took four of us to half-carry and half-drag Weber to his and Bretti's room, and even then we slipped and slid.

"I think I've put my back out," Beilke grumbled.

"No excuse – you're still down for dawn!" I said.

We deposited Weber on his bed.

Schulte gave him a thoughtful look. "Do you want a hand undressing him?" he asked Bretti.

"Sod that! Just put a blanket over him."

"He is rather muddy," said Schulte.

"Lovely curly hair he's got," remarked Eichner.

"Bit longer than regulation, as well," Schulte agreed. "Especially on top."

I could guess what they had in mind.

"I'm going back to the mess," I said. "I've got more drinking to do."

"Me too," said Horstmann, whose only contribution had been to open the doors for us.

I couldn't help laughing as we slithered along the duckboards. "Half bald or completely?"

Horstmann laughed as well. "Find out in the morning, no doubt!"

"How does the parachute work, anyway?" I asked Fellmann when we got back to the mess.

"You don't have to do anything – there's a line that's attached to the aircraft. You just jump out and the parachute will open."

"Just make bloody sure the line's attached!" Otto said cheerfully.

"The Chief's giving you a briefing in the morning, anyway," Fellmann added. "So you can all have a quiet night's sleep!"

My nerves were infinitely better the next morning. I was still going off to stake my life, but now I knew that I wouldn't burn and that I could push any attack as hard as I liked without fear of structural failure, and that gave me a huge feeling of security.

And then I was suddenly very angry when I thought of all the men who needn't have died. *No use, Franz. Put them out of your mind and get on with your job.*

We had two very hot fights, and everyone seemed to go in just that bit harder and to push that bit more. Sobek was learning fast and was actually quite useful, chasing a Nieuport off Teuffel's tail, but yet again I had the frustration of not seeing my intended victim go down.

I've lost my bloody touch, I thought with considerable annoyance. *It must be because I broke the Rule of the Series by having leave.*

That's bollocks – the boss got one on his first patrol back. It'll come back. You scored well before and you will again.

We found a very bleary Weber sitting at the breakfast table, with a monk's tonsure and the odd small cut on his scalp, and we burst out laughing. The Chief assumed a very severe expression, and everyone except Weber knew that he was struggling not to laugh as well.

"Brettschneider, would you do Weber's familiarisation straight after breakfast?"

"Yes, sir."

"And Weber, this isn't a monastic order."

Weber blushed. "No, sir. Sorry, sir."

"Don't worry," I said quietly as I lit his cigarette. "You're not the first. The boss is more interested in how you fly."

"Thanks." He took a drag with an attempt at nonchalance, and almost choked.

Poor little sod. Doesn't smoke, doesn't shave, probably doesn't fuck – and he'll be lucky to do any of them before the fellow with the scythe gets him.

I wrote to Karl, to tell him about the parachutes. *I wish the Chief had gone to see you,* I thought as I sealed the letter. The boss had told me during the handover that there hadn't been time – after the trials he'd been stuck at the Technical and Testing Commission, and had had to give talks in factories.

God knows what that was supposed to achieve – I can't imagine the munitions workers being impressed by a fighter pilot.

"Becker, would you fly against Weber this afternoon?" said the Chief.

"Yes, of course, sir."

"That's your boozing sorted out," Beilke said. "You'll be awash with champagne!"

"Anyone fancy Claudette's?" asked Eichner. "Been a week or so."

"Sounds good to me," said Horstmann. "We can set off straight after the last flight."

"You up for that?" Bretti said to Weber.

"Er…"

"Don't miss the chance of a fuck," said Benner. "You never know what's coming."

We all started laughing.

"Well, I shall be, for a start!" Otto said.

"And me!" said Sobek.

"And me!" we all said, more or less in unison.

"Better take the truck, then," said Horstmann.

"Er…" Weber said again.

"Look," said Bretti, "it's a really nice place. The girls are pretty—"

"But I'm not an officer."

"Neither am I," said Otto. "Someone will lend you a coat – just keep it on in the salon."

"But are they clean?"

"Use a condom," I said.

"I don't know…"

"Well, I do," Bretti said firmly. "You're coming with us, and that's the end of it."

When the time came to leave, Weber still hesitated.

"You don't want to die a virgin, do you?" Teuffel said.

"And after Becker slaughtered you this afternoon, you can't really think you'll survive!" Otto said.

"Get in the bloody truck," Horstmann said.

"But I've got no hair!"

Horstmann rolled his eyes. "Don't look in the sodding mirror, then!"

He hesitated again at the whorehouse door. Bretti took a firm grip on his arm, and Benner pushed him from behind. I went up to Claudette.

"Ah, good evening, sir," she said. "It's so good to see you back."

"Thanks – we've got a virgin who needs deflowering."

"Oh – the very young one?"

"That's right."

Weber was gazing at the girls, like a boy with his nose against the sweet-shop window.

"Who do you fancy, then?" Eichner asked him. "What about that slim brunette?"

He went beetroot red. "Er..."

Claudette swept up to him in a cloud of perfume and frills, and he looked quite taken aback. He obviously thought she wanted to take him to bed, and he recoiled visibly.

Otto caught my eye, and I only just managed to stifle my laughter. Claudette was easily forty-five and had never been known to go upstairs with anyone. Presumably she had done in her youth.

"I have just the girl for you," she said. "Emilie!"

"Well," Horstmann muttered to me. "I'd rather like her myself."

"Hard luck!"

Emilie was nicely buxom, with a fair-sized behind, and long dark hair. *I wouldn't mind, either*, I thought as she and Weber headed for the stairs.

"Well, he should be happy," Bretti said, "and the rest of us had better get down to business before the crimson-collared bastards turn up."

This has been a pretty fair day, I thought after dinner. I was feeling nicely mellow on all the fizz Weber had bought me, topped up with a few brandy chasers. *Flying over the Front is so much better with a means of escape, and flying against Weber got me let off the afternoon patrol, and I had an hour with Cécile to finish things off. About as good as a day gets round here – except for the lack of a victory.*

"You don't mind the Chief being back?" Horstmann asked as we got ready for bed.

"God, no. Being in command's all right for a few days, but I wouldn't want to make a habit of it... I'm just glad he did come back."

He gave me a quizzical look.

"He brought Mrs Chief to one of the receptions. I tell you, if I had a wife like that I'd get myself posted to Berlin."

"That good?"

"Fucking gorgeous. He's a lucky bastard."

I didn't say that Mrs Chief was expecting – that wasn't my news to give out.

"Well, I've got the lovely Susanne, so I'm not jealous at all!"

He got into bed and turned his light out. I did likewise, with a feeling of profound loneliness, and lay awake for quite a while, staring at the ceiling, wondering what Karl was doing.

My frustration continued for the next fortnight. I managed to wing a Camel but the bastard just headed west in a steep dive, obviously under control. I'd hit him, I was certain of that, but not badly enough.

This won't do, I thought after yet another unsuccessful patrol. Benner had got one, but I was still stuck.

I went to change into a dry shirt and to try to clean the oil off my face. *I am so fucking pissed off with this. I've lost my touch completely. I've got to score again soon—*

What you mean is that you want to kill again, to burn some poor bastard to a frazzle, or send him hurtling earthwards to smash to pieces. Do you want to do it, or do you need to?

Revulsion at myself gripped me, so strongly that I had to hold on to the edge of the chest of drawers. *What the fuck am I turning into?* I didn't want to meet my eyes in the mirror.

You're just a fucking murderer – that's why they gave you that pretty blue cross, because you're so good at it.

I sat down heavily on my bed. *Get a grip, Franz, for fuck's sake get a grip. You don't have any choice. As Johnny said, 'It's not a fucking tea party.' And if you start thinking like this then you'll be bugger all use to anyone, and you'll get someone killed. You can make peace with your conscience 'after the war'.*

The door opened and Horstmann came in. "Jesus, I swear I can wring this bloody shirt out… What's up, Becker? You look like you've seen a ghost."

"Oh, nothing. I was stupid enough to start thinking, that's all."

He gave me a very serious look. "Put more schnapps in your coffee, then. Or go to Claudette's more often. Otherwise you'll go round the bend."

"Yes, you're right."

"I know I'm fucking right."

The weather broke, and I didn't know whether to be happy or sad.

"Can we go to Claudette's?" asked Weber. "That Emilie's really something."

"Have a different one this time," Otto said. "You don't want to start getting attached to a tart."

"That's for sure," I agreed. "It just gets messy."

It seems like half a century since Lensch was killed, and poor little Marie sobbed her heart out in the car.

"My ambition is to collect the full set," said Eichner.

"Full set of what?" asked Benner. "Diseases? Crabs?"

"You say the nicest things," Horstmann said.

"But I'm missing three," Eichner continued, unperturbed. "And every time I think I'm going to have one of them, there's a bloody staff officer gets there ahead of me."

"I still want that Emilie again," Weber persisted.

Otto rolled his eyes.

When we got there, Hans Lethen von Thingummy and Whatnot was there with the other fellow, and suddenly all I could see was Westermann having that stupid argument with him and calling him out. *And then poor Westermann got fried…*

"*Franz.*" Otto sounded impatient.

"What?"

"Have a glass of champagne."

"Thanks."

I realised that Emilie was sitting on Lethen's knee, and that Weber was looking on unhappily.

"Choose another," I said to him. "Variety and the spice of life and all that."

Anne came over, took Weber by the hand and led him towards the stairs.

"Lucky bastard," grumbled Beilke. "They don't do that to me."

"That's because he's an innocent young lad and you're a hairy-arsed bastard," Horstmann said. "Come on, you want the child to be happy before he gets killed, don't you?"

"Well, if you put it like that…!"

I think I'm going off commercial sex, I thought as I went back downstairs. *It's a good physical release and I suppose I feel better for it, but it doesn't give me what I really need.*

And what is that, exactly?

All I could think was that I wanted to be lying in Karl's arms, and that raised the question of what I was.

I can't be queer. I do prefer women – it's just that he and I… We're not lovers, and it'll soon be irrelevant anyway.

Weber was positively glowing on the way back. "She was even better than Emilie!" he said happily.

"No," said Sobek, "you're just getting better at fucking."

Just what I was thinking.

Late in the evening, Otto sat beside me on the small sofa. "You're very quiet this evening," he said.

"Am I?"

"You don't want to start thinking, you know."

I laughed. "That's just what Horstmann said this morning."

"Well, he's right, so drink up!"

We lost Schulte the next day – we took off, and suddenly he wasn't with us. The rest of us got into formation and headed for the Front.

Wonder what happened. Maybe he had engine failure or something.

Half an hour later I'd forgotten about him completely – we were scrapping with two flights of Camels, and some of the buggers were far too sharp for comfort.

But not all of them. I turned in behind one who must have been a novice, as he used hardly any bank, and got in so close that the tang of castor oil penetrated my scarf and balaclava. The Triplane shook as the guns fired, the tracer going into where the back of his seat must be – and he reared up and fell into a spin, and I only just missed him.

At last. At long fucking last.

When we formed up to fly home I wondered where Schulte was, and then remembered and wondered if he was all right. As we flew overhead our field, I saw the remains of a Triplane in the trees at the western end, but didn't have time to look closely. There was a chance that the fuselage had crumpled and taken the sting out of the impact – at least I hoped so.

Uhlig's solemn face told me otherwise.

"Well, sir?" he asked as he lit my cigarette.

"One Camel."

"Well done, sir!"

"Thanks – what about Schulte?"

He shook his head. "Engine failed on take-off and he went into the trees. Braun's sorting out the body."

Another gone…

We all froze at the funeral, standing in our best uniforms in the snow and the icy wind. It had been bloody cold in the hangar during the night as well, and I felt as if I hadn't thawed out from that.

Poor little sod. He was only eighteen. At least it was quick.

Weber was very pale, and I realised it was his first experience of violent death. And that made me think of Anton, and I really didn't want to.

I'll be quite happy if I never sing this again, I thought as the band struck up 'I had a Comrade'. *Every time, I see the men I knew who are dead – and there are so many now that I always leave some out…*

Beilke photographed the grave for Schulte's family and for the squadron album.

"Is everyone in there?" asked Weber.

"Yes," said Beilke. "Have a look."

Weber put the album on the dining table and we all gathered round.

"Gosh, Kramer, I didn't realise you'd been here so long," said Weber.

"Oh, well, off and on," Otto replied.

"Oh, and here's Becker, already," said Sobek.

And there was Johnny.

"What happened to him?" asked Benner.

"Went down in flames," I said, and almost sounded matter-of-fact about it.

"Thank God we don't have to worry about that any more," Teuffel said.

And there was Karl's Pour le Mérite portrait. His beautiful clear eyes gazed at me, and I could almost hear his voice and feel his touch. If I could have stopped them turning the page I would have done. I was almost overcome with longing for him. *I wonder how you really are – you just gloss over your health in your letters. I wish I were with you.*

We had a decent wake for Schulte, and I drank enough to pass out. I woke in the early hours to the sound of rain drumming on the roof.

Oh dear. No dawn patrol unless that stops – and even if it does, the field will be like a swamp.

I lay for a while, listening to the rain and Horstmann snoring – and suddenly I was in the shell-hole with Kurt, holding him and listening to his cries of pain as the rain lashed down on us – I woke shivering, soaking wet and half frozen. My first, appalled, thought was that I'd wet the bed, and then I realised water was pouring through the roof.

"Oh, fucking hell!" I shouted, switching my light on.

"Becker, for Christ's sake!" Horstmann sounded half asleep. "What's the bloody matter?"

"The fucking roof's leaking. I'm fucking soaked!"

I leapt out of my bed and started pulling it across the floor. Horstmann, the bastard, lay in his nice warm nest, laughing at me as I capered about bollock naked.

"You could give me a hand, you rotten sod!"

"Bet you wouldn't say that to Fellmann!"

"Oh, sod Fellmann!"

"No thanks!" he laughed.

"Oh, shut up!"

"Come on, Becker, where's your sense of humour?"

"Bad dream."

"Ah."

I got dressed quickly. "I'll see you in the mess," I said. "It's too cold to sit round in here."

"You're early," Fellmann remarked.

"Roof's leaking – my bed's sopping wet."

"Oh, shit! Better get that sorted out for you – you boys need your beauty sleep."

"Wasted on me!"

Schmidt and Kessler mended the roof, cursing in the wind and rain. The Chief gave them a very decent quantity of rum when they'd finished.

I could do with some of that myself, I thought, and poured a generous slug into my coffee. It helped a bit, but I couldn't get Kurt out of my mind.

It would be better to fly and have something else to think about, rather than sitting round all day, trying not to hear the rain and hoping I don't shake in public.

"What dreadful weather," Teuffel said with a mournful shake of his head. "The only thing to do is drink."

"Terrible, really," Benner agreed, and ordered another bottle of brandy.

By dinner time we were all very well lubricated, and the furniture paid the price. Eventually we headed for bed. Horstmann and I managed to stay upright on the duckboards, but Benner wasn't so fortunate. There was a loud splash, followed by even louder swearing. Everyone was laughing too hard to help him as he crawled onto the duckboards.

"Mis'ble b'st'ds!" he shouted, which just made us laugh harder.

Back in our room, I half-fell onto my bed and took my boots off.

"You goin' leave y'bed there?" Horstmann asked.

"Why not? Wass problem?"

"Y'shld purri' back. They fixed tha' part'f the roof."

"Y'righ'. Gi'me hand?"

We dragged the bed back across the room and I practically fell into it. The drink didn't work. I was too scared to sleep because I was sure I'd have a nightmare, and I lay there trying not to think.

I must have fallen asleep eventually, because the rain woke me, rattling on the window. It was still dark and I had no idea what time it was. I pulled the covers over my head and tried, unsuccessfully, to shut out the sound. Even imagining I was in Karl's arms didn't help.

After an eternity, it got light. Horstmann woke up, and we talked for an hour or so, then dragged ourselves out of bed and sloshed over to the mess, the mud clinging to our boots.

Around lunchtime the sky cleared, and a brisk, cold, northerly wind set in. The Chief and I inspected the field but it was so wet that we could hardly stand up. Even the gravel strip was slippery.

"Rain's melted the snow," the Chief remarked. "Still, might be all right in the morning."

It wasn't.

Another glorious day of doing sweet fuck all, I thought as I settled into an armchair after breakfast. *No war for us today…*

Otto wound up the gramophone and put on the first soppy, sentimental song that came to hand. I picked up an old *Berlin Illustrated* and leafed idly through it.

"Hey, Becker, have you seen this?" Sobek was holding out a magazine, folded back on itself.

"Very nice," I said appreciatively. "Who sent you this?"

"A friend. He works at the printers. That one's going up on my wall, but you can have one of the others if you like."

"Thanks."

Sobek's choice of pin-up was a bit too plump for my taste – but there were plenty to choose from: tall, short, dark, fair, big tits, small tits…

I think I'll go for a fuck this evening. Been a few days now.

"Horstmann, fancy Claudette's this evening?" I said.

"Yes. Why not?"

"Otto?"

"Definitely. Poor little fellow's fed up with fingers."

"That's settled, then. You coming, Sobek?"

"You bet I am!"

"Anyone else?"

Everyone said yes apart from Benner, who looked unhappy about something.

The day passed in lethargy, with the agreeable thought of a girl at the end of it. That would stop me thinking about the bloody war, for an hour anyway.

I should answer Alfred's last letter, but I really can't be bothered.

My bad nights caught up with me and I fell into a sort of half-sleeping torpor, which turned into a rather pleasant erotic fantasy about—

"…patrol before it gets dark," I half-heard the Chief say.

The words barely penetrated my reverie, and at first I didn't realise what he'd said. I didn't know that he and Fellmann had been out to look at the field.

"Aren't you coming, Franz?" Otto was looking at me with a rather bemused expression.

"Oh, are we going already?"

"Come on, Becker!" the Chief said, rather impatiently. Suddenly, his earlier words sank in.

Oh, shit. He said we're going flying. That's the last thing I want to do. I thought I was safe today. I thought nothing would happen apart from eating, drinking and a spell of fornication.

I tried to look enthusiastic. I could see the others having the same struggle, and I had the ungracious thought that the boss was just grabbing the chance to increase his score. That was bollocks, of course. No one could have been more dedicated than the Chief – and anyway, I was doing my best to increase my own score.

Make the best of a bad job. Make sure you get one.

The airfield was still very wet underfoot, and I had to scrape the mud off the soles of my flying boots before I got into the cockpit. I didn't want my feet slipping on the rudder bar.

I hope the strip's dry enough to take off – and landing could be a bit interesting. That's right, Franz, assume you'll be back to land... My hands were shaking and my mouth was dry.

The weather was starting to close in again. We ran into the first layer of cloud at about seven hundred metres. It was very thin and we were soon through it, but there was another wispy layer above it, and another above that. *How can such thin layers hang in the sky? I wondered. And what causes them?*

Widemayer wanted to study the weather. I wonder if he'll ever recover.

We broke through into clear air. In the west, the sun was hidden behind vast ramparts of cloud, grey, black and almost purple against the light, their massive, unreachable tops brightly gilded. *God knows how high those anvils are.* I felt utterly dwarfed. I looked at the other aircraft. *We are less than ants, tiny black specks crawling across an immense void...*

Franz, what the fuck are you doing? Stop looking at the fucking clouds and start looking for the enemy, you stupid bastard. Two-seaters won't be up – they wouldn't be able to see enough. The only men who'll be up here will be hunters like us.

Nothing. No one. Only us. Only the sound of the engine, the bitter cold beginning to chill my bones, and those awesome towers of cloud.

The Chief will take us home soon. We've all shown willing, but there's no one to play with. We'll go home and thaw out, and then we'll go to Claudette's.

The Chief wagged his wings and my stomach turned over. There was a formation below us and slightly to the south. *They might be Pfalzes... or Halberstadts...* but I knew they weren't. They were fucking Camels. Four of them.

The sudden nausea was so intense that it was actually a pain in my stomach. *Why in God's name am I doing this? What a bloody stupid way to go to war.*

The Chief started a slow descent, and Horstmann, Beilke and I followed. The rest of the Jasta stayed at altitude, watching for trouble.

If they see us and turn for home we'll never catch them... We can't use the sun, not this evening.

The Chief was doing a fine job of stalking them. They hadn't seen us. We were above and behind them. The Chief rocked his wings again and the four of us dived steeply down. My nerves had gone and I was completely calm, my hands and feet quite steady. The Camel I'd chosen as my target was growing larger. *Not yet...*

They saw us and scattered. Mine turned right, tight but not tight enough. No one behind me, closing the gap, thirty metres, still closing – as I fired he tightened the turn. I was close enough to see the holes I was making in his wing. No bloody good, that. I turned tighter still – the guns fired a few rounds more and fucking well jammed. Both of the bastards.

"Fuck it!"

I unclipped the hammer and gave the cocking handles several almighty whacks, still close behind the Tommy. I couldn't free the jam.

He'll realise. He must realise soon. Bastard fucking things.

I broke off, diving away as fast as I could, twisting and turning, watching behind – my heart leapt into my throat as one of the Camels came down after me, turning into position to fly straight towards me. *Oh Jesus, he knows.*

Fear ran cold down my back as I hammered at the guns again. They were stuck fast. I was completely defenceless.

I was almost at the top layer of cloud. I put the nose down vertically. Two long seconds later I plunged into the cloud, and hurtled out of the bottom of the thin layer. I went down through the next layer to be sure, the wind tearing at my collar, the wires screaming – I was in the clear between layers, and I eased carefully out of the dive. He hadn't followed me.

I'd got away. I was alive.

I was soaked in sweat, and I realised I was still clutching the hammer. My hand shook so much as I tried to re-stow it that I almost dropped the bloody thing. *Fucking bloody guns.*

Where the fuck am I? The cloud beneath me was solid. *When in doubt, fly east…*

I flew east, looking for a hole in the cloud, and after five minutes or so decided I wasn't going to find one. I was down to a thousand metres and I began a shallow descent, holding the controls central. The cloud rushed towards me, and I was engulfed in cold, clammy, featureless grey. It got quickly darker, and I remembered the huge clouds in the west.

I went down and down, and there was no change in the cloud. *How much lower, for God's sake?* I eased the control column back slightly, centralised it. The altimeter unwound more slowly…

The cloud thinned and I was beneath most of it, banked slightly to the left, only a thin layer between me and the ground. I dropped down through that, and tried in vain to recognise something, anything. Belgium looked flat and brown and featureless.

The wind was westerly when we took off, and I flew east, so I must be on our side of the lines – but where? The visibility was very poor and I could see almost no distance.

We turned south to attack the Camels. I'll try heading north.

There was an airfield, with huts, canvas hangars and aircraft – but what type?

They look like Pfalzes. I'll have to do a lowish pass and have a look. If it's an Allied field I'll soon find out. It's got to be German, surely.

As I crossed the fence I saw the black crosses on the parked aircraft. *I just hope they see mine, otherwise I'll get shot down by my own side. Some trigger-happy machine-gunner will shoot first, just in case.*

No one shot at me and I pulled up, flew a quick circuit and landed, keeping the stick well back. Fortunately the ground wasn't too soggy.

A short, slightly balding Leutnant sauntered over as I was unwrapping my scarf.

"Bullert," he said. "Welcome to Croulshouten."

"Where the hell's that?"

He burst out laughing, and I remembered my manners.

"Becker," I said, and we shook hands.

"Get your map and I'll show you," he said. "Get a bit lost, did you?"

"Out of my skull."

"What the hell were you doing up in this? It's fucking shite!"

"Our Old Man thought it was a good idea."

"Who's that, then?"

"Kralewski."

His eyes widened. "What did you say your name was?"

"Becker."

"Franz Becker?"

I was beginning to get embarrassed. "Yes, that's right."

"Well, bugger me! Come into the mess and meet the others. We've got a bloody good cook – pinched him from a Brussels hotel. We'll give you dinner and you can fly back tomorrow."

"That's really kind of you – I'd love to, but I'll have to get back. They'll be wondering where I've got to. I had to drop out – both guns jammed solid. The Chief will want to talk to me."

"Yes, of course. Bastard, that, isn't it? He get away?"

"Apparently."

"Bad luck. Where's your base?"

I told him, and we looked at the map together.

"If you head north for about seven kilometres you can pick up this road and follow it," Bullert suggested.

"Yes, that should do it." *I'll have to stay good and low, and I should just make it by dark.* I didn't want to lose time refuelling, and I reckoned I should have enough, just about. "Thanks. Sorry I can't stay to dinner. Can one of your fellows give me a start?"

"I'll send someone over. Nice to have met you."

"You too."

A few minutes later I was climbing into the murk. I levelled out just below the cloud and flew north, looking for the road. In the grey gloom I could see barely a kilometre ahead, and I began to wish I'd accepted Bullert's invitation.

I could have reported to the Chief by phone…

Yes, and some well-meaning armourer would have fixed the guns during the night, and you'd have been left with no evidence for your story.

I was sure the Chief would believe me, but I hadn't been exactly enthusiastic about the patrol and I didn't want him to think I was starting to turn yellow.

I must have missed that bloody road. Surely I've been going long enough… There it is. I turned to follow it.

The cloudbase was getting lower and it had started raining. There were troops on the road. *I hope they can see the crosses. I'm bloody low enough – but some of them just shoot at any aircraft they see…*

Suddenly it was pissing down. The windscreen streamed with water and I could hardly see through it. I put my head over the side and my goggles were instantly in the same condition. I shoved them onto the top of my head, and the wind and rain lashed my face and stung my eyes. I retreated behind the windscreen, my eyes watering. I could barely see which way was up.

I should be there. Where the fuck's the airfield? If I don't see it in the next five minutes – Jesus fucking Christ! I flung the Triplane onto her right wingtips and the chimney of the sugar factory flashed past, towering darkly over me in the gloom. *Christ, that was close!*

It was almost too dark to land. The mud gripped the wheels and she nearly turned over, but to my relief the tail came back down. It was impossible to taxi, and I shut down where I was. Uhlig and Zaffke came out with a crew to pull the aircraft in, and we waded through the sticky mud.

My heart was racing and my hands were trembling. *I don't want another afternoon like that. I really don't.*

The Chief was waiting for me just inside Hangar Two. I kept my hands buried in my pockets as I walked towards him.

"What happened, Becker?"

"Guns jammed, sir. Then I got lost."

The drumming of the rain on the canvas roof rose to a terrific din – there must have been hail in it – and then eased off abruptly.

"So did we – but obviously not as lost as you."

I told him the rest of it.

"Oh, well, not to worry. Horstmann winged one of the Camels, but none of us scored – unless you did?"

"No, sir. Bloody things jammed on the second burst."

Out of the corner of my eye I could see Schwarte having quite a bit of difficulty with my guns. The Chief noticed as well.

Good. That raises me above any suspicion.

"Well, you're not the only one," he said. "I'm finding a lot of oversized rounds."

"Me too… You'd think our going through the belts would sort that out, though."

Anyone with any sense spent wet days remeasuring every round and replacing any that weren't exactly right – and not just to murder effectively. I'd just had a sharp reminder of how terrifying it was to be disarmed, and surrounded by enemies with functioning guns and lethal intentions.

The sudden heat as I entered the mess made me realise just how cold I'd got. Horstmann, Otto and Sobek were sitting together playing cards. Otto looked up as I sauntered towards them, brandy glass in hand.

"It's the wandering Franz Becker! Where the hell did you get to?"

"Bloody double gun jam, got chased into the clouds by one of those sodding Camels, then got bloody lost. I landed at some godforsaken place called Croulshouten, which was about as wet as here, and where some helpful fellow gave me directions – and here I am."

"Navigation never was your strong point," Otto said.

"If he's airborne he's lost," Horstmann remarked.

"Too bloody right. I'm lost half the time on the ground as well," I said. "From what I've heard, you lot couldn't find your way either."

"No." Otto started laughing. "I think even the Chief was beginning to wonder what the hell we were doing up there. It was bloody filthy."

"I nearly hit the chimney of the sugar factory," I said. "I swear the bloody thing attacked me." I was trying to make a joke of it, but I had to shut up because my voice started to tighten.

"Probably," Horstmann said. "We really ought to knock the bloody thing down, before it knocks one of us down."

"It is Belgian," Eichner said. "I had a jam as well. Bloody nuisance."

"Isn't it," I said. It was all I could say. I didn't trust myself to drink the brandy – my hands were shaking too much.

"What do we expect?" Horstmann said. "Everything gets soaking wet, and then we take it up to where it's minus God knows what, and get offended when it freezes."

The corner of his eye started to flicker, and he rubbed it with an irritated gesture, then busied himself searching his pockets for his cigarettes and lighter.

"Blast it – my lighter's out of fuel."

I fished mine out of my pocket and slid it across the table to him. I daren't try to light his cigarette.

I can't do this, not any more. It's too much. I should have taken Karl's advice and become an instructor. I've done my bit, surely.

For fuck's sake, Franz, you're here to fight. Stop moaning and bloody well get on with it.

The atmosphere that evening was oddly subdued. Everyone just got pissed, without any of the usual malarkey.

Benner was even quieter than the rest of us, and a couple of times I noticed him staring at the floor with a very worried expression. I didn't like to ask what the problem was.

I only realised the next day that the trip to Claudette's had been totally forgotten.

II

"Hey, weren't we going to Claudette's yesterday?" Bretti said over a very late breakfast.

"God, so we were," said Beilke. "How about tonight?"

"Definitely," I said. "Even if the field's fit for use, we'll be done by dark."

"And hopefully without blundering about in the murk!" Sobek added. "I didn't realise you chaps flew in that sort of crap!"

"We don't usually," Otto replied.

"No, but those Camel bastards were up," Horstmann said.

"Bastards is the word," said Eichner. "Going after Becker when he'd got a jam."

"Well, that's how it is these days," Teuffel said with a sigh. "Chivalry's dead and buried."

"All the more reason to get your end away while you can!" said Bretti.

"Count me out," Benner said, very downcast and staring at the floor.

There's definitely something wrong, but I doubt it's anyone's business but his own.

After lunch, the Chief and I slithered across the field. Even the gravel strip was too greasy to stand on, and the mud was starting to reclaim it.

"I wonder if Fellmann can get another delivery," the boss said. "But maybe there's no point. What d'you reckon?"

No point at all, I wanted to say. "Worth a try."

When we got back to the main hut I went to the Ops Office. Fellmann was on his own, smoking one of Karl's cigars.

"Ah, Becker!"

I sat down. Something in his manner made me reluctant to get straight down to business.

"Bloody good cigars, these," he said. "Have you heard from Karl lately?"

"Yes – had a letter yesterday."

"How's he getting on?"

"He doesn't say. You know what he's like."

"Yes… That's the trouble." He lowered his voice. "I'm trying to get him posted to the Technical and Testing Commission, to make sure he can't come back."

"That's a bloody good idea – but we don't have to worry. There's no way he'll ever be fit for the Front again."

Fellmann just looked at me. "He's a Leussow. My uncle's from one of those families, and believe me, it's all 'With God for King and Fatherland.' You know what they tell you on your first day at cadet school?"

"'Gentlemen, you are here in order to learn how to die.'"

"Exactly."

The conversation I'd had with Karl on my last day with him came back, far too clearly. 'That's what we're for, to bleed and die for Prussia…'

"I hope you succeed – I mean in getting him posted, not in dying for the Fatherland!"

Fellmann laughed. "I'll keep you informed. I don't want…" He went completely scarlet.

Don't want Karl to go the same way as Johnny? Neither do I.

"Thanks – I really appreciate it Changing the subject completely, can you get us some more gravel? It's a pain only flying when the field's frozen."

'Gravel… David's spunk would be gravel, don't you think?'

I could almost feel Karl's touch, and it was my turn to blush. I wriggled in my seat.

Fellmann raised an eyebrow, and I went even redder.

"Going to save that for Claudette's girls, are you?"

"Well—"

"I can spot a stiffie at two hundred metres, duckie!" he said, in his campest manner.

I laughed. "Why does that not surprise me?!"

"But I'm quite lost as to the erotic possibilities of *gravel* – I mean, *why*?"

"It was a joke Karl made, about Michelangelo's David and his spunk being gravel."

Fellmann's laugh rattled the windows. A moment later the boss put his head round the door.

"Going to share the joke?"

Fellmann did, and it was the Chief's turn to laugh.

"Poor Mrs David!"

"Oh, I expect she's marble, too," Fellmann said, but the look he gave me said, *I can guess where the two of you were when Karl said that.*

There was absolutely no point trying to deny it.

I wish I knew what I wanted, I thought as we went into the salon at Claudette's. *It used to be so simple…*

Weber knew what he wanted, all right, but Emilie was stroking the thigh of some carmine-collared bastard. The boy gave him a filthy look and got one in return. *Better stop this going any further*, I thought, remembering Westermann. I took hold of Weber's arm, and sat him down firmly with his back to them.

"Don't get attached to any of the girls," I said.

"I'm not—"

"Becker's right," said Teuffel. "You paid to fuck her and now he's going to do the same. You think any of them actually *want* us?"

"Well..." Weber's face fell slightly.

"They're all French or Belgian," Bretti said, "and we're filthy Boches. They just want our money – probably all saving up to retire."

"Find yourself a nice girl back home, and get fond of her," I said.

Fat chance of that happening.

"And in the meantime, just enjoy a fuck for its own sake," said Eichner. "It's better than wanking, after all."

"Look, why don't you have a bounce on Christine?" Bretti suggested. "She's great fun – and those tits are quite something!"

"Never mind that whopping great arse!" said Horstmann.

Before Weber could say another word, Bretti was waving Christine over.

"My friend was just saying how lovely you look," he said.

Weber went scarlet. Christine gave him a very kindly look, took his hand and led him away.

"Easy job for her," Eichner remarked.

"Yes – she probably wishes we were all seventeen!" I said, and shut up as Jeanette came and sat on my lap, her tits in my face and her hand on my cock, just as she had once done to Karl's pa.

Don't think about the dead.

When we got back Benner was more than half pissed, and was staring at the floor again.

"What's up with him?" Otto asked me. "He looks like a wet Wednesday."

"God knows. Girl trouble, I expect."

He was so gloomy after dinner that Bretti convened the Court of Riotous Behaviour. Benner pleaded guilty, downed the wine glass of booze and left the mess.

We looked at each other, shrugged, and got on with drinking.

Whatever was on Benner's mind was obviously eating away at him – he was morose to the point of grumpiness, and it was affecting his flying. He made a completely reckless attack on an SE5, and was very lucky to escape in one piece.

"What the fuck is wrong with that bastard?" Horstmann demanded a couple of weeks later.

"Benner?"

"Who else? He almost rammed me today – he's fighting like a lunatic."

"Yes, I'd noticed that too."

So, of course, had the Chief. "Becker, have you got a moment?" he asked as we passed his office door.

"Of course, sir." *It's not as if I've got anything else to do…*

"Close the door and have a seat… What's wrong with Benner?"

"I don't know, sir. He's been getting worse for the past couple of weeks."

"Whatever it is, it needs sorting out."

I sighed. "Yes, sir, I agree. I'll have a word with him."

Easier said than done, that. Then I had an idea.

"Benner, fancy coming to practise our circles?"

He looked at me, and then shrugged. "All right, then."

"Whose idea was this, anyway?" he asked as we walked out to our improvised range.

I told him about Karl. "…and the Chief thought it would improve everyone's marksmanship if we had the weekly competition," I finished.

"Makes sense. Ground's fucking cold, though."

He made a complete mess of his first two attempts.

"Fucking hell, I can't get this right today," he said with disgust as he reloaded.

"Look," I said, "if something's bothering you, we might be able to sort it out."

He laughed. "The only thing that'll sort me out's a bullet in the head."

"Is that why you're attacking without thinking?"

"Am I? Probably. I'd blow my brains out, only I'm too much of a coward."

Bruch, staring emptily at the ceiling…

"We had a fellow who did just that – he'd got too scared of going on patrol."

Benner turned his head towards me. "You think I'm scared of the fucking Tommies?!"

"Well?"

"It's not them I'm scared of. I'd just rather be killed than… than die… than what I'm likely to get."

"Benner, what the fuck are you talking about? Are you sick or something?"

He laid the rifle on the ground, his shoulders sagging.

"Look, why don't you go to the hospital and get yourself examined?"

"Because I'm far too fucking scared of what the doc might say."

"So what do you think you've got?"

There was utter terror in his eyes. "I caught something from my best girl."

My guts turned to water. *Jesus Christ, I'll have it now. I'll die rotting and insane, just as Papa warned me. But I always use a condom and I haven't had any symptoms…*

"And you've been fucking Claudette's tarts and given it to all of us, you bastard."

"*No.* Becker, I swear I haven't! I don't fuck those tarts without a condom – I thought I was cured but it's come back, and every morning it's the same thing."

I didn't want to know what happened every morning.

"You're going to see the doctor," I said. "And I'll have to tell the Chief."

"They'll send me to the Knights' Castle." Slang for the VD hospital.

"Only if you've got syph—"

"Don't say it!"

"Big S."

He was visibly shaking, as I would have been in his place.

"Lousy way to find out she'd been cheating on me," he said, with an attempt at flippancy.

"Benner, if any of us have caught it we'll fucking kill you."

"You'd be doing me a favour."

"I think you'd better tell the boss yourself, right now. And then go straight to the hospital."

"All right. You won't tell the others, will you?"

"I'll give them all a lecture about protecting themselves," I said. "Though given our likely life expectancy they might not listen."

He looked slightly less worried in the evening. We'd had such a hot fight that I'd forgotten the whole business, and walked into the mess on legs that were still trembling.

"You look like you could use a brandy," Benner said to me.

"That's for sure."

"Well, aren't you going to ask me?"

Ask you what? "Oh – yes. What did he say?"

"He reckons it's the clap rather than the other thing, but they're doing some tests and he'll let me know. I'm warned off Claudette's, anyway, condom or not."

"Half the staff swine are probably diseased," I said.

"What's that, Franz?" Otto asked.

I repeated it.

"That's for sure!"

I went to the Ops Office. "Fellmann, you know that film they're showing back home, about not getting nasty diseases?"

"Yes."

"Do you think we could get a copy to show here?"

He raised both eyebrows. "Is that why Benner went to the hospital this afternoon?" he asked quietly.

"You'd have to ask him that," I replied.

He gave me a warm smile. "Always the soul of discretion! I'll get onto HQ – they'd probably be glad to show it."

"And can you use your contacts to get hold of more condoms?"

"Could be tricky with the shortage of rubber, but I'll try."

"Thanks... In the meantime, I've got a brief lecture to give," I said with a sigh.

It was very brief indeed. I went to my room and fetched a box of Venus condoms, then rapped on the mess table.

"Right," I said. "Everyone know what these are?"

"Of course we bloody do!" Horstmann retorted, and there was a chorus of similar comments.

"Everyone use one?"

"Of course we bloody do!"

"It's getting harder to replace them, though," Eichner said.

"Yes, I know. Fellmann's working on a fresh supply. But if you run out, you stay here and use your imaginations. No one is to fuck Claudette's tarts – or anyone else, for that matter – without one."

"We're not likely to live long enough to die of the pox," Teuffel said.

"That's no reason to give it to someone else," I said.

Beilke turned to Benner and gave him a sharp stare. Benner went scarlet.

"This is because of you, isn't it?" Beilke said, his tone matching his expression. "That's why you buggered off this afternoon."

"I give you all my word that I have never fucked Claudette's tarts bare," Benner said.

"If I've caught something from you I'll bloody well kill you," said Eichner.

"You can't have done. I promise."

"You're more likely to get something courtesy of the carmine-collared," Horstmann said. "God knows what they get up to. Benner's given us his word, and that's good enough for me."

"Thanks."

A nasty little thought crept into my mind. *But what if one of them sucked his cock and then did the same to one of us…?*

I rapped on the table again. "And don't get any of them to put her mouth round it, either. Just in case."

The others exchanged looks. This time there was no rejoinder.

And of course the thought wouldn't go away – except when we met the Tommies, who were becoming far too numerous.

"Please, dear God, let us have those new Fokkers soon," Bretti said after one particularly nasty patrol.

"No point thinking about it," Horstmann said.

Ten minutes later we all had something else to think about. The Chief came into the mess and rapped on the table.

"Gentlemen, I've just had a call from HQ. Claudette's is closed until further notice – there was a health inspection last week and one of the girls was found to have…" He paused, distaste in his face. "Gonorrhoea."

We all looked at each other. *Could have been a lot worse, and anyway, I've always been careful.*

"And I'm sorry to have to tell you that all Claudette's customers have to be tested, for that and for… er… the other thing."

"Fucking marvellous," Horstmann said.

Everyone looked at Benner.

"I told you all, I've always used a condom there," he said. "And no, I didn't ask any of them to put her mouth round it."

Beilke gave a snort of disbelief.

"For fuck's sake, isn't my word enough?" Benner demanded angrily.

The Chief rapped on the table again. "Gentlemen, there is no point in recriminations. We don't know where the disease has come from – we're hardly the only customers."

"That's for sure," Horstmann said. "I'll bet it's one of those staff swine."

"In the meantime, we have a job to do," said the Chief. "The hospital's going to let us know when someone will be coming to take samples, and they've sent us an information sheet about diseases and their symptoms."

"That'll be fun reading," said Beilke.

Bretti looked very unhappy indeed. "I hope I didn't catch anything when my condom split."

"Well, you'll find out in a couple of weeks!" Teuffel said.

I read the information sheet with mounting relief, until I got to the end: 'It is quite possible to be infected without having any symptoms at all.'

Fucking wonderful. If only we could fly... I had to laugh at myself. *A few days ago I'd have been quite happy with a bit of guaranteed life, but now I just want something to take my mind off appalling diseases.*

A doctor turned up with two orderlies, and they took blood samples from us all.

"We'll get the results back to you as soon as possible," the doctor said.

"Have you got mine yet, sir?" Benner asked.

"Give us a ring in a week's time."

"I really could do without this," said Sobek. "My girlfriend will kill me if I take something home."

"Why the fuck are you worrying about that?" Teuffel replied.

"My girl will kill me too," said Otto.

"And mine," added Horstmann.

"The whole idea makes my skin crawl," Beilke said.

Mine too.

Eichner just shrugged. "I'm far more bothered about Tommy bullets," he said. "Let's face it, none of us needs to worry what diseases he might have."

"But if we have got… you know… then they'll take us away to the Knights' Castle and then we really will die of it," Bretti said. "It would be better if the whole thing hadn't been discovered."

He's got a point there, I thought as I lay awake trying not to think that I might have Big S. I didn't even want to say its name in my head. *And I'd never be able to touch Karl again.*

You won't anyway. You'll be lucky to see the spring – and you can always blow your brains out before it takes hold.

A few days later a truck arrived, and got stuck just inside the airfield gate.

"Ah, that'll be the *gravel*," Fellmann said, looking at me and raising an eyebrow.

"Well, we'd better all get spreading, then!" I said. "Then maybe we'll be able to fly tomorrow."

Of course it took longer than we thought, but we managed an evening patrol two days later.

It wasn't Tommy bullets that Eichner needed to worry about, but Weber's lack of lookout. I was hot on the heels of a Nieuport and suddenly fragments of aircraft went everywhere. Half a wing just missed me and I dived sharply. As I turned I saw a parachute open.

Of course the Nieuport got away, and I was soon fending off a Camel. Bretti came to my aid, and then another Jasta joined in and I bloody nearly hit one of them.

When we formed up I realised Eichner and Weber were missing, and wondered whose parachute I'd seen.

Otto parked next to me. "What happened?"

"I don't know." I told him what I'd seen, and just as I finished Sobek joined us.

"I think it was Weber's parachute," he said, "but I'm not certain."

Nine pilots assembled in the mess.

"Well, gentlemen," said the Chief, "we must expect Weber's replacement to be just as inexperienced… It seems ironic that the survivor should be the man who caused the collision."

"That's what happened when Boelcke died," I said.

"Indeed… did anyone see Eichner's parachute open?"

There was a pause, and then Sobek said, "Yes – that is, it started to, but it got caught on the tail."

"So the bloody things don't always work," said Horstmann.

"Does anything work every time?" Bretti said.

"So Eichner is almost certainly dead, and Weber's probably a prisoner," said the Chief. He sighed heavily and went to his office.

"Shit," Otto said. "We've never lost two in one day before."

"At least there's no funeral and no guard of honour," I said.

"And we're going to get two more children with no idea what the fuck they're doing," said Benner. He got up and left the mess.

Bretti wound up the gramophone and put on the Liesl song. "At least we won't catch the clap from dear Liesl!" he said, and we raised our glasses and started to sing, and then we belted out the English dying pilot song, and then another of our favourites.

Benner came back with a huge smile on his face. When the song ended he jumped onto the table. "*I do not have the pox!*"

A massive weight dropped off my shoulders.

"The champagne's on me!" he added, and we all cheered.

You'd think we'd have more respect. Eichner's dead and Weber might be too…

We drank to Eichner's memory after dinner.

"Why couldn't that stupid bastard have collided with a Tommy instead of with Eichner?" Beilke asked.

"The answer is in the question," Bretti said obliquely.

"Hey?" asked Teuffel.

"Because he was – or is – a stupid bastard, of course," said Otto.

"Bloody university types," Teuffel grumbled. "Too fucking clever for your own good."

"Hey, count me out of that," Bretti protested. "I'm a career officer like you."

We heard the next day that Weber was indeed a prisoner.

"Jammy fucking bastard!" was Beilke's verdict, delivered in the Chief's absence. "Couple of weeks at the Front and then safe in a camp somewhere."

"While poor old Eichner – who was far more use – is in a hole in the ground," said Horstmann.

"If there was enough to bury," Sobek added.

The next day a Sopwith carrying white streamers flew low over the field and dropped a canister. It contained photographs of Eichner's funeral and of his grave, and a very courteous letter from the CO of the Camel squadron that had buried him.

"You can say what you like about the Tommies," Otto said, "but they do things properly."

"Yes," said Horstmann. "They're very smartly turned out. Almost to Prussian standards."

"*Almost*," agreed Beilke.

"Though things have slipped since the old Regular Army passed away," Fellmann added regretfully.

"Indeed," said Horstmann. "You do wonder if things will ever be quite the same again."

"They will if enough of us survive," Beilke said.

"The Tommies will never be as smart as us, anyway," said Fellmann. "You'll never get them doing the parade march."

Beilke laughed. "No, they swing their arms instead, don't they – really strange, that looks!"

"Do they?" asked Otto.

"Yes – right up to shoulder height."

"How odd."

"Maybe they think we look odd," said Sobek. "Everyone has his own point of view, doesn't he?"

"You know, I'd never thought of that," Horstmann replied.

"I must say, I prefer the way we do it," said the Chief.

Möller knocked on the mess door. "Excuse me, sir, gentlemen, but there's a letter from the hospital."

"Thank you, Möller," said the Chief. "Put it on my desk, would you?"

"Certainly, sir."

That'll be the test results. The jolt of fear was almost as bad as when we spotted the Tommies. I could see the same apprehension in my comrades' faces.

"I'll call you in alphabetical order," said the boss, and went to his office.

That meant he called me first. My heart pounded as he handed me the paper, and I hardly dared look at it.

'Wassermann test – negative. Gram test – negative.'

My hands shook with relief. *No pox, no clap. Thank fuck for that.*

"Send Beilke in, would you?" the Chief said, with a frank and genuine smile.

"Yes, sir."

The measure of happiness in the mess rose with each man who returned smiling, and that evening we had the most magnificent mess-wrecker of a celebration.

"All we need now is for Claudette's to reopen!" Sobek said cheerfully.

"I'm fucked if I'm going to that bloody place again," said Beilke. "I don't want another fright like that."

"Bet you ten marks you can't keep it in your trousers for a month," Bretti said.

"You're on – if only because I won't be around to pay and you won't be around to collect!"

"So what happens to the debt if one of them dies?" asked Teuffel.

Horstmann thought for a moment. "Well, Beilke has to last a month. If he doesn't then the bet's off. If he does, and he's kept his trousers buttoned, and Bretti's dead, then Bretti's estate has to pay up."

There was a murmur of agreement.

"Tell you what," said Bretti, "I'll give Fellmann the ten marks now – but I'll be getting them back!"

Schwarz and Schmidt joined us from Valenciennes – the former looked about twelve, but the latter was off two-seaters and had been in the infantry before that. We could all guess which would last longer.

A few days later we got into a very nasty fight – it started off with a squadron of Camels, and as we were all up that was manageable, especially as two of them were obviously novices. I got one of them and was very glad I couldn't watch him go down, because I'd glimpsed a small flame coming from the cowling...

Two minutes later a flight of SE5s arrived, tipping the numbers against us, and they all knew what they were doing. One of them got straight onto little Schwarz, who was on his first patrol, and Beilke was after him in a flash.

Two Tommies promptly attacked Beilke and for one splendid moment I thought they were going to collide with each other, but they managed not to. *Time to help* – but there was another flight of sodding Camels diving into the fray and I had to turn to defend myself.

Whatever I did there was a Camel behind me, and I threw my poor Triplane into one skidding turn after another, hoping to throw their aim off. Bullets pinged off the struts and the edge of the windscreen—

I'm not going to get out of this one.

There was an SE5 in front of me and I gave it a burst, but to no effect – and Beilke was fending off three of the bastards. The Chief joined their fight but Beilke was spinning.

Hope he's bluffing.

The first Camel flight buggered off, and a few minutes later the SE5s left as well. *I just might get out of this after all—*

There were now ten of us to four Camels. Funnily enough they didn't like that much, and tried to leave.

Nice to have the upper hand again, I thought as we chased them westwards. Horstmann sent one spinning down, and shortly afterwards the Chief took us home.

I'm alive after all. How many more times can I write myself off?

"Blimey, sir, that's a lot of holes," Uhlig said.

He wasn't joking. All the aircraft were in a similar state – except Beilke's, which of course wasn't there.

"We were outnumbered," I said as he lit my cigarette. My hands shook so badly that I almost dropped it.

"Let's go and warm up," said the Chief.

"You forget what summer feels like, don't you?" Otto said as we walked to the mess.

"Well, it's on its way," Schwarz said cheerfully. "It's nearly the end of February."

Summer on its way? What is the stupid sod talking about?

Bretti and I exchanged looks.

"Don't know what summer he thinks we'll see," he muttered as he poured himself a mug of cocoa, and added a healthy slug of rum.

"The eternal summer in Heaven, I expect," I said.

"Rum in yours, Schwarz?" Teuffel offered.

"No thanks."

Teuffel looked at me and shrugged.

"I'd like rum in mine, please," said Schmidt, clearly aware what a bad situation we'd been in.

"Do you think—" Sobek began, but the Chief rapped on the table.

"Gentlemen, on numbers that patrol was a success, but…" He paused. "Did anyone see whether Leutnant Beilke pulled out of the spin?"

We all looked at each other. *That says it all. I've never known the Chief lose track of someone before.*

One by one we shook our heads.

"Then we just have to hope," the boss said, and continued the debrief.

Horstmann and I were in no mood to celebrate. Time passed and we waited, but Beilke didn't call.

All the aircraft were holed, and by the time the patches had cured the sun was almost on the horizon. None of us was sorry, apart from Schwarz. He said something about how brilliant it would have been to get another patrol in, but no one answered.

"This isn't looking good," Otto said to me.

"No."

"Time to start drinking properly," said Bretti. "Pity Claudette's is still shut."

The medics weren't allowing the place to reopen until they'd found the source of the infection.

"Yes – just what I need right now," Teuffel said with a sigh.

"I hope he's not in No Man's Land," said Schmidt.

"Shouldn't be," said Bretti. "We were only just over their side when it started, and the wind's pretty fresh."

Some time after it had got dark I thought I heard the phone, but the gramophone was on and we were singing.

Fellmann put his head round the door. "Pipe down, chaps – the boss is on the phone."

Teuffel took the needle off the record. In the silence we heard the Chief say heavily, "Yes, do, please… We'll send someone. Thank you very much."

He came into the mess. "That was General von Schutte's adjutant… Long story short, they saw Beilke spinning – he came out of it and bailed out shortly after. It took them a while to find him – apparently it was hard to tell where the parachute had come down – but he'd been hit several times and it was too late. They're putting him in a coffin – Fellmann, would you…?"

"Right away, sir." Fellmann headed for the hangars.

"I don't know what time they'll be back," the Chief continued, "but you all know what to expect."

He headed for his office, and the unenviable task of writing to Beilke's family.

"I suppose I'd better sort his things out," Otto said.

He'd moved in with Beilke after Weber got shot down. "I'd rather share with someone I know," Beilke had said. We'd teased him about his faith in Otto's longevity, and now it was he who was dead.

"I'll give you a hand," I said.

"It was a good way to go," said Bretti.

"Yes," Horstmann agreed. "Far better than some of the poor sods."

"That's for sure," said Teuffel.

"You know what really gets to me?" Otto asked as he opened the door of their room. "It's the way everyone's stuff is just *left*, as if he's about to come back."

I knew what he meant. A book lay open on Beilke's bed, and there was a pile of photographs on the table that he'd obviously been sorting out.

"He was a good bloke," I said. "Be very hard to replace."

"Especially these days. Where are we going to get another ace?"

"And who's going to take the photos for the album?"

That question was answered a couple of minutes later. Beilke had left a note for us all, in which he'd put fifty marks for us to have a party in his memory – and he'd left his camera to Fellmann.

We took the money to the mess and gave it to Fellmann.

"And the camera's yours," Otto added, handing him the note.

"Oh, good – we can keep the album going... Talking of money – Bretti, you'd better have your ten marks back."

"I don't want it – this isn't how I wanted that bet to end."

"No, of course not – but the bet's off now."

"Put it with the fifty," Bretti said.

I had a letter to write as well, to tell Karl that another comrade had gone. *There are fewer and fewer left*, I thought as I sealed it.

It was midnight before Braun and co arrived with the coffin. Beilke was chalk white, but quite presentable in his best uniform.

"Lucky Braun got there before rigor mortis set in," Horstmann remarked.

Schwarz was almost as pale as Beilke. *Yes, war kills – and your introduction to that has been a rather gentle one. And you won't have to see what Beilke looks like after three weeks or so.*

"If only they'd got to him sooner," Benner said.

"I doubt it would have made any difference," Teuffel replied. "He looks like there's no blood left."

"Probably just as well he was dead," said Bretti. "Or they'd just have tortured him trying to save him."

"Indeed," I said, thinking of Hauschke.

We buried Beilke late the next morning, and then went on patrol. The band had played the Funeral March from Beethoven's Eroica Symphony, and the music went round and round in my head as we suited up.

"Time to get our own back," said Schwarz.

"Forget that idea," I said. "Beilke was a soldier and he knew the stakes."

"That's right," said Bretti. "Just concentrate on learning the job."

I hope we don't have another patrol like the last one...

I ended the day with mixed feelings – I was very pleased with myself because I'd managed to get a Bristol Fighter, and they were bastard things. It was luck as much as anything – I'd disabled the observer with the first burst and then the pilot was relatively easy, because there was no way he could turn as tight as my Triplane.

At the back of my mind was the sneaking thought that I'd done something to avenge Beilke after all – inappropriate though that was.

There's hardly any of the old crowd left now – only the Chief, Otto, Horstmann and Bretti. And me, of course. I definitely know more dead men than living ones.

With sixty marks in the kitty we had a truly splendid wake, and were all magnificently hungover when a new pilot arrived at lunchtime the next day. The Jasta had managed two patrols by then, courtesy of the longer days, but without result.

"Which school has he been dragged out of?" Schmidt muttered to me.

"God knows."

Zeitler had passed out top of his course at Valenciennes. We knew because he told us within five minutes.

Horstmann laughed. "I doubt the Tommies will give a shit!"

The boy looked offended, which was a complete waste of effort.

Otto took him to their room, and the second they were out of the hut Teuffel said, "Shall we run a sweepstake on how long he'll last?"

"Why not?" Sobek said. "Might as well get some fun out of it."

"How shall we do it?" asked Schmidt.

"I reckon everyone writes down his guess – five days, three weeks and so on – and puts in five marks," Benner suggested. "Fellmann can be stakeholder. The money goes to the man whose prediction was most accurate."

"Yes, that should work," said Horstmann. "And if the winner's already bought it then the money goes to his family."

"Or his wake," Bretti said.

"What if there's a tie?" I asked.

"They all have to be different," Sobek said. "If it's in between two then the prize is split."

"Fair enough."

"Do we let Zeitler play?" Horstmann asked, and we all laughed.

Schwarz was looking at us as if we smelled, and we laughed harder.

"Won't work if he wins!" Bretti said.

"Yes, it will – it'll pay for the wake!" answered Teuffel.

"Are you running one on me?" Schwarz demanded.

"Of course," Horstmann said solemnly.

"But Becker and I are already out of the running," said Sobek.

Schwarz glared at us both. There was no point telling the truth – he wouldn't have believed us.

"So what are you putting for Zeitler?" Teuffel asked him.

"You might as well play," Benner said. "There's not much fun round here."

"Especially not for you!" said Bretti.

Benner pulled a face.

Schwarz shrugged. "Two weeks, then." He handed Teuffel his five marks.

"Jolly good."

"So what had you put for me?" Schwarz asked me, late in the evening when we were both well lubricated.

I grinned at him. "Omertà."

"What's that mean?"

"It means my lips are sealed!"

Zeitler proved to be so mouthy that the Chief dispensed with half his familiarisation.

"You're flying against me after lunch," he said to the boy the next day, and told him the stakes.

We all gathered to watch. The boss turned him inside out.

"Five," said Bretti as the Chief got on Zeitler's tail once again.

"This is getting expensive," Horstmann said.

You could see who was the victor, and who the vanquished, as they walked towards us. The boy looked as if he'd been hit by a truck.

They went into the Chief's office, and the rest of us went to get dressed for flying.

Zeitler managed to survive his first two weeks. By then it was early March, and the longer days and the hint of spring were doing their best to lift my spirits.

I have got through my last winter of the war. There won't be another because my chances of seeing December are nil, and because we can't— I didn't want to finish that sentence. I knew my poor country couldn't take much more.

The point was underlined every time we flew, as every time we met a more numerous enemy. There was still no sign of the promised Fokker D.VII, and our Triplanes were becoming more and more tired. Mine climbed with marked reluctance, as if she'd had enough of war. Fellmann had requested a new engine, but it was taking time to arrive.

I wish the fucking thing would just fail, preferably over our side. Then I could have a few days' rest. The longer days and better weather might be good for the soul, but I'm getting knackered from the extra flying.

I knew I was getting nearer the edge of the precipice. Every time we flew my nerves were just a bit worse. Some mornings the sick fear was so bad that it was all I could do to keep my coffee down, and I'd long forgotten what a good night's sleep was. Either I lay awake staring at the ceiling, trying not to think, or I had nightmares. The burning dream recurred every few days, and the fucking shitting thing was always exactly the same.

You've got a parachute now – you won't burn, I told myself as I lay shaking yet again.

But what if I can't get out?

Maybe I could get a posting to Döberitz – then I could see Karl. We could walk hand in hand under the limes, and then go upstairs to bed... And when I had nightmares he'd chase the ghosts away. Maybe the war would end before I had to come back here, and slowly, bit by bit, I would start to get better.

And there are fairies dancing round the hangar.

Horstmann wasn't quite as far down the slope as I was, but the twitch at the corner of his eye was more frequent. We were far from alone – the atmosphere in the mess was often strained, and the only way we could relax was by getting pissed.

Claudette's reopened, but it was a while before we felt like going back.

"It's the safest time of all," Sobek pointed out. "And Benner's banned."

"I know," said Bretti. "But that was a hell of a scare."

"Sod it," Teuffel said. "I'll be dead next week, or the week after. I'm having a fuck while I can."

"I bet you all want to know where the infection came from," Fellmann said.

"We can guess that," said Horstmann. "It was the carmine-collared."

"And that's where you're wrong! It was an Artillery Captain."

"How the fuck did you find that out?" asked Schmidt.

"Oh, I know everything!"

"Bet you don't know when my new engine will be here," I grumbled.

"The day after tomorrow, so there!"

"Believe that when I see it." I lit another cigarette, wishing the tremor in my hands would stop. "If it doesn't come, then I'm pinching Zeitler's Triplane and he can sit on the ground."

That was crap, of course. We couldn't afford to leave anyone on the ground.

The next day we were in the middle of lunch when the phone rang. A minute later, Möller came into the mess.

"Excuse me, Squadron Commander, sir, gentlemen – I'm very sorry to disturb you." He turned to Fellmann. "You're wanted on the phone, sir – I asked if I could take a message, but it's a Hauptmann Dietlein and he insists on speaking to you."

"Oh, all right. Do excuse me, sir, everyone."

He came back with a huge grin on his face.

"Well, you'll never guess what that was about."

"Go on," said the boss.

"The good Captain and his men have an undamaged Sopwith Camel and it's ours. We just need to collect it and then you can all have some fun."

"How on earth did they get hold of that?" asked Otto.

"Pilot made a forced landing near the village they're resting at – he was trying to set it on fire and didn't understand 'Hände hoch', so they shot him."

"Shit!" said Zeitler. "What, just like that?"

Horstmann shrugged. "What did he expect?"

"Yes, but if he didn't understand—"

"You know what a rifle bolt sounds like," I said.

"Oh. Yes. Is he dead, then?"

"No," said Fellmann, "but he's on his way to hospital, so we won't be able to entertain him."

"That's a shame," Horstmann said. "We might have learned a new song."

"So why are *we* getting the Camel?" asked the Chief.

Fellmann hesitated and started blushing. "I don't really know, sir," he said awkwardly.

"Yes, you do," said the Chief. "You did another of your deals, didn't you?"

"Well, sir, I... er... I didn't think you knew about that."

The boss started laughing. "Fellmann, I've known for God knows how long that you trade Becker's and my pictures for all sorts of things. Just let us know when you need more photographs signing."

"Oh – yes, of course... How did you know?"

The Chief pretended to think. "What's the word, now? Oh, yes – omertà!"

Fellmann blushed harder, and once again I wondered where he'd learned it. "Ah... yes... er... that's right, sir... Braun and co are on their way to collect it, anyway."

It arrived, and we stared at the beautiful instruments in the cockpit. They were edged with brass.

Brass, for God's sake! They can afford to put instruments like this in combat aircraft, that by their very nature are expendable, and we can barely afford ordinary metal parts. All this wealth is lined up against us, and we're running out of everything.

The aircraft was in perfect condition, and while we were flying Braun's boys replaced the roundels with crosses.

There was just enough daylight for the Chief, Horstmann and me to fly the thing – and it was a truly sobering experience. The Camel's only vice was its propensity to spin. Apart from that, it was formidable.

Now I know why the Tommies are doing so well.

"Fucking hell," said Horstmann, echoing my thoughts. "I almost wish I hadn't flown it."

"Why's that?" asked Sobek.

"You'll find out in the morning."

In the intervals between patrols we all flew it against each other. Even Zeitler was reduced to silence after he'd run rings round Schwarz's Triplane.

"What did you think of that, then?" Günther asked him.

"Er... bit of an eye-opener," was all the boy said.

"Like fucking Christmas for me," Günther said.

"Yes, but you've done three months already," said Schwarz.

Günther had been poached from another Jasta to replace Beilke.

"I spent most of that sitting on the ground looking at the shit weather," he said, "and I reckon it's good to know what we're up against."

"Even if we can't find many flaws," Benner said.

We weren't quite so happy a couple of days later when the Chief said it had to go to Valenciennes.

"I suppose it would be rather selfish of us to keep it," Otto said, and we couldn't really argue.

My new engine arrived, and I was amazed by the transformation. My tired old Triplane leapt into the air, and climbed as if she had a firework up her arse.

"Nice not to have to throttle back for you any more," said Horstmann.

"I'm struggling to keep up now," Sobek said.

"Yes, I noticed," I replied. "I'll have a word with Fellmann."

Who sighed. "Another fucked engine – you chaps do thrash them."

"What do you expect us to do?"

"I know... I'll get the order in."

I had a letter from Alfred, who was back from the Alpine war and who was busy training storm troops. I laughed when I read that, and the next sentence didn't disappoint.

'If they imagine I'm staying here once things kick off they're wrong,' he wrote. 'There's only one place I'll want to be, and I'll move Heaven and Earth to get there.'

Good old Alfred, just as belligerent as ever. 'Once things kick off...' We'd heard rumours about a build-up to a really big spring offensive, but nothing unusual was happening in our area. The Ypres sector was as always – a cauldron of simmering violence, on the verge of exploding.

'I had a letter from Karl,' he went on, 'and I'm hoping to get the chance to go and see him. He probably told you we bumped into each other near Verdun – that's nearly two years ago and we've got a lot of catching up to do.'

You haven't mentioned seeing him at the Adlon. Karl was right about you wanting to keep that quiet. I hope you do go and see him – I'd like your opinion on how he is.
Karl himself barely enlightened me, of course. I knew his medical board was coming up, but his letters said so little about his health that I wondered whether he'd tell me the results.

The rumours of a spring offensive got louder.

"My cousin reckons it's going to be the biggest bombardment in history," said Horstmann.

"Do you think you should be repeating that?" Zeitler asked.

Horstmann rolled his eyes. "This isn't some café in Berlin with God knows who listening – and if any of you turns out to be a spy I'll shoot him myself." There was a pause, and then he continued, "And there'll be God knows how many divisions waiting to go in."

"1914 all over again," said Otto.

"Hopefully not," I said.

"Maybe this time we'll break through," said Schwarz.

"And have the manpower to follow it up, not like Verdun," Horstmann said.

"We could take Paris and win the war," Günther added. "That would be something."

I've heard all this before, I thought with sudden weariness, *and for most of us it's going to be completely academic.*

"Champagne on the Champs-Élysées," Teuffel said.

"French tarts!" Bretti added gleefully.

"I'm going to get ready," I said.

Otto limped out of the mess after me. "You don't believe it, do you?" he asked.

I sighed. "I'd like to – but there've been so many disappointments… We just have to do what we can."

"Maybe we'll be ordered south."

"Who knows?"

The afternoon was already well advanced, the sun on its way down as we climbed. Above us a layer of cloud was spread like gold lace across the pure blue of the sky. *Such loveliness, and all we can find to do is kill.*

Half an hour later I sent a Bristol Fighter down in flames with a frontal attack. The pilot was so surprised that he only managed to get off a few rounds at me.

The Chief gave me a rather straight look as he started the debrief. "Well, Becker, that was a very bold attack." He turned to Zeitler and Schwarz. "Gentlemen, remember that Leutnant Becker is a very experienced fighter pilot, who knows when such an attack is likely to succeed. When you have his score you can think about doing the same thing, but until then follow Boelcke's Rules."

Horstmann gave me a very sharp look as we changed. "What the fuck did you do that for?"

I shrugged. "Seemed like a good idea – and it did work out."

"Don't start behaving like Johnny. You know where that ends."

That sobered me up a bit. "Don't worry – it was a one-off."

"Just use your fucking brain."

"No chance – it's been too well pickled!"

Two days later I got a letter from Karl.

'My dear Franz, many congratulations on your continued success – you're leaving me well behind!'

He went on with some inconsequential stuff.

'But I'm beating about the bush instead of giving you my news. I had my medical board yesterday' – I hardly dared read the next words. *They can't have passed you fit, surely* – 'and you'll be pleased to hear they rejected me, and gave me three more months' leave.'

Thank God for that. The war just might be over by then.

'They did a lot of tests, but wouldn't say what was bothering them, just that I need more time to recover. So it seems I'm stuck here while the rest of you have all the fun.'

That just shows how things have changed since last summer. We had the upper hand then...

'It's so frustrating, and I feel quite guilty that I'm doing nothing, so I've applied for the Technical and Testing Commission. The interview's next week, so I'll let you know.'

Good. With a bit of luck they'll take you and then you'll be safe for good.

'I think often of January, and hope you'll be able to come and stay again soon. Watch your tail and break a leg!
Ever yours,
Karl.'

I think of January often as well – what wouldn't I give to be in Brandenburg with you? The longing that swept over me was so powerful I could hardly breathe. All I wanted was to be in Karl's arms, with his voice in my ear and that lovely silken skin against mine...

"Becker's got another love letter!" said Bretti.

"Bollocks!" I retorted. "No one sends me love letters."

He laughed. "Apart from half the women in Germany!"

"Come on!" said Schmidt. "Show us her picture!"

I could feel myself going beetroot red. Fortunately I did have two letters from lonely women, and I fished out one of the pictures and handed it over.

"Very nice," Bretti said appreciatively.

"She's yours," I said, and left the mess before anyone could say another word.

I put Karl's letter in the drawer with the others. There was quite a pile of them.

'Don't look at him like that in public,' Johnny said. 'It was – soppy.'

His voice was so clear that I actually turned round, but of course I was alone.

I went to see Fellmann.

"Karl's applied for Technical and Testing," I said.

"Thank God for that – with his contacts he'll probably get it as well. Let's keep our fingers crossed."

"He just wants it as an interim, though – he says they've given him another three months' leave and he's getting bored."

Fellmann sighed. "Let's hope someone has more sense than he does – I'll never forget how he looked lying on that stretcher. God knows how he's alive at all. His right lung must be completely buggered."

"That's just what I think… The Chief won't have him back, anyway."

Fellmann just looked at me. *The boss isn't immortal*, his face said.

"It might be down to you."

"Me? How d'you make that out?"

"Because if – God forbid – the boss joins the Great Army, you'll be in command."

"Bollocks. Anyway, that would be dead simple – I'd just send Karl home."

There was something in Fellmann's eyes that I couldn't quite read, and I didn't want to try.

"When's Karl's medical?" Otto asked me later.

"He had it last week – they've given him another three months' leave."

Otto just looked at me. "Why? I mean, surely he should have had a medical discharge?"

Suddenly I understood exactly why, but I didn't want to think it, let alone say it. *Because once they do that, they've lost him. This way they can still use him, if he improves.*

Shit. There must be something I can do…

The next morning I knocked on the Chief's door after second breakfast. He'd downed a two-seater on the dawn flight, and was in a good mood.

"Sir, I had a letter from Leussow. They've given him another three months' leave."

"That is good news," he said. "He mustn't come back until he's fit. This is no place for someone who's not up to it – the fellow would be a danger to everyone, not just himself."

"I'm a bit concerned they haven't given him a medical discharge – you'd think after an injury like that…"

"Yes, you would… Look, I'll put in a word – I've got a couple of contacts in Hoeppner's office – but we have to recognise that he may well be fit in three months' time."

"Thank you, sir." Hoeppner was the Commanding General of the Air Service, so if anyone could get Karl into Technical and Testing, he could. "It might be over by then."

The Chief smiled. "Let's hope so."

And then we can all go home, and you'll be there to celebrate the birth of your first child. And so might I…

Hang on – it's nearly nine months since Maria and I went to bed. If I did make her pregnant, then I could be a father already.

I ran that thought through my mind a few times, not sure whether I liked it or not, and dismissed it as speculation. Johanna had written that the Hertels still hadn't come back, and that there was no news of them.

Well, if Maria still wanted me she'd write. I get letters from all over Germany, after all. Stuff her.

In the early hours of 21st March I was woken by distant thunder. It got steadily louder until the hut was vibrating, the windows rattling.

Horstmann started yelling in his sleep, and I went over and shook him.

"*Sound the alarm!* Oh, shit, sorry, Becker – I thought I was back at the Somme."

"I'm not surprised, with that racket."

He listened for a moment. "It's started, then."

"So it seems."

I got back into bed and lay listening to it. *That's a bombardment.*

"Must be bloody heavy if we can hear it," Horstmann said. "Poor bastards."

"Indeed."

For a moment I actually felt sorry for the men on the receiving end, shivered as I remembered pressing myself into the mud as the shells exploded all around – and I hadn't experienced anything as heavy as this one.

It must feel as if the earth itself is erupting. It must be unbearable. But the worse it is for them, the better. It really might cut the wire and leave the trenches full of corpses so our fellows can just walk in. This time we might succeed.

The atmosphere in the mess was electric, as if the distant battle had sent a current running through us all. Everyone's eyes were shining.

"When are they going to want us?" Zeitler asked.

"It's a bit much being here when it's all happening there," said Teuffel.

"Yes," Bretti agreed. "That's the biggest battle in history and there must be hundreds of Tommies and Frenchies up."

"The war's going to be decided without us," Benner said with a sigh.

"We might get ordered south," said Otto. "I mean, they might need everybody."

"Well, gentlemen," the Chief said, with an approving look at us all, "we can help by giving the Tommies plenty to think about here. I wouldn't be surprised if they tried an attack in this sector, to take the pressure off their chaps to the south."

Just one more effort, I thought as we suited up. *Just one more push from us all and it'll be over.*

The Chief seemed to have a point. The Tommies did seem to be turning it up, and we ran into a huge formation that really gave us something to think about.

Poor Schwarz didn't get long to think about anything. One moment he was at the head of a five-man tail-chase, with Benner trying to get a Camel off his tail, and the next he was spinning, and I didn't see whether he got out because there was a French Spad XIII trying to get behind me.

The olive-green Jasta had piled in as well, and one of them was straight on the tail of the Spad. Sobek left the fight with a stationary propeller, I spotted an SE5 trying to linger on the edge, and the silly sod broke right when he saw me coming.

I got him with the second burst and then had a merry dance with his patrol leader, and more Camels arrived, diving down from some ridiculous height, and on it went.

And then I realised to my horror that I only had about twenty rounds left, and that the fight showed no sign of ending.

The only thing I could do was bluff, and hope no one noticed I wasn't actually firing.

About a year later the Tommies all buggered off westwards. We left the pursuit to our olive-green colleagues and headed home.

Uhlig clucked and shook his head. "Lot of holes again, sir."

"Have a look at the belts," I managed to say. I was shivering so much my teeth were chattering, and I'd bitten halfway through my fag.

"Bloody hell. What belts?"

"What's this?" asked the Chief.

"Almost out of ammunition, sir."

"You and me both. That was rather warm. You've got a lot of holes – but then so has everyone. Especially Schwarz, no doubt."

Sobek phoned in and said that he'd managed to reach the Gotha base, but that his engine was well fucked. Fellmann swore, and sent Zaffke and Schiffer in the truck with the spare.

"Had to shut it down because the vibration was so bad," Sobek told us when he got back. "Then I found I was heading for No Man's Land and got it started again. So I reckoned I'd keep it going till it packed up, and it held out all the way to the Gotha boys."

Schwarz hadn't been so fortunate. We were in the middle of dinner when we heard that he'd managed to land, and was on his way to hospital. Fellmann gave it another couple of hours before ringing them – and came back into the mess with a very sober face.

"I'm very sorry to say he was dead on arrival," he said. "Braun will fetch his body in the morning."

"Poor little sod," said Günther.

"Lousy timing, when it's all about to end," added Zeitler.

Horstmann just looked at him. *Yes – how many times have we been told that this offensive is the one that will break through?*

But this time we'd really done it. By the time we'd buried poor little Schwarz, the papers were full of the huge gains our troops had made. The English and the French were falling back kilometres every day.

Hope filled us with renewed energy and enthusiasm. Victory was in sight. We flew and flew, but suddenly I wasn't as tired as I had been.

"It's like the lecturer saying, 'And finally,'" Otto said. "You realise it's nearly over and it perks you up no end."

"Papers!" said Fellmann, entering the mess with his arms full. There was almost a fight over the illustrated ones.

The storm troops were the heroes of the hour, and there were several pictures of granite faces under steel helmets. I looked closely, but none of them seemed to be Alfred. *I wonder if he made it to the Front, and, if so, whether he's still in one piece.*

"You can't help wondering why some clever general didn't think of this before," Horstmann said.

"Isn't that an oxymoron?" asked Kleber, who'd arrived a couple of days earlier to replace Schwarz, and who was also horrifyingly young. 'Just done my Abitur,' he'd told us, 'got my place at Tübingen for after the war...'

He was the only one who could still say 'after the war' without inverted commas in his voice. Even Zeitler had started doing that.

"Yes, it probably is!" said Otto with a laugh.

"Bloody university types," Teuffel grumbled again. "What the fuck is an oxymoron?"

Kleber explained.

"Oh, right," said Teuffel. "Well, then, yes – a clever general is indeed an oxymoron."

"They do seem to have found one this time, though," Bretti said.

"So why the fuck couldn't this have been done at the bloody beginning?" Horstmann demanded.

Why indeed? Anton would probably have been killed, but Kurt might be alive, and Friedrich, and Johnny, and the Major. Karl would still be the youngest son and he wouldn't have been shot, and Verdun would never have happened, nor the Somme... We'd be back at Heidelberg, with a fine adventure behind us and stories to tell the girls.

No point thinking about it. No point dwelling on the millions of men who wouldn't have been mutilated to death.

"Let's just hope we can push it right home this time," I said.

"Indeed," agreed Horstmann.

"You are such a pair of cynics," Zeitler protested.

"No, they're not," said Bretti quietly. "We've all seen it before – well, nothing quite like this, but—"

"Exactly," said Zeitler. "Nothing quite like this."

"So when are we going to get our turn?" Benner asked. "I'm getting pissed off with being stuck here in a sideshow."

Not quite my choice of word, but I can see his point. The papers were full of the exploits of Richthofen's Fighter

Group and the other squadrons that were fighting over the battlefield.

"If this is a sideshow then God knows what the main event is like," Horstmann said to me the next day as we peeled off our sweat-soaked underwear. It had been another bastard of a patrol.

"Can't be much worse – anyway, you should be happy with that Camel."

"Oh, I will be, once it's confirmed."

Teuffel was also grumbling about not heading south. "They're getting all the glory," he said, flourishing the paper.

"Glory has its price," Horstmann said.

"You can talk, being as you just got one."

"So do the same!"

It took a week, but he did it, and that left him one short of being an ace.

The aerial activity was frantic, and we seemed to spend more of the daylight in the air than on the ground. The Tommies were definitely more numerous but they were also less experienced, and within the next fortnight the Chief got two more, putting him on thirty-seven. Bretti also stood on the verge of acedom with four, and dear old Otto actually sent an SE5 down in flames.

"I can't believe it," he kept saying. "I've actually shot something down."

We were in the middle of celebrating when Möller came in and went up to the Chief, who left the mess. Five minutes later he came back and had to bang hard on the table to get everyone's attention.

"Gentlemen – that was General von Schutte's Chief of Staff. A fresh offensive is planned in the Ypres sector" – he was drowned out by cheering – "and we'll receive our orders in the morning."

"Bloody good news," Horstmann said.

"Our turn for some of the glory," said Benner.

"Bleif! Champagne!" bellowed Fellmann, the windows rattling.

When it arrived, the Chief raised his glass. "To victory."

"To victory!"

The party got going properly after that. None of us stopped to ask why they needed to open a new offensive if the first one was so successful. That thought sneaked into my mind in the early hours, and I dismissed it.

They're doing it to hit the Tommies in two places at once, I told myself. *That's all. It doesn't mean there's a problem.*

III

If we'd thought things were hectic before, we soon found out how much worse they could get. The days were longer and the fighting more intense than I'd ever known. In between patrols we collapsed in the mess or went back to bed.

The bombardment went on day and night, but I was so fucking knackered that I slept through much of it.

"Who said he wanted a share of the glory?" Horstmann grumbled one morning over second breakfast.

"Teuffel, wasn't it?" Sobek asked with a grin.

Teuffel started. "What?"

"You were the one who wanted a fight," Sobek reminded him.

"Oh – and no one else did?"

Zeitler was nodding in his chair, his breakfast half eaten.

"Do you think he'd notice if I nicked his ham?" Kleber asked.

"Probably not," said Otto.

Zeitler did notice. "Give that back, you bastard!"

Kleber stuffed the ham into his mouth. Zeitler lunged at him, and Kleber leapt up and ran towards the door.

Zeitler caught him and wrestled him to the ground. "Rotten thief!"

Horstmann opened one eye. "Bloody puppies playing," he said, and closed it again.

"Better hope they've got teeth, then!" Bretti said.

Horstmann just grunted.

"Papers!" Fellmann came into the mess with the latest delivery. "This time you can read about yourselves!"

And there on the front page was the Chief, now a forty-victory ace. We'd been too exhausted to have much of a party, but we'd garlanded his aircraft with a '40' and Fellmann had taken a photo, for the album and no doubt as illegal tender as well.

There was quite a long piece about the squadron to go with it, and pictures of all of us who'd enjoyed recent success: my score now stood at thirty-one, Horstmann's at eight, and Teuffel was a freshly minted ace.

There were several articles about the battle, on the ground and in the air.

"Buggered if I recognise any of this," said Benner.

"Me neither," Otto agreed, and read out a particularly purple passage, full of shit about young knights of the sky.

We started laughing.

"If the coverage of the ground action's as bollocks as that, we've got no chance of knowing what's happening," Schmidt said.

"We never have had," I said. "We're best off using our eyes."

I turned the page. There were several photographs purporting to be from the front line, but they were obviously posed. One was of a sniper taking aim while his observer gazed through his binoculars.

If they're in the front line I'll eat my hat. The trench is far too clean. They're far too clean. There's no one else in sight. And the observer's not wearing a steel helmet and his head's way above the parapet. The sniper's taking a chance as well, tin hat or not...

I wonder if Taschner's still alive? I could see them only too clearly in the dawn light, Karl rolling the two of them from one shell-hole to the next. *God knows how they got away with it.*

"That's a bit posed, isn't it?" Horstmann commented.

I laughed. "Just a bit. Not how Karl would have done it at all."

"Quite... have to say I've always been in two minds about that job."

"What do you mean?" Not that I really needed to ask.

"Bit cold-blooded, isn't it? Shooting someone who's coming at you with a bayonet is one thing, but hiding yourself away and putting a bullet into some chap who's minding his own business – I wouldn't be happy doing that, and I've always wondered what sort of man can be. Don't misunderstand me – Karl's a good bloke and I like him well enough, but I don't like thinking about what he used to do."

"As he said, the fellow who's minding his own business today will come to kill us tomorrow."

"There is that, but even so I'm glad they never asked me to do it."

"No chance – you don't shoot well enough!"

Horstmann laughed and changed the subject, and five minutes later it was time to suit up again.

I found I couldn't stop thinking about Karl dragging Taschner slowly back. I told Horstmann about it as we were changing after the last flight. He shook his head, then sat on his bed and looked at me.

"Becker, there are two things you must remember about Karl. The first is that he's too brave for his own good—"

"You don't need to tell me that!"

"I know, but hear me out. You and I don't have that sort of lunatic courage, and we're better off without it. If we got hit as badly as him, we'd lie in our hospital beds thinking, *Oh joy, my war is over*, and looking forward to a medical discharge and a pension. I'd be dreaming of going home to Susanne and you'd be dreaming of whoever it is – don't deny it, I've seen you staring into space looking doughy. Anyway, the Leussows of this world lie in their beds thinking, *How soon can I get back to the Front?*"

"I don't believe he's like that," I said, knowing I was talking crap.

"Yes, he is. You may have known him longer than me, but I've only known him as a soldier and I know what I've seen. He's like that storm troop mate of yours, the one who's always in hospital."

"Friedemann."

"That's the fellow. There's nothing to choose between them. The second thing you need to remember is that Karl is – well, a Leussow."

What the fuck else would he be? "Is that today's statement of the glaringly bloody obvious?"

"You know what I mean. How many of them have died in uniform? His parents fed him honour, duty, and the family history for breakfast, lunch and dinner every day."

"That's just what Fellmann said…"

"Exactly. Karl's going to try to come back, and you need to be aware of that."

"They won't let him. He has to get through his next medical board."

"How closely do they look at anyone these days? He's an ace with the Blue Max. When he says he wants to come back, they'll pass him fit."

"He can barely climb the stairs, for God's sake. He's an invalid – I hate saying it, but it's true. There's no way he can ever fight again. *It's completely impossible*."

"Sorry, Becker. I didn't mean to annoy you."

You always have to open your big mouth. I understand why you've said it, though – I know Karl's thinking exactly the way you described. But I can't see that he'll be passed fit.

"Let's go and eat," I said.

"Anyone for Claudette's?" asked Sobek.

"Bloody good idea," Schmidt replied.

Seven of us squeezed into the squadron car. Offering to drive got me the best seat – Horstmann sat in the other front seat, with Bretti on the floor between his legs, while Sobek, Kleber, Schmidt and Günther squeezed themselves into the back. The Mercedes felt awkward with the extra load, and I had to be careful to brake early. There was one nasty moment when we nearly hit the back of a truck.

"Watch out, Becker – someone might get hurt!" Horstmann said, and we all laughed far harder than the joke deserved.

Claudette had a new girl. Horstmann was rather taken with her, and as Anne and I passed them he was caressing her very shapely behind.

"You're not hanging about," I said.

"In more ways than one!" he replied.

The girls looked at each other.

"You want us both together?" asked the new girl. "We make a nice show for you."

Helena and Marion, head to tail on the huge bed in Kempinski's, and Karl going to join them…

Horstmann looked at me, rather doubtfully. "What d'you reckon, Becker?"

"I'm not doing four in a bed with you!" I said, laughing, and carried on upstairs with Anne.

That was probably my last fuck, I thought on the way home. That idea was far too depressing, and I did my best to banish it with booze.

As we were undressing, Horstmann said, "It's got nothing to do with Susanne, you know."

"What hasn't?"

"Going to Claudette's. I'd never do it at home, but a chap needs to relax – especially when things are as hot as they are just now."

"Why the fuck are you telling me that?"

"She believes I'm faithful."

"So far as I know, you are. Paying a tart isn't the same thing at all."

"You know that and so do I – but women are a bit funny about these things. She'd be very upset if she found out."

"Well, I won't tell her – I'm not likely to meet her, anyway, am I?"

"You won't say a word?"

"Horstmann, I swear on everything I hold holy—"

"Not much value in that!"

"All right, I give you my word: I shall never breathe a word to Susanne about tarts. Now stop being such an old woman and let me get some sleep!"

He put his light out, and, a moment later, asked, "What was that about not doing four in a bed with me?"

"I don't know you well enough!" I replied cheerfully.

"So have you, then?"

"*Omertà!*"

"I'll bet it was with Karl and those dancers in Berlin."

"*Omertà!*"

"So what was it like?"

I laughed. "*Omer-bloody-tà!*"

"Bastard!"

"That's me!"

You'll just have to use your imagination, and I'll bet that's pretty fertile. I'm certainly not telling you anything about it.

A couple of days later the Chief brought down another two-seater, this time by shooting the engine to pieces. The crew landed unharmed near one of our heavy batteries, and the aircraft was only slightly damaged. The boss was keen to get a salvage party there before someone else did.

"Becker, would you go with Braun and co, invite the crew for dinner?"

"Of course, sir."

That'll make a nice change, get away from the airfield for a few hours. My Triplane was grounded with a broken rib in the right middle wing and wouldn't be ready before the next morning, and I wasn't sorry to have a rest.

The downed aircraft was surrounded by curious artillerymen.

"Didn't realise they were so bloody flimsy," said one.

"Wouldn't get me up in one of those," remarked another. "Look, it's made of cloth!"

I smiled to myself. *They're a bit stronger than you think – but perhaps not that much.*

The two Tommies were standing next to the fuselage, looking rather apprehensive. *So would I, surrounded by armed enemies.*

"Was it you who brought us down?" asked the pilot.

"No, it was my – my chef – er…"

My bloody English! It was all right when I wasn't tired, but I just couldn't think of the English for 'Chief'.

"Your CO?"

"Yes. Yes. My CO."

Silly bugger, Franz. A chef is someone the English have in their kitchens.

"We never saw him. The first thing we knew was when the engine stopped. It was damned good shooting."

"He is a good man. You meet him later, at the airfield. We would like you to come and eat with us."

"That's awfully kind of you," said the observer.

"It's our pleasure."

They climbed into the back of the truck, seeming quite happy even though Zaffke and Schiffer were sitting opposite them with rifles.

I half-envied them. *No more patrols for you. You can have a nice rest, and the only hazard will be the boredom of prison. No one's going to try to kill you tomorrow, not like me…*

When we got to the airfield, I cut one of the numbers from the fuselage for the Chief. Like many fighter pilots, he was very fond of his collection of bits and pieces. It wasn't something I'd ever gone in for. I just kept a record in my log book of what I'd shot down and when.

"I say," said the pilot, "can I have the other one?"

"Of course."

I cut it out for him, and then the observer decided he wanted the one of the roundels, so I cut that out as well. I was just about to take them into the mess when the sound of engines announced the return of the Staffel.

There's the Chief in the lead, Benner, Sobek, Otto, Teuffel, Zeitler... Where's Horstmann? Oh, yes, hidden behind Kleber. No casualties. Good.

The Englishmen were standing beside me as the squadron broke formation and, one by one, came in to land. As Horstmann turned onto his final approach, the nose of his Triplane dropped suddenly and then rose again as he blipped the engine.

Something's wrong. Yes, the wind's beginning to gust up, but Horstmann's an experienced pilot and he can cope better than that.

Each time Horstmann cut the power the nose dropped, and then rose again with each blip. As the Triplane lurched drunkenly earthward, the babel of German and English voices got louder.

"I say, that doesn't look right, does it, Jenkins?"

"Lost 'is fuckin' elevator if you ask me," said Kessler.

"Reckon you're right," said Uhlig.

Shit. He'll never do it. How's he going to get the nose up for landing? The only way he can raise it is by adding power, and that'll make the Triplane climb. He needs finesse, and you don't get that with a rotary.

He made it down to twenty feet. A gust caught the aircraft and the nose went up. He had no way of lowering it again and the Triplane stalled, hit the ground right wings down and cartwheeled, crumpling into a mass of wood and fabric.

"*Jesus Christ!*" I heard myself shout as I began running across the field towards the wreckage. I almost forgot that three of the squadron hadn't landed yet, almost forgot to look out. *He's dead. He must be dead – but if he's alive we've got to get him out before it burns.*

Horstmann was trying to drag himself out of the wreck. It was beginning to smoulder.

"Are you hurt?"

"Don't think so. Fucking foot's stuck."

We grasped each other's wrists, and I pulled as hard as I could.

"Shit! *It won't come loose!*" The flames were taking hold and I could hear the fear in his voice.

I pulled harder, with no result. *Oh Christ, he's going to burn – we've got to get him out!*

Two pairs of hands joined mine on Horstmann's arms, and I noticed with a shock that one pair had khaki sleeves. Schwarte started pulling at the wrecked fuselage, and Horstmann wriggled like a hooked fish, trying desperately to free his foot. The fire was leaping higher and it was getting bloody hot.

He came loose with such a jolt that all four of us fell in a heap. We picked ourselves up and ran, sliding on the wet ground, Schwarte hot on our heels. We weren't a moment too soon. The Triplane's fuel tank exploded and we threw ourselves flat in the mud.

"Jesus, the magazine!" Horstmann had read my mind. The magazine was right next to the fuel tank, a particularly thoughtful touch on Fokker's part. His words were still hanging in the air as the firework display began.

"Be a bit rough to get shot by your own aeroplane," I said. "How much did you have left?"

"A hundred rounds or so. I like to keep a bit in reserve."

"*Normally* very prudent!"

We couldn't help laughing. The fireworks were soon over and the five of us got up, plastered in mud. Horstmann and I turned and looked at the wreck. The fire had almost burned itself out.

He turned to me. "Thanks, Becker. I owe you a drink for that."

He embraced me in a muddy hug that damn near squeezed the air out of me, and I hugged him back, laughing with relief that he was still alive, that we'd got him out in time. He hugged Schwarte and Teuffel as well, and then stopped dead, looking with astonishment at the English pilot.

"I don't think we've been introduced," he said.

The Tommy looked blank, and I made the introductions in my schoolboy English. They shook hands, with much warmth on Horstmann's side.

Horstmann turned to me. "Becker, will you translate?"

"If I can."

"Will you tell this gentleman that… that he's a very brave and chivalrous man and that I'm very grateful to him? He didn't have to come and help me, after all."

I translated as best I could – I had to substitute 'honourable' for 'chivalrous' – and then added, "I would like also to thank you. This man is my friend but he is your enemy. You did not have to…"

I was trying to remember how to say 'risk your life', but the Englishman, who was blushing dreadfully, said, "Horrible way to go. I couldn't stand and watch that. Besides, you've been decent to us and one good turn deserves another."

Chivalry isn't dead after all. I didn't have the words to tell the man how impressed I was by him. *Would I have risked my life to rescue him, just after being brought down by one of his squadron-mates? Surely he must have his Antons and his Kurts, his Langemarck or his Somme – and yet he went to help Horstmann.*

Why on earth are we fighting each other?

"What happened?" the Chief asked Horstmann.

"Elevator cable broke, sir. I'd taken a few hits – it felt a bit stiff now and then on the way home – it would suddenly get a bit stiff and then free off, but it seemed to be holding. It must have gone as I turned finals – the nose dropped in the turn and I couldn't pick it up. It wasn't going too badly till that bloody gust caught me and I couldn't get the nose down. I thought of putting the power on, but the nose would have gone up even more and I didn't like the idea of that."

"No, quite. Nasty one. Well, the main thing is you're all right – hang on, you're bleeding."

Bugger me, so he is. Blood was running down Horstmann's face and dripping from his jaw. I hadn't noticed, because of the liberal coating of mud.

"Am I?" He got out his handkerchief and wiped his face. "So I am. I expect Fellmann can fix it."

"Time for a glass or two and then dinner, I think," said the Chief. "Oh, I almost forgot our guests."

I made the introductions. "This is the man who brought you down," I said to the Englishmen, and then I turned to the boss. "The pilot helped save Horstmann's life."

"Did he, by God?"

The boss welcomed the Tommies in fluent, almost unaccented English. I'd forgotten that he'd spent six months with an English regiment before the war.

"That was jolly decent of you," he said. "Bloody good show. We owe you a drink or two, I think."

"It was jolly decent of you not to riddle us with bullets," said the observer. "It would have been much easier."

"I flew two-seaters for nearly a year. I know what it's like."

They wandered towards the mess, chatting affably. Horstmann and I went to our room to clean ourselves up.

"I haven't been this muddy since I was in the trenches," I said as I stripped off.

"Neither have I. I did think airmen didn't get covered in mud."

"There is no escape from the Belgian mud… You'd better get that seen to."

The gash on his forehead was quite deep and still bleeding.

"Oh, Fellmann can sort it out," he said again.

"You need stitches," Fellmann said. "I'll take you to the hospital."

"Bugger that – I'm not turning up there with just a cut. You can patch it up, can't you? It'll scar whether it's stitched or not, and I'm hardly a beauty."

"Ooh, I don't know. That fine, manly face!"

"You be careful, Fellmann. I might take you seriously. I'm getting a bit bored with Claudette's tarts – *ow! Bloody hell!* What the fuck's that?"

"Iodine. That'll teach you to be lippy. Now keep your mouth shut, or you'll get some more as a punishment for making me late for dinner."

Horstmann kept quiet as Fellmann sewed him up and bandaged his head, and a few minutes later the three of us joined the others in the mess. Horstmann insisted on buying champagne for the Englishmen, as did I, and they got quite merry.

"Teach us a song," Bretti said. "We are bored with the old ones."

"All right, then," said Sawyer. "What d'you reckon, Jenkins – what about the dying pilot?"

"We know that one," I said.

"Ah," said Sawyer. He thought for a moment, then stood on a chair and began solemnly, "We meet 'neath the sounding rafter, And the walls all around are bare…" and finished, "So stand to your glasses steady, This world is a world of lies. A cup to the dead already, Hurrah for the next that dies."

The Chief was staring into space, and I didn't think he was listening as Otto and Zeitler argued over the translation. When they got to 'a world of lies', I thought I saw him nod slightly.

"I like that," said Horstmann. "Hurrah for the next that dies – that pretty well sums it up." He raised his glass. "To the fallen."

There was a pause.

"What did he say?" asked Jenkins.

The Chief translated, and there was a moment of awkwardness.

"In English we often say, 'Absent friends,'" Sawyer said tactfully.

The Chief translated that.

"Yes, that will do very well," said Horstmann with a smile, and we all drank to those who were no longer with us.

"Now we need to learn the song," I said.

"We'll write it down for you," said Sawyer. "Then you'll just have to learn the tune."

"Pity Karl isn't here," Otto said. "He'd have the tune off in no time."

"I'll give it a go," said Kleber, and sat at the piano.

"Now you teach us one," said Jenkins, so we taught them the Liesl song.

Zeitler was quite surprised that I knew so many rude English words, and the Tommies were astonished.

"My best friend is part English," I explained.

"Your best friend?" Jenkins's face was a picture.

Otto laughed. "And he's Prussian."

"Well, bugger me," said Jenkins.

"Britain and Prussia were allies for centuries," the Chief said quietly. "I regret the present situation more than I can say."

"I suppose we tend to forget that," said Sawyer. "The pub in my village used to be called The King of Prussia, and it had Frederick the Great's portrait on the sign."

"What did he say?" asked Horstmann, who had probably understood 'Prussia' and 'Frederick'.

I translated, and he sighed. "Makes a real nonsense of this business, doesn't it?"

The party came to an end when the escort arrived to take our guests to prison. Even then the escort had to wait nearly half an hour, because just as they were about to leave, Sawyer said something about Aldershot.

"You were at Aldershot?" the Chief asked.

"That's right – from '10 to '13."

"I was there in '13!"

The two of them got lost in reminiscences and stories of mutual friends, the war forgotten.

"Are you going back to England after the war?" asked Sawyer.

"I hope so," said the Chief, and for the first time I saw a shadow in his face.

"If you do, look me up and we'll have a game of tennis. It would be such fun."

"Do you think, after this, that I'd be welcome?"

"Look," said Sawyer, "we've got more in common with you than with those back home – they've got no idea."

A slight smile flickered across the Chief's face. "I know what you mean. Well, thank you for the invitation, and I hope I'll able to take you up on it. I'd like my wife and child to see that… well, that war is made by politicians and not by men like us."

"Amen to that," said Jenkins.

Eventually they made their unsteady way outside to be collected by the escort, who'd been well fed in the kitchen and were in no great rush to leave.

I should have asked them if they knew Karl's brother-in-law, I thought, far too late. *But that's stupid – there are millions of Tommies, so why would they?*

"They're just like us," said Benner. "What the fuck are we doing?"

"If you find out, please tell me," Bretti replied.

"We have a job to do," the Chief said, "and the better we do it, the sooner this whole business will be over."

"Indeed," said Horstmann.

"Did you say, 'wife and child', sir?" asked Fellmann.

The boss's face lit up. "Yes – my wife's expecting. The baby's due in June, if all goes well."

"Congratulations," Fellmann said, echoed by us all.

"I think that calls for another bottle," I said, and we drank to the health and future of the Chief's family.

The next morning Horstmann was hobbling on a very swollen foot, and had a fine collection of bruises.

"Well, it hardly matters when you've got nothing to fly," the Chief said. "You can give Fellmann a hand with the paperwork – I've been too busy to get it all done."

Horstmann pulled a face and headed for the office.

A brand-new Triplane arrived a couple of days later, flown by our old friend Wendt. He jumped down and took his helmet off, and Zeitler and Kleber stared at his burned, melted face.

"Don't gawp," Fellmann said severely, and they both blushed and looked at the ground.

"Just be thankful you've got parachutes," said Schmidt.

"Bloody luxury!" Wendt said, and then added cheerfully, "Still, if I hadn't been fried I'd probably be dead by now."

"There is that," said Bretti.

As we sat down to lunch Wendt looked round the table, and sadness flitted across his face. *It must be like this at every squadron you deliver to. Next time you come here, you probably won't know anyone.*

"I'm sorry we can't stay and talk to you," said the Chief, "but as you'll appreciate we're a bit busy these days."

"'Fraid you're stuck with Fellmann and me," Horstmann said.

"There are worse fates," Wendt replied, with an attempt at a smile. All it did was stretch his scars into an even more frightful pattern.

"Horstmann, come and sit in your new Triplane," said the boss. "See if you can operate the rudder."

It was plain that he couldn't, even if he could have got his flying boot on.

"Jammy bastard," I said, and he just grinned.

He and Wendt stood by the hangars and waved us off. A couple of hours later, we came back without Schmidt. He'd fallen victim to a Camel.

"I do seem to bring you chaps bad luck," Wendt commented. "Last time I was here you got attacked by the Tommies."

"And Patschke crashed on take-off," said Horstmann.

"That's it – and one of your ground crew got shot dead… Fellmann, could I borrow your spare uniform again?"

"If there's a funeral, yes, of course."

There was.

We're taking over this cemetery. There are more pilots' graves than civilian ones now… And once again it's spring and we're putting a young man in the earth, who should have had his life in front of him.

The previous spring felt like a century ago. *I've got so old, and so weary of this whole business. I don't know how much longer I can find the energy to go on.*

The post brought me a batch of letters – most of them were addressed in unfamiliar feminine writing, but one was from Karl and another from Alfred. *I should put Karl's to one side and read it in private later – though what makes them think I look 'doughy' I just don't know, and anyway, I'd better read it now while I'm still here.*

I put on what I hoped was a severe expression and opened the letter.

After the usual teasing about my score, Karl went on, 'I've just come back from Berlin, where I had an interview for the Technical and Testing Commission. Long story short, they don't want me! The whole thing was horribly embarrassing, because I was late. General von Brandt, who's an old friend of Pa's, had set it up and he was waiting for me in the anteroom. I could have died, but he was very kind – as were the interviewers.

Anyway, they said that I wouldn't be able to cope with the workload, and that I should go home and grow food! I had to point out the illogicality of telling a man to go and plough his fields when you've just said he can't do an office job, and to be fair they saw my point.

Apparently I can have Russian prisoners as labourers – and I can tell you, I need them. There are only old men and women left here – the men aren't up to the ploughing and the women don't know how, and it's easier to do it myself than to tell them what to do.'

I didn't like the idea of him ploughing his fields. *You could barely walk two hundred metres in January, so unless you're a lot better I don't see how you can manage. And what if you collapse? How are the old men and the women going to get you back to the house?*

'I was thoroughly fed up with being rejected, no matter how they put it. There was one old boy who'd caught it very badly in 1870 (lance in the belly – he was a Dragoon, in Great-Uncle Heinrich's regiment. Small world!), and he said it'll take longer than I realise and I just have to be patient.

By the way, I think I'm safe from any Mahlke matchmaking. The lady came here yesterday afternoon, all of a flutter. Her worthy husband has been ennobled (!), so her daughter is Clara von Mahlke and has no need of a Karl Leussow! How about that?!'

I had to smile at the almost waspish tone, and the way he'd written, 'Clara von Mahlke', but 'Karl Leussow'.

Horstmann caught my eye and raised an eyebrow. *Shut up and get on with your flower letter*, I almost said, but instead I finished reading Karl's, wishing I could hear his voice...

I put it down with a sigh and a strong feeling of sympathy for him. *Being told you're fit for nothing must be horribly depressing. Maybe talking to that old cavalry officer did some good – Karl's got no way of knowing how fast he can expect to get better.*

I opened Alfred's letter and started laughing.

"What's the joke?" Horstmann asked.

"You know that storm troop mate of mine who's always in hospital?"

"Yes?"

"Guess where he is!"

Horstmann started laughing as well. "What's he got this time?"

"Hang on a mo – 'it's a trivial bloody cut, just got a small shell splinter in my left biceps, no damage to the joint or the bones, but the bastard of it is that the muscle's cut almost right through' – and he says he can't use his arm properly. No strength in it."

"Won't be able to fire a rifle, then," said Otto.

"No."

"Don't those storm troop fellows use carbines?" asked Kleber.

"Same difference," Otto replied. "Still need your left arm."

"He should be out of it for a while, then," Teuffel commented.

Let's hope so. The best thing for Alfred would be a permanent posting to Döberitz, though he wouldn't see it that way.

"How's Karl?" Otto asked.

I almost asked how he knew I'd got a letter from him, but I didn't want to hear the answer. I gave him a summary of Karl's news – I would have handed him the letter, but there was a sentence that could have raised his eyebrows. Karl was always very discreet, but he'd put, 'it's really rather dull here without the sight of your ugly mug in the morning', and I didn't want anyone reading something into that.

There wasn't time to write back before we went flying again, and the fight we got into was so hot that I really didn't think I was going to get back.

Horstmann was sitting by the stove in the mess, the lucky sod. He got up and moved when we came in.

I sagged onto the small sofa beside him and ordered a brandy. I was trembling so much that I almost spilled it.

"Did I miss much?" he asked.

"Oh, fuck off!" Teuffel retorted.

Horstmann just raised his eyebrows and said nothing.

"Sorry," Teuffel said later, and bought him a beer.

"Don't mention it – I'm hoping to be back with you tomorrow."

That was optimistic – it was a whole week before Horstmann could fly again. The rest of us were quite green with envy. His narrow escape must have shaken him more than he would admit, though, because I had to wake him from nightmares almost every night. It had shaken me as well – suppose he'd crashed off the airfield, and no one had got to him in time?

I couldn't help imagining being trapped in the wreckage with the fire taking hold, and the harder I tried to stop thinking about it, the more persistent it became. It haunted my nights, and even going to bed well pissed didn't stop it going round and round in my head. And when I did sleep I had the burning dream, and Horstmann had to wake me.

How much longer can it go on?

Zeitler got his first, and we had a big party because it was also the squadron's hundred and fiftieth victory. He looked as if Christmas and his birthday had come at the same time.

"Just remember this is only the beginning," Benner said to him. "Don't start getting too clever."

"No, I won't," Zeitler said. "There's a big difference between Valenciennes and this."

Good. You've realised that rather quicker than some fellows do.

In place of Schmidt, Fellmann managed to poach Jantke, already an ace. To Horstmann and Bretti's delight, he came from Potsdam.

"That's redressed the balance a bit," Bretti said. "It hasn't been quite right since we lost Beilke."

"Stuff where he comes from," said Günther. "I'm more interested in the seven victories."

"Yes," Horstmann agreed, "it makes a change from getting schoolboys in uniform."

"Oh, come on!" Kleber protested. "I left school last year!"

Everyone except Zeitler laughed.

"Know what a razor is yet?" Sobek teased.

"Of course I do – I shave every morning!"

"Tell you what," said Benner, "don't bother for a week and see if we notice."

"All right, I will."

To my joy the weather broke, with strong winds and heavy rain.

"Thank fuck for that," Sobek muttered to me over a very late breakfast.

"You and me both."

No one was unhappy to have a rest. For the first time since I'd known him, the Chief didn't fret at the imposed inactivity. *You're just as knackered as we are*, I thought but of course didn't say.

"I hear Karl got rejected by Technical and Testing," Fellmann remarked to me over coffee.

Bloody hell – does nothing escape you?

"Yes," I said, noticing that Fellmann wasn't looking as cheerful as I felt. "Why the serious face? If he's not even fit for that, then there's no way he'll be fit to come back."

He gave me a very doubtful look. "Once they accept him for T and T, they're stuck with it – I've never heard of anyone getting back to operational from there. And that'd be one more Pour le Mérite who isn't over the Front scoring more victories."

Shit. "You mean they're keeping their options open."

"That's about the size of it."

"But they told him the workload would be too much."

"They had to say something, didn't they?"

"You haven't seen him."

"No. You're right," he replied with a smile, and I went back to reading and listening to the rain pattering on the mess windows.

Two days of that left the airfield a swamp again. Even the gravel was sinking into the mud.

"We might have to get more *gravel*," Fellmann said, and he, the boss and I laughed, to the complete mystification of the others.

Even after a couple of days of sunshine it was still very slippery and left to ourselves we wouldn't have flown, especially as the cloud had rolled back in again with a solid base at about three hundred metres.

"Maybe tomorrow," Otto said, settling himself on the sofa with a pot of coffee and the *Berlin Illustrated*.

Bretti wound up the gramophone, and I sat down to write to Johanna. She was still trying to convince Mama to let her become a nurse, and in her last letter she'd said that she was going to join the Red Cross and that the parents could poke it.

What on earth do I say to try to dissuade her – though she would be doing valuable work, and why should I want to protect her from reality? All the same, she is my little sister...

Bretti was about to put another record on when the phone rang. It was for the Chief.

"Yes, sir," we heard. "One moment, please, sir, I'd like to write that down... Yes, sir, we'll be there."

We looked at each other. *That did not sound like a quiet day writing letters or whatever.*

The Chief came into the mess, his face very serious. "That was Schutte's Chief of Staff... Would you all come into the Ops Office, gentlemen?"

Möller had to leave so we could all squeeze in.

"We're to join the Junkers J.Is in strafing the Allied troops," the boss said.

A ripple of silent disquiet went round the room. The J.Is were designed specifically for ground attack work. They were armoured and could take a lot of hits without damage, unlike our Triplanes. We would be far from our normal area of operations, and very vulnerable to ground fire.

"Our troops will be attacking on a front from *here* to *here*," the Chief continued, indicating the positions on the wall map, "and our task is to assist them by causing as many casualties and as much pandemonium among the Allied troops as we can. We rendezvous with the J.Is over Houlthust Wood at 11:30."

Terrific. Fucking terrific. This isn't our role at all – but what can you do? Orders is orders...

We took off, joined formation and followed the boss to Houlthust Wood. We arrived at precisely 11:30 and the Junkers turned up about half a minute later. The visibility wasn't very good, and we didn't see them until they were quite close.

That's not good. If the Tommies are up as well we'll be straight into the fight without any preparation.

The Chief led us into formation on the J.Is. 'Furniture vans', the crews called them, and I could see why. *Ugly boxy things, don't look as if they're really capable of flight – and they must be fucking heavy. Whoever thought of building metal aircraft?*

Down we went, through the haze and the intermittent rain, down to twenty metres above the ground, shooting up the trenches and the roads their reinforcements were marching up. I saw the khaki figures clearly as some ran and others dived for cover, saw white faces looking up at us.

The next lot were more alert, and we flew through a hail of rifle and machine-gun fire.

What the fuck am I doing here? This is not my idea of fun at all.

Suddenly I wished I were flying one of those ugly, boxy aeroplanes instead of my fabric-covered Triplane. There was no room to manoeuvre so close to the ground. All we could do was pour lead at the Tommies, and hope they didn't hit anything vital.

I felt horribly vulnerable as we turned to fly parallel to the front line, all of us following the Chief as if glued to him. We raced over a mass of Tommies who were barely a hundred metres from our fellows – the Chief's aircraft flicked over, hit the ground and burst into flames.

He's dead. There can't be much left.

There was no time to think about him. I signalled to the aircraft on my left to formate on me, and they closed the gap. We carried on, over a road crammed with lorries and troop columns, and it seemed that all the time we flew through a wall of lead.

We had used nearly all our ammunition and most of our fuel. It was time to go home.

As we flew back I shook from head to foot, my heart thumping. My throat was so dry I could hardly swallow. *How in God's name did the rest of us escape? The air was practically solid with all that stuff in it…*

The mood was very sombre as we assembled for the debrief. I felt that task fell to me, as I'd taken over command at the time. At the end, Horstmann, Otto and I looked at each other.

"Someone has to be acting CO," I said. "Even if the Chief survived, he'll be out of it for quite some time. I expect Berlin will send us a new boss."

He can't have survived that. No one wanted to say it, but it was in everyone's faces.

"It should be you," Otto said to me. "The boss made you his second in command."

"This is different," I said. "It should be a Regular officer – Horstmann, you're the most senior and the most experienced."

"You're our top ace now," Horstmann replied.

"I agree," said Bretti, and the others backed him up.

"You know it doesn't work that way," I said.

"Hoeppner can appoint who he likes," Horstmann answered. "In the meantime it's up to us, and we'd all be happier if you led us."

You really don't know how bad my nerves are – but I couldn't really argue with them all.

I wrote the combat report, with the bare facts of the Chief's crash. It still hadn't really sunk in. Part of me still hoped that he was in hospital, that he'd been thrown clear on impact. It was inconceivable that he could be dead.

In the afternoon I led the squadron in a repeat performance. *I hate this wretched business. I hope the weather improves soon, so we can go back up high where we belong. Aircraft against aircraft* is one thing, but this grubbing about at ground level with half the British Army shooting at us is another matter entirely. If I have to do much more of it I really will lose my nerve. It's bloody terrifying.

All of us got back safely, but Zeitler, who was last to land, ground-looped.

I'd better have a word with him. He should be able to do better than that. It's not as if there's much wind today.

He taxied about halfway in, then stopped and shut the engine down. He didn't get out.

"Fellmann! *Fellmann!* Bring the first aid kit!" I shouted as we started running across the field towards Zeitler's Triplane.

His bare head was resting against the rim of the cockpit, and he was almost crying with pain. I could smell blood but I couldn't see it.

"Zeitler, where are you hit?"

"Left – left leg, sir. I'm sorry – can't taxi."

I squeezed his shoulder. "All right. We'll get you out in a minute. You'll be fine."

Braun and Zaffke brought a set of steps. Möller followed, clutching the first aid box.

"Where's Fellmann?"

"He's on the phone, sir."

"What the hell's he doing on the bloody phone?" *Get a grip, Franz. Shouting at Möller won't achieve anything. We need to get Zeitler out. Job for a strapping great Brandenburger, I think.* "Zaffke, can you lift him out without hurting him?"

"I'll do my best, sir."

Zeitler was a slightly built lad, and he looked like a child in Zaffke's arms. Zaffke lifted him out carefully, trying not to bang his leg, carried him down the steps and put him gently on the ground. Zeitler whimpered a bit, but to my relief that was all.

Braun started cutting off his flying boot with the shears from the workshop.

"Well done, Zaffke," I said, and sat down beside Zeitler. "When did it happen?" I asked.

"Over the – the long road."

We'd strafed the long road a good fifteen minutes before the end of the low runs. Add to that the time to fly back to the airfield…

"Why didn't you break off and come home?"

"It – didn't hurt too much – at first – only the last – last few minutes. It's—" The words died in a cry of pain as Braun took Zeitler's boot off.

I squeezed his shoulder again. "Well done, Zeitler. You've done a bloody good job. Fellmann should be here in a minute and he'll give you a shot of morphine."

You're a bloody hero. I couldn't find the words to say it without sounding sentimental.

I looked round. Fellmann was running across the airfield.

"Fellmann, where the bloody hell have you been?"

"Sorry, Squadron Commander, sir. Schutte's Chief of Staff. Wanted to thank us for a good job. I couldn't get a word in edgeways."

"Oh, well, better late than never," I said.

"I – lost my – flying helmet," Zeitler said. He could hardly speak.

"Oh, don't worry about that," said Fellmann as he stuck the needle in Zeitler's arm. "You won't need it for a few weeks, and then we'll give you a nice new one."

Zeitler's leg was a mess, the calf muscle torn right open. Fellmann did a very neat job of patching him up.

"Just as well he's out cold," he said. "That would have been rather unpleasant."

"We'd better get him to the hospital," I said. "Zaffke, could you put him in the back of the car?"

"Yes, sir."

"I'll go with him," Fellmann said, "make sure he doesn't fall off the seat."

"Thanks… Uhlig, you drive."

"Yes, sir."

Well, that's you out of it for a while, I thought as they drove out of the gates. *Should be a nice Heimatschuss, and no doubt the girls will give you lots of attention as you hobble round on crutches…*

It won't do that Fellmann's the only one who can give those injections, though. Suppose we get bombed again and he's killed or injured? He'll have to teach Möller to do it, or a couple of the mechanics.

I gathered the others round. "Well done, gentlemen—"

The phone rang.

"It's for you, sir," Möller said to me. "It's Excellency von Schutte's Chief of Staff, Oberst Brinkmann."

I went into the Ops Office and picked up the receiver. "Becker, sir."

"Ah, Leutnant Becker," said a slow and rather deliberate voice. "Excellency von Schutte would like to speak to you. One moment, please."

Fucking hell. The only other general I've spoken to was Lentzke's father.

"Becker." The General sounded younger and more vigorous than I'd expected.

"Your Excellency."

"I'm very sorry indeed to have to tell you that Oberleutnant von Kralewski-Zentzytzki is dead. Our chaps retrieved his body about an hour ago. I presume you'd like to bury him yourselves?"

For a moment I almost couldn't answer him. I'd known that the Chief was almost certainly dead, but had been hanging on to that 'almost'.

"Thank you, Your Excellency," I said heavily. "We'll send a party to collect him."

"There's no need. We'll deliver him to your airfield as soon as possible, with a suitable escort. This is a very sad day, a very sad day indeed."

"It certainly is, Your Excellency."

"I expect you'll be taking over?"

"No doubt Berlin will decide, Your Excellency."

I'm starting to get sick of saying that. I wonder if he gets fed up with hearing it? I realised I was standing to attention, and remembered Karl leaning back in the Chief's chair, smoking as he talked to Grimnitz.

"Yes, no doubt they will. My deepest condolences to your squadron... I've enjoyed talking to you. I wish it had been under happier circumstances."

"Thank you, Your Excellency."

You enjoyed talking to me? Why, for God's sake?

I went back into the mess. The mood was suddenly even more sombre as everyone saw my expression.

"The Chief is dead. They're sending us his body," I said quietly, and began the debrief again. "Well done, gentlemen."

I looked at each of them in turn. No one had turned back with 'engine trouble' or a 'gun jam'. Everyone had flown through that hail of lead, time and again, without flinching. And Zeitler had carried on even after he'd been hit. *He should get something for that. I'll have to put in the recommendation.*

"From a purely military viewpoint the day was a complete success. We gave valuable assistance to our infantry for the loss of one pilot killed and one wounded, and one aircraft lost. However, we – and our country – have lost someone who can never be replaced."

I paused, trying to frame the words.

"Oberleutnant von Kralewski-Zentzytzki led this squadron for eighteen months, and under his leadership it has become one of the most successful on the Western Front. It is now up to us to honour his memory by ensuring that our success continues."

Everyone nodded, and I saw resolution in every face.

"General von Schutte sends us his condolences, and they're allowing us to arrange the funeral," I finished.

"If we're organising the funeral, we need eight Pour le Mérites," Horstmann said. "For the pallbearers."

Shit.

"The General said he's sending a suitable escort," I said. "In the meantime I'll get Fellmann to see who he can get hold of."

"Pity Karl's not here," said Otto. "We'd only have to find six."

"And that would be so easy!" Bretti retorted.

"I'm not sure it matters too much in the circumstances," said Jantke. "Yes, that's the protocol, but it's not that easy when everyone's up to his eyeballs."

"Where are they going to sleep?" Benner asked.

"I'll get Fellmann onto that as well," I replied. "Some of us might have to sleep on the floor for a night or two."

"Bugger that," said Horstmann. "We have to fight. If anyone should sleep on the floor it's the fucking staff."

There was a murmur of agreement.

"Maybe Claudette could put them up!" Kleber said, and we all laughed far too hard.

I went to the hangars to give the ground crew the news.

"This is a very sad day, sir," Braun said, and the others echoed him.

"Yes," I said. "It was a good way to go – over very quickly. Braun, they're sending us his body. I don't know when it will arrive, or whether there'll be anything for you to do – though I have to say the coffin will almost certainly be closed."

"That does seem likely, sir, from what you told us earlier."

"Can you have the aircraft ready for dawn?"

"We'll do our best, sir."

"Thank you."

I could see the unspoken question in their eyes.

"We'll have to wait and see what Berlin says – I'll let you know as soon as I hear."

"Thank you, sir," Braun said.

"I've held you up long enough," I said, and went to the Chief's office.

The wake was just getting under way. *That was quite a day. I'd like to get pissed as well, but I'll have to stay relatively sober. And in the meantime I've got the sodding paperwork to do, to request two pilots and another Triplane. And I'll have to go through the Chief's things – and oh, fuck. I'll have to write to his wife. Better get that done first. At least I can tell the truth about his death.*

I fetched the next of kin book from the Ops Office. It was an index book – each new pilot wrote the relevant details in it, and when he was killed, or injured badly enough to be taken off the strength, his name and the address of his family would be struck through.

There were a lot of crossings-out.

I sat at the Chief's desk with a very heavy heart. Yes, I'd sat there before, but always with the knowledge that he was coming back. This time I felt like a usurper.

The squadron without the Chief was unthinkable. *It'll always be his Jasta, no matter who takes over. He was a bloody good bloke, in every way...*

And what I remember most is how kind he was: to Lentzke, to Karl when he was in hospital, and to Karl and me. He probably thought we were lovers – many men would have posted one of us away, but he just noted it and left us alone.

I'm putting the letter off.

I picked up my pen and started to write, but all I could see was Elise's face lighting with joy and love as she looked at the

Chief, and all I could think was that their child would never know its father. *He'd have been a good father...*
She knew the odds.
It took me four attempts, but finally the letter was finished.

'It was a privilege to know your late husband and to serve under him,' I concluded. 'Our country is poorer without him.'

The party was getting louder.
"Are you coming to dinner?" Fellmann asked.
"Yes – I'll be there in a moment."
I hadn't realised how late it is. Sorting the boss's things out can wait until morning.
We drank to the Chief and to the future of the Jasta. The evening seemed likely to turn into a proper piss-up.
Why not? They've had quite a day. They need to unwind.
I left the party shortly after dinner and went to the hangars. I looked at my Triplane and wondered how on earth I'd come back in one piece.
"Don't count the holes, sir," said Uhlig. "You don't want to know."
"Have you all had something to eat?"
"Yes, sir – we had a break about two hours ago. We're all right – we'll have them ready for the morning, no problem. There's a lot of patching but no real damage. We washed out the cockpit of Zeitler's aircraft. Smells a bit of disinfectant, but that's all. No blood or nothing."
"We can keep that one in reserve, then. You're doing a good job, as always."
When I got back to the mess the others were belting out all the Air Service songs, plus the ones we'd learned from the Tommies.
"This world is a world of lies..."

I remembered the faraway look on the Chief's face. *You were only too aware of time running out, just like the rest of us. It must have been so hard to leave your beautiful Elise, knowing you were unlikely to see her again or to hold your child.*

The song ended.

"Good night, gentlemen," I said, and went to bed, where I lay staring at the ceiling, wishing I were in Brandenburg, in Karl's bed with his arms round me.

That will never happen. I shall never see you again...

A few hours later all our remaining aircraft were lined up in the dawn, and all our remaining pilots blinked at them with hungover eyes. It was a fine, clear day and we went back to our usual duties with great relief.

I knew everyone was out for blood.

"Gentlemen, our late commander was a soldier to his core, and he knew the stakes. Don't be distracted by thoughts of revenge – just do the job to the best of your ability."

There was a chorus of, "Yes, sir!", and I hoped they meant it.

The good weather brought the Tommies out in force, but we were on good form. Horstmann, Jantke and Günther got one each, and I gifted Sobek his first.

After second breakfast I went to the Chief's room. Just as Otto had said, everything was left as if he were about to walk in, all of it suddenly irrelevant. *Here's a sweater he'll never wear again, books he won't read.* The finality was overwhelming.

This is so fucking depressing... His wife's photograph stood on his bedside table, and I didn't want to look at it. There was another photograph, of his family: his parents surrounded by their two sons and three daughters, all the men in uniform.

I didn't realise he was one of five. I wonder where his brother is... He must be dead – the Chief never mentioned him.

Going through his things was horribly intrusive, and I looked at as little as possible. Elise's letters were in a neat stack in a drawer, and there was the usual collection of rude pictures, which I decided to chuck in the stove in his office. The squadron was well enough supplied with pornography.

There was a slim notebook in his bedside table. I turned it over in my hands a couple of times, unsure whether I should open it or not.

It might be something his wife wouldn't want to read, but if I send it back then she will...

I opened the book cautiously. It was a diary, and I closed it again quickly.

I had no idea the Chief kept a journal. Do I burn it or send it home?

It was only about half full, so either he'd started recently or it was just the latest volume – in which case he'd probably sent the notebooks home as he finished them, like Horstmann.

I wonder what sort of things he's put in it. And what might he have written about Karl and me? The temptation to have a peek, just to check that there was nothing about his suspicions, was almost overwhelming. Almost, but not quite.

This belongs to his widow now. If she doesn't like something in it, then that's her problem. And if there is something about Karl and me, then that's our problem. I wrapped it carefully in one of the Chief's spare shirts and put it in the bag.

In the top drawer of the chest were the boxes containing his medals. He'd never flown in uniform so they were all there, including his Blue Max. I took them to his office and got the black velvet cushion out of the cupboard.

This is going to be quite a display. We must remember to photograph it, for the album and for his family.

Don't forget you're working backwards. Left when the cushion's lying on the desk becomes right when you carry it at the head of the procession – stupid bastard. That's no different from fastening your own onto your best tunic.

Precedence was a bit tricky – I knew his Prussian awards came first, but he'd had medals from a couple of the smaller states, and I had no idea which order they went in. I scratched my head for a moment, and then remembered there was a fairly recent formal portrait of the Chief in the album. I knew he would have got it right.

The finished display was impressive – yes, I'd seen him wearing them at Schmidt's funeral, but the medals gleamed far more against the black background than they had on field grey.

"Fellmann – have you got the camera?"

"Yes." He came into the office. "Wow. That's magnificent."

Horstmann knocked on the door. "Sorry to interrupt, Squadron Commander, sir, but it's ten o'clock."

"So it is…"

"Wow," said Horstmann. "That looks splendid."

"I'll take some pictures," Fellmann said. "And I'll sort out the accommodation for the escort."

"Thanks."

I thought it was going to be two funerals. Günther left the fight in a spin, and we were very relieved when he phoned in to say his engine had seized solid, but he'd landed without damage.

This is not the war it was…

When we got back from the afternoon flight, there were four strangers in the mess – very smartly turned out strangers who made us all look very scruffy, especially in our flying uniforms.

Base swine, I thought, trying not to react to the carmine collar patches.

They had the grace to stand as we came in. Four pairs of eyes went straight to my Blue Max, probably thinking how out of place it looked against my oil-stained tunic.

"Leutnant Becker?" asked a tall, thin Oberleutnant.

"Yes, sir."

"Naucke. We, er… we've brought your late commander's body… I'd just like to say how very sorry we are. He was an inspiration."

"Thank you. Yes, he was – it's rather strange without him, to be honest."

"His Excellency apologises, but it wasn't possible to find another seven holders of the Pour le Mérite who could attend."

"That's all right…"

He was ours, and we don't want a load of strangers taking over.

"But then I expect you'd rather carry him yourselves, anyway," Naucke added.

"Yes, thank you, we would. Is your accommodation satisfactory?"

"Oh, yes, perfectly," he said with a smile.

I made the introductions and then went to the boss's office to fetch the cushion. As I passed the Ops Office I put my head through the door.

"Fellmann," I asked quietly, "where are the staff fellows sleeping?"

"Well, two are in the Chief's room – we put another bed in there – one's got Zeitler's bed, and the fellow with the splendid moustache is with me," he said with an archly raised eyebrow.

I shook my head and laughed. I hadn't noticed a splendid moustache, but then I wouldn't.

I took the cushion to Hangar One, where the ground crew had already formed a guard of honour. The coffin was closed, which was hardly surprising, and I wondered how much of its contents was the Chief, and how much parts of his Triplane, and how much earth, to make up the weight… That brought back Johnny's pitiful remains, and the soldiers shovelling earth into his coffin.

It was a good way to go. He couldn't have felt a thing. I stood there for a while, remembering a fine man whom I had admired and respected, and then went back to his office to make the arrangements.

We buried him the next day in the pouring rain. It was as if the sky itself were mourning him. The squadron left the airfield in a slow, solemn procession, the coffin covered with wreaths. We were all soaked long before we got to the cemetery, which was so packed that men had to stand outside in the road.

All the Fourth Army staff seemed to have come, and pilots from several of the neighbouring squadrons as well. Once again I listened to the sonorous German service, and once again we sang 'I had a Comrade', engraving words and tune still more deeply on my heart.

Two days later I received formal notification of my appointment as CO of the squadron, and of my promotion to Oberleutnant.

IV

I looked at myself in the mirror, at the stars on my epaulettes. *I should be proud – I started the war as a private, and now I'm the commander of a fighter squadron.* But I wished the circumstances were different, and I was very much aware that I had to carry on the Chief's legacy.

Two new children arrived, Geissler and Mersch. I remembered how the Chief had welcomed me when I was new, and tried to give them the best reception I could.

It wasn't easy. I had to fight my profound, weary cynicism, and my awareness that they would soon be feeding the crows. Both were young and keen, and made me feel a thousand years old.

If only it were possible to combine bright-eyed enthusiasm with experience. If only acquiring the latter didn't destroy the former.

I got Horstmann and Jantke to do their familiarisation and then flew against them myself, with the same stakes that the Chief had used: one glass of champagne to me for each time I would have killed them, and a bottle of brandy from me if they got on my tail. My mess bill was never in danger, and I was so far in credit with champagne that I shared it with the others.

"Makes you wonder how long they'll last," Horstmann commented, and I wondered whether they were running another sweepstake. I knew they wouldn't discuss that in front of me.

A few days after the funeral, I came down with a streaming cold. I ignored it and carried on flying.

"You'll fuck your ears up, sir," Horstmann said bluntly, when I came back stone deaf yet again.

"Bollocks," I replied. "It'll be all right."

That was crap – I could hardly hear my own voice and there was an echo in my head.

"Well, at least I don't have to listen to you sneezing and coughing."

I had, reluctantly, moved into the Chief's old room. I liked sharing with Horstmann and I didn't want to be on my own with no one to wake me from my nightmares, but the unwritten rule was that the CO had his own room.

"No, you've got Geissler snoring instead!"

Horstmann pulled a face. "You haven't heard him – I don't know where the volume comes from!"

That afternoon my ears failed to clear at all during the descent. I pinched my nose and blew as hard as I could, several times, but I couldn't get the pressure to equalise. The discomfort was tolerable until I was overhead the airfield. As I began my approach the sudden agonising pain made me cry out, and almost blinded me. For one horrible moment I thought I'd be unable to land.

I managed a rough landing, and was in so much pain that I couldn't get out of the cockpit.

"Where are you hit, sir?" Uhlig asked.

"Ears – it's just my ears," I managed to gasp, and climbed out with some difficulty.

Otto came up to me as I leaned against the side of my Triplane, almost sick with pain.

"Sir, are you all right?"

I could hardly hear him. "My bloody ears," I croaked. "Tell Jantke to lead the next patrol. I can't fly like this."

"Of course. Can I do anything?"

"No. I'm going to my room."

I had to go and lie down. The pain was vile, like someone drilling into my head from both sides at once. My ears were ringing with a horrible scratching noise, like a bad violinist, and I thought my eardrums were going to burst.

There was a knock at the door. Someone said something I couldn't make out.

I sat up. "Come in!"

It was Fellmann. "Kramer said you weren't well, sir."

"It's my ears."

"That's what you get for flying with a cold. Let me have a look."

"It's all right. It's just the pressure, that's all."

I had to make a real effort to sound civil. *Fellmann should become a doctor after the war. He'd be the sort who bosses his patients about.*

"You'd better let me see. You might have burst a drum."

"All right – but just look. No poking."

"Would I poke?" he asked with a raised eyebrow.

"Given half a chance."

I wonder how you got on with that staff officer, the one with the 'splendid moustache'…

He had a good look. "I can't see anything nasty. If it gets worse I'll drive you to the doctor."

Bugger that. "Thanks."

"And no flying until you're better. Everyone's relying on you, sir."

"Don't worry. I've worked that out for myself."

You don't tell me not to fly. I'm the bloody CO, not you…

I kept my mouth shut. Fellmann was just trying to be helpful. It wasn't his fault that I was in pain and feeling very grumpy. If it was anyone's fault, it was my own.

He left me in peace. After a couple of hours, the pain had diminished enough for me to get up and go to my office. On the way, I put my head round the mess door and called Horstmann in.

"I'll say it before you do," I said. "You were right. I'll have to stay on the ground until this is sorted out. You, Jantke and Bretti lead the patrols. Take it in turns or come to whatever arrangement suits you all."

"Yes, sir. Are you going to see the doctor?"

"No. It'll come right."

Good to have you three to delegate to. I should have taken your advice in the first place. That could easily have happened when we were diving to attack, and I'd have been bugger all use to anyone.

I remembered what the Chief had said about Karl coming back: that an unfit pilot was a danger to everyone. *I've got to supervise myself as well as the others – for the first time I don't have an immediate superior close by. The responsibility's all mine.* It felt a bit like stepping out into a gale from the shelter of a wall.

I never realised what being in command would be like. Everyone has moved away from me – even Otto's careful to say 'sir' in public, though he does still call me Franz in private, thank God.

There was a small mountain of paper on my desk.

Bloody stuff's been breeding again – better get it done, being as I can't fly.

"Bleif! Pot of coffee, please!"

"Right away, Squadron Commander, sir!"

He put the tray down, looked at the paper, and gave me a sympathetic smile.

"Thanks."

And now I have to deal with all the crap I used to put to one side when I was just acting CO. No one else is going to do it.

My ears were just as bad the next morning – and even more paper had appeared. I ploughed through as much as I could, and joined Fellmann for a mid-morning coffee and cigar.

"Now I understand why the Chief spent so much time in his office," I said.

He laughed. "I think there's some rule about an aircraft needing its own weight in paper before it can take off! Anything I can help you with?"

"I don't think so – you're doing everything you used to do for the Chief, aren't you?"

"Yes."

"Well, then, I'd better do the rest of it... You'd think we'd have heard about Zeitler's commendation by now."

"Yes – it'd be a bit mean of them not to give him anything. That leg must have been bloody painful."

Yes, and he'd have had every justification for pulling out of the formation, and either coming back or landing somewhere on our side of the lines, but it didn't seem to have occurred to him to do either.

"Telegram, sir," said Möller.

"That shuts us up," I said to Fellmann. "They've given him the Iron Cross Second Class."

"Bit thin, that – they almost give those out with the rations these days. But you have to start somewhere."

The medal arrived a couple of days later, and I sent it to Zeitler's home with his goblet for his first victory. *Those should cheer him up. Brave young fellow, and he was starting to be useful.*

"How are the new boys doing?" I asked Horstmann.

He shrugged. "Struggling, as you'd expect."

I saw that myself once I was fit to fly again. Poor little Mersch made the novice's error of failing to watch his tail, and was on his way down in flames before I could get to him.

I'll be able to say the funeral services in my sleep soon, I thought as we made our way to the cemetery yet again.

It was a glorious spring day. The birds sang and the trees were covered in blossom, and I looked at them with black gloom.

There won't be another spring for me. My time must run out soon, and then it'll be the Latin mass, but the same song as they put me in the earth…

That's if there's enough left to bury. Otherwise they can just fill in the hole.

The next morning I was in the middle of putting in Sobek's and my victory claims when Fellmann came into my office, looking pale and shocked.

"What's the matter?"

"This, sir."

He handed me a telegram. I read it in disbelief. The words danced before my eyes and I had to read them again.

Richthofen was dead. The master, with that incredible score of eighty, had been shot down Tommy-side.

"Jesus Christ," was all I could say. It was unbelievable.

I wrote a message to his Fighter Group, expressing the squadron's sincere sympathy at their loss, which was also the loss of all the Air Service and of the entire nation. 'We shall strive to honour his memory by following his example,' I finished.

"Send this, would you?" I said to Möller.

"Of course, sir."

I sat back and stared at the wall. I'd only met Richthofen that one time at the aircraft trials, but he'd been the inspiration for the whole Air Service for so long that it was hard to accept that he was dead.

I hope he died quickly, like the Chief. I hope he didn't burn. He died as he must have expected to – like the Chief, and like Karl's brother Friedrich, he was a soldier to his fingertips.

He's irreplaceable. They don't make many like that.

I went into the mess and rapped on the table, as the Chief had done so often.

"Gentlemen, I have to tell you that Rittmeister von Richthofen is dead, shot down on the English side."

I could see stunned disbelief on all their faces.

"I've sent a message of condolence to the Group," I added, "and if anyone can think how we can commemorate him, apart from the obvious, please let me know."

"What about a memorial service?" said Otto.

"Or a wake," said Bretti. He saw my expression and added hastily, "I mean a proper one, not an all-night piss-up."

"When have we ever had a wake which was not an all-night piss-up?" I asked him. "Not for Richthofen. It's not appropriate."

"I think a service would be the best thing, sir," Sobek said.

I agreed, and decided on the following Sunday, exactly one week after Richthofen's death. "Fellmann, would you organise it, please?"

"Of course, sir."

A few days later we heard that the Tommies had buried Richthofen with full military honours, and the photographs showed they'd made a fine job of it. Apparently there was an argument over whose bullet had killed him – their new Royal Air Force had been credited with the glory, but some ground troops had put in rival claims.

"What was he doing so low down?" Jantke asked.

"God knows," Otto replied.

"Bit rum, them fighting over who got him," said Horstmann.

"I suppose that's to be expected," Benner said.

"I still don't know why he was so low," Sobek said. "It just doesn't make sense."

"Maybe they were doing a bit of strafing," said Günther.

"Hardly matters, does it?" Bretti said.

"Except that if he made a mistake, then so can any of us," said Geissler.

Good point – and made by the newest member of the squadron.

"Quite," Horstmann agreed.

In place of Mersch we acquired Sandberg, fresh from Valenciennes. *Another bloody novice* – and then I noticed that his pilot's badge was tarnished and dented, and that he didn't look as overawed by my Blue Max as the very young fellows did.

"What were you doing before that?" I asked.

"Oh, I was on two-seaters."

Thank fuck for that.

I was pleasantly surprised when I flew against him the next day. He didn't turn tight enough – none of the new fellows did, except for the rare one from another Jasta – but his lookout was superb and I didn't manage to jump him.

He'd done so well that I put him down for dawn the next day. Fellmann raised his eyebrows slightly but said nothing.

"He's more switched on than most of them," I said, "and we need everyone we can find."

I was pleasantly surprised by Sandberg's first patrol as well. *Hope you last, because you just might be useful…*

My run of good luck continued, and I got an SE5 that day and a two-seater the day after. That took me to thirty-four – if they were confirmed, of course.

I was expecting the squadron to have a party, but I wasn't prepared for Fellmann detaining me in my office with a load of trivial paperwork, which he insisted was urgent.

"Fellmann, why are you pestering me to get this done now?" I asked, rather grumpily. "Surely it can wait till morning."

It had been a bloody long day and I was bloody tired. All I wanted to do was have a few drinks and some food, and fall into bed in the – probably vain – hope of sleeping without nightmares.

"I just need you to sign this," he said, putting yet another document in front of me.

"All right – but it's the last one."

I've had enough of today, I thought as I headed for the door.

"Just a minute, sir," said Fellmann, getting right in my way.

"What is it now, for God's sake?"

Fellmann was looking over my shoulder. I tried to turn round but he caught hold of me, and just as I was about to protest he released me, apparently in response to some signal or other.

I turned round. The entire squadron, pilots and ground crew, was assembled in the mess, under a banner that read, 'Happy Birthday, Squadron Commander!'

"Happy birthday, sir!" said Horstmann, advancing on me with a glass in each hand. He handed one to me and turned to the others. "Three cheers for the Squadron Commander!"

I blushed furiously as they cheered and then chorused, "Happy birthday, sir!"

"Well, bugger me – thank you, everyone. This is a surprise."

In more ways than one. I'd completely forgotten my birthday.

The glass was full of Horstmann's lethal spring punch. There was champagne as well, and Bleif had outdone himself in the kitchen.

After the meal I stood up and thanked them all, and then they got on with the serious drinking. I sat on the small sofa talking to Otto and Horstmann, and trying to get just pissed enough to sleep, without drinking so much as to affect me in the morning.

Last year Johnny was here, and Karl, and we had such a piss-up, and they threw me up in the air and dropped me. No one's going to do that to me now. I'll just laugh when they do it to each other.

It used to be so easy – get as pissed as I damn well wanted, and deal with the dawn when it arrived.

I said, "Good night", and went to my room.

On my bed was a letter from Karl, and a parcel from my family. *Fellmann, you cunning bastard – these must have arrived in today's post, and you kept them hidden.*

What if I hadn't come back?

Wouldn't really make any difference, would it? I thought as I opened Karl's letter.

It was written on headed paper, from some Institute in Bad Kissingen. His sense of humour had got the better of him, and he started off, so respectfully, in the third person.

'Most esteemed Herr Oberleutnant Becker!

May I be permitted to offer my sincere congratulations to Herr Oberleutnant upon his well-deserved promotion and upon his recent victories in the air.'

Karl, for Heaven's sake! No one uses that starchy, formal third person any more – not in the Air Service anyway.

'It gave me the greatest pleasure to read in the *Military Weekly* of Herr Oberleutnant's success, which I have no doubt will continue, and to reflect that he is now closer than ever to obtaining the title of Ace of Aces. I should also like to wish Herr Oberleutnant every success in his new command, and to say that I am very much looking forward to serving under Herr Oberleutnant in the near future.'

I couldn't help laughing. *You piss-taking bastard – I can see you smiling as you write.*

'Seriously, Franz, I was very happy to read of your promotion.'

That's better. Although he'd made me laugh, it had felt very odd being addressed in that stilted way by Karl. 'Du' was much more natural.

'You richly deserve the command of the Staffel and I'm sure you'll lead it well. In fact I can't think of anyone who would do a better job. I just wish I were there to drink your health and congratulate you in person – and, of course, to follow you in the air.

I cannot tell you how grieved I am by the Chief's death. I can hardly believe he's gone. He was a fine man and an exemplary leader. He was a soldier through and through and did his duty with total dedication, to all of us as well as to the Fatherland. It was a good way to die – and no doubt was what he expected – and this time at least we know that he died quickly and didn't suffer. I count myself fortunate to have known him.

As you can see from the address, I've escaped from the farm for a couple of weeks. One of the doctors in Berlin recommended this Institute (horrible word – sounds as if we're all mad), as it specialises in treating us poor crocked-up bastards. They've had plenty of practice, after all.

There are quite a lot of us here, as you'll realise, in various stages of decrepitude, and the local ladies quite fall over themselves to make us feel at home, and very generously offer their own therapy (which – as you'll imagine – is rather more pleasant than anything provided by the Institute). There are more women than a fellow could do justice to.

There are parties almost every night, dancing, cards, and so on, and sitting on a park bench in uniform, looking peaky, almost guarantees attention from some kind creature. It really is quite overwhelming.

The treatment at the Institute is very good, though I'm fed up with being told how lucky I am. Every doctor I've come across says, "A few centimetres to the left and the bullet would have gone through your heart or your spine or both." Very tedious.

Anyway, I have exercises in the morning (rather painful), and then later in the day I suffer the attentions of a very good masseur (grit my teeth for that, I can tell you). He's helping the stiffness in my chest a lot – apparently the scarring is very tight and that's causing most of the trouble.

It would probably have done me a lot of good if I'd come here from hospital, but I just wanted to go home. With all this attention and a bit of luck I should be fit again soon.

Things would be even better if we were on holiday together, but hopefully the war will soon be over and then we can do whatever we want.

Franz, be sure to watch your own tail as well as everyone else's. I hope you're still doing well, and that I'll soon be reading of your next victories.

Have a very Happy Birthday, and break your neck and legs!
Ever yours,
Karl.'

The paragraph about the social life in Bad Kissingen sounded completely false. *If you were well enough to carry on like that you'd have been passed fit last month. Even the Technical and Testing Commission didn't want you – and now you're apparently dancing the night away, and leaping into bed with every woman who'll have you. Bollocks. Utter bollocks.*

The paragraph about his treatment sounded more convincing, but even that wasn't quite right. *What about the pain in your lung, and coughing up blood? You haven't mentioned those.*

I read the letter again. His words about the Chief rang true, but that was almost all. *I wish you weren't so bloody determined to come back. You won't be 'serving under Herr Oberleutnant in the near future' or at any other bloody time if Herr Oberleutnant has anything to do with it.*

Something struck me. I read the paragraph about Bad Kissingen again, carefully. 'There are parties every night...' But he didn't say he'd actually *been* to any of them. He didn't say anything definite about the women, either.

I'll bet the truth is that you sit and chat with some of the other 'crocked-up bastards' for a couple of hours in the evening and then go to bed, while the fitter chaps go to the parties and enjoy the women. The treatment must be pretty tiring, and you weren't strong to begin with.

It was a nice piece of deceit. I'd only seen through it because I'd read the letter three times.

Horstmann's right. Karl is going to try to come back. The Chief's not here to send him home – I'm in command and it'll be my decision. Unless he's a hell of a lot better than he was in January, he'll be going back the day he gets here. I'm not having a sick pilot in my squadron, however brave or high-scoring he might be.

I read the very last part again: '...then we can do whatever we want'.

I left my parents' parcel for the morning, got into bed and imagined that I was with Karl in Brandenburg, and fell asleep with his arms wrapped round me and my head on his shoulder.

Two hours later I was staring at the ceiling, wide awake and wishing the dawn would come – and when it did, I wished it hadn't, because I knew it was going to be another day of hard fighting.

Fellmann did a fine job of organising our memorial service for Richthofen, and sent out dozens of invitations. The village church was packed, with men standing at the back.

We had a reception at the airfield afterwards, which was a complete surprise to me. I was about to congratulate Fellmann on putting together such a fitting occasion, but he was deep in conversation with a moustachioed staff officer, who kept putting a hand on his arm.

You came to the Chief's funeral, I thought suddenly. *Ah. You must be the fellow with the 'splendid moustache', in which case I won't intrude.*

I did tease Fellmann later, though. "That your new beau?"

"I don't know what you mean, sir!" he said with an archly raised eyebrow.

"No, *of course* you don't—"

Horstmann knocked on the open office door. "It's time I was off, sir. Fellmann, could you give me a lift to the station?"

"Of course."

"Well, Horstmann, enjoy your leave," I said.

"Thank you, sir."

There was to be a memorial service for Richthofen in Berlin on 2nd May, which would have been his twenty-sixth birthday, and I'd decided to send Horstmann to represent the Jasta. I couldn't justify going myself – things were far too hot for that – but he was overdue for leave, so I tacked some onto the official trip. Spending a day in Berlin would hardly be onerous, being as he was from Potsdam.

"Take the lovely Susanne boating on the Havel, or whatever you fancy doing," I said.

I can guess what you'll be doing some of the time, you lucky bugger, I thought, and couldn't help imagining the two of them entwined.

Horstmann just grinned and left.

We were so busy that I rather regretted sending him away. Bretti shot down his fifth, making him an ace. We had a party for him, but it was very restrained compared to our wild nights of the year before. Benner and Günther got one each, taking them both to three, and I shot down a DH4, which brought my total to thirty-five. That was all over the papers, along with the portrait photos taken in January. I didn't read any of it, didn't even look at it.

The others did, though. I went into the Ops Office and noticed an article pinned to the wall. 'Germany's highest-scoring living ace!' read the headline, and beneath it was my photograph.

Where the fuck do they get that idea?

The article listed the top ten aces, and I realised with a shock that the headline was true. I was in seventh place overall. Richthofen and the Chief were ahead of me, but they were both dead, like the other four. That was not a comforting thought. I felt like asking Fellmann to take the bloody article down.

"You're doing bloody well, Franz," said Otto later, in my office.

"I hadn't realised I'd got that far! I'm not sure about having that article on display, though. It feels like showing off."

He shook his head. "Everyone's very proud of you. I mean, you should hear the way the young lads talk about you. They're very proud to be in your Staffel. It makes them feel… well, you remember how it was being led by the Chief. We all felt we had the best leader there was, and it gave us all confidence and made us feel we were a cut above the rest."

I was blushing. "Otto, I'm not the Chief." *How can I inspire anyone?*

"You're doing a bloody good job. I mean, it's reflected glory for everyone else, isn't it? It does them good, gives them a bit of a lift – and God knows we could all do with one."

"I suppose so."

It was very hard for me to believe, especially considering how bad my nerves were – and yet they weren't getting any worse. The extra responsibility gave me less time to think. Some days I was pushed to find time to eat. I wasn't all right, not by a long way. I chain-smoked and bit my nails and lay awake and had nightmares and fits of shaking, but I was coping. I still got that cold, calm feeling when I attacked.

Deep down inside I knew I was heading for exhaustion, but I told myself I'd worry about that when it happened.

I didn't even feel like going to Claudette's. A couple of times Bretti or someone had asked for permission for a group to go, and I'd said yes, and thought that I really must go by myself some time. It was just too much effort.

Horstmann came back from leave looking relatively well. I wondered what the lovely Susanne had thought of the tic in his eye and the fresh scar on his forehead.

She must be worried sick about him. Must take courage to love one of us. I wonder how the Chief's widow is doing... Is it better to love like that and then lose the other, or not to love at all?

You're hardly likely to find out, are you, Franz?

"Tell me about Richthofen's memorial service," I said. "Who was there?"

"The family, of course, including his brother Lothar, who's convalescent – you remember he was shot down in March."

"Yes."

Lothar also had the Pour le Mérite, and was arguably even deadlier than his late brother.

"And the Empress went and sat with them."

"Did she? That's quite something."

"That's what I thought. The whole thing was done very well indeed. There was no coffin, of course, but they had a catafalque, with four machine guns and the cushion with his decorations. I thought the Chief had one or two, but you should have seen that lot. It was really impressive. They played Brahms's German Requiem and I haven't been able to get it out of my head since – you know, 'For all flesh is as grass, and all the glory of Man is as the flowers of the grass.' Sums it all up very well, that."

"'And the grass is withered, and the flower thereof falleth away'... Yes. Indeed it does."

"Who's going to think about us a hundred years from now?" Horstmann asked. "No one. We'll be forgotten, like the chaps from all the wars before."

"Yes... Who thinks about anyone who fought at Waterloo, apart from the generals?"

"Quite. Anyway, there was a really good turnout. The streets were packed as well."

"Wonderful how he could inspire people."

"Yes... And Karl was there."

"*Was he?*" *Good.* "How was he?"

"Didn't look well at all. In fact I thought he looked bloody awful. It was a bit of a shock. I hadn't seen him since before he was shot down and – all right, I know no one thought he'd survive, but that's nearly ten months ago and he's as thin as a rail. That's what I noticed most. His uniform doesn't fit any more. It just hangs on him."

"I know." *Still. That's not good.*

"He said he'd just come back from a spa – can't remember which one – and I thought, *Well, it didn't do you much bloody good, then.* He came to Potsdam for the day, had lunch with me, if you could call it lunch. Afterwards I suggested we take a walk to Sans Souci, but he said something about how long it would take him to get home and buggered off. I think he couldn't manage the walk but didn't want to say so."

Surprising that Karl passed up the chance to visit Sans Souci, given his admiration for Frederick the Great... But I've seen pictures of the palace and I know it's on a hill.

I thought of all those steps up the terraces, and I was certain that Karl knew he couldn't do it and didn't want Horstmann to see.

So much for dancing the night away at Bad Kissingen. I knew that was crap.

"He talked about coming back," Horstmann went on.

"And what did you say?"

"Told him he shouldn't even be thinking about it after an injury like that. 'How can you fly with a fucked lung,' I said to him, 'up at five thousand metres?' But he wouldn't listen. We'll just have to hope the doctors have more sense than he does."

Good old Horstmann, blunt as ever.

"He's so bloody stubborn," I said.

"Yes, I know. He sends his regards, anyway. I gave him yours, as I thought you'd want me to."

"Thanks... How did you tear yourself away from the lovely Susanne to have lunch with Karl, anyway?"

"She was on duty."

"Well, she must be busy." *More than enough 'crocked-up bastards' to keep a nurse occupied, after all...*

"That's for sure."

I'd better ask him. He'll never forgive me if I don't. "So how is she?"

He chattered on about her, gazing across the room with a faraway stare. It made me want to laugh and yet I was jealous of him, because I would never know what it was to love and be loved like that.

Fellmann said he needed to go to Schutte's HQ – something about a trade and delivering more photographs. He'd taken a new portrait of me as an Oberleutnant, and I'd signed a batch of them. He had that same faraway look in his eyes as he made the request.

"Going to see the Splendid Moustache, are you?"

He raised an eyebrow. "Now that would be telling!"

I laughed. "All right, you can go!"

"Don't you want to know what it's about?"

"Apart from your liaison?"

He put on a pained expression. "I am doing this for the good of the squadron, sir... They might be able to get us a couple of D.VIIs rather quicker than otherwise."

"Oh. I see." I was impressed. "Fellmann, if you can get us a D.VII or two then you can have Schutte's entire staff, with my blessing!"

He gave a mock shudder. "You wouldn't be able to pay me enough for most of them, I can tell you."

"I don't want to know! Be off with you!"

We'd barely noticed that the Flanders offensive had stalled. We knew the front line had stayed in the same position for several days, but we were too busy to think much about it – or perhaps we didn't want to think about it. The implications were all too clear.

I almost forgot to write to Karl in time for his birthday on 10th May.

It's his first birthday alone, and he must be feeling horribly lonely – he had company at Bad Kissingen, and then Richthofen's memorial service and lunch with Horstmann, and now his house must feel emptier than ever. I don't suppose he'll feel like celebrating. We had such a party for him last year, and since then his life has been brutally altered.

The day itself started misty, but in the evening the weather cleared and the dear old Allies were out in force. We got into a massive dogfight involving us, a flight of Camels, one of Nieuports and another of Pfalzes. I don't know how we didn't all meet in the middle. I had to break off my attack on a Nieuport when I was nearly rammed by Kleber, who was going after it hell for leather.

Must mention it to him in the debrief, I thought as I climbed back up, *mustn't forget…*

Otto was under attack from two Camels, twisting and turning. As I turned towards them his aircraft threw out a white trail of petrol, the tank holed.

Get out. Get out before you burn.

He made a last desperate turn, skidding round, trying to bring his guns to bear on his attackers – the white vapour turned abruptly to black smoke.

"*Get out, Otto!*"

I was closing the distance between us, but too late.

"*Get out!*" I screamed into the slipstream, into the roar of the engine.

He made no attempt to jump, didn't move at all. In a few seconds his Triplane was ablaze from nose to tail. I watched, appalled and helpless, as it began to fall like an autumn leaf, and then plummeted earthwards—

My left middle wing was suddenly torn with holes and the air by my ears cracked. My stomach curdled as I flung the

Triplane onto her wingtips, hot and cold all over, my heart pounding.

You bloody idiot, you bloody fool, watching Otto instead of your tail, bloody fool, bloody fool... The words danced round and round in circles, like the deadly dance in the sky.

The Tommy was still firing bursts, but missing me completely. *Novice. Old hands don't waste ammunition.* He couldn't turn well enough, and I started pulling away from him. He realised he wasn't going to get me and broke off.

I don't know how much more of this I can take, I thought as I flew home, trembling and soaked in sweat. *I can't afford another lapse like that. That's how you die, how Karl nearly died. It would be a bit much to be shot down by a novice – but that's what'll happen if you make yourself an easy target. Think how he would have crowed.*

Otto's dead. He must have been hit. I hope he was unconscious. I hope he wasn't trapped there, too crippled to get out, seeing the fire begin, feeling the heat of the flames...

I shook from head to foot and it was all I could do not to be sick. *Parachutes don't necessarily save you. You can still burn.*

I thought, with sudden horror, of the burning dream. *My right knee's smashed, every time. Will I be able to get out if that happens? Or will I sit there, like Otto, and fry? Is that what's waiting for me?*

When we landed I felt so ill that I almost couldn't do the debrief. Sandberg had returned hit in the arm, which gave me an excuse to put it off while Fellmann patched him up and then helped him to the car. Everyone else was unhurt.

Everyone except Otto. All I could see was his burning aircraft, and him sitting there motionless before the smoke and flames hid him from view.

I'll dream about it, I know I will. And now I have to write my combat report, and write to Karl. And to Otto's parents.

I went to the mess to get a large brandy to take into my office. It was going to be difficult, especially the letter to Karl. I had to tell him that our last friend from university was dead, that he'd burned. It was no use trying to fob Karl off with vague statements.

At my office door I almost bumped into Horstmann. He looked very shaken.

"Did you see, sir? What happened to Kramer?"

"Yes."

There was a long pause and then he said, "I thought those days were over. I thought that now we have parachutes, that wouldn't happen."

"He must have been hit," I said. "Maybe he was already dead, or unconscious."

"Maybe."

I could see what he was thinking: *Or maybe he just couldn't move.*

"I've got to do my paperwork," I said. My voice shook.

Horstmann stood close beside me. "I'm very sorry, sir," he said quietly. "I know he was an old friend of yours. He was a good bloke."

"Yes, he was. We were at university together, and then at Langemarck... Would you help Fellmann organise the funeral?"

"Yes, of course."

I went into my office, closed the door and sat at my desk. The room disappeared and all I could see was Otto's burning Triplane. The distance between our aircraft had only been two hundred metres or so, but it might as well have been all of infinity. There was nothing I could have done to help him, absolutely nothing.

We fight and die alone in this business. All I could do was watch him burn, and I nearly got myself killed doing that.

I managed to write my report, containing the brief sentence, 'Unteroffizier Kramer killed, seen going down on fire.'

I wrote the usual lies to his parents: 'He was killed outright, and we can be certain he didn't suffer.' I added my habitual sentence saying that he had died bravely for the Fatherland. *That part's true, anyway, and I had to lie about the rest of it. How could I tell his mother that her son burned to death?*

Besides, I told myself, what I'd written could be true. Otto had sat completely motionless. He could easily have been dead. But I hadn't been close enough to see. All I really knew was that he hadn't – apparently – tried to get out.

I picked up a fresh sheet of paper. 'My dear Karl,' I wrote, and was unable to write another word.

I was seized by the worst fit of shaking I'd ever had, and I couldn't hold my pen, let alone write. I was trembling from head to foot and I had to make a huge effort not to be sick. I was burning hot and couldn't breathe. I had to open my collar. I was in desperate need of air, but I didn't know if I could walk to the window.

My heart was banging at some horrific rate and I wanted a crap, but that would have meant walking down the corridor and to the outhouse, and I couldn't let anyone see me.

Someone knocked on the door.

Oh, God – I can't see anyone. I made a massive effort to calm myself, to find my voice to call out something, anything—

To my colossal relief, I heard Horstmann say, "Can I help you?"

"I wanted to ask the Old Man something," said Geissler.

"He's a bit busy at the moment," said Horstmann. "Maybe I can help?"

"I had a gun jam today, and the Old Man was going to show me how to try to avoid them."

"Oh, right. Let's go to the hangars."

I heard their footsteps going away. *Thank God. I owe Horstmann a bottle of brandy for that.*

I had to keep my problems hidden from the youngsters. They trusted me and relied on me, and I couldn't let them see that they were putting their weight on rotten wood.

I hope no one else turns up.

My shaking had diminished, as had the other problems, and I managed to light a cigarette and take a large gulp of brandy. My shirt was soaked in sweat and I felt dreadful.

Only a few weeks ago, I thought that losing the Chief, Otto or Horstmann would hit me hard, and now two of them have gone.

I managed to finish the letter to Karl. My writing showed the state of my nerves only too clearly, and I knew what he'd think when he read it, knew how worried he'd be. He'd made me smile in Brandenburg – we'd been talking about his time as a sniper, and he'd said, 'You used to worry about me. I found it rather touching.'

We worry about each other in roughly equal measure… He'll be upset about Otto and he'll be just as aware as I am that, out of the five of us who enlisted together, only he and I are left. Please, God, don't let them ever pass him fit.

I'd finished my brandy, but I didn't feel ready to face the others. I walked rather unsteadily to the door.

"Bleif! *Bleif!*"

Not quite Fellmann's standard of voice projection, but not bad.

"Coming, sir!"

That'll slow down the service in the mess.

Bleif appeared in the door. "Sir?"

"Bring me another brandy, would you? A large one."

"Very good, sir." He was back with it in two seconds flat. "May I offer my condolences, sir?"

"Thank you. You'd better get back before they die of thirst."

After I'd drunk that I was steady enough to join the others. I could hardly face dinner, but I made myself eat something. I thought of Karl, picking at his food, and understood how it felt to be so profoundly disturbed.

Horstmann didn't eat much either. No one else seemed to be as affected as the two of us, and I wondered if we were the only ones who'd seen.

Sandberg and Fellmann arrived back from the hospital just after dinner, the former with his arm in a sling.

"Welcome back," I said. "What did they say?"

"Should be able to fly in a couple of weeks, sir – it was really just a graze and they've stitched it."

"Good. You can help me with the paperwork!"

"Thank you, sir," he replied, rather wryly. "Pity it's not my right arm!"

Yes – and I'll bet you wish you were on the train home.

I got thoroughly drunk. I'd been drinking pretty steadily all evening, and when I was really beginning to feel it I drank two more large brandies very quickly, and went straight to bed. The full force of the alcohol hit me as I was undressing. The room reeled and I thought I was going to be sick, but I fell into bed and passed out.

And I had the fucking burning dream and was sick out of the window. I rinsed my mouth with water, and sat smoking and shaking. *That dream's really starting to get to me.*

There was a knock at the door.

"Sir," Bretti called out, "we're due in the hangar in fifteen minutes."

"Thank you."

The face in the mirror was white as a ghost and deeply lined, with bleak, bloodshot eyes. I looked about fifty.

Fifteen minutes later I was in my best uniform, gongs and all, standing in the hangar by Otto's sealed coffin and trying not to imagine what might be inside. Bretti, Jantke and Sobek made up the rest of the guard of honour, and after we were relieved I went back to my room, while they headed for the mess.

I was dreading the funeral. *It's nearly three years since Kurt died, and since then no one close to me has been killed.*

I went up at dawn. I had to fly. I daren't stay on the ground, and I was needed. I knew Otto would have understood.

I shot down a two-seater and landed relieved, because I'd felt fine as soon as I dived for the attack. Otto's death had shaken me badly, had brought me nearer to the edge, but I could still function.

The funeral was every bit as awful as I'd feared. Otto had been a Catholic, so this time it was the requiem mass. *It's just one funeral after another. When is it going to stop?*

All through the service I saw Otto's face, saw the five of us going off to volunteer, remembered Kurt after Langemarck, asking if we'd seen him, and our joy a couple of weeks later when we got his letter from hospital.

All the effort they went to, to get his leg to heal, all those operations, and in that coffin there might or might not be the incinerated remnants of the surgeon's work. It's such a waste, all of it, such a fucking waste.

My throat was tight as we sang 'I had a Comrade', and it was almost too much for me.

It goes right through you, that song. The poet must have lost a good friend, to have written like that about the helplessness of watching your friend die, and being unable to do a bloody thing about it.

Anton, Kurt and now Otto – the first two died in my arms and I had to watch Otto burn to death, and I couldn't do one single damned thing to save any of them.

The funeral was over, and everyone was waiting for me to lead the way back down the lane to the airfield.

We went straight up again. There was no time to mourn.

Heimann arrived a couple of days later, another youth straight out of the fighter pilot school. *And you're supposed to* replace Otto, with his hundreds of hours of combat experience. It would be funny if it weren't so fucking tragic. You'll only survive if the war ends soon.

There was no end in sight. We were still flying over the same areas, and it was obvious that the offensive in the North was finished. The newspapers were coy about our casualties, but Horstmann said he'd heard the total was somewhere between a quarter and a third of a million.

I've always had a problem with those enormous numbers. I can't imagine them.

I thought back to Ypres in '14. Rumour then had said we'd lost one hundred thousand men in two weeks. Having seen the carnage I could easily believe it – but that's the population of a town.

We can't keep losing men like that. If we don't win this spring it's all over. This is the last throw of the dice. We all know that, but no one wants to say it.

I took advantage of my Triplane being grounded for repairs to go to Claudette's. I wasn't feeling particularly frisky, but it had been some time and I hoped a fuck would help me sleep.

I opened the door into the salon. Westermann was sitting there with Johnny, Lensch looked round for Marie, Otto was wearing my coat. Hauschke got up as I stepped in, and then Karl's pa came down the stairs.

"Ah, Oberleutnant," said Claudette. "It's lovely to see you—"

I turned and left as fast as I could.

I sat in the car, shaking, trying in vain to light a fag.

Jesus fucking Christ, what was that about? They're dead, they're all fucking dead, so how were they sitting there like that?

Was that Valhalla? Were they trying to tell me I'll be joining them soon?

Bollocks, Franz. It was just your imagination. You've been there often enough with them. Now get a grip and go back in. They're not there at all, as you'll see.

I don't think I'll be able to fuck after that.

A few minutes later I felt a lot steadier. I got out of the car and went back into the whorehouse, and this time all I saw was Anne and Jeanette.

So now I've started seeing things.

"Forgot my cigarettes," I said as casually as I could.

I paid for both of them, and watching them together and then joining them blotted out thought.

I did feel better afterwards, but in the middle of the night I thought about my hallucination and wished I hadn't.

No more Claudette's for me, I decided in the morning. *Not if that's going to happen. I'll just use my imagination instead.*

A week after Otto's funeral, we received orders to move to another airfield. The squadron that had been based there had been moved south and HQ wanted us further south as well.

"Must be building up to something new," said Horstmann.

"Let's hope it bloody works this time," Jantke said.

I decided I hadn't heard.

The new airfield was quite a bit larger than the old one, and the surface was a lot better.

"Won't be needing *gravel* here!" Fellmann said, and we both laughed.

"And no tall chimneys," said Bretti.

We never did get round to blowing up the chimney of the sugar factory. No doubt it'll scare whoever moves in to our old field.

Our new accommodation was better as well – it was in huts again, but they were rather bigger. The CO of the previous squadron had occupied a very nice large room, which took up the end of one of the huts and looked out over the airfield. It was airy and private, and I liked it – and it felt far more mine than the Chief's old room ever had.

The best discovery of all came in the evening. A lorry pulled up outside the mess hut.

"Ah – that'll be the delivery," said Fellmann, and went outside.

"Fellmann should have been a magician," said Horstmann. "He does love producing rabbits."

"That does not look like rabbits," said Sandberg.

"Unless they've started living in barrels," Sobek agreed.

Ten minutes later, we had glasses of cool beer in our hands.

"Fellmann," I said, "where on earth has this come from?"

"Well, sir – there's a brewery about five kilometres away, and the Pioneers got it working again. I managed to negotiate a very good price."

"Bloody well done," I said. "Three cheers for Leutnant Fellmann!"

He went scarlet.

"I suppose you'll need more photos signing," I said once it was quiet again.

"Yes, please, sir!"

The quality of the food improved significantly as well, and there was real coffee. I didn't ask him where that had come from. *Better not to know. Probably meant for some general or other. Best drink it in happy ignorance.*

Our move was soon crowned with success. The next day we jumped a flight of SE5s. I sent one down in flames, for my thirty-sixth victory, and climbed back up, looking for another target.

Sobek's victim went spinning down, and the fight was over as quickly as it had begun. The remaining Tommies dived for home, and our Triplanes were too slow to pursue them.

Oh, for a Fokker D.VII! What I could do with one of those!

About half an hour later we spotted some two-seaters, but they were some way off and we didn't have the fuel to go after them.

It was an easy kill, I thought that night. *We used the early morning sun and they didn't see us coming. My victim never knew* what hit him – at least I hope he didn't. I'm as sure as I can be that I shot him. He might have been dead by the time the fire began. I didn't have time to watch him going down – not that I wanted to. Too much like Otto. I wish they didn't burn. I wish I could bring them down unharmed.

Hypocrisy, Franz. Sheer fucking hypocrisy. Your reaction to seeing enemy aircraft is to want to destroy them, and when you succeed all you feel is exhilaration. You can feel as bad as you like about it later. It won't change a thing.

No doubt he'll get his revenge when I'm asleep...

I closed my eyes, and all I could see was burning aeroplanes: Otto's, then my latest victim's, and then Johnny's Albatros ablaze from nose to tail, his burning body falling out and hurtling down, tumbling over and over.

I lay wide awake, sweating, feeling the tremor spread from my hands to the rest of my body. It was hopeless. I got up and lit a cigarette, my hands shaking.

I wish I could sleep, just sleep until daylight without dreams. Come on, Franz, you must sleep. You'll be up before the dawn and you need to sleep.

There was no peace for me and the night was endless. Even imagining Karl was with me didn't help. I needed his arms around me and his voice in my ear.

I dragged myself out of bed for the dawn flight, so tired I didn't even feel human.

And I have to fight like this. Too many nights like that and I'll be with the others in Valhalla.

When we got going the adrenaline woke me up, but it wasn't good to rely on that.

I should take some leave, hand over to Horstmann, and go and have a good rest. I could go and stay with Karl. We could pretend the war's over...

Fat bloody chance. There's no way I can take leave.

A few days later there was an official letter in my post. The CO of the squadron that had taken over our old airfield had been killed, and recommendations for a replacement were requested.

I thought of Horstmann at once. He was more than capable of leading a squadron, and I'd always felt that he should have succeeded the Chief rather than me.

I'll miss him if he gets it. He's a very useful member of the Jasta, and I'll have to work harder when he's gone... Maybe he won't get it.

Don't be selfish, Franz. Horstmann deserves his own squadron and you know he does.

I picked up the letter and went outside. Horstmann was lounging on the grass, reading. Sandberg was leafing through some magazines, while Sobek and Kleber played cards.

Very keen fellow, Sandberg. He's desperate to get back in the air, but that arm needs a few more days.

"Horstmann, do you fancy a walk?" I said.

"All right. Where to?"

"Just round the airfield. I feel like stretching my legs."

When we were out of earshot of the others, I said, "Remember when the Chief was at Adlershof and you were acting CO?"

"Yes, of course. What about it?"

"How would you like your own squadron?"

He looked at me in puzzlement. "You're not leaving us?"

"No. Absolutely not." *My nerves aren't that bad.* "Read that."

He stopped walking as he read it, then looked at me, his eyes alight. "You're going to recommend me?"

"If you'd like me to."

"You bet I would!"

We continued walking.

"I can't promise you'll get it, but I'll certainly put you forward. I think I can make out a pretty good case in your favour."

"Thanks, Becker – I really appreciate it… But if I leave, you'll get another child in my place."

"It doesn't matter. I'll be sorry to see you go, though."

"I'll be sorry to leave."

He stopped and so did I. We faced each other and our eyes met. *How difficult it is to say what one means…*

"You'll keep in touch? If I get it, that is," he said finally.

"Of course I will."

I sent the reply that afternoon, with full details of Horstmann's experience and a strongly worded recommendation. I couldn't be sure he'd get the command, of course, but two days later we received a telegram saying he'd been awarded the Knight's Cross of the Hohenzollern House Order, in recognition of his mounting score.

We had quite a party. I'd taken him off the dawn flight the next day, so it wouldn't matter how pissed he got. I had the feeling that it was going to be our last party together for some time, and it very nearly was.

A few days later the gong itself arrived in the squadron post, and the same day a telegram came saying that Horstmann had got the appointment, with immediate effect.

We gave him a farewell dinner, at which he tried to make a speech. He'd had rather a lot of champagne, and his voice was somewhat slurred.

"And I'd like to propose a toast to our splendid Oberleutnant," he said.

I went scarlet with embarrassment.

"I hope he won't take offence if I say that he's the second-best CO I've ever had. We've had some bloody…" His voice cracked. "Oh, bugger it! Break a leg, the whole bloody wonderful lot of you."

He downed his glass of champagne in one, and sat down amid cheers and applause.

When the party was in full swing, I left the mess quietly and went to my room, just as the Chief used to do. Some time later there was a knock on my door.

"Come in!" I called out, and put the light on.

Horstmann staggered in and sat on my bed. "I'm gonna fuckin' miss you," he said. "Ws fuckin' nice of you to 'range this."

"I didn't, really. I only recommended you for it."

"Yeh, well, all th'same…" He threw his arms round me. "Look after y'self."

"I'll miss you too," I said truthfully.

He took off with us the next day, and we escorted him to our old airfield. He rocked his wings and broke formation, peeling away from us, descending.

Goodbye, Horstmann, and good luck. We circled overhead until he'd landed and then continued towards the front line.

V

Now there's just me and Bretti from the old crowd, I thought after we landed. I looked at Bretti during the debrief, remembered him arriving the previous summer as an officer cadet, in awe of us all and especially of Karl. *Now you're a Leutnant and an ace, and a very useful fellow – and how long before you join the Great Army?*

Is there some way of keeping Bretti safe? I wondered, and realised there wasn't. We needed all the experienced men we could get.

That point was underlined when Horstmann's 'replacement' arrived: another skinny kid who didn't actually need a razor. This one was called Albrecht, and he looked about fourteen.

"Am I getting old or something?" I asked Fellmann.

He looked at me and raised an eyebrow. "Well, now, you are looking a bit tired…"

"Oh, shut up! It's just that the new boys look like – well, boys."

He sighed. "That's because they are boys. And after nearly four years of war you and I are getting a bit worn, with all respect, sir. I feel about a hundred, and I haven't had to fight."

No – you've just had to watch one man after another disappear. And you lost Johnny… I hope things work out with the Splendid Moustache.

"Just let me know if you need to make another trip to Schutte's HQ," I said.

He gave me a beautiful smile, without a hint of archness. "Thank you, sir."

Suddenly I felt just like the Chief, and had a glimmer of understanding of his kindness.

Over lunch I looked round the table at the pilots, sharply aware of my responsibility. *An officer's first duty is to his men, as the Prussians insist.*

Quite right too, but how do I reconcile that with leading them off to possible death?

That's what they're here for – my job is to make sure they fight effectively and without unnecessary losses.

Losing Horstmann had diluted the experience level, but I still had Jantke, Teuffel and Bretti, all of whom were bloody useful. Benner was pretty handy and Sobek and Kleber were coming on well, so that was six good blokes out of ten. Sandberg was still a bit of an unknown quantity, but I reckoned he had potential.

Provided we don't have any disasters, we should be well set up.

I went to my office, to deal with yet more paper. There was a letter from Karl, which had obviously crossed with mine about Otto. He mentioned Richthofen's memorial service and meeting Horstmann, but said nothing much about his health.

Reading his words was almost like hearing his voice.

I miss you dreadfully, I thought, longing for his embrace. I realised a minute or so later that I was staring absently across the room. *If I were in the mess they'd be exchanging glances and rolling their eyes – nice of Fellmann to put all my mail in my office.*

I lit yet another cigarette and picked up the latest missive from HQ. Apparently we had to conserve fuel.

I laughed. *They should come here and see what we have to do. Yes, I could 'conserve fuel' by cutting the number of patrols, or the number of aircraft in each one – but that would get the Allies even further towards aerial superiority over the Front.*

They'll be asking us to conserve ammunition next, and spare parts, and then we won't have an Air Service at all...

I'll ignore this until they restrict the quantity they send. In the meantime we'll carry on as usual.

But the God of War must have heard my thoughts about the Jasta being well set up, and decided to punish my impertinence.

That very afternoon, when I went to my office after flying, I found Fellmann waiting for me, looking glum.

"What is it?"

"This, sir," he said, handing me a cable.

It was a posting for Jantke, back to his old squadron, with immediate effect.

"Can't we do something about it?"

He shook his head. "Believe me, I've tried. Their old CO had a complete breakdown, pretty much like Widemayer, and he's in hospital, so they want Jantke to take his place."

I sighed. "Well, it's good news for him, I suppose. Bit of a bastard for us, though."

"I'm working on getting someone with experience to replace him, but you know how things are, sir."

"I do indeed."

I wished he hadn't mentioned Widemayer, or that another pilot had had a breakdown. *It's only a matter of time before mine...*

I pushed that thought away smartly. *If you start thinking like that then it really will happen. Just focus on your job.*

I called Jantke into my office. "Have a seat."

"Thank you, sir." He looked at me expectantly, but with a slight hint of apprehension.

"You'll be pleased to hear that you're to have your own squadron." I handed him the cable.

His face lit up. "Oh, that's fantastic! Well, that is, obviously I'll be sorry to leave you, and I'm very sorry indeed about poor Pohlenz – I wouldn't wish that on anyone."

"No, of course not – but being as he isn't fit someone has to take over, and I'm happy for your sake that it's you. I'll be sorry to see you go."

"Thank you, sir – I've enjoyed being here."

"You'd better pack," I said. "Fellmann can take you to the station."

He hesitated.

"It does say, 'with immediate effect', and they're without a CO."

Bugger it, I thought as we waved him off. *I hope Fellmann can get someone from another Jasta.*

It was all too clear that evening how much we needed another experienced man. We got into a terrific fight – Teuffel sent an SE5 down in flames, but he, Bretti and I had to rescue the new boys over and over. How we didn't lose one I don't know.

"That was fucking exhausting, looking out for them all the bloody time," I heard Teuffel say.

I was in my office, writing my combat report, and both my door and the one into the mess were open as usual.

Bretti's reply was too quiet for me to hear.

"I don't give a fuck," Teuffel replied.

"Yes, well maybe you should," Bretti said. "One of them might hear you."

"So what if they do? It was just the truth."

"Have you forgotten what it's like, being new?" Bretti asked. "We have to help them stay alive and learn the job, and it's just too bad if it's hard work for us."

Nice, Bretti. You've grown up even more than I'd realised.

"Well, I suppose so."

"Anyone for Blanche's?" asked Benner.

"Are you allowed now?" Bretti retorted.

"Yes – clean bill of health. So there!"

"I'll ask the Old Man if we can borrow the car," said Günther.

He knocked on my office door, and I pretended I hadn't been listening.

"Yes, you may," I said in response to his polite request, and he went to collect the starting handle from the Ops Office.

I'll go by myself some time – now it's a different house of joy, I might not see the dead sitting there.

Getting an experienced Jasta pilot proved too much to hope for, despite my position in the aces' league table and Fellmann's contacts. Richthofen's Group still had far more clout than us, even without their famous leader.

Fellmann did manage to pull some strings, though. The new man, Richter, was off two-seaters. He and Sandberg hit it off at once and, like Sandberg, he had his wits about him. *We just need Sandberg to be fit, and then we'll be back up to strength.*

Karl wrote again.

'Many thanks for telling me about Otto, though the news made me far sadder than I can say. I suppose it was to be expected, but it's hard to grasp that you and I are the only two left.'

That was all he said about it, but I knew Otto's death would have hit him just as hard as it was hitting me.

I kept seeing him, sitting there motionless as his Triplane caught fire, and there was no one in whom I could confide. Like the Chief, I had to keep the mask firmly in place.

I sighed, lit another fag, and picked up the spares order.

There was a knock at the door. *Blast it, I never get any bloody peace. The second I settle down to something, someone disturbs me, every bloody time.* I forced myself to assume a friendly expression, or at least one that wasn't irritated.

It was Sandberg, without his sling.

"Come in, Sandberg. Have a seat."

"Thank you, sir." He sat for a moment, as if trying to work out what to say, and then blurted out, "I'd like to fly, sir. My arm's all right now."

"Fellmann still dresses it for you, doesn't he?"

"Well, yes – it's a bit awkward doing it myself—"

"I meant it's not healed yet."

"It's a lot better now, sir. It doesn't hurt. And it's my left arm and I hardly need it to fly." He paused, looking a bit guilty. "I don't know if I should tell you, sir, but I went up yesterday afternoon, while you were all away."

"Did you now?" I suppressed a grin with some difficulty, did my best to look severe. "With whose permission?"

"I know I shouldn't have done, sir, but I wanted to know if I could do it, and it was fine. No problems at all." He was blushing furiously.

"Well, it's just as well you weren't jumped by half a dozen marauding SE5s, isn't it?" I dropped the severe expression. "You can come on the next patrol, Sandberg—"

"Oh, thank you, sir!" He looked as if I'd given him a million marks, rather than the chance to get killed.

"But any sign of pain or feeling unwell and you're to break off and come home, you understand? No heroics."

"No, sir – I mean, yes, sir."

"Off you go, then. Briefing's at two."

Good for you, I thought as he left my office. *Wonderfully keen fellow. Very nice to see. You'll be very useful if you last long enough.*

I kept a particularly careful eye on him during the patrol, but he flew well and I could see no reason to keep him on the ground any longer. *Good – we're almost back up to strength, at least for the moment.*

Careful, Franz – remember what happened last time you thought that?

This time the God of War delayed his retribution by two days, probably liking his revenge cold. We lost Geissler, Tommy-side, shot down by a Camel pilot who was far too hot for comfort. I found myself dancing with him a few minutes later, and the bastard could fly.

Albrecht and Heimann looked very shocked during the debrief, especially the former, who'd just lost his roommate.

"Sobek, would you help Albrecht pack up Geissler's things?" I said.

That might make it a bit easier, having someone more experienced there.

"Of course, sir."

"At least this time there's no funeral." It was Benner who said it.

Heimann looked at him, rather dismayed. "But he won't get a Christian burial."

You what? Where have you been for the last three and a bit years?

"Just like millions of others," Bretti said quietly.

"That's right," said Teuffel. "God alone knows how many are lying where they fell."

"My brother was at Verdun," said Richter. "He said the whole place was putrid, bits of bodies rotting everywhere."

"Same as the Somme, and Flanders," added Sandberg. "We're lucky in this business – a lot of us do get a decent burial."

I left the mess and went to my office, trying not to think about the men I'd known who had rotted into the Flanders mud.

"That's another pilot and another aircraft that we need," I said to Fellmann.

He sighed. "Poor little sod had only been here five minutes – but then that's always the way."

"Indeed."

"I'll see if I can get someone with a bit more experience – it would help if we had another ace or two."

"Get Bretti and Teuffel to sign some photographs."

He grinned. "Oh, I'm ahead of you there, sir!"

The next morning he came into my office, obviously bursting with excitement.

"What is it, Fellmann?"

"You're going to like this, sir."

You always used to tease the Chief like this. "Go on!"

"We're getting two Fokker D.VIIs."

"And Christmas is coming."

"No – they're at the Aircraft Park, waiting to be collected."

I felt my face start to crack into a huge smile. "Say that again."

He obliged.

"That is the best news I've had for God knows how long – how soon before we can have some more?"

Fellmann arched an eyebrow. "Greedy! I'm working on it, sir."

"Does that mean you need to go to Schutte's HQ again?"

"Well, now you come to mention it…"

"All right – end of the week, then."

Fellmann practically glowed with happiness. I had noticed that he phoned Schutte's staff more often than was operationally necessary.

Better hope the General doesn't object to the liaison, or we'll be last to get anything.

I went into the mess. There was the usual between-flights mixture of gramophone, cards and chatter. I waited until the song ended, and banged on the table.

Silence fell, and everyone looked at me.

"I've got some news," I said, "which will please Teuffel most of all."

The new aircraft had to go to the men with the highest scores. Nothing else would have made sense.

"There are two shiny new Fokker D.VIIs waiting for us at the Aircraft Park – and we're hopeful of more in the near future."

That's a bit thin, but there's no other way of sweetening it for the rest of them.

"So when are we going to collect them?" Teuffel asked. He looked every bit as relieved as I felt.

"Right away. Bretti, you and Benner can lead for the rest of the day. I don't know what time we'll be back."

I headed for the hangars.

"Braun, we're getting two D.VIIs," I said.

"Bloody good news, sir! The more we get the better – the rotaries are all wearing out. Don't like the synthetic oil."

"Who likes synthetic anything?" I said with feeling.

We'd recently been sent more synthetic honey, and margarine made from God knows what, and Mama's letters complained about bread that was part sawdust.

"Quite, sir."

"So which aircraft do we hand back?"

"Well, sir, being as we're still one short, I think we should get rid of Leutnant Günther's. It's going to need a new engine otherwise."

"Right. Teuffel can fly that, and I'll get Heimann to fly me there in the LVG."

Braun gave me a look, and it took me two seconds to revise that plan. *I'll fly us there, and Heimann can fly the LVG back. That way he won't kill me if he fucks up.*

My memories of flying the D.VII prototype back in January were more than a bit hazy – I remembered having a very good overall impression, but that the handling had been far too sensitive and the top wing a bit too high. Fokker had solved both problems, and the result was the most superb aircraft I'd ever flown. The speed, rate of climb and manoeuvrability were excellent. *This is bloody lovely.*

When we got back the Jasta was flying. We had the two D.VIIs refuelled and then flew against each other overhead the field. It was the best fun I'd had for months.

"Bloody hell," said Teuffel afterwards. "I can't wait to get after the Tommies in that."

"You and me both. Give the bastards something to think about."

"So this is what all the fuss is about," Fellmann said. "Quite a machine."

"You can say that again," said Teuffel. "Flies like a bloody dream."

"So I saw…"

The ground crew were all gathered round, giving the aircraft a very close examination.

"How does she fly, sir?" Uhlig asked me.

"Bloody lovely!"

The sound of engines cut through the conversation as the Jasta returned. Or rather most of it. Bretti wasn't there.

Oh God, not Bretti.

Sandberg jumped down from his Triplane.

"Where's Leutnant Brettschneider?" I asked.

He shook his head. "I'm sorry, sir – I don't know. He left the fight in a hurry, over our side, and we were too busy for me to watch what happened."

"Was he in control?"

"Yes, as far as I could tell. He wasn't spinning."

"Let's hope it was just an engine problem or something. Any victories?"

"Yes, sir – I got a two-seater," he said proudly, and then a huge grin spread across his face.

"Well done," I said warmly, shaking his hand. "Very well done. I'll let you get on with your debrief, then you can come and make your report."

"Where the devil has Heimann got to?" asked Teuffel. "I know the LVG's slow, but we've been back ages."

"I'll give the Aircraft Park a call," I said.

But when I got to my office, Möller greeted me with a very long face. "Sir, I'm very sorry to have to say – the Aircraft Park rang – Heimann took off in the LVG, but the engine failed. He tried to turn back and spun in."

"Dead?"

He nodded. "I'm afraid so, sir."

"I see. Thank you."

I went straight back to the hangars, to arrange for Braun to fetch the body. By the time I'd done that, Sandberg's victory celebration was starting.

Shame to spoil it, but I have to tell them…

They all looked at each other, suddenly serious.

"Er… is there any news of Bretti?" asked Sobek.

I shook my head. "It's probably taking him a while to find a phone."

But it's nearly two hours since Sandberg saw him leaving the fight…

Quite a day this has turned into.

The phone rang and I jumped half out of my skin.

"Yes, one moment, please, sir," said Möller. He came to my office door. "It's for you, sir – it's Staff Doctor Lennig."

Oh, shit. I hope Bretti's not badly hurt.

"Ah, Oberleutnant Becker," said Lennig. "This is an unexpected pleasure – not often I talk to someone famous."

Get to the fucking point.

"I've got your Leutnant Brettschneider in my hospital – got a couple of bullet wounds and a broken ankle, but nothing too serious."

Thank fuck for that. "How many is a couple, sir?"

He laughed. "Exactly that. Two. One through his left thigh – he's a very lucky chap. It missed the bone and the major blood vessels, or we'd be having a rather different conversation – and the other broke his left humerus. Upper arm, that is."

"And the ankle?"

You said, 'nothing too serious', and he's got two broken bones – but then you're used to dealing with blokes who've been mutilated by shellfire.

"That was his bad landing – he said to tell you he's very sorry, but he had to parachute out. He said he was starting to feel bad and didn't know if he'd be able to land."

"Please tell him that's what parachutes are for, sir, and not to worry about the aircraft. Where are you?"

It wasn't a name I recognised, and I had to look at the map. The hospital was about twenty kilometres away, and I cursed under my breath.

"Please would you tell him that I'll try to get over to see him, sir, but that it might not be possible – and give him all our best wishes for a good recovery?"

A good, slow recovery.

"Yes, of course. He should be all right – the ankle needs surgery but young fellows tend to mend well."

"Thank you very much for everything you're doing, sir."

"Not at all – and best wishes to all of you. Break your neck and legs, as I believe you fliers say!"

I laughed. "That's it!"

As I replaced the handset, Fellmann and Möller looked at me.

"Leutnant Brettschneider is in hospital – should make a good recovery but he'll be out of it for a couple of months."

"Good," said Fellmann, and I could see he didn't care what I thought about his saying that.

"And he had to bail out, so now we need two pilots and one more aircraft. Preferably a D.VII."

"I'll see what I can do, sir," Fellmann said. "Mind you, I don't think I can get a D.VII *and* an experienced pilot. It'll probably be one or the other."

"At least we only lost one today," Teuffel said when I gave the pilots the news. "I was beginning to think it might be two."

I suddenly realised I hadn't written to Heimann's parents. *Such a fucking waste – somehow it would have been better if he'd died in combat.*

That just shows how warped your ideas have become – surely any normal man would think it better to die in an accident than be deliberately killed by someone else. But then what's normal about being a fighter pilot?

Shut up and write the fucking letter.

And then I couldn't resist getting on the phone to Horstmann.

"Horstmann? Becker here. Just thought you might like to know we've just collected two nice new Fokker D.VIIs!"

"Piss off, Becker, you bastard! I've been begging for those ever since I got here and all I get is bloody excuses. I sent a cable yesterday to Berlin saying that we can't fly excuses and when are the bloody D.VIIs coming – and now you tell me you've got the damn things!"

"Ah, well – I have Fellmann!"

"Fuck Fellmann!"

I burst out laughing. "Not bloody likely!"

He couldn't help laughing as well. "It was an expletive, not an instruction!"

Horstmann told me, much later, that he'd been so cross he'd got on the phone to HQ to try to speak to Schutte, but had been forestalled by his adjutant. He'd done Horstmann a favour. Shouting down the phone at the General would not have been a good idea.

I had to curb my enthusiasm for the D.VII a little. Neither Teuffel nor I knew the aircraft well enough yet, and I wanted us both to do more familiarisation before we flew them against the Allies. As the war was not going to stop while I learned all the ins and outs of the Fokker D.VII, I had no option but to continue flying my Triplane over the Front.

So I left Teuffel to fly his D.VII to his heart's content while I climbed into my Triplane to lead the dawn patrol. I hadn't realised just how knackered the poor old beast was. It was quite a shock after the new D.VII, and for a moment I wanted to turn back.

It was good enough yesterday, I told myself sharply, *and most of your squadron are going to have to continue flying them, tomorrow and the day after and so on, until more D.VIIs arrive. Forget your D.VII exists and get on with it.*

We buried Heimann after second breakfast. The cemetery was a bit bigger than the one near our old base, but once again the pilots' graves were starting to outnumber the civilians'. I couldn't help looking at the others and wondering who was going to be next.

Here's a cup to the dead already, And hurrah for the next man who dies…

I managed to fit in another flight in my D.VII just as the sun was setting.

Overnight the ground crew repainted the new aircraft in the squadron's sky blue, and added my white knight and Teuffel's rearing horse.

Well, I thought in the morning twilight, *let's see how this goes.*

As we climbed up Teuffel got into position on my right wing, and I found I had to throttle back so the Triplanes could keep up.

It wasn't long before we found a flight of SE5s. Even at altitude the D.VII answered swiftly to the controls and still had power in reserve. In short order, two of the enemy went down burning: one for Teuffel and one for me, raising my score to thirty-seven. We were off to a good start.

Half an hour later we spotted a big fight and joined in, and I saw Horstmann's Triplane waltzing prettily with a Camel. They were going round and round as if choreographed. *Beautiful flying. All that needs is a bit of Strauss. If only the purpose weren't so deadly.*

As soon as I'd finished debriefing, I sent an urgent request for more Fokker D.VIIs.

'The difference in performance between these new aircraft and the Fokker Triplane is very marked,' I wrote. 'At present I have to put up mixed patrols and it is impossible to exploit the Fokker D.VII fully in these circumstances. In particular we are unable to take full advantage of the high-altitude capability of this aeroplane. The Staffel will be much more effective when we have been fully re-equipped.'

Much good it'll do, I thought as I signed it. *It's a pity Fellmann can't exchange photographs for aircraft. If we had all D.VIIs we wouldn't have to stop climbing when the Triplanes run out of breath. The Triplanes aren't really good enough any more and it's very hard on the new boys.*

I'll have to try to think up some new tactics, see if there's some way of using the D.VIIs to their best advantage.

It turned out that Fellmann was right about not getting a D.VII *and* experienced pilots – to be fair, he did manage one of the latter. Lehmann turned up in a brand-new Triplane, and he'd done a month with another Jasta. That was in sharp contrast to Grünwald, who actually had spots.

"How old is Grünwald?" I asked Fellmann.

He checked the records. "Seventeen, sir."

"You're sure?"

"That's what it says here... I know, he doesn't look it."

"It's the spots – when Karl was a sniper one of his oppos had spots, and I found out after he'd been killed that he'd been fifteen most of the time – just had his sixteenth birthday."

"Well, it's possible Grünwald's fibbed about his age. I'll see what I can find out."

"No, don't bother. He's here and we'll do our best to keep him alive."

Fellmann nodded. "Oh – the hospital rang. Bretti's on his way home."

"Good." I lowered my voice to a murmur, aware that the office door was open. "Let's hope he's out of it."

"Quite."

High summer was approaching, and we were flying through all the hours of daylight. I could only put the whole squadron up twice a day – the rest of the flying had to be shared out, otherwise we'd all have been exhausted in no time.

Dawn was so bloody early that there was hardly any point going to bed, and the last flight ended as the sun touched the horizon. We slept when we could during the day, but that was bloody difficult with the noise of aircraft taking off and returning, and the telephone ringing.

I wished it would rain for a few days, so I could stay in bed in the mornings and sleep, but the weather held.

Thank fuck I've got Teuffel and Benner as patrol leaders, or I'd be dead on my feet by now. Maybe I shouldn't have thought that. I hope the God of War wasn't listening.

Superstitious crap, Franz. There is no God of War, any more than there's a god of anything else.

There was still no sign of the promised D.VIIs. Our enemies grew ever more numerous, and with mixed patrols we couldn't exploit the aircraft's advantages, especially its high ceiling. It could climb to seven thousand metres, well above all the Allied types, while our tired old Triplanes were pushed to make six thousand.

I didn't relish the idea of spending much time at seven thousand metres – it meant using the oxygen system, and no one liked that. You breathed the stuff through a tube held in your mouth, and it was thoroughly unpleasant. The tube had to go through your scarf or balaclava or whatever, and even a tiny hole let in enough frigid air to chill your bones. The tube itself got bloody cold, and the gas dried your throat out – as if it weren't dry enough already. Between five thousand and six thousand I could manage without being on oxygen continuously, but not above six thousand.

You'd be above the Spads, though. Above every bloody thing, in fact.

I had an idea. "Teuffel, would you come to my office for a moment?"

"Of course, sir."

"Shut the door and have a seat... I've been thinking about how we could use the D.VII's high-altitude capability, and I'd like to run it past you."

He looked at me expectantly.

"Suppose Benner leads the Triplanes while you and I climb to our maximum altitude. If the Triplanes maintain five and a half thousand metres or so they'll be in the right place to engage SE5s or Camels. We'll be able to watch from above, and when they attack or get attacked we can enter the fray, and the Tommies won't be expecting us."

Teuffel's face lit up. "That sounds like a good plan, sir – the only thing is, what if they get jumped by a large formation? Someone could be dead before we get there."

"That is the snag... I'll sleep on it, decide in the morning."

I didn't sleep on it, of course, but it gave me something to think about as I lay awake. *Teuffel's right, it could all go hideously wrong – but you can't keep them all alive, Franz. They know the stakes they play for – but are you sure you're not just desperate to increase your score?*

Worth a try, I decided as I shaved.

I gave everyone a very careful briefing. Teuffel was thrilled that he was finally going to be able to use his D.VII properly, but it did feel like glory-hunting. A niggling voice in my brain muttered that I was just trying to get to forty victories.

Would the Chief have done it? I didn't have an answer. *In a way I'm looking after them even better by being higher*, I thought, probably trying to convince myself.

Teuffel and I took off first, and held over the airfield whilst the Triplanes got airborne and formated on Benner. We left them beneath us as we climbed higher and higher into the frigid air, turning frequently to keep them in sight.

At five thousand metres the wind was like an icy knife. At seven thousand the cold was blasting through my clothes, and the oxygen tube threatened to stick to my lips. My throat was so dry it was practically sticking to itself.

After twenty minutes at that altitude I'd had enough – and then I saw a flight of Camels, off to the south, at about the same altitude as the Triplanes. I rocked my wings and pointed them out to Teuffel.

Benner hasn't seen them – but he suddenly rocked his wings.

The morning sun was still quite low, and I was itching to position Teuffel and myself up sun from the enemy, but we had to shadow Benner as he led the rest of the squadron east and up, the others keeping formation pretty well considering their level of experience.

The Camels were heading north. They must have seen the Triplanes and they were closing the distance fast. Benner wasn't going to be in the best position. *You want to attack them, not the other way about, but that's not what's going to happen.*

I led Teuffel into position to the east of the other aircraft. They were going to need all the help they could get.

My heart hammered as we waited for the right moment, tension running through me like an electric current, my right foot jittering on the rudder bar, sweat running down my back—

The Camels were almost upon the Triplanes. Benner was turning to meet them.

Now. I rocked my wings again, half-rolled and stood my D.VII on her nose. Teuffel dived beside me, the wind rising to a banshee wail in the wires. The Triplane formation scattered as the Camels attacked, one of them settling onto Lehmann's tail.

I was perfectly positioned and the Camel pilot hadn't seen me. Teuffel peeled off after his chosen victim, and I fired a burst at mine. His aircraft pitched up sharply and then fell into a spin. As I climbed back up I saw Sobek's victim hurtle down, burning. Benner was going round and round with a Camel, but he was holding his own.

Albrecht flashed past me, hotly pursued by a Camel and I dived after them, firing a warning burst at the Camel pilot. It was too late. There was a plume of smoke from Albrecht's aircraft, followed by a blaze of flame. The Camel pilot broke right, and as I followed him I saw Albrecht's parachute open.

We were still at five thousand metres, and at that altitude the D.VII turned very well. I was gaining on the Tommy, he was almost in my sights – I had to break off as one of his colleagues came to his rescue, but Sandberg was turning in behind him.

Lehmann was under attack, Sobek was going to his aid – a Camel passed sideways beneath me and I flung my D.VII after it. *Must be a novice, he's not turning tight enough.*

As I closed the range he tightened the turn, desperately, hopelessly trying to escape. For a split second I almost felt sorry for him – then I fired and his aircraft reared up and then went into a dive which became steeper and steeper.

The Camels broke off, diving away. It was time for us to go home as well. We didn't have much fuel left.

My first double. I was especially pleased that I'd brought each one down with the first burst. *That was good flying and good shooting, Franz. You're getting better at this, nerves or no nerves.*

As we flew home I felt cold and shaky, as always, but with one uncomfortable addition: *I'd almost felt sorry for my last victim.*

I couldn't afford emotion. *If you don't watch out, you'll start seeing men instead of targets, like that time you looked through Karl's telescopic sight, and then where will you be? If you think like that you'll hesitate, and there are plenty up here who won't. Keep feelings like that for later. Don't have them in the air.*

I'm really not sure about that experiment. In a way it was a success: we destroyed three enemy aircraft for the loss of one of ours, and three enemy airmen are probably dead, while one of ours has been shot down, but is probably alive. But I can't help feeling that I used my pilots as a decoy, and that it's better to keep the squadron together.

"Teuffel, would you come to my office, please?" I asked as we all walked towards the main hut.

"Of course, sir."

I closed the door and lit both our cigarettes.

"Well done," I said, "but what did you think of the plan?"

He thought for a moment. "Well, sir – it worked out very well, but… well, if there'd been more Tommies it could have got very messy before we'd got there."

"My thoughts exactly. Thanks."

I told everyone that we would not be doing that again, I think to their general relief. I looked at their young faces and realised how much trust they placed in me, and felt the full weight of the responsibility.

More emotion, Franz. Won't do.

I'd just finished debriefing when the phone rang. Fellmann had been ringing round to try to find Albrecht, so far without result, and I hoped it was someone calling back with good news.

"It's for you, sir," said Möller.

I took the phone. "Becker."

"Hello, sir," said a chirpy voice. "It's Albrecht."

"Ah, good! Are you in one piece?"

"Yes, sir. I'm a bit bruised, but I'm all right."

"Good, good. I saw you jump. Tell me where you are and Fellmann will come and fetch you."

Fellmann pulled a face. *It's too bad. I can't spare the time. I'll be airborne again in a couple of hours, and before that I have to write my combat report.*

They arrived back in the middle of the afternoon. Albrecht looked rather cheerful, and was instantly surrounded by the others, all asking him about his parachute jump. I was curious as well, and stood listening as he described what had happened.

You're dead lucky it's '18 and not '17, or you'd have burned. The English still burn, the poor sods, like Teuffel's today. Why don't their people give them parachutes? Albrecht's alive and will fight again this evening. Teuffel's victim is dead. How can they afford to waste trained men like that?

Albrecht flew well in the evening flight, and I was very pleased to see it. We met a flight of Spads and he attacked without hesitation. *Brave fellow. If he has been shaken by the jump this morning then he isn't showing it.*

I left them in the mess celebrating Benner's fourth victory, and paid my usual evening visit to the hangars.

"Everything all right, Braun?"

"Yes, sir. Usual patching to do, and we're replacing the barrel of Leutnant Günther's right gun – it's getting worn and we don't want any of you to miss!"

"Neither do we!"

Zaffke came up to me. "Excuse me, sir – may I ask if there's any news of Leutnant von Leussow?"

"Yes, of course – he's busy on the farm. He's got some Russian PoWs as labour, so things should go a bit better."

"That's good to hear, sir. Would you give him my regards, please?"

"Of course... I won't hold you fellows up any longer – you're doing an excellent job as always." I turned to leave. "Oh, Braun – we're doing the spares order tomorrow, so would you give Leutnant Fellmann the list?"

"Very good, sir."

It was the most beautiful June evening, and I strolled slowly back across the grass to my hut.

It's almost a year since I stayed with Karl, and we had those two days with Helena and Marion in Kempinski's, and then I went home and – went to bed with Maria. If she did get pregnant then the baby will be about three months old...

And the Chief's baby was due in June.

I'd had a very gracious letter from his widow in reply to mine. 'We both knew how likely it was that he would be killed, but life is short and all we can ever do is live and love to the fullest while we can,' she'd written.

I've got bugger all chance of seeing my child, too – if there is one.

As I was undressing I caught sight of myself in the mirror. *It's just as well I met Maria last year – no one would want to go to bed with that.* My face was deeply lined, my eyes sunken with strain and fatigue, and my cheeks were falling in.

And then there was my expression. *We all look like that. Anyone who survives a few months gets that look in his eyes.*

The youngsters called me the Old Man – it was the usual term for a CO but I felt they meant it, even though I was barely older on the calendar than they were. I felt so old.

One lives through an entire lifetime here. All that awaits me now is the grave.

That was far too depressing.

It's nearly a year since Karl and I became – what's the word for it? We've never been lovers exactly, but at the same time we're more than just friends.

I sat on my bed and reread his last letter.

'The promised Russian prisoners arrived a few days ago, and you should see them. The poor sods make me look fat. The first thing I did was get Henning to take them into the kitchen and give them some food, for which they were absurdly grateful – it was just thick soup and bread, and you'd have thought it was dinner at the Bristol.

Anyway, they're working well – I make sure they get a good meal every day, and they're living in one of the estate cottages. I imagine it's rather better than the PoW camp, even if they do have to work for their supper.

One of them speaks some German. He said he had a farm back home, but his wife wrote that the Red government has taken it. Must be bloody awful, that, to have your land stolen by the people you've been fighting for. He couldn't believe the state of my soil – ran some of the prime sand through his fingers, clucked and shook his head, and then asked, "How anything grow?"

"Shit," I replied, but of course there isn't much of that with the horses gone.'

It was almost like having Karl sitting next to me, talking softly into my ear.

I hope you're not working too hard – hang on, it's June. You must be due for your next medical board. I don't want to see you back here – I'd rather never see you again than that.

I fell asleep in his arms, but woke sweating and shaking and lay staring at the ceiling, wishing I could sleep without nightmares. Two minutes later, Schiffer brought the shaving water, and I dragged myself out of bed for another fucking long day.

A long bastard of a day – we lost Benner, shot down Tommy-side. I saw him jump out of his burning Triplane, and his parachute open – but of course I was far too busy fending off the Tommies to watch.

The next day we heard that he was a prisoner, in hospital with a broken leg. And that afternoon, Albrecht fell victim to a Spad and crashed in No Man's Land. Set against that, Teuffel and Sobek got one each, so the Jasta was just about breaking even.

This time last year we had it almost all our own way. Now we're fighting for survival.

Some days later, we heard that an infantry patrol had found a charred wreck with an incinerated pilot inside it, possibly Albrecht.

"Nice thing to come across," Sandberg commented.

No Man's Land has always been full of corpses, I didn't say.

"No doubt they've seen worse," said Günther.

"Are we getting him back to bury?" asked Lehmann.

Sobek laughed. "You really imagine that patrol went to the bother of scraping up what's left and bringing it back?"

Lehmann blushed. "Well, I suppose not."

"Being on patrol's hazardous enough," I said, rather more kindly. "You don't risk men's lives for a corpse. We'll say our own goodbye to him."

"I'm quite happy to have no funeral," Fellmann said to me, late in the evening.

"So am I." I stretched, my eyelids heavy from fatigue and bad nights. "See you in the morning," I said, and left the mess.

I felt bloody awful. *I should take leave, go and help Karl on the farm – but it's just not possible. Even if I get an experienced man in Benner's place, things are so busy that no one can go away.*

I realised I still hadn't been to the whorehouse. I didn't even know what Blanche's was like. I just didn't feel like it.

It's not good to feel like this. It's not healthy. I ought to make the effort. But I had very little enthusiasm for the idea, and I was afraid I'd get into the bedroom and find I couldn't do anything. That would be terrible.

I'll wait until I'm desperate, then I'll go. I've never liked paying anyway. That just felt like an excuse. My loss of interest in sex was another, frightening, symptom of stress. It went with the fits of shaking and the nightmares.

If the war doesn't end soon I shall end up exactly like Widemayer. If I don't get killed first.

We got Müller and Steinwarz, both as green as the grass, and two new Triplanes.

"I'm sorry, sir," said Fellmann, looking very down in the dumps.

"Don't worry about it – experienced men are thin on the ground these days. Thin in the air as well."

It was a feeble joke, and it didn't even raise a smile.

"Look," I said, "I know how things are. We can't have what isn't there."

"No. I suppose not."

I realised suddenly that he hadn't asked to go to Schutte's HQ for a while, nor phoned them every other day. *Something must have gone wrong with the Splendid Moustache.*

"Er… are your contacts still there – at HQ?"

"What? Oh, no, sir, not any more. Got posted away."

"Ah. Sorry to hear that."

"To the front line, in fact."

"Ah…" *Not because of you, I hope*, I thought, but couldn't say. "Let's hope, then."

"Indeed."

It would be rough after Johnny, but there's nothing I can do.

Teuffel was scoring well, as if to make up for the dilution of experience – he got two-seaters on two successive days, while Sobek managed a Camel. I gifted victories to both Kleber and Richter, which made them happy.

I'd have over forty if I didn't keep giving them away, I thought as we took off for the last patrol one evening.

And that was my lucky day, because I got on the tail of an SE5 and there was no one nearby to give him to.

The ground crew garlanded the nose of my D.VII with a large '40', and we all posed in front of it for Fellmann to take the picture, and then he took one of me sitting outside the mess. I tried to look fearless and warlike, but – to my eyes, anyway – succeeded only in looking old and tired.

I really am getting past it, I thought as I signed the prints. I didn't have the energy for even half the party.

We all held our breath when a fresh offensive began near Montdidier on 9th June. The youngsters were fired with enthusiasm, and afraid the war would end before they could really get stuck in. I dimly remembered feeling the same in the training camp in September '14, with Anton, Kurt, Otto and Karl. That was ancient history.

We stayed in Belgium, as we had during the Kaiser's battle. The young men fumed, but I was relieved.

That's not how you felt in March, Franz – you were frustrated not to be ordered south. That's only three months ago, but my attitude has changed. And I try to tell myself my nerves are no worse...

The bad dreams came every night, and when I didn't dream I stared at the ceiling, waiting for the dawn. The slight tremor in my hands was perpetual, and my eyes were shadowed.

This business is ruining me. One way or another it will destroy me, and all I can do is keep going until it does.

Karl's letters said nothing about his health or his medical board. *I wish you'd give me a clue as to how you are. I can't imagine they'll pass you fit. Even if they do, if you come back here you'll have to convince me that you really are fit, and if you aren't I'll send you home. I'm not having anyone unfit in my squadron. That just gets men killed.*

The offensive lasted five days and was abandoned.

That was the fourth offensive of the year, and all four have stalled. If we don't win a decisive victory soon we're finished, and they will all have died for nothing.

There wasn't time to brood on things like that. All we could do was shoot down as many enemy aeroplanes as we could, and leave the direction of the war to the generals.

Alfred wrote. He was in rest, having had a hot time of it in the Montdidier offensive. He'd come out of hospital just in time to take part in it.

'Well done on your promotion and your recent victories – I think sometimes of our little group in Flanders in '14 and how strange it is that you and Karl are famous, when almost everyone else is dead and I'm still a foot-slogger. Still, they've given me the Hohenzollern House Order, in spite of my being a mere company commander and not a dashing knight of the air!'

Yes, I know – we're the glamour boys and you're poor bloody infantry. Elite poor bloody infantry, though, as you're well aware. The Hohenzollern is bloody good going, though, and you deserve it after the fighting you've done.

I didn't say that in my reply, of course, just took the piss out of the storm troops and 'mud-grubbers' in general.

What really struck me was that he still seemed to be enjoying 'the best fight of my life', while for me the blasted war couldn't end soon enough. *I wonder what you really think, Alfred.*

I received a personal message of congratulations from the King of Württemberg on my fortieth victory, and a box containing the Knight's Cross of the Military Merit Order.

Very nice of him. Another ribbon for my chest, this time yellow with black edges. That brings the total to seven.

They're not charms, Franz. They won't stop you getting killed.

The medal itself was a white enamel cross with a blue ring in the middle. 'Fearless and loyal,' said the motto, in gold letters. *I'm not sure about that – my loyalty's not in doubt, but there's plenty of fear.*

"Congratulations, sir," said Fellmann. "That means another portrait!"

"I never thought I'd escape!" I said. "And I suppose we'll have to have another party as well."

"That'll please the others, anyway."

I put the gong in the drawer with the others. *If I'm not careful I'll lose one of those cases*, I thought, and ordered a large one from Berlin so I could keep them all together.

It was a close, sticky day, and during the early part of the afternoon the clouds began piling into huge white turrets, massive outcrops which looked as solid as rock and which dwarfed us into atoms.

How can all that water simply hang in the sky? The sheer size of the things was awe-inspiring, and as we flew round them they grew visibly, their crisp tops dazzling against the blue sky.

Very pretty, and bloody dangerous. The Tommies could be using them to set up an ambush…

We twisted and turned between the clouds. Where the sun hit them they were almost blinding, but I had to stare at them, trying to see where the Tommies might be lurking. In their shadows it was freezing cold, and their walls showed a thousand shades of translucent grey.

If only I could appreciate such beauty for its own sake, instead of straining my eyes and every nerve. If only survival weren't at stake...

We flew round into the sunlight again, and something glinted above us. Camels! They had the advantage of altitude, and we were badly placed for a fight. I continued the turn, trying to get the cloud between us and them before they could see us.

It was too late. They were already diving down and we scattered, turning to meet them. They knew what they were doing and we turned and turned, the enormous clouds forming a Roman amphitheatre with the gods enjoying the spectacle of slaughter...

Suddenly I was engulfed in damp, featureless grey. I lost sight of my opponent at once, and a few seconds later had no idea if I was still turning or not. It didn't feel like a turn. I could see nothing. The turbulence threw my Fokker about as if she were made of paper. I was completely enveloped in cloud, and I couldn't tell which way was up.

I levelled the wings cautiously, I thought, but in the wild air it was impossible to tell. The altimeter said I was climbing. I closed the throttle and still went up. *The cloud must have been growing from beneath us as we turned. If I keep going straight I'll come out of it...*

There was no straight. No up, no down, no left and no right. Fear ran cold down my back and curdled in my stomach. The airspeed was winding up even though the throttle was closed. I tried to pull the stick back but it wouldn't move.

There was a coating of ice on the flying wires and the wings, and as I watched it got thicker. The controls were frozen. I had no control over my aircraft. None at all.

The cold feeling changed to a hot sweat. *How long do I do this before I jump out?*

An endless series of hard, vicious jolts threw me about like a pea on a drum. I'd never felt anything like it. My weight was alternately on the seat and in my straps, and I had the sensation of spinning. I was beginning to feel sick, from the sensations and from sheer terror. Airspeed and altitude fluctuated wildly, and I could make no sense of either.

I'll have to get out, I thought, my mouth dry, my heart thumping against my ribs. *What was the cloudbase?*

Think, Franz, get a grip…

About fifteen hundred metres, I think… That's high enough to jump if I can't regain control. I don't want to abandon my nice new D.VII.

I'll sit and wait. I'll come out of it eventually…

I dropped sickeningly, the altimeter unwinding. The ice began to melt, and then to break off in chunks. The airspeed was increasing, the wires screaming. I pulled back. Nothing. I tried again with all my strength and the stick moved – and then hit the backstop. I was pressed into my seat, my cheeks sagging. The sensation became heavier and heavier. The throttle was closed completely, and I was going faster than a D.VII ought to go.

I'll have to jump – the cloud cleared suddenly away and the ground appeared, tilted at a horrifying, unbelievable angle. *That can't be right* – but there was no time to think. I levelled the wings and eased carefully out of the dive. I was running with sweat and all I wanted was to be on the ground with a large brandy.

Fucking hell, that was frightening. At least when I'm being shot at I've got control of the aircraft and a chance of survival, but in that cloud I was completely at the mercy of the gods.

I thought again about the Roman amphitheatre, and wondered if they'd enjoyed the spectacle.

Now where the fuck am I?

I flew east, on the basis that it was safer than west, and after a few minutes recognised the old walled city of Bruges. I knew my way home from there.

In the warm air near the earth, the last of the ice melted away. I was shaking from head to foot, my hands wet inside my heavy gauntlets, and I felt horribly sick.

It was the turbulence, I told myself. *That was enough to make anyone feel sick. At least the D.VII stayed together. If that had been an Albatros it would probably have broken up, and if the turbulence hadn't done it the airspeed would have done. And last year we didn't have parachutes.*

Uhlig met me as I parked, relief all over his face.

"You were last seen vanishing into a cloud, sir," was all he said as he lit my fag.

"You'd better give her a thorough check," I told him. "I came out of that cloud at one hell of a speed."

My pilots crowded around me, and I was glad to see that they were all there.

"Any of you get into those bloody clouds?" I asked.

"No, sir." It was almost a chorus, just like bloody school.

"Well, don't."

The sun was lighting the cloud tops gold and grey and white. I looked at them and shivered as I thought of the cold, clammy, featureless grey, the sickening turbulence, the horrifying speed when I came out of the bottom, the ice on the wings and the frozen controls.

I am never, never doing that again, and I shall do my best to put the fear of God into this lot, to put them off ever doing it either. There are ways of dying, and I don't fancy that one.

I told them all about it, in great detail. Their expressions were quite something.

"Bloody hell," said Teuffel. "I've flown in cloud for short periods but I didn't realise all that could happen."

"Neither did I," I said. "And I didn't intend to fly into the bloody thing – I was just suddenly in it."

"Christ, it's getting dark!" said Sobek.

There was a brilliant flash of lightning, followed barely a second later by the most almighty bang. The wind was suddenly violent.

"Jesus, the aircraft!" shouted Fellmann, and I turned round just in time to see Sobek's Triplane lift into the air, turn over and slam into Lehmann's.

"Four men on each aircraft!" I ordered, mindful of Uhlig's accident the summer before. "The D.VIIs first!"

The heavens opened in a mighty deluge, so heavy that I could barely see across the field. *Don't think, Franz – just work.*

We slipped and slithered, but managed to get all the remaining aircraft safely into the hangars.

"Well done, everyone," I said.

We were all soaked through and out of breath.

I didn't realise we'd got so unfit. Better start playing football or something between flights.

"Jesus, I'm soaking!" said Müller.

"Me too," Steinwarz added.

"Well, at least we can all get dry," I said. "It's not like being in the trenches."

"Were you in the trenches, sir?" asked Müller.

"Yes – until early '16."

We headed for the huts. The deluge got heavier, drumming on my head, and I knew what was about to happen.

I can't have one of those episodes in front of my pilots.

I turned round. "Fellmann—"

And then I was in the shell-hole with Kurt, the rain pouring down on us as his blood ran into the water—

"Come on, sir. *Come on. Now.*" Fellmann was holding my arm and pulling me towards the huts. The others were all ahead of us.

"Did anyone see?" I asked, my voice shaking.

"No, sir. Only me."

"Thanks."

"No need. Are you all right now?"

"Yes. See you in a few minutes."

I went to my room, stripped off and dried myself, trying not to hear the rain on the roof. *Put some dry clothes on, go to your office and have a brandy, Franz.* But I was almost afraid to go out again.

So put your cap on, you stupid bastard.

I made it to the main hut, and sat in my office with a brandy and a fag, while the most spectacular thunderstorm went on outside.

Fellmann came in, trailing water. "Lehmann's Triplane's badly damaged, sir, but Sobek's is repairable."

I sighed. "So that's another aircraft we need... Still, it might have been two."

"Why didn't you jump?"

"Didn't want to lose my nice new D.VII – especially when I'm only likely to get a Triplane to replace it."

"You're far harder to replace. We don't want to lose you," he said firmly.

I looked at him and raised an eyebrow.

He blushed. "You know what I mean – and it's not like that."

"Sorry – couldn't resist teasing you."

The storm didn't stop until too late for us to fly again. I wasn't sorry – I was very tired and more than a bit shaky.

I'd had a worse fright than I'd realised. In the evening, after a few brandies, I felt a bit steadier, but when I got to bed reaction set in and I lay trembling and sweating.

If that had happened a few months ago, it would have been exciting and interesting, but now my nerves are too frayed for things like that.

It was a very long time before I fell asleep, and then I had the fucking burning dream, exactly the same in every detail as it always was.

VI

We didn't only need a new aircraft. The next day we lost Richter – he collided with a Camel, right in front of Teuffel, who nearly got taken out as well, and who shook so violently after the patrol that Lehmann had to light his fag.

"Sorry, sir," Teuffel said to me.

"Whatever for? Just get Schwarte to light them for you after flights."

"Oh – I see."

That's why Uhlig always lights your post-flight cigarette, I could see him thinking.

I smiled and clapped him on the shoulder. "A fellow's entitled to get a bit wound up by a thing like that – and I really don't want anyone who has no fear. They're just bloody dangerous."

"I'll second that," said Günther. "We had a fellow like that in my platoon last year – fucking idiot, he was. Got killed in no time, just lucky he only took one other chap with him."

Fellmann was waiting for me, obviously bursting with some secret or other.

"Don't ever play cards, Fellmann," I said. "You'll be cleaned out in no time."

"We're getting another D.VII."

"I like hearing things like that. When?"

"Next week."

I looked at him. "What the fuck use is next week?"

"That's what I said to them, sir. But the answer I got was 'Shut up and be grateful' – phrased a bit more graciously, but not much."

"Oh, well… We're going to need another pilot, I'm sorry to say."

"Yes, I heard. I'll see if I can poach someone."

"Do you need more photographs signing?"

"Yes, please – and I'd better take a fresh one with all your gongs, now you've got another."

The latest addition was the Knight's Cross of the Military Order of St Henry, from the King of Saxony. Of course I was very happy to get it, but I had no idea why – I had no association whatever with Saxony. It went very well with the others – it was a golden cross edged in white with a blue ring, rather like the Military Merit cross from home, and the ribbon was a very pretty shade of pale blue with yellow.

This is getting ridiculous, I thought as I spruced myself up for the portrait. *There are plenty of fellows like Alfred who've served for years, risked their lives, and been smashed up over and over – and I've got all these baubles, just because I'm in the Air Service and managed to shoot down a few aircraft.*

I left the gongs on my best tunic. It was only a matter of time before the next funeral, though Richter wouldn't get one as he'd gone down Tommy-side.

A few days later, Fellmann said, "Oh, sir – that new D.VII should be available in two days' time. And I tried to get another to replace Richter's Triplane, but no joy."

"Never mind."

I'll give it to Sobek. He's been here a bit longer than Günther.

"And at least the experience level is going to go back up." Fellmann looked very uncomfortable as he said that.

"Managed to poach someone, have you?"

He looked at me in blank astonishment. "Karl's been passed fit."

My office seemed to spin before my eyes. "Fellmann, that's not funny."

"No, sir, it isn't. And it wasn't meant to be. He's on a refresher course at Valenciennes and he'll be here in a few days' time... I thought you knew."

There was no point trying to pretend.

"No. He didn't tell me." My voice seemed to come from some way off, and I was burning hot, sweat running down my back. *Shit. Shit, shit, shit.* "He can't be fit."

"Just what I think – but we know how it is these days."

"I'll send him home."

"Sir – it might not be that simple. If they say he's fit then you'll need evidence to the contrary."

I was starting to feel very sick. I remembered Sobek and the others laughing at a cartoon of a doctor examining a skeleton and pronouncing it 'fit for active service'.

Karl's a Pour le Mérite, things are getting desperate – of course they've passed him fit. And he didn't tell me because he knew what my reaction would be.

"Well, I doubt it'll take long to find that," I said. "He'll never manage at altitude."

"No... surely they should have found him a ground job."

"Who do we know who could change his posting?"

Fellmann thought for a moment. "No one comes to mind, sir, but I'll have a think."

I couldn't think of anyone either. *This has to be stopped, because otherwise—*

I didn't want to finish that sentence. I lit a fag, my hands shaking visibly. I needed Karl to be safe. The thought of him flying over the Front when he wasn't fit was unbearable.

"He can have the new D.VII, anyway," I said. "I was going to give it to Sobek, but..."

"...but they do have to go to the highest scorers," Fellmann finished.

Our eyes met. What I'd really meant was that it would give Karl the best chance of survival, and we both knew it.

There has to be some way to stop this happening – but Fellmann's right. I need evidence. I'll have to wait until Karl gets here, and hope he doesn't get killed before I've got it. But the second I have that proof, he'll be grounded and Berlin can poke it.

An hour later, I really believed I would get to the Great Army ahead of him. It started as a scrap between us and two flights of Camels, and I was sure one of them was the same fellow I'd met a few days before. He was shit-hot and turned that thing on a sixpence, and I just couldn't get on his tail.

Things turned really nasty when a squadron of Spads joined in. There were at least two of their aircraft to each of ours and it was every man for himself. I saw Günther in trouble but was too busy fending off two Tommies to go to his aid, and Teuffel was coming to help me out but got engaged by a Camel—

And then, thank God, one flight of Camels buggered off, and Horstmann's Jasta joined in and saved our bacon. A Spad went down in flames, and I was pretty sure it was down to Horstmann himself.

I shook all the way home, and told myself it was the cold wind chilling my sweat-soaked clothes. Uhlig lit my fag, as always, and I was shivering so badly that it almost fell out of my mouth.

"Jesus," said Teuffel. "That was a bit hot." There was an audible tremor in his voice.

"That's for sure," Günther agreed. "I'm not sure how I got out of that."

"You didn't," Sobek said. "Not unscathed, anyway."

He pointed to Günther's right leg. Blood had soaked through his overalls and flying boot, and was puddling around his foot.

"Well, bugger me! I thought I felt a bit of a thump."

He suddenly went pasty white, and Müller grabbed him just as he started to sway.

"Sit down," I said, and Müller and I propped him against the wheel of his Triplane. "Lehmann, go and get Leutnant Fellmann. And bring the brandy."

"Yes, sir."

"Sergeant, could I have the shears, please?" asked Müller politely.

Braun looked slightly surprised. "Yes, all right."

"I'll get them, Sarge," said Schwarte.

Müller started cutting off the leg of Günther's overalls, with a very confident air. *Oh, to be seventeen.*

Günther looked very sideways at Müller's fresh, downy face. "I hope you know what you're doing," he said. "Maybe we should wait for Fellmann."

"Best to get started," Müller said. "Hm – entry but no exit." He turned to Fellmann, who had just arrived. "Could you give me the first aid kit, please, sir?"

Fellmann looked at him. "You're not going to try to get that out?"

"No – but the bleeding needs to be stopped."

Of course it bloody does. Everyone knows that.

"So are you a medical student or something?" Günther asked suspiciously.

"No, I haven't done my Abitur yet – my old man's a vet and I help him in the holidays."

"A *vet?!* That's supposed to reassure me?"

"Yes. Look," said Müller, rather impatiently, "the principles are the same, whether it's you with a bullet in you or a cow that's cut herself. And we're wasting time arguing."

"Go on, then," said Fellmann. "You might be able to improve my knowledge. I've done the Army first-aid courses, but that's it."

"This might hurt a bit," Müller said.

"Can you manage without morphine?" asked Fellmann.

"Give me the brandy," said Günther. "I'd rather be awake!"

Müller did a bloody neat job.

"Well done," said Fellmann, surprised and impressed.

He wasn't the only one who was impressed. The phone rang in the middle of dinner.

"I'm very sorry, Squadron Commander, sir," said Möller, "but it's for you. It's Assistant Doctor Eicke."

"Oh, all right. Do excuse me, gentlemen – and don't wait for me."

There was the usual crap about talking to someone famous, and then Eicke said, "Who's your first-aid whizz?"

"Oh – that's War Volunteer Müller," I replied. "His father's a vet."

Eicke laughed. "Well, tell him from me that his work was bloody good. It was a shame to disturb it, but I had to take the bullet out – otherwise I'd have put Günther on the train just as he was."

"That's quite a compliment – I'll pass it on."

Müller positively glowed when I told him. After dinner, I called him into my office.

"Müller, would you like to transfer to the Medical Service?"

His face fell. "Aren't I doing well enough, sir?"

"Yes, of course you are."

"Well, then I'd like to stay, please, sir. I've got plenty of time to become a vet or a doctor or whatever after the war."

What the fuck can I say to that? That there is no 'after the war' if you stay here?

"Just let me know if you change your mind," was all I said.

Two days later, Wendt turned up in a nice new D.VII, and I could see everyone wondering who was going to get it.

"I'm sorry to have to abandon you," I said to Wendt, "but we're all off again in half an hour."

"Oh, that's all right," he said. "I'll lie in the sun for a bit and talk to Fellmann."

I'll tell you all who's going to get the new toy after the patrol. I pushed the idea away smartly, because I'd been doing my best to forget that Karl was coming back. It was casting a very dark shadow over all my time on the ground.

Maybe he'll fail the refresher course... but that was really stupid of me. *Of course he won't – or, rather, if Karl fails then who in God's name will pass?*

Everyone got back safely, and they gathered round me for the debrief.

When I started in this business I could never understand how the Chief could keep track of everyone, and now I do it myself, without even thinking about it – except when it gets ridiculous...

"Grünwald, if you don't keep your bloody eyes open you'll be feeding the crows. You nearly rammed Lehmann. You've got to look out the whole bloody time. Never lose sight of what's going on around you..."

A lorry stopped in the lane outside the airfield. A tall, lanky figure climbed down out of the cab, pulled out a haversack and a bag, and started sauntering towards us.

The straight back and the easy, almost graceful walk were horribly familiar. His cap was stuck on his head at an angle, shading half his face. I didn't want to believe what I was seeing, had almost convinced myself that I was wrong – but then there was a glint of gold as the sun caught the order at his collar.

The light dimmed suddenly, and the ground seemed to crumble.

I realised that I'd stopped talking, and that the others were following my gaze. His uniform was creased from travelling. I could see the pilot's badge, the Iron Cross, and the two black and white ribbons looped through his buttonhole. And then he was standing in front of me.

He saluted me as smartly as if I'd been a general. "Leutnant von Leussow reporting for duty, Squadron Commander, sir!"

Oh, God, no. I'd hoped that somehow it wouldn't happen…

"What's wrong, Franz? Don't you want me in your Jasta?"

I don't want you in anyone's bloody Jasta. I want you at home, or behind a desk in Berlin. Anywhere safe, in fact.

"Of course I do, but—"

"Well, then – here I am!"

His eyes were blue and warm, and something inside me turned over in that usual stupid way.

The others were staring at us. I don't think they'd heard anyone call me 'Franz' before.

I made the introductions. The boys couldn't take their eyes off Karl's Pour le Mérite. I could, though, and I saw that his face was lined and strained, and his tunic loose.

"Leutnant von Leussow has returned to us from convalescent leave," I said by way of explanation.

They looked as if they wanted to say something, but didn't quite know what. *He must look rather imposing…*

"That's all for now. Remember, look out! Schiffer! *Schiffer!* Take Leutnant von Leussow's bags to my room and put another bed in there."

"Franz, you don't have to do that."

"I know I don't."

We started walking across the field. When we were out of earshot of the others, I said, "How in God's name did they pass you fit? You did tell them the truth, didn't you?"

"Now that would be telling."

I could hear that teasing tone in his voice. *Oh, for God's sake! Can't you take this seriously?*

"You should be at home." *You lied to that medical board. I know you did.*

"I can't stay at home any more," he said, his voice suddenly sober. "I've been there long enough. More than long enough."

"Karl, for God's sake, what do you want? A hero's death?" I could hear my voice getting louder and more impatient.

Keep your hair on, Franz. Shouting at him won't achieve anything. You know how bloody stubborn he is.

"I can't stay at home any more, Franz," he repeated quietly. "I have to be able to look in the mirror."

He stopped, and our eyes met. His were grey-blue and very calm. *That's what we're for, you said, to put on a uniform and bleed and die...*

"If you're fit to be here I'll eat my hat."

"Boiled or roasted?" he asked with a grin.

"You're the most pig-headed of pig-headed Prussians, you know that? Don't any of you have any bloody sense? You had a ticket out, for fuck's sake, but you have to come back."

"Franz, if you won't have me, someone else will. This," he said, fingering his Blue Max, "will get me into any Staffel I apply for."

That stopped me dead. That's exactly what you'll do.

I sighed. *It's better to keep you here, with me. And as soon as I have proof that you're unfit, I'll ground you and then get you sent home permanently.*

"If I were going to send you away, I wouldn't have had your bags taken to my room, would I? For fuck's sake, Karl, you've done your duty. You could have retired with honour. Why push your luck?"

"There's nothing else I can do. You'd be exactly the same."

"No, I bloody wouldn't. If I'd copped it that badly I'd stay at home, or work for the Technical Commission, and thank my lucky stars I didn't have to fight any more."

"You wouldn't, you know. You think you would, but it's not that simple."

We were going round in circles, and I knew I was wasting my breath.

"Come and see your new aeroplane, then," I said.

As we neared the hangars, Zaffke came out. He stared at Karl in disbelief.

"Hello, Zaffke – how are you?"

"Sir… I… er… this is a surprise." *And not a good one*, his face said clearly.

Karl just grinned. "There's a definite lack of a warm welcome here," he said. "I've just had our dear Squadron Commander almost shouting at me, and now you don't seem pleased to see me!"

"Zaffke probably feels as I do – that we'd rather see you anywhere but here."

"Well, never mind. I'm sure you'll get used to it!"

"So here she is," I said. "A brand-new Fokker D.VII, and I think you'll like her."

"She really is beautiful," he said appreciatively. "Thank you."

"Not at all… Look, it's lunchtime, so let's go and eat and then you can fly her to your heart's content."

Zaffke's eyes met mine behind Karl's back, the dismay in them eloquent. *Yes, I know, but we've been outmanoeuvred, for now anyway.*

Fellmann had much the same expression. "Hello, Karl," he said. "It's good to see you."

"You could sound as though you mean it!" Karl retorted, and gave Fellmann a playful punch on the arm – with his left hand. "There *is* a definite lack of a warm welcome here – first Franz, then Zaffke, and now you! I don't believe you want me back!"

We don't. Me least of all.

I expected Wendt to recognise Karl, but he didn't – and then I remembered that Karl had been shot down before Wendt started bringing us Fokkers.

As we all sat down, Steinwarz said to Karl, "Did I see oak leaves on your cap, sir?"

"Yes. I was a sniper – oh, back in '15."

"So was my brother."

"Oh, right."

I could see Karl wondering the same as the rest of us – *Is that 'was' as in killed, or as in moved on?*

"He was at Verdun," Steinwarz continued.

Karl's face froze, that old awful shadow spreading across it.

Yes – now you're back men are going to say things that let the demons out. I wonder if you'd thought of that.

"When was he there?" His tone matched his face, and I could see Steinwarz thinking that he'd put his foot in it.

"July."

"After me, then. I was there at the beginning, in the Brandenburg Corps... Did your brother make it out?"

"Yes – he got blown up, lost his right hand."

"Ah." Karl lit a cigarette and took a long drag. *That's interesting – you can smoke again.*

"So what happened to you?" Teuffel asked. "I mean, Oberleutnant Becker said you were back from convalescent leave."

Karl smiled. "Got shot down – forgot to watch my tail."

"Jesus," said Sandberg, "we've all done that."

"Amen," said Wendt. "That's how I ended up like this."

The lesson doesn't need underlining, I thought, and said nothing.

"Well," Karl said after lunch, "I'm off to fly my lovely new aeroplane."

And we're off over the bloody Front again...

Sobek got a Spad, taking him to four and the threshold of acedom, but I had to rescue Lehmann, because, in spite of the conversation over lunch, the silly sod attacked without looking behind, and bloody nearly got shot down.

I called him into my office.

"Lehmann, I'm thinking of fining you all five marks for every hole you collect," I said severely.

"Sorry, sir." He sounded just like a schoolboy.

"If you get that many again I'll have to think about posting you out," I went on. "It's not the standard I expect."

His face crumpled, and I almost felt guilty – which was stupid because I was trying to keep him alive.

"No, sir. I'll do better this evening, I promise."

"Tomorrow," I said. "All those patches will have to cure."

I went outside. Karl was sitting on the grass outside the main hut, enjoying the sun.

"So, what do you think of your new steed?"

"Beautiful, really beautiful – I wish we'd had those last year. When am I on patrol?"

"Not until you've flown against me – and that won't be until tomorrow morning. We've got one more to make today."

He looked at me closely. "Do you go on all of them?"

"No – Teuffel takes one a day."

"Well, I'll be able to take at least one of the others soon."

I was so knackered that I fell asleep sitting beside him, and only realised when he shook me awake.

"Oh, shit! I needed to get the spares order done."

"I can do that while you're flying," he said.

"Thanks."

Everyone but Karl and Lehmann went on the evening patrol. When we got back the two of them were sitting in the mess. Karl was trying to get Lehmann to talk, but the boy was obviously in awe of him.

The ice needs breaking.

"Would you play something?" I asked Karl. "I haven't heard you since January."

He played one of Chopin's nocturnes, and he had obviously been practising. It was beautiful. Grünwald slid quietly out of the door, and came back a few minutes later, clutching a book.

He went shyly up to Karl. "Excuse me – I sing a bit. Could we…?"

He held out the book.

"Schubert," said Karl. "How lovely. Of course we could. You'll have to forgive the wrong notes. I used to accompany my sister, but that's years ago now. What shall we start with?"

"'Rose on the Common.'"

Well, I'll be damned. I never knew Grünwald could sing like that.

It was almost like the old days. I closed my eyes, and for a moment the clock turned itself back a year, as they moved on to the old Air Service songs…

When the party for Sobek's victory was getting going, I said quietly to Karl, "This is where I bail out."

"I'll come with you – otherwise I'll disturb you when I come in."

We both knew that wasn't the reason.

He closed the door behind us and put a chair under the handle, and then I was in his arms.

"Karl, I would be so pleased to see you, if only it weren't here—"

His lips landed so gently on mine and stopped any more words. And I really did fall asleep with my head on his shoulder, and the most absurd feeling of being, at long last, home.

I woke in the small hours, filled with guilt. *This is all your fault, Franz – you dreamed of lying in his arms like this, you wanted it more than anything, and all your wishing has made it come true.*

But you will have to pay.

That was the end of further sleep. There wasn't much room in the single bed anyway, and I detached myself carefully and got into Karl's bed instead, where I lay trying to dispel the awful, black foreboding.

Schiffer knocked with the shaving water, and I realised the chair was still against the door.

"One moment!" I called out, and moved it.

I wondered whether Schiffer had noticed that we were each in the other's bed, and decided I didn't care.

Karl mumbled something and went back to sleep. *Lucky bugger*, I thought as I forced myself out of bed. I was so tired that I felt as if I'd died and been dragged out of my coffin to go flying. That thought made me shiver.

You'd better bloody wake up, or you'll be back in your coffin by nightfall, for good. And then who'll look after Karl? I have to survive, or no one will send him home, and then he'll be killed as well...

Bloody fool. You're getting sentimental.

We had a couple of encounters with the good old Tommies, but I didn't score. During one of the fights I realised that Müller and I were going after the same aircraft. I wasn't on form and it took me three bursts to cripple the pilot, and then I broke off and let Müller finish him off. His first kill would mean much more to him than my forty-first would to me.

He was beaming after we landed, looking very full of himself. *Next time you can do it without my help.*

Now for Karl. Let's see what he can do.

He was lying in the sun beneath the window of our room, flat out on the grass, gazing up at the sky.

"Right," I said. "Off you go. I'll be debriefing for about ten minutes and then I'll be after you."

He grinned. "You're dead, Franz!"

I wasn't dead. I let him jump me, to see how he'd deal with the resulting dogfight. Not well enough was the answer. If it had been for real I would have killed him.

He probably doesn't realise how strong the D.VII is. It's not an Albatros. I told him so in the debrief.

"Not good enough," I said. "Not aggressive enough. We'll do it again this afternoon."

I could see the disappointment in his face.

"All right." There was a pause, and then he said, "How many forty-victory aces have they got, anyway?"

"You'd only need to meet one once," I said. "It's bugger all use if you get killed first time out. You can do a lot better than that. These will take a lot of punishment before they break."

I told him about my encounter with the storm cloud, and finished, "...and while I'd rather you didn't break one, don't forget these days if it does happen, you can jump."

"True... Is there anyone I can practise against before this afternoon?"

"Sandberg. Be interesting for you to match that against a Triplane."

I had a small surprise in mind. I had a quiet word with Sandberg and told him to delay their take-off until we'd been gone an hour. I planned to arrive back with enough fuel left to bounce Karl. I needed to know if he would see me coming.

It worked beautifully. They were scrapping right overhead the airfield. *Karl's doing much better – but then he would feel he had to beat Sandberg.*

We'd come back good and high, and I dived down, hoping to surprise him. I'd briefed the rest of the patrol to stay out of the way.

I was almost behind him. *He hasn't seen me, no marks –* and then he broke into a hard climbing turn, using most of the D.VII's power and performance.

Good. Very good. That's much more like it.

After ten minutes I had to break off for lack of fuel, but I'd seen enough.

"Much better," I said to him. "You're down for dawn tomorrow."

His face lit up. "Thanks, Franz," he said warmly.

"So you'd better get that painted overnight... By the way, how did your refresher course go?"

"Very well. As I'm sure they told you."

"I thought you were still at home."

"I wanted to surprise you."

"You certainly did that."

For a moment I felt quite cross with him. *You've always been determined to come back, and you've never wanted me to know just how much that injury has affected you. Yes, I got a good look at your scars, but I found out about the pain and the coughing blood by accident.*

I'll bet I don't know the half of it. I'll bet your medical notes would make very interesting reading. Now that's a thought – but I don't suppose anyone would let me have a copy. Even if they did I probably wouldn't understand them, or be able to work out their likely effect in the air. I'll just have to watch you and assess you myself.

We had a party for Müller's first victory. Karl played the piano, and we sang all the Air Service songs, the Liesl song, all our favourites. I noticed that Karl was pale and very tired, but he made the effort to play for a good couple of hours.

At about eleven he got up from the piano, finished his brandy and stretched.

"Sorry, chaps, but I'm off to bed. Got an early start tomorrow, and I mustn't disappoint our dear Oberleutnant."

All I want is the excuse to drag you off to the doctor, I thought as we headed for our room, *and if you last a couple of weeks I know I'll find it. I can only pray that you'll last that long.*

In the early morning I shook so badly that I couldn't fasten my shirt, and felt so sick that I had to sit down. Karl noticed, of course. He couldn't help but notice, but he didn't say anything.

I wonder how you'll be when the bullets start flying. It can't be easy, fighting again after an injury like that. I'll be watching and you'd better go in hard, or you'll find yourself back at that fighter pilot school as an instructor. I wonder how difficult that would be to arrange...

In the twilight by the flight line, he seemed considerably calmer than I was. *I'll be all right when we attack, but will you? Or will that calmness evaporate?*

We had two inconclusive engagements, and in both of them he flew well and aggressively. *Perhaps I was wrong, perhaps you are all right.* But after we landed he looked grey and exhausted, and went back to bed. I wrote my report and then went to wash the oil off my face, and he was so deeply asleep that he didn't stir.

I know you're not well, but I can't prove it yet. If you keep flying like that you'll be very useful, and I'll have no excuse to ground you.

"How did he get on?" Fellmann asked me.

"Very well."

Fellmann pulled a face. "Nothing you can do yet, then?"

"No... can you find out whether they need another instructor at Valenciennes, or any of the other fighter pilot schools?"

"Yes, will do, sir – but..."

"Yes, I know. I'll need an excuse to send him there."

That afternoon, as we were changing out of our sweaty clothes, Karl asked, "What are the tarts like round here?"

"I don't know."

"You don't know? Are you all right?" He looked at me closely. "No, you're not, are you?" he said, concern in his voice and eyes.

"I'm fine, Karl. I just haven't had time to go to the house of joy."

"Well, then – it's time you did. You can't be out here without ever having a fuck."

I put my arms around him. "Now that you're here…"

He laughed gently and stroked my hair. "Franz – you know how it is. We don't fuck and we both need women as well."

I couldn't argue with that – and the contact between us had revived my libido, and the thought of a nice warm girl was very appealing.

"I suppose that makes me the same sort of wretched pervert as you!" I said with a smile.

"There is no hope for either of us, so let's give in to vice while we can!"

He played the piano again in the evening, and Grünwald sang 'Singing on the Water'. *The last time I heard this was in Karl's house. 'Come back in the summer and we'll take the boat out on the lake…' It must be just like this, with the evening light shimmering on the rippling waves.*

Karl's eyes were very bright. *The memory of home's almost too much, isn't it?* I remembered the look in his eyes as we'd watched the sun set the summer before, that terrible intensity as if he knew he would never see another sunset at home.

And this time? What are your chances of making it back to Brandenburg?

"May tomorrow vanish on shimmering wings, Like yesterday and today, Until I, on higher, shining wings, Myself disappear from changing time," sang Grünwald.

You won't fall for Prussia if I can help it.

"That's enough culture," said Teuffel. "Let's have something a bit livelier!"

"All right," Karl said, and played the introduction to 'Ten Thousand Men'.

We sang for half an hour, and then he got up.

"Franz, we have an appointment," he said, "in case you've forgotten."

The others looked at us in surprise. They obviously thought their Old Man was a boring old fart – I left their parties early, none of them had seen me really drunk, and I never went to the whorehouse with them. That was more than enough to make me a boring old fart. It wasn't something I wanted to be, but I had to keep some distance between them and me, in the interests of discipline, and I'd changed. Once I'd been as keen on parties and tarts as anyone, but now I just couldn't see the point of them.

"I'm taking our dear Oberleutnant to the fleshpots," Karl announced loudly. "Anyone else coming?"

Karl, for Christ's sake, I thought, turning red... but no one wanted to come with us. *Going to the house of joy with me is probably the last thing they want to do.*

"This is just like old times," he said cheerfully as we got into the car.

Oh, for God's sake! Who are you trying to convince?

He caught sight of my expression in the twilight, and his face was suddenly sober.

"Well, no, it isn't really, is it?" he said.

Stupid of me to wonder who you were trying to convince. If anyone needs to imagine the old days are back, you do.

"They wouldn't want us to mourn for ever, Franz. The best way we can honour the dead is by living our own lives to the full."

"Is this living to the full, coming back here?"

"What is there fuller?"

"You told us all in '14 that we were bloody fools for thinking that."

He smiled. "Let's go."

I still had misgivings about going to Blanche's. *Oh, well, if nothing else I can have a drink while Karl goes upstairs, and it'll be pleasant seeing women for a change...* But once I had a couple of glasses of champagne inside me and a half-naked girl on my knee, nature took over. I just hoped I wouldn't have a fit of shaking in the bedroom.

I didn't. I actually managed to forget the war completely. I fell asleep afterwards, the first genuine, relaxing sleep I'd had in weeks, broken only too soon as she shook me awake to tell me that my time was up.

Karl was right to drag me here, I thought as I went downstairs. *I should do this more often.*

"Karl, we'd better get back," I said. "It's nearly eleven."

"Oh, Christ, so it is."

On the way home he asked, "So what are the others like? Teuffel seems pretty hot."

"Yes, he is. Sobek, Sandberg and Kleber are coming on well too, but they can't see anything apart from what they're doing themselves. They don't have an overview."

"Neither will I, to start with."

"It'll come back. Your experience is going to be very useful. But, Karl, tell me truthfully: how do you feel? I don't mean what did the doctors in Berlin say. I mean how do you feel?"

I don't know why I bothered asking. I had as much chance of flying to the moon as of getting a truthful answer.

"I'm fine, Franz. Don't worry about me."

I'll be watching, and I know I'll find something wrong with you.

"How's the farm?"

"Coming on. We'll have more of a harvest this year. The Russians were working well when I left, and Mahlke's estate manager said he'd keep an eye on them while I'm away."

"*Von* Mahlke's estate manager," I said naughtily.

"You've never met him." I could hear the disgust in his voice.

"How long will it be before he's accepted?"

"He won't be. His grandchildren will, probably, depending on who his children marry."

"So you're still not marrying Clara?" I teased.

"Absolutely not. At present I don't want to marry anyone."

"It's going to be rather hard for them, isn't it, if everyone thinks the same as you… I take it young Hans is still alive?"

"He was last thing I heard."

I parked the car behind the hangars, and as we walked to our hut I heard Karl humming 'Singing on the Water'. The last words of the song came into my mind, about leaving Time on higher, shining wings.

Very appropriate for a fighter pilot, that. I probably will leave this world on shining wings, high up, when I make that last mistake and someone fills me full of lead…

And how much more time have I got?

That night I had the bloody burning dream, and Karl woke me.

"It's all right," he said into my ear, as he held my trembling body tight against his.

"Oh, shit," I heard myself mumble. "What the fuck are we doing here?"

"God alone knows…"

"It has to end soon," I said. "How can it have gone on so long?"

The next day it rained, to my great relief.

"Do you want to visit Otto's grave?" I suggested. "We could invite ourselves to Horstmann's for lunch."

"Yes. Thank you. I'd like that very much. Be good to see Horstmann again as well – though no doubt he'll bang on about Susanne!"

I didn't ring Horstmann, and the look on his face when Karl got out of the car was quite something.

"Karl – well, bugger me! This is a surprise!"

"We thought we'd come and say hello," I said, "and visit the cemetery."

"Ah, yes – hope you don't mind if I don't. We had yet another funeral yesterday and I'd rather not see it again until the next time. Are you staying to lunch?"

"If we may."

Horstmann rolled his eyes. "Of course you may, you stupid bastard. See you later, then."

The pilots' graves had taken over the cemetery. Reading the names of the men I'd known was almost too much for me. *Here's the Chief, and Johnny, and Otto...*

Karl stopped for quite a while at Johnny's grave, and I wished I could forget him falling blazing through the sky, and the pitifully small bundle in the coffin.

We paused at each of the others' and stopped again at Otto's. Neither of us spoke. After a minute or so Karl sighed, and we saluted the dead and left the cemetery, then walked in silence down the lane to Horstmann's airfield. All I could see was Otto in his burning Triplane, and sweat ran down my back.

Horstmann and his pilots gave us a true Air Service welcome. Most of them were just as young as my fellows, and seemed a bit stunned at having two Pour le Mérites to lunch.

The tic in Horstmann's eye had got worse. It used to be confined to the outer corner, but now his whole eyelid jumped and twitched. My hands shook, and every now and then the tremor spread to the rest of me, and I felt hot and cold and sweaty.

Karl sat there talking to us, completely calm, his eyes clear and steady. *Perhaps what we all need is eleven months off. Perhaps that's the answer – get a bullet through you and have a nice long rest.*

Karl excused himself and left the room.

Horstmann leaned close to me. "What the hell is he doing?" he said quietly. "And more to the point, what the hell are *you* doing allowing it? You know he's not fit."

"Yes, but I can't prove it."

"What are you waiting for? For him to black out at five thousand metres, in the middle of a fight? Get him examined, before it's too late."

"They passed him fit in Berlin. And you know how things are these days. Look at your boys. They're completely green, just like half of mine. You think they're going to tell an ace he's not fit to fly? And please don't say, 'I told you so.' I know you did."

"I wasn't going to…"

Karl came back, and Horstmann changed the subject, going on about the lovely Susanne. Karl tried to catch my eye.

Oh no, you don't. I stared at Horstmann instead. If my eyes met Karl's we'd both be helpless with laughter, and it would be very unkind.

I wondered if Horstmann bored his pilots with Susanne, or whether he kept his personal life to himself.

The rain had stopped, and the sun was trying to break through.

"Horstmann," I said, "it's been most kind of you, and we've enjoyed seeing you very much, but we'll have to go. It would be good to talk all day, but you know how it is."

"Yes, I do. Come again soon."

"No, you come to us. Don't leave it too long."

Karl got into the car first, which gave Horstmann the opportunity to whisper, "Becker, do something, for God's sake."

There was no time for me to answer.

We got back and took off almost at once. Sandberg got a two-seater, but just as the fight was running out of steam Teuffel's D.VII burst into flames. He jumped out, but the parachute had already caught light, and he fell like a stone.

The mood during the debrief was very sombre. We were all relying on our parachutes…

"How often does anything catch fire that fast, though?" asked Sobek.

"It only has to happen once," Lehmann said.

"Quick death, though," Karl said. "Better than burning."

"Yes," said Sandberg. "Much better."

Lehmann and Grünwald looked at Karl, and I could see the realisation in their faces: *We are here to die and we'll be lucky if we go home.*

Well, you had to understand that some time.

I went to the Ops Office.

"Fellmann, could you chase up the replacement for Günther?" I said. "And we'll need—"

The door opened and a youth came in, dressed up in uniform. He stopped dead when he saw me, and bowed smartly.

"Good afternoon, Herr Oberleutnant."

"Good afternoon. And you are?"

"Buckow, sir, reporting for duty."

I looked at Fellmann.

"This is Officer Cadet Gustav von Buckow," he said. "And I'll get onto them for a replacement for Teuffel – hopefully I'll be able to poach. Oh – and I had a call from the Air Defence Officer. Teuffel came down in No Man's Land."

"Thanks." I turned to the new arrival. *Christ, you look about twelve.* "Well, Buckow, you'd better come and meet the others."

Karl looked at Buckow as I introduced them.

"Any relation of Werner?" he asked quietly.

"Yes, sir – he's my oldest brother."

"Well, how about that! How is he?"

Buckow looked awkward. "As well as we can expect, sir. He's in that Institute in Düsseldorf that specialises in facial injuries."

"What – still?"

Buckow shook his head. "Again…"

He obviously didn't want to talk about it.

"Give him my best wishes when you write – and we're very informal here. You say 'du' to everyone apart from the Oberleutnant."

"Oh. Thanks… So how do you know Werner?"

From Karl's shadowed expression, I knew the answer.

"We were in the same company at Verdun, and then later I saw that he'd caught it badly at the Somme."

"Another of the Brandenburg mafia!" I teased Karl later.

"More quality, you mean!"

"Quality? Come on – he's a child!"

"Well, let's see what he can do."

The answer to that was 'not much', and the same went for Teuffel's 'replacement'. Fellmann's attempts at poaching had failed dismally, and Stoll looked frighteningly young.

And we have to turn them into fighter pilots, and trust them to watch our backs. I really didn't want to dwell on that, or to say it out loud.

Karl still hadn't given me an excuse to ground him. He was obviously very tired after every flight and had that grey tint in his complexion, but he was flying well. A week or so after his return, he shot down an SE5.

"That makes twenty-four!" he said gleefully. "Watch out, Franz, I'm right behind you! Only sixteen more and I'll have caught you."

"By that time I shall have fifty. I've got a position to uphold, you know!"

"Of course, Herr Oberleutnant!"

Later that same day, I shot down a Bristol Fighter, my forty-first.

"See?" I said. "You're not going to catch me up after all!"

"Ah – but you're flying less now I'm here!"

That was true – and Sobek was now capable of leading, so I had two competent patrol leaders and could lighten the load on myself.

I needed to. I shied away from the word 'exhausted', but I knew I wasn't far away from it. What I really needed was leave, but I daren't take any. Karl could run the Jasta easily, but I needed to keep an eye on him.

If I go away, he'll be killed.

It was a stupid, irrational belief, but I couldn't get it out of my head. And I daren't take leave because I didn't think I'd be able to fly again afterwards. Leave would ruin me. I just had to carry on.

One lovely hot day, I was lying on the grass beneath the mess windows. Karl was leading the patrol and I should have been doing my paperwork, but it was very pleasant idling, and that spot was a good sun trap.

I didn't intend to eavesdrop, but the window was open and I could hear every word.

"He's a decent sort, and he plays the piano beautifully, but he's a bit old for a fighter pilot, isn't he?" Grünwald said.

"How old do you think he is, then?" asked Müller.

"Well, he looks about forty-five, even older than the Old Man."

Thank you very bloody much. I know I look a bit battered, but forty?

"They're as thick as thieves, those two," said Kleber. "Can you imagine any of us calling the Old Man by his first name?"

"Christ, no," said Müller.

I smiled to myself.

"And they share a room," Grünwald said.

"The Old Man used to share with Horstmann," said Kleber. "I expect he got lonely."

"They go back a long way, if you ask me," Müller said. "Where did Leussow get his Blue Max, anyway?"

"Well, I was having a look in the photograph album the other day," said Grünwald, "and there's a Leutnant Karl von Leussow in there – I'll show you."

I heard the sound of pages being turned, and then Grünwald said, "There he is. Look."

There was a brief silence.

"Yes, but that's a young man," Müller said.

"It's him, though, surely," said Kleber. "It's the same face. It's just lined now."

He read out the dates when Karl had joined the Jasta, when he'd received his Pour le Mérite, and when he'd been wounded.

"It must have been bad," said Grünwald. "He's only just come back, and the Old Man said he was back from convalescent leave."

Kleber said, "No wonder he's going grey, if it's taken him nearly a year to recover."

Going grey? I'd had enough. I stood up and leaned in through the window.

"Can I help you, gentlemen?"

They went scarlet, and Grünwald started to stammer something.

"Just remember you can be heard when the window's open," I said. "The Karl von Leussow in the album is indeed the one we have with us now. And yes, he was badly injured, and no, he's not 'a bit old for a fighter pilot', any more than I am. We are both twenty-three."

"I'm sorry, sir," said Müller. "We didn't mean—"

"You're wasting your breath," I said, and went back to sunbathing.

The silence from the mess was deafening, and after a couple of minutes they left, no doubt to continue their conversation in private. I'd had to make the point. I didn't want Karl overhearing their juvenile speculation.

I could understand why Kleber thought Karl was going grey. The hair at his temples had always been ash-blond, and in some lights it was almost silver. His face was still drawn and lined, and that would make ash-blond hair look grey – especially when he'd just been flying, and his face had that greyish hue.

I didn't like that colour at all. It reminded me of how he'd looked when he was in hospital, half dead. Something snagged in my mind, someone else who'd looked grey, when I was a child – or maybe I hadn't actually seen it, maybe I'd only heard my parents talking…

I'll ask Alfred next time I write, though I don't know when I'll get an answer. If I tell him as much I can about Karl's injury and the way he looks now, maybe he'll have some idea what's wrong.

No time like the present. I got up, dressed, and went to my office. I was halfway through writing the letter when Fellmann came in.

"It's almost time for the next patrol, sir," he said.

"Thanks."

I finished the letter in the evening. *I'm clutching at straws*, I thought as I sealed the envelope. *I really need to get Karl examined by a doctor – but on what pretext?*

And there was something else, something I didn't even want to admit to myself. Karl's company was delaying my slide into the abyss. Our shared intimacy and the solidity of his embrace helped me to feel steadier.

When I send you home I'll be on my own again, and then it'll be only a matter of time before I fall apart completely or get shot down. But that has to be, because if you stay here you'll die.

A few days later, Sobek was flying with half the Staffel and I was enjoying the sun again, this time with Sandberg, Lehmann and Grünwald. *We'll all be as brown as anything soon. The Tommies will think we're Indians if they shoot us down.*

There was no need to be dressed ready to fly. If the telephone rang we would just put our flying suits on and leap into our aircraft. It was warm enough now to fly like that – at least, most of us thought it was. Karl still wore his uniform under his flying suit, making some joke about wanting to look his best for the ladies of Paris if he were captured. I think he just felt the cold rather more than we did.

He strolled over in shirt and trousers and joined us. I wasn't sure if he'd strip off or not – he wasn't self-conscious about his scars with me, but that was in private.

Lehmann and Grünwald were sitting together, talking. Karl undressed, folded his clothes neatly and lay between me and them, face down.

"Nice, this, isn't it?" I said.

"Mm. Lovely. Don't let me go to sleep. I don't want to get burned."

I opened one eye and was aware that the two youngsters were looking at Karl's back. Half an hour later, he turned over and lay spread out, his eyes closed. Their conversation died.

I glanced at them, and saw that their eyes were riveted on the scar on his chest. It didn't look any prettier than it had in January.

He opened his eyes and looked at them. "Seen enough?" he asked.

"Sorry," said Grünwald, "we didn't mean to stare."

"Yes, you did," Karl said. He sat up. "Have a good look." He turned his back to them. "Entry here and" – turning to face them – "exit here. One Vickers machine-gun bullet, fired from a Sopwith Camel. The moral of this story is watch your tail when you attack. I was lucky. His guns jammed, otherwise I'd be even thinner."

"That can't have been much fun," Sandberg said quietly.

The livid scar on his arm showed clearly, and I thought suddenly that, out of the five of us, he and Karl were the only ones who had ever been wounded. Yes, I'd got that cut on my arm in that trench raid, but that didn't count.

Karl smiled. "No, it wasn't." He looked at them. "To save you having to speculate, the scar on my leg dates from spring '15 and was kindly donated by an English shell."

He lay down and closed his eyes. After a couple of minutes the two kids stretched out in the sun as well.

A while later I looked at him, and saw for the first time what Kleber had been talking about. The hair at Karl's temples was completely grey. I hadn't noticed before – I'd just assumed it was the colour it had always been – but now, in the bright sunshine, I could see the difference.

Sad, that a man who's still young should be turning grey. It was hardly surprising, having regard to what had happened to him, but I still didn't like to see it.

Johnny was killed in early July. I'd better check the date in the album. Karl will remember and I don't want to seem to have forgotten. It wasn't exactly difficult to work out the anniversary of their father's death. He'd died three days after Johnny.

The shocked, hurt look in Karl's eyes when he came out of the Chief's office that day had never really gone – it had dimmed but was there constantly, behind every other expression.

It's going to take him a very long time to get over it all, I thought, and then realised there was nothing to say he ever would. Every now and then I caught him staring into space, his eyes deeply shadowed, and I was painfully aware that there was nothing I could do to help him.

I could save his life by sending him home, but I couldn't undo the past.

On the anniversary of Johnny's death, I said, "Karl, if you want to borrow the car today, you can."

"Thanks – but I'm needed here."

I couldn't argue with that.

"I paid my respects the other day," he added, "and Johnny would understand."

"Yes, he would."

In fact, he'd probably prefer you to fight.

"Tell you what," I said, "why don't we raise a glass to him in my office after flying?"

He smiled. "Yes. Good idea. And we'll ask Fellmann as well."

I can't believe it's a year ago. Almost every pilot who was in the Jasta then is dead now. Karl, Horstmann and I are the only ones left.

Karl was very quiet for the rest of the day. During the early afternoon flight I saw his D.VII going hard after a Camel. We were up at nearly six thousand metres, which put the Camels right at their ceiling while we still had power in hand. He sent the Tommy plummeting earthwards in an ever-steeper dive, over the vertical—

Karl was spinning. For one horrified moment I thought he'd been hit, but he couldn't have been. No one was near him.

"What are you waiting for?" Horstmann had said. "For him to black out at five thousand metres, in the middle of a fight?"

There was no time to think about it, no time to do anything except hope he was all right.

I saw him a few minutes later, circling with another Camel, his D.VII easily recognisable by the black and white stripes around the fuselage. *Thank God for that.*

As we flew home I was shaking with relief, and trying to work out what to say to him. He'd given me the proof I needed.

Or had he? It could be that he'd manoeuvred too sharply in the thin air and lost it. I'd done that myself, and he'd only been flying the thing a couple of weeks. I couldn't prove he'd passed out.

"What happened to you, then?" I asked in the debrief.

"Pulled it too tight and spun off the turn," he said. "Even Mr Fokker's wonder-machine gets a bit breathless up there."

I've still got no proof. I could ask him to see a doctor, but everyone knows what the Army doctors are like. They'll think he's fit enough to die for Germany, and they're probably right.

In the evening the three of us met in my office, with a bottle of champagne.

I filled the glasses and raised mine. "Leutnant Johann von Leussow – may he rest in peace."

The other two echoed me.

We drank, and then Karl said, "You know, I really can't imagine Johnny resting in peace."

We laughed.

"No," Fellmann agreed. "Quite out of character!"

"Neither can I!" I said at the same time.

Karl raised his glass. "Here's to you, Johnny, you old bastard – give the devils hell from all of us!"

We emptied the bottle reminiscing about Johnny and the old days in the squadron, and then joined the others in the mess.

The next day poor little Grünwald was killed, and the day after that Kleber came back long before the rest of the patrol, flew his approach far too fast, and hit the ground in a series of bounces, breaking the undercarriage off his Triplane. It skidded drunkenly to a halt, and he made no effort to get out.

"Fellmann!" I shouted, and we ran across the airfield towards the wreck.

There was blood everywhere. Poor Kleber was bent over, clutching his stomach and groaning, literally writhing in pain. God knows how he'd managed to get down.

"I'll forgive you the bad landing!" I said.

At least you've brought us the aircraft back. You'd have been perfectly entitled to parachute out. Unless you couldn't get out, of course...

Otto sat, unmoving, in his burning Triplane – I shook my head and the image disappeared.

Stop it, Franz. Think about Kleber instead.

The fuselage isn't too badly damaged, but we're going to have to lift him out. Poor sod. It'll half-kill him – unless we can spare him the agony of being hauled out fully conscious.

"We'll get you out and on your way to hospital," Fellmann said, "and then you can go home and have a nice rest, and see lots of pretty German girls."

The ground crew were on their way, and Karl was bringing up the rear. I noticed he was walking – but then a pilot doesn't have to be able to run.

"Fellmann, can you knock him out while he's still in the cockpit?"

"Oh, I should think so… Hold him steady for me, would you, Karl? I don't want him moving at the wrong moment."

"Of course."

Karl leaned into the cockpit and wrapped his arms around Kleber. He said something to him, very quietly, something that I couldn't hear but that seemed to reassure him, and he actually kept still for Fellmann to get the needle in.

Karl held him until he passed out. I was rather surprised. *It's not as if you know him well. I'd do that for a friend, of course, but I'm not sure about anyone else. It's too close, too personal.*

"All yours," he said, and straightened up.

As he turned away from us I caught a glimpse of his face, creased in a mixture of pity and anger. Looking at Kleber made me angry as well.

I don't believe he even has to shave. He should be at school, not out here. And now the poor little sod's got a stomach full of lead.

Zaffke and I lifted him out of the aircraft. He was limp and heavy in our arms, and didn't make a sound. Fellmann had knocked him out thoroughly, and I hoped he hadn't overdone it.

That's one advantage of wearing nothing under our flying suits, I thought as Fellmann started to examine him. *Less clothing to cut away.*

I didn't look too closely. It reminded me too much of Kurt. Fellmann patched him up as best he could, and we wrapped him in a couple of blankets and put him carefully in the back of the car. Lehmann got in, to keep him on the seat, and Fellmann set off slowly for the field hospital.

Kleber shouldn't wake up for quite a while, which is just as well. The thought of being jolted over all those potholes with an injury like that makes me feel quite sick. I don't suppose we'll see him back. I hope he makes it.

I turned back to the Triplane, to try to assess whether it could be repaired. Karl was leaning against it, white as a sheet, sweating visibly, and looking very sick.

Quite unlike your usual composure.

"Are you all right?"

"Yes. Yes, of course I am."

Seeing Kleber like that must have brought back all your memories of hospital.

"I could do with a brandy," I said. "Nasty, that."

"Yes. So could I. It reminds me…"

"I thought it might."

Where do you find the courage, after what happened to you, to come back and risk it happening again? No doubt you pushed it to the back of your mind, refused to think about it. And now you've seen someone else badly wounded, and you can't pretend any more that it couldn't happen.

If only that would make you see sense.

"What did you say to him, anyway?" I asked as we walked towards the lavatory block to wash the blood off ourselves. "It obviously worked."

"Oh, nothing really…" He kicked a stone savagely. "Just the sort of platitudinous crap I hope I'll never have to say to you."

"The sort I said to you a year ago, you mean."

"Actually, you didn't… At least, if you did, I don't remember it!" He grinned at me. "You're too honest, Franz. I'm sure you never told me I was going to be all right."

"Well, if I had I'd have been right, wouldn't I?" I retorted. "After all, you're here now, which I'm sure is more than the doctors expected."

"All right, all right! You win!"

I nearly commented on his having held Kleber longer than was necessary, but kept my mouth shut. *Maybe someone did something like that for him, after they'd got him out of the wreckage of his Albatros, and he wouldn't want to be reminded of that.*

I wonder if anyone will do that for me, when it's my turn? I hope it never will be. I hope I'll either get through unharmed or be killed outright. I certainly don't want to be shot in the stomach. Poor Kleber's problems are only just beginning.

I dreamed about Kurt that night, in the shell-hole, holding him as the rain poured down on us… I woke feeling sick and miserable, and lay staring into the darkness, listening to Karl snoring quietly.

Tomorrow we're going to have to bury Grünwald. It's unbearable. Completely unbearable.

VII

The morning of Grünwald's funeral, Karl shot down another Tommy, bringing his score to twenty-five. He was scoring better than I was – I'd only managed six since Otto's death nearly two months earlier – but then he always had done. His temperament was cooler than mine, and he'd always been a first-class shot. He was fighting as if he'd never been away, and he was an effective and aggressive patrol leader.

On the face of it, he was an asset and I should have been very pleased to have him back, but I wasn't. It wasn't only that I was afraid he'd be killed. Something was disturbing me, something I couldn't put my finger on.

I wish we had a squadron doctor. I'd like to be able to discuss you with someone who sees you every day, someone who sees the same things I see but who understands them. Fellmann's medical knowledge is rudimentary, but perhaps that's better than nothing. I'll have a chat with him after the funeral.

When we got back from the cemetery, I took him aside.

"I'd like to ask you something, in private," I said. "Come to my office."

We sat together on the same side of the desk.

"Fellmann, I know you're not a doctor," I began.

He raised an eyebrow. "But you think you've caught something nasty, and you'd like me to take a look!"

I laughed. "Nothing of the sort!" I hesitated. "It's Karl."

"Oh – you think he's caught something nasty!" We laughed, and then he said, "I know what you mean. That grey colour, especially after flying."

"That's just it. And a few days back, he spun in the middle of a fight – he claims he just pulled the turn too tight, but…"

"But you think he passed out."

"Yes. With that lung, at altitude…"

"Mm… As you said, sir, I'm not a doctor, but… well, I've been unhappy about him for some time. I don't like that greyish colour at all, but we're back to needing proof."

I sighed. "Indeed. Thanks, Fellmann."

"It's a pity the aircraft trials have finished."

I'd forgotten there'd been another set of trials. "Yes, it is."

That would have been perfect. I could have sent Karl to Adlershof for three weeks, but it's too late.

I wish Alfred would answer my letter, but no doubt he's up to his eyeballs in muck and bullets. If he's still alive.

That evening I watched Karl, trying to analyse exactly what was wrong, but without success. Some time after dinner I got into an intense discussion with Sobek and Sandberg, about – of all things – Einstein's Theory of Relativity. Sandberg had been studying maths till early '17, and he claimed to understand it. Neither Sobek nor I could make head nor tail of it.

"If you ask me, Einstein's mad," said Sobek in the end.

"Whether he's mad or not, I can't see what it has to do with me," I said. "The D.VII's pretty quick, but I'm sure it doesn't go fast enough to start getting heavier – if that's what happens."

"That's exactly it," said Sandberg, and launched into another incomprehensible 'explanation'.

He lost me completely and I looked round, wondering if Karl had been listening and what he thought about it. His chair was empty, and I realised it was some time since I'd heard his voice. *I expect he's gone for a piss. He'll be back in a minute.*

But he didn't come back.

This might be my opportunity. I'll bet you're feeling ill. It's very smoky in here and I'll bet it's got to your lung. If I can only catch you, get some proof, I can ground you...

I got up and left the mess. As I went down the steps, I saw him leaning against the side of the hut.

"Lovely evening," he said, gesturing at the twilight.

I looked at him closely. He seemed pale and drawn, but that late evening light takes the colour out of everything and I couldn't be sure.

He smiled. "Fancy a stroll?"

"Yes, all right."

He linked his arm through mine and we ambled slowly across the airfield, towards the pale blue and gold of the western sky.

"Karl, I... look, I'm rather worried about you – I mean..." The words tumbled out awkwardly.

He squeezed my arm against his body. "Let's not talk," he said.

His voice was so warm and soft that I felt it touch me, and I realised I didn't want to talk either. It was enough just to have each other's company, and all at once I was at peace, with myself and with the world. We stopped in the middle of the airfield and stood there together, and it was as if the earth had ceased to turn, as if time had ceased to flow.

The light faded slowly from the sky, and we turned and went to our room.

I put the chair under the door handle. His eyes were blue in the electric light, and softer than I could ever have imagined them, and then he was in my arms and nothing else existed.

In the middle of the night, as I lay awake trying not to disturb him, I resolved to find a way of sending him home, however I had to do it. I would be miserably lonely without him and I would never see him again, but it would be God knows how many times worse if he were killed.

But the next day was so busy that I didn't have time to think until the evening, and then I was too tired to do anything except have a few drinks and go to bed.

The following day I had a much-needed lie-in while Karl led the dawn flight, and I was enjoying a leisurely breakfast when they returned. Karl came and sat beside me.

"How did it go?" I asked.

"No victories, no losses." He poured himself a cup of coffee and lit a fag. "There are far too many of them and not enough of us. It's not the war it was last year."

"I know."

"I winged a Camel, but the bugger wouldn't go down and I had more sense than to keep after him, so he got away. Sobek nearly got one as well, but that was it."

"Oh, well, c'est la vie."

"Indeed."

We lingered over breakfast for half an hour or so, and then I said, "Oh, well, time to go flying."

"I think I'll go back to bed."

He got up and stopped suddenly, bent over, gripping the back of his chair, his knuckles white. His eyes were narrowed and his lips compressed, and he seemed to be having trouble breathing. I glanced round. None of the others seemed to have noticed.

After a short while he straightened and turned to leave the table. *Now I've got you.*

"Would you come to my office, please?" I said quietly.

He nodded, still apparently unable to speak, and followed me. I closed the door behind us.

"Sit down," I said, indicating one of the chairs in front of my desk.

I sat behind the desk and looked at him. He was impassive, sitting very straight, his eyes still. His face had that grey tint again, as if he'd been flying.

I wish I could get to the bottom of this... It took me a moment to frame the words.

"Karl, I'd appreciate a straight answer. What's wrong with you?"

He smiled. "I'm fine, Franz."

But you're not. I know you're not.

I made an effort to keep my voice steady and unemotional. "Just now, when you got up, you seemed to be unable to move for a good half-minute and you seemed to be in pain. And the other day you went into a spin at altitude, for no apparent reason."

"I pulled it too tight and lost it, that was all."

"Maybe. But what about just now?"

He looked at me steadily for a few seconds and then shrugged, as if admitting defeat. "My chest still hurts sometimes, that's all," he said reluctantly. "I didn't want to tell you, because I knew it would worry you."

"So badly that you can't move? Like in January?"

For a moment I thought he wasn't going to answer, then he gave another shrug.

"Now and again."

"Has this happened in the air?"

"No." He answered a fraction too quickly.

"That day you spun, perhaps?"

"*No.*"

Too fast again, and with a touch too much emphasis. *You're lying – but how in God's name do I prove it?*

"Karl, I'd like you to stay on the ground for the rest of today—"

"Franz—"

"I've got behind with my paperwork in all this fine weather and I'd appreciate it if you'd deal with it for me."

"Franz, I didn't come here to shuffle papers."

It's not a request. It's an order, however I might phrase it. I'm your CO. You know that.

"I know, but it would be a great help."

I could see the set of his jaw and the obstinate look in his eyes. I knew that expression only too well. The silence lengthened, and I thought he was about to argue.

Don't make me pull rank, Karl. Please just do as I've asked. I don't want to give you a direct order, not about this.

If I have to say, 'You will not fly again until I give my express permission', then you'll stand rigid before me, bring your heels together and say, 'Very good, Squadron Commander, sir', and the gulf between that and 'du' will be just too much.

The words hung, unspoken, between us.

He sighed. "All right, Franz."

Thank God for that.

"Thanks. It's all here. Do what you can – a lot of it's bureaucratic rubbish. Sign the letters per pro., just let me know what you've done. See you later, then."

As I went to pick up my flying jacket and helmet, he took hold of my hand and kissed my palm.

"Franz, I appreciate what you're trying to do," he said, still holding my hand, "but this is war, and there's a limit to what we can do for each other."

I squeezed his hand. "I know. Believe me, Karl, I know."

But war's for the fit, I thought as I walked out into the sunshine, *not for someone who should have been invalided out. You're going to see the doctor later, and I shall write to Berlin today for a copy of your medical report. If they won't give it to me then I'll have to think of something else. I'll get onto Hoeppner himself if I have to, but you're going home as soon as I can arrange it.*

I don't know who passed you fit, but he needs his head examining. There's no way you should be here.

When I got back from the flight, I went straight to my office.

"How's it going?" I asked him.

"Nearly finished. There wasn't as much as you made out."

"Right. We're going to the hospital, and while I visit Kleber you're going to see one of the doctors."

He smiled. "All right."

You took that very calmly. No doubt you were expecting it, and no doubt, having been passed fit in Berlin, you think you won't have any difficulty here.

I sighed. "I shall want to talk to the doctor myself," I said quietly.

"Don't you trust me to tell you the truth, Franz?"

"Quite frankly, no. You didn't tell me what was going on, did you?"

"Hoist with my own petard!"

When we arrived at the hospital, I noticed that he was rather pale.

"I don't care for these places much," he said.

"No, I'm sure you don't. Do you want to see Kleber?"

"Not particularly. It's not as if I know him well."

I don't suppose you ever want to see the inside of one of those wards again, and I can't say I blame you. I'm not too keen either – but it's part of my duties.

They weren't too horribly busy, and after about ten minutes we found a doctor who agreed to look at Karl.

I spent fifteen minutes or so with Kleber, who was half conscious and intermittently aware that I was there. One of the nurses told me that he was doing well and should soon be on his way home, and I wasn't sure if he was lucky or not. I wished him a good recovery and went to find Karl.

I tried not to look at the other patients as I left the ward, but I couldn't avoid seeing one fellow by the door, whose head was covered in bandages. They were soaked with blood and pus, and disintegrating. The bandages were paper, ordinary crêpe paper. *Oh, Christ – what use is that?*

I left quickly, shivering in the July heat. *I didn't realise we don't even have proper bandages any more...*

I was suddenly very afraid, and my hands shook more than ever. *I hope to Christ I don't end up here! Thank God Karl didn't come into the ward. That's the last thing he needs to see – but perhaps it would be better if he did see it.*

Perhaps I should take him to see Kleber, whether he wants to or not. That might be exactly what he needs – to see how much worse it'll be if he gets injured again. His imagination will make far more out of paper bandages than mine can.

I found the doctor's office and knocked on the door.

"Come in!"

Karl was sitting fully dressed in a chair, chatting to the doctor, a middle-aged man with glasses and a receding hairline.

"So, Doctor, how is he?" I asked.

"Fit enough."

Oh, Christ. "Yes, but can you be a bit more specific?"

"It was a serious injury, but I've seen worse. It takes a few months to get back to normal after something like that, but there's no reason why he shouldn't fight."

"He was in so much pain this morning that he couldn't move."

He shrugged. "That's to be expected."

Oh, fuck. Fuck. "We have to fly very high – six or even seven thousand metres."

"There's no reason why he can't continue."

"Thank you." *For nothing.*

What a bloody waste of time – or, rather, worse, because all I'd done was undermine my own position.

Bloody bastard doctor. No doubt he believes it's his duty to get men back to the Front as soon as possible, and that anyone who can hobble can fight.

He saw straight through me. He must have realised how desperate I am to keep Karl alive – and what did Karl say to him?

That's the trouble. I left them alone. I should have gone in with Karl, should have told the doctor exactly what the problem was. Karl probably told him all sorts of rubbish about being perfectly all right, and I don't suppose that bastard even examined him.

Now what am I going to do? I wondered as we drove back to the airfield. *When the report arrives from Berlin I might have some ammunition – unless it contains more of the same crap.*

I've now got very little justification for keeping him on the ground, especially with the situation in the air. I could have him transferred to one of the fighter pilot schools as an instructor, but he'll get himself posted straight back to the Front, to someone else's Jasta. I can't argue that he's incompetent. I could send him on leave, but if I do that he'll just apply to another squadron.

The problem is that he's determined to continue fighting, and the establishment is on his side.

'Do something,' Horstmann had said. *Do what, for Christ's sake?*

I had to let Karl return to flying, at least until the report from Berlin came. I certainly needed his help, not least in training the new arrivals.

Herzog and Schlenz were waiting for me in the mess. Two more green, bright-eyed youths who looked as if they should still be at school.

"They make me feel a thousand years old," I said to Karl in private.

"They probably think we are a thousand years old," he answered cheerfully. "And compared to them, I suppose we are."

"You could really help me with them," I said carefully. "They'll need a lot of practice before they fly over the lines. I'd like you to concentrate on that for the next few days."

He looked at me, steadily but with more than a hint of dismay. "Franz, you don't mean that's all you want me to do?"

Yes, that's exactly what I want, but I know if I say that you'll apply for a transfer.

"No, not at all. You know I can't spare you to that extent. I'll have a word with Fellmann, get him to arrange for you to do half the patrols you're doing at present."

He couldn't argue with that – well, he couldn't argue anyway, but I thought I'd found a way of reducing his exposure to danger. I could see he didn't like it very much, but I was pretty sure he'd accept it without trying to leave.

He smiled. "All right, Franz." I was surprised by the warmth in his voice. "I'll do whatever you need me to do, you know that."

For a moment I was suspicious. *You'll say that to my face, but plan to leave behind my back.* But his expression seemed genuine enough.

I actually felt happy. *I can sleep a little easier now. I've just reduced your chances of getting killed. At last I've managed to achieve something.*

"You've done a bloody good job with Buckow," I said.

"I am impervious to your flattery!"

I remembered saying that to him in Brandenburg, and what had followed…

He leaned towards me and murmured in my ear, "Now that's something to look forward to!"

"Just bugger off and do their familiarisation," I said, my voice thick.

When we got back from the patrol he was sitting on the grass with Schlenz, taking him through their mock combat. His hands flew through the air, his face and voice animated, and it was just like watching him talk to Bretti the summer before.

I could stand here and look at you all day—

'Don't look at him like that in public,' Johnny said, and I started and almost dropped my flying helmet.

I wonder if anyone noticed…

Their problem, I thought as I went to the Ops Office.

To my astonishment Zeitler was sitting there, talking to Fellmann.

"Welcome back!" I said. "How's your leg?"

"It's fine, thank you, sir."

"Good, good – I'm very pleased to see you."

His face lit up. "Oh, thank you, sir!"

"Not at all. Fellmann," I said, "would you send all our sheets to the hospital? I'll get everyone to strip his bed."

"Of course, sir." He looked slightly bemused, and I could see him wondering what use a few sheets would be.

"For bandages," I said. "They're using crêpe paper."

"Jesus," he said quietly. "I didn't realise things were that bad."

"Neither did I."

I went into the mess and rapped on the table.

"Gentlemen," I said, "when I visited Kleber earlier today, I noticed that the hospital has run out of proper bandages and is making do with paper. So we're all going to take the sheets off our beds, and send them there to be cut up."

"They were reusing bandages when I was in there," said Zeitler.

Karl was staring at the floor. "And last year," he said quietly.

"What the fuck use is paper?" asked Sandberg. "It must fall apart in five seconds flat."

"It's going to be rather uncomfortable sleeping without sheets, though, in this weather," said Steinwarz, and then had the grace to look embarrassed.

"Try it with a fever and a hole in you," Zeitler countered, and Karl nodded slowly.

"You mean they don't have sheets in the hospital?" asked Schlenz.

"No, of course they bloody don't," Karl said, looking up with eyes like flint. "Not in the field hospitals, never have had. Not where I've been."

The boys looked at each other.

"Just be grateful you sleep in a bed, and not a muddy hole," Karl added.

"Quite," I said. "The infantry would give their eye teeth to live as we do."

"I'll second that," said Sobek.

"Me too," Buckow agreed. "My brother told me plenty about it."

Sandberg stood up. "Well, I'm off to get mine now."

Everyone followed him out of the mess.

"What was Steinwarz thinking?" Karl asked as we entered our hut. "I know he's a bit of a mummy's boy, but really!"

"Yes... at least he realised how bad it sounded."

Karl started stripping his bed. "Paper bandages... Jesus Christ. The poor bastards." After a pause, he said, "So what are they using for plugs, then? They can't use paper for those, surely."

I looked at him. "What do you mean?"

"You don't know? Well, I suppose you wouldn't." He started folding his sheets.

"Karl, what the fuck are you talking about?"

He took a deep breath. "If you have a deep... a deep... if there's a deep hole in you, they plug it with gauze so it heals from the bottom. Then when they change the dressings they... they pull it all out and... and... and so on." His voice was shaking and he broke off abruptly.

He looked quite sick, which was rather how I felt.

I really didn't want to hear that.

So now you must realise that if you get hit again it could be very nasty indeed, I thought as we got ready to fly. *Maybe, just maybe, that might weaken your resolve to continue...*

Trouble is, you'd never admit it, not in a thousand years.

As we headed back to the mess, I saw that Zeitler had a noticeable limp.

"You're sure your leg has healed up?" I asked.

"Oh, yes, sir, it's fine," he said. "I just have to keep exercising it. That's what they said in the hospital and it does seem to work. If I walk round the airfield every day it'll be perfect in no time."

I did what the Chief had done with Horstmann, in what seemed to be another age – I got Zeitler to sit in a Triplane and operate the rudder. He didn't seem to have any problems with that, so I reckoned he could cope all right, physically at any rate.

He seemed to be rather uneasy at being back – entirely understandably, being as his last flight had resulted in a very painful injury.

"Could you take Zeitler on his first patrol?" I asked Karl later. "He might feel a bit more confident being led by you, because you… well…" I didn't quite know how to put it.

"Crocks' outing, you mean?" he said with a smile.

"No – I just thought…"

"I know what you mean, Franz. I'll let you know how he gets on."

"Thanks."

There was a party, of course, to welcome Zeitler back. It made a good excuse, anyway.

"So how was the homeland?" Sobek asked him.

Zeitler shrugged. "All right, I suppose."

"I bet you had girls falling over you," Sandberg said with envy.

"Well, some…"

"Oh, come on!" said Sobek. "Wounded hero? They all go for that."

A smile started to creep across Zeitler's face. "Well, there were one or two!"

"I hope there were more than that," Sandberg said. "Let me loose among German women and you'll never see me again!"

Herzog and Stoll were looking rather doubtful, and Schlenz looked downright embarrassed. *Oh, Christ – you must be virgins. Someone should do something about that before it's too late.*

"Anyone for Blanche's this evening?" asked Sobek. "All this talk of women's making me randy."

The three boys looked even more doubtful.

"I reckon the three of you should go," said Lehmann, clearly thinking just like me.

"Yes," Müller agreed. "I went last time and I should save some money."

What for?

I left them to it and went to the Ops Office.

"Fellmann, when are we getting a new D.VII? We must be well overdue for one."

"I'm working on it, sir."

I lowered my voice to a murmur. "And please, please, see if you can get us someone experienced next time?"

"I'll do my best."

I went to my office while most of the Jasta went flying. Karl came back without Müller.

"Went down in flames, Tommy-side," he said. "Damn thing caught fire faster than you can say 'burn' and then exploded. The tracer must have caught and set the fuel tank off."

The phosphorous tracer always was dodgy stuff, especially stored so close to the petrol tank.

"Poor sod."

"He wouldn't have felt much – it was one hell of a bang."

"Well, that's something... How did Zeitler get on?"

"All right. Pretty nervous before we took off, but that's fair enough."

"How did you feel, the first time back?"

"Oh, after all this time at war... We're used to it, aren't we?" he said with a smile. "Just more of the same shit. Anyway, he flew very well – I saw him going hell for leather after a Spad. Didn't get it, but that would have been a bit much to hope for."

"Anything else?"

"Yes – I got one of those Bristols. If it's confirmed, of course."

"Well done! Where did it come down?"

He shrugged. "Tommy-side as well."

"You really are catching me up."

"Only because you give so many away – and I'd have done the same if anyone had been near enough."

In the past couple of days I'd given victories to both Lehmann and Buckow. Starting to score improved pilots' confidence no end, even when they knew I'd set it up for them.

"Thanks for looking after Zeitler," I said.

"I didn't really look after him, Franz. That's impossible, as you know."

Don't I just. My best efforts to look after you are proving hopeless.

My idea of keeping him out of trouble by getting him to train up the newcomers proved short-lived. I'd reckoned without the Tommies. They were putting up so many aircraft that I had to let Karl return to full-time patrols.

It was a pity in more ways than one. He was very good with the novices and they learned well from him. *Maybe I could recommend him for a posting to one of the fighter pilot schools on that basis – but there's no way that'll succeed, not with his scoring rate. The top brass want to keep him at the Front, and I can see their point.*

There must be some way of getting him away from here. There must be some errand I could send him on, to Berlin, perhaps, some nice long errand that would take at least a fortnight...

If only I could think of something. Perhaps I should remind Berlin that Karl's the last of his line. I knew what his reaction to that would be, and I knew he'd never forgive me if he found out. Maybe I should write to Hoeppner's office and suggest that Karl should be examined by a specialist, preferably in Berlin.

I wish I knew what's wrong with you. I wish that bloody medical report would arrive.

We heard there was a nice new D.VII for us at the aircraft park, and I thought of sending Karl to fetch it – but it was going to be Sandberg's, so it made more sense for him to take his old Triplane there and swap it.

Fortune smiled slightly, in that Müller's replacement had done a month with another Jasta, even if his score stood at zero. Weiss was a tall, skinny fellow, with an air of steady calm. He'd spent three years in the infantry before transferring to the Air Service.

"He'll be bloody good once he gets a bit more experience," Karl said to me. "Just the sort of fellow you want alongside you... He does put it away a bit, though."

"We all do that."

"Mm."

Weiss turned out to have such a dry sense of humour that the youngsters often took him seriously. Buckow didn't, but then he was from a military family and his brother had been in the front line.

"It's good to have another proper Front swine here," Sandberg said.

And good to have another potential patrol leader. Weiss had been rock steady in every fight I'd seen him in, and he used his eyes and brain well, even if he didn't make full use of the Triplane's capabilities.

If someone else can lead then I can keep Karl on the ground a bit more, until that report arrives.

"Be handy to have another patrol leader," he said to me as we undressed. "We'll be able to take some of the load off you."

"Oh, I'm all right," I replied.

"Of course you are," he said, and wrapped his arms round me.

I had the fucking burning dream, and he woke me and held me tight as I shook, his embrace solid and reassuring. The unworthy thought occurred that maybe I should let him stay, that if he really wanted to die for Prussia then I shouldn't stand in his way. Yes, it would half-kill me, but I wasn't likely to outlive him by much.

Bollocks, Franz. You're being selfish. You've got used to his being here, to the daily intimacy and to not being alone with your demons. You have to send him home.

He'd put the light on and his eyes looked into mine, their usual hardness completely absent. The war receded into the distance.

"Penny for them, Franz?" he asked, his voice matching his eyes.

"I was just thinking that the war almost disappears when we're like this."

He smiled, and stroked my eyebrow. "It can't go on much longer – then we can go home, and you can come and stay for as long as you like."

Endless days of peace in Brandenburg, sitting on the terrace with Karl… *I've never felt such harmony with anyone as I do with you. I could easily spend the rest of my life living with you.*

In that mythical fairyland called 'after the war'. It'll have to end bloody soon for either of us to have a chance.

We assembled in the mess in the beginnings of the dawn, in the usual atmosphere of anticipation and apprehension. My coffee cup rattled in the saucer, Sobek's hand shook slightly as he lit his fag, Buckow cracked some joke that made Stoll laugh rather too loud, and Weiss poured a hefty dollop of schnapps into his coffee – hefty even by our standards.

I saw Sandberg raise an eyebrow. *Yes – we might need to keep an eye on that. This isn't the trenches – you have to be a bit soberer for our business.*

We got into a very hot fight with Camels, Nieuports and SE5s. A Jasta of Pfalzes joined in, but we were still heavily outnumbered. I saw Stoll going down out of control, but apart from that we escaped without casualties, and I evened the result by getting one of the Nieuports. We were lucky to get away so lightly.

I hope it's not going to be like that from now on, I thought as I taxied in, trembling and soaked in sweat. *I can do without too many of those.*

"Bloody hell," said Lehmann. "That was a bit hot."

"You can say that again," said Sobek, and Lehmann did.

We all laughed, rather too hard.

All the aircraft were holed, Buckow's quite badly. I told him off, but couldn't put my heart into it.

"Still glad you made the move?" Karl asked Weiss over second breakfast.

"Well, let me see... No lice. No mud. No shelling. No snipers—"

"Apart from Leussow," said Steinwarz with a grin.

"Doesn't count," Weiss said. "Nice hut, good food, flying... on balance I'd say this is *marginally* better."

"You left out good company," said Schlenz.

"That's because I haven't made my mind up about you bastards yet," Weiss said.

"Let us know when you do," Sobek said.

Weiss kept the deadpan expression. "You might not want to hear!" He poured himself another coffee and added a glug of schnapps.

Karl looked at me. His face didn't change, but I knew he was thinking the same as me.

As long as he keeps functioning and doesn't drop anyone else in the crap, I won't make an issue of it.

We lingered over second breakfast, and then I dragged myself to my office, where the usual heap of paper awaited me.

Karl was leading the second patrol, and I gave myself a break to wave them off. Buckow, Sobek and Herzog went to play cards in the sun, and I went to write to Stoll's parents.

About an hour later, the phone rang. Fellmann answered it.

"Yes... I see, thank you." His voice was very heavy.

Oh, Christ, who is it this time? Not Karl, please—

"Hold on a second, I'll write that down... Yes, we'll be there in a couple of hours. No, we'll bring one."

Shit. Who's dead, then? I held my breath.

Fellmann came into my office, deathly white and looking very awkward.

No. Please, no.

"Sir..." He faltered.

"Get on with it."

He took a deep breath. "Karl's been shot down – he's – I'm so sorry."

My office moved before my eyes, and something inside me started to crumble.

You knew this would happen. You should have sent him away.

"We'll take the truck and bring him back," he said.

"I'm coming with you." I got up and put my old tunic on.

"Why don't I arrange everything, sir, and come and get you when we're ready?"

"Thank you."

There's a mistake, I thought stupidly – *but there can't be. They'll have looked at his identification disc – but that's if they could.* Fellmann didn't say what had happened. The pilot might be unidentifiable. *The wreck might have burned. It might be someone else.*

"We're ready, sir."

We went out into the bright sunshine. *Karl can't be dead, not on such a lovely day. There's a mistake, there must be a mistake…*

"Let's sit in front with Braun, sir," Fellmann said. "Schiffer, Schwarte and Zaffke are in the back."

With the coffin.

"I'm so sorry, sir," Braun said with genuine sympathy as we got in.

"What…" My voice was a croak, and I tried again. "What did they say? And who phoned?"

"It was a Leutnant in Transport, sir." Fellmann's voice was quiet but firm. "He said a Fokker D.VII crash-landed beside the road. His men got the pilot out but he was already… it was too late."

There's no mistake. The sunlight dimmed.

We said nothing more until Braun pulled off the road into a field, and stopped.

There was Karl's D.VII. The fuselage was intact, but the left wings were a complete mess and the undercarriage had gone. *You must have hung on just long enough.*

There was a small group of soldiers standing round it, and I made my way towards them. My legs were like rubber and I could hardly feel the ground.

I was dimly aware of someone saluting, and returned the courtesy automatically. The group parted, and I saw Karl lying on the ground, soaked in blood, and for one awful moment I thought I would actually faint.

His goggles were on his forehead, and his eyes stared sightlessly at the sky. I looked into those eyes for the last time, and gently closed them. Then I sat beside him and took him in my arms, holding him tight. His head fell onto my shoulder and

I rested mine on it, desperate for the feeling of his living body against mine, just one more time.

'That's not me, Franz – not now.' The words were as clear as if he'd spoken.

I laid him carefully on the grass, wondering why I was being so gentle.

All I could feel was a terrible, numb emptiness. Part of me had been ripped out, and I knew I could never be the same again.

For the second and final time, I took his Pour le Mérite from round his neck and put it in my pocket. I unpinned the pilot's badge and the Iron Cross and put them in my pocket as well, and took the signet ring from his finger.

Slowly I got to my feet and turned round. The others didn't want to look at us.

Fellmann stepped forward. "I'm so very sorry, sir," he said, and once he'd broken the ice there was a quiet chorus of sympathy.

"Thank you." My voice sounded strange and distant.

Zaffke looked at me, reproach in his eyes. *You knew he wasn't fit*, they said.

You will never, in all eternity, be as sorry as I am. I should have sent him home...

"Let's see where we can wait," Fellmann said.

Schiffer was hovering, looking very uncomfortable.

"What is it?" I asked.

"Sir, you... er... the blood," he said very quietly.

I looked down. My tunic was covered in Karl's blood and so were my hands. The ground shifted sideways under me and I was almost sick. I'd had blood all over me before, many times, but this was different.

I took my tunic off. I didn't want to look at the wretched thing. *I don't think I can wear that again, no matter how thoroughly it gets cleaned.*

"Throw it away," I told Schiffer. "There's no reason for you to have to deal with that."

I wiped my hands on the grass. My head was starting to swim, and I had a growing feeling of disorientation.

A balding Leutnant stepped forward. "Traub, sir. This is an honour."

"Becker," I replied, "and this is Fellmann."

"Come this way," he said, and led us into the first of a row of houses. "Have a seat. Schlumm! Tea and rum, please!"

"Right away, sir!"

"Can I wash my hands?" I asked.

"Yes, of course – in there."

Karl's blood was drying round my fingernails, and I scrubbed and scrubbed to remove it, unable to stand the sight of it.

I'll have to join the others – but I just want to be out of here.

Traub handed me a mug with more rum than tea in it, and I started to feel a fraction steadier.

It can't take long to put Karl in the— We'll be ready to set off soon, surely.

"I'm very sorry for your loss," Traub said. "We – er – we saw him land, and got there as fast as we could, but he was already dead. Then when we got him out, we saw the Pour le Mérite and we realised he was someone special…"

He was that, all right.

"And Berger – my Sergeant – who follows the war in the air, said he recognised the aircraft markings, then we looked at his tag, and…"

His voice turned into a meaningless buzz of sound.

"Did you see the fight?" I heard myself ask.

"No, sir – we just saw him coming in to land, and it looked all wrong, as if he wasn't really in control – but then he must have been dying…"

My cigarette had burned right down, and I realised ash was dropping all over my trousers. *How much longer, for Christ's sake?*

There was a knock at the door.

"Excuse me, sir," said Braun. "We're ready."

"Thank you." I turned to Traub. "Thanks for the tea."

Fellmann took my arm as we approached the truck.

"Let's sit in the front again," he said, gently but firmly. "It'll be better to look at him once Braun's…"

"Made him presentable?" My voice broke slightly. *Get a grip, Franz.*

"Exactly. You want a better memory."

Better than the one you have of Johnny.

All I could think, all the way back, was that Karl was lying in a box a couple of metres behind me, and that he would never again speak to me or hold me.

The Jasta was back. *Why couldn't it have been someone else? The young fellows get shot down all the time – why couldn't it have been one of them?*

I turned to Braun. "I'll bring you his best uniform."

"I'll do that, sir," Schiffer said.

"Thank you."

The remaining pilots were in the mess, talking very quietly. As we entered the room they fell silent, and looked at me.

"Your report, Sobek, please," I said.

"We'd had two engagements – we lost Steinwarz in the first one, had to parachute out – and then we were on our way back when we saw a big fight going on and we joined in. Leussow got one. I was going to go for him but he got there first – sent him down in flames."

"Yes, I saw that," said Buckow, "but I didn't know who'd done it."

Hopefully it'll be confirmed – but it hardly matters now what his score is.

"Two, then," Weiss added. "I saw him shooting the crap out of one of the bastards – just flew straight at him, blasting away. He bloody near rammed him – just pulled up at the last second, skimmed over the top of him."

"Frontal attack, then?"

"Yes. Sent him down vertical."

That's two you took with you, then. You went just as you wanted to.

"I'll organise the funeral, sir," Fellmann said, his eyes very sympathetic. "We'll give him a proper send-off."

"Thank you."

I focussed on the squadron. *We're three pilots and three aircraft down in one day – and we need replacements urgently.*

Fellmann followed me to the Ops Office.

"We'll need another three pilots – preferably someone experienced – and three more new aircraft, preferably D.VIIs," I said.

"Yes, sir – I'll get onto it right away."

"Lehmann can help organise the funeral."

"I'd like to do that, sir," said Sobek.

"Yes, of course."

I realised that Herzog and Schlenz were standing beside him, looking at me rather uncomfortably. They obviously thought the Old Man was a real hard case.

No one could be more aware than I am of what's happened – but I've also just lost a patrol leader and the second ace in the Jasta, and that leaves us truly stuffed. Unless Fellmann can get a suitable replacement – and he won't be able to get anyone as experienced and capable as Karl – I'll be stuck with more children, who might be some use if they live more than five minutes.

The feeling of unreality was getting stronger. I went into our room and was shocked by how normal it looked – the sun was pouring through the window, there was a sweater lying on Karl's bed, and his hairbrush and razor were in their usual places.

He'll walk in, make a joke about something, take me in his arms – but of course he won't.

The shock was starting to wear off, and the appalling emptiness was getting worse.

Don't stay in here, Franz, I told myself. *Go and do something. You've got a squadron to run, and you've just lost three pilots in one day.*

Braun will have finished soon. I have to get the cushion ready so Karl can lie in state properly.

I went to my office, and got it out of the cupboard in the corner. The velvet seemed to soak up the light and darken to absolute blackness. Fellmann looked up as I passed his door, saw my expression and what I was carrying, and lowered his head back to his papers.

I remembered Karl carrying the cushion at Johnny's funeral, his face pale but composed. *We'll do it properly for you, Karl. A funeral with full military honours for a man who'd never wanted to be a soldier, but who'd been one of the best.*

I took the cushion back to our room, put it on the table, took the three awards out of my pocket and put them beside it. *That just leaves the Iron Cross Second Class and the Knight's Cross with Swords of the Royal Hohenzollern House Order. I'll have to look through his things for them.*

I hesitated. It seemed such an improper thing to do.

He won't mind, and I'll have to pack them up anyway, to send them home – but to whom? Henning, I suppose. And I'll have to try to get a letter to Elisabeth.

I found the two crosses easily enough, in the top drawer of the chest, each one in its case. I took them out carefully and put them with the others on the table. We kept the pins in the cushion, and I took them all out.

Now I could begin.

First, at the top, the Pour le Mérite. I'd thought it might have been damaged in the crash but it was as good as new, better than mine, which had a couple of chips out of the enamel.

You hardly wore it, I thought sadly. *Five weeks before you were shot down, a few times on convalescent leave, and about three weeks now.*

I remembered his jubilation when he'd got it, the first of his old military family to receive such a high award, and the Chief lending him his, and the party we'd had.

The blue and gold cross gleamed on the black velvet. I spread the ribbon out and pinned it in place. The old bloodstains showed clearly, discolouring the two white stripes.

Oh, Karl, Karl... My vision blurred and I shook my head, closed my eyes tightly. I had to keep control. I couldn't let myself give in to grief. The others were relying on me.

In the middle, the Iron Cross Second Class and the Hohenzollern, the former on the left, the latter on the right, in accordance with the order of precedence, each on its black and white ribbon. It felt strange, so strange, to be touching these things which had been so personal to him, to know that he would never, ever, wear them again.

At the bottom, the Iron Cross First Class and the pilot's badge. *There should be a wound badge, but being as they're new he hasn't got his yet. I don't suppose he will now – the Prussians don't make posthumous awards.*

He wouldn't have minded.

'They'll be giving us medals just for being here next,' he'd said scathingly.

I propped the cushion against the wall and took a step back. The effect was sombre. Apart from the Pour le Mérite and the small amount of blue and green on the Hohenzollern, the entire display was black, white, silver and gold. It had an austere Prussian dignity that I found entirely appropriate.

I sat on my bed for a moment, my mind and heart full of him. *It's my fault. You'd be alive if I'd done what I knew was right. I killed you, as surely as if I'd shot you.*

I knew that that was ridiculous, that nothing could have saved Karl from himself, that if I'd refused to accept him he would just have gone to another squadron, but the guilt was so bad that I felt sick.

It was abruptly overlaid with anger. *Why did you have to come back here? Why couldn't you have accepted that your war was over and stayed at home? If you'd done that you'd still be alive and I'd be able to see you again... We'd be able to sit and drink and talk together...*

I'll never hear your voice again. One day I'll forget what it sounded like.

And I'll never feel your arms around me, or your touch. Never.

Don't sit there torturing yourself, Franz. For God's sake, find something to do.

I went to my office, lit a fag and sat staring at the wall.

Fellmann came in. "One bit of good news, sir – Steinwarz has been picked up. He's got two broken legs but apart from that he's all right."

"Good. One funeral is quite enough."

"Indeed." He lowered his voice. "How are you?"

"Let's not talk about me." *Because I can't.*

He nodded in understanding. "What music would you like, sir?"

"One of Beethoven's funeral marches for the procession – the one from the 'Eroica' if they've got the music – and then in the service we'll sing 'Now thank we all our God', and at the end, of course, 'I had...' er... the usual song." The song whose name I couldn't bring myself even to say, and which I would have to sing without faltering, just as Karl had sung it for Johnny and his father.

Fellmann looked a bit puzzled for a moment. "Are you sure about the hymn?"

"Leussow family tradition – you remember?"

His face fell, and I regretted having to remind him about Johnny's funeral.

"Oh – yes, of course."

"And we'll have a couple of really good marches on the way back," I said.

"Yes… Which ones did you have in mind?"

"'The Glory of Prussia', of course – it was his favourite, and they sang it at Verdun, on the first day… and then the 'Hohenfriedberger'. After all, he did get two victories before they killed him."

And it seemed appropriate to play Frederick the Great's victory march, being as he'd been Karl's childhood hero.

"And they're good, rousing tunes," Fellmann agreed. "What about his old regimental march?"

"That's a bloody good idea. I'll ask Zaffke what it is."

"Sobek's organising the gun carriage and so on," he said, "and we're trying to get as many Pour le Mérites as we can."

"That's going to be difficult. Have you told Horstmann?"

"Yes – he said he'll come if he can, but you know how it is."

"I do indeed." I looked at my watch, and just then Braun knocked at the door.

"Sir, I… er… Leutnant von Leussow is in Hangar One."

"Thank you, Braun. Thank you very much indeed."

"I took the liberty of making out the roster for the guard of honour, sir," said Fellmann. "Starting at 2pm."

"Thank you… Fellmann, you've got me down at two and again at six."

"Yes, sir."

"That won't do – I'll have to fly."

He looked at me very doubtfully. "Do you think that's a good idea, sir?"

"There's only Sobek and I who can lead now. We'll have to share the work."

He nodded. "All right – I'll change it."

"I'd better put the cushion in the hangar," I said, and went to my room to fetch it.

The room was unbearably empty, and I left quickly.

Karl's coffin stood on trestles in the hangar, with Zaffke, Schiffer, Uhlig and Bauer forming the guard of honour.

There was a space for the cushion at the foot of the coffin, and I placed it there carefully and then stood beside him.

The light filtered through the canvas onto his still face. Braun had done his job well. Karl looked so peaceful, as though he were asleep, as if I could touch him and wake him. Death had taken the lines of strain from his face, and he looked so young.

"Thank you very much, Braun," I said. "He looks so..." My throat closed up and I couldn't finish the sentence.

"He was a very brave man, sir," he said, "being here at all with those scars – and that was a terrific fight he was in."

"Well, they were outnumbered." I actually managed to sound quite controlled. God knows how – the emptiness inside me had grown into a huge void, and I was falling into it.

"Yes..."

I could see that there was something he wanted to tell me, but that he wasn't sure whether he should or not.

"Go on."

"He... er... he'd been hit four times, each time from a different direction."

"It couldn't have been one burst?"

"No, sir." He hesitated again.

"Braun, I've been in this filthy business since October '14. I've seen it all. Tell me."

"Well, there was one from the side, through his left calf." He began awkwardly and became more fluent as he spoke. "And another that broke his right shin – that was from directly in front. The third was from the left and behind, broke his left arm and grazed his ribs. And the one that was probably fatal went right through his lower body, from the right and a bit behind."

"Jesus Christ."

I looked at Karl's serene face. *You bloody mad idiot. You stupid fucking cunt. Why the fuck didn't you disengage after you'd been hit the first time? You'd still be alive, you'd be safe in hospital, and I wouldn't feel like this.*

I was suddenly boiling with anger, so much so that I had to turn away.

I managed – just – to remember my manners. "Thank you for telling me," I said in a choked voice.

I left the hangar. *Why did you do this to me, you bastard?*

Get a grip, Franz. You're flying in an hour's time.

The others were eating lunch, in silence. *That's not like them at all – but then we don't often have two killed and one wounded in one day.*

"Do excuse me, gentlemen," I said, far more steadily than I expected. "Briefing will be in half an hour."

"Would you like some lunch, sir?" Bleif said.

"No, thank you – I'll have it after the flight."

As I went to my office I heard the murmur of voices, and a few minutes later Lehmann knocked and came in.

"Sir – I could lead the next patrol. You must have an awful lot to do – and half the aircraft are holed and won't be ready until this evening."

"Thank you, Lehmann – but I'll lead."

I have to fly, because I must have something else to think about or I'll go mad. Karl would want me to go on fighting.

Lehmann looked quite crestfallen.

"You can lead tomorrow morning, before the funeral," I said.

"Thank you, sir!"

He was like a dog with two tails, and I tried to remember when I'd last felt excited at the prospect of a fight. *Probably just before Langemarck, before I realised what war is.* Becoming a fighter pilot had restored my enthusiasm for a time, but I was only too aware that it was about killing the other fellow before he killed you.

Twenty minutes later, I went into the mess and rapped on the table.

"Gentlemen – we have lost two good friends today. Leutnant von Leussow was a soldier and he died as he expected to. He once said to me, 'Live by the sword, die by the sword – or in our case the bullet.' Pilot Stoll had only been with us a short time, but he knew the stakes. Don't allow your judgement to be clouded by thoughts of vengeance. We can honour them best by fighting to the best of our ability."

There was a muted rumble of agreement.

As we went out to the flight line I pushed Karl out of my mind. I had to focus completely on the patrol – and that might stop me feeling anything. Even fear, because I didn't care what happened to me. *If I get killed then they can put me next to him*, I thought as I scanned the huge blue expanse of the sky.

I gifted Buckow a Tommy. He must have been on his first flight over the lines – the poor bugger had no idea what to do – and part of me couldn't help thinking, *That's one for you, Karl.*

When we got back I went in search of Zaffke, and found him in Hangar Two, making a new rib for Schlenz's Triplane.

"That's beautiful work as always, Zaffke."

"Thank you, sir," he said politely, but with reserve.

"I... we're sorting out the music for the funeral," I said, "and we thought of playing your old regimental march on the way back. If the band's got the music, that is."

He smiled under his moustache. "That's a very good idea, sir – they should have it, it's in the Army March Collection. The 'Prince Friedrich Karl March', it is, sir."

"Thank you, Zaffke... Did Braun tell you about his injuries?" The sheer awfulness of it all hit me again, and I struggled for composure.

"No, sir," he said, with a note of surprise, and I realised that Braun had told no one except me.

"Ask him," I said. "Say I told you to."

"Yes, sir, I will."

You'll realise, when you hear, that he must have chosen to die – but why? I don't understand it, I thought as I went to change.

As I opened the door to our room I had the sudden, powerful feeling that Karl was there, waiting for me – but of course the room was empty and silent. Desolation flooded into me.

It's always going to be like this.

His things were still scattered about his bed. *I'd better pack everything up and have the bed moved out. Then I can pretend he's at home in Brandenburg – and it won't matter whether that's true or not, because my chances of seeing the end of the war are nil.*

I pulled his two bags out from under his bed. It only took a few minutes to clear out his side of the wardrobe. Spare shirts, socks, underwear, monogrammed handkerchiefs, all stacked neatly on the shelves, spare boots...

That's all we need. Life here is reduced to the bare minimum. Just enough until it's our turn to die.

In the top drawer of the chest were two thick sweaters. Under one of them was the photograph of his family taken on Elisabeth's wedding day. Uncle Heinrich glowered from his wheelchair, Elisabeth sat between her parents, looking nervous in her wedding dress, and the three sons stood behind, Friedrich in his cadet's uniform, Johnny and Karl in suits. All dead, all except Elisabeth.

I didn't want to look at it, and I put it in one of the bags.

Under the other sweater were two letters on top of a couple of books. The sight of his writing was almost too much.

The top letter was for me.

'To be opened only in the event of my death,' it said, just like the one I'd burned the year before. *I wish I could burn this one as well*, I thought as I sat on my bed and opened it.

'My dearest Franz,

If you are reading this then I have got what I wanted. Please remember that – I flatter myself that you might miss me, and it might help.

Long story short, my heart is giving out due to the injury I received last summer. The medical review that I thought would be a formality turned into half a day of tests, during which they brought in a heart specialist. At the end of all that I was told that I was not fit for service in any capacity, and that I would be given a medical discharge and a disability pension.

Apparently the combination of severe blood loss and infection did rather a lot of damage. I'd put the pain and shortness of breath down to the injury to my lung, but the real problem is my heart and there is nothing that can be done.

I had to really push the specialist for a prognosis, and eventually he told me that I might have another five years, if I "go home and live quietly". I feel reasonably well now, but in a year or so I'll start to go downhill, and then it'll be an ever-steepening dive. I decided that I'd rather die with my boots on, and so I wrote to Hoeppner, who gave me permission to return to the squadron.'

That was an easy decision for you. Death in war, death for Prussia, was far better than a slow, painful decline at home. And of course Hoeppner had understood Karl's request perfectly, and had probably hesitated for all of half a second before granting it.

I would do the same. I've no desire to die for the Fatherland, but I too would choose a quick end over a slow one.

I stared across the room. *So that's why you didn't break off – because each hit took you closer to the death you wanted. What was it like, knowing that you would fight until you were dead or unconscious – grim determination or exultation? Was it 'Come on then, you bastards – who's coming with me?'*

The next part of the letter knocked me flat.

'Death frees me to say what I never dared say in life: I love you, Franz. I love you with all my heart and all my soul. I never imagined that love could be like this – I live for the sight of your face and the sound of your voice, and there have been times with you when I thought I would die of joy. I would give everything I have for your survival and your happiness.

Goodbye, my only love. Maybe we shall meet again in a better place.

Forever yours,
Karl.'

His writing blurred as my eyes filled with tears, and then a bolt of pain went right through me as I realised that I loved him too, and that it was far too late to tell him.

You stupid fucking cunt, Franz – how could you have been so fucking thick? Wasn't it bloody obvious – that wonderful, deep contentment you felt lying in his arms, wanting to live with him in Brandenburg, dreaming of walking hand in hand under the limes and then going up to bed? What other name is there for that but love?

I never expected to fall in love with a man. That's why I didn't see – because it was so far beyond anything I'd ever imagined.

And what if I had realised, if I'd told him I loved him? Would he still have wanted to die, or would he have accepted those few years if he could have spent them with me?

I'll never know, I thought miserably.

He sat beside me, his arm round my shoulders. 'Read the first part again,' he said gently. 'It was over.'

"Karl—"

But he had gone, and the love and tenderness had gone with him.

A black wave of grief hit me, and I found I was crying. I wanted to bang my head on the floor and howl, but such a total loss of control would only have made it worse.

Get a grip, Franz. I forced myself to my feet and went back to the chest.

The other letter was addressed to Jacob Feinstein, Feinstein and Co, Berlin, and Karl had written in pencil, 'Please post this if I'm killed.'

There was a note on the books: 'Keep the "literature" if you like!'

I opened one. It was pornography: expensive, beautifully illustrated pornography, and I had to laugh in spite of the situation – and two seconds later I felt even more miserable, because I realised that he'd intended to make me laugh, and the lack of him was unbearable.

There was a knock at the door.

"Sir," said Schiffer, "it's a quarter to six."

Why – oh. I'm due in the hangar.

I put on my best tunic and made myself as presentable as I could. My eyes were slightly puffy, and I was shocked by the look in them. *Come on, Franz, you can do better than that. Karl managed when Johnny was killed.*

Zeitler, Buckow and Herzog were waiting outside the hangar. We took over from Sobek, Lehmann, Weiss and Schlenz.

Lying there is the man I love, and will love for ever more. I wish I'd understood that. I wish I'd made it possible for him to tell me what he felt. Was that what he wanted to say in Brandenburg? 'There are things the other might not want to hear…'

I wish I could be alone with you, to look at your face and tell you I love you. You can't hear now, but I'd be able to say it.

'You are alone with me, Franz. No one can see inside your head, can he? I love you and I shall always be by your side.'

I almost started, because his voice was so clear. *Am I going mad or do we really live on?*

As we left the hangar, Sobek took off with the others, the evening sun glinting on the wings.

I watched them until they disappeared.

VIII

I took the gongs off my best tunic – which was now the only one I had – and went to my office.

"I'd like to go over the plans for the funeral with you, sir," said Fellmann. "I need to be able to make the final arrangements now."

"Yes, of course."

"We've got the Lutheran padre and the band, but there's a bit of difficulty with the pall-bearers, as we expected. I telephoned all the squadrons who have a Pour le Mérite, and they said he'd try to get here, but of course they can't promise."

"I don't think we can worry about that," I said. "We'll plan on the basis that none of them can make it. We certainly can't delay the funeral."

Not in this heat...

"No, quite. I also rang all the other squadrons in the area, and they all said they'd try to send a representative, but of course it depends on operations."

"Indeed."

The death of one Leutnant does not stop a war, and we all knew how hot things were. We were fighting, increasingly desperately, for Germany's survival.

"And I've borrowed the usual gun carriage and black horses."

"Well done."

He looked very awkward. "I presume you'll be leading the procession, sir?"

"Yes." I hardly knew where I would find the strength.

"The bandmaster said he's got all the music you wanted. I think it's going to go off all right, sir."

"Yes, I'm sure it will. Thank you."

"Shall we go and have a brandy? I think we both need one."

"Yes. Good idea."

The mess was empty and we sat together in a corner. It was very quiet and private, and I wasn't sure what Fellmann was likely to say.

If he gets personal I'll deny everything. It's no one's business but mine now.

"They don't make many like him," he said.

"No." I didn't know if I could talk about Karl.

There was a very long silence, then Fellmann said quietly, "Sir, – I just wanted to say – well, I do understand what you… I mean, I know I've always said things that were a bit off colour, but it's my way of dealing with the world—"

"You don't have to explain," I said, wondering why he was suddenly telling me his problems.

"No – but we've known each other quite a while now, and I just wanted to say that I know what you—"

This is not a conversation I want to have.

"I don't want to talk about it. I've just got to deal with it."

The words came out far more harshly than I'd intended, and his face fell.

Shit.

"I appreciate your sympathy and what you're trying to say – but it's time to change the subject," I added, not unkindly.

"Of course, sir," he said, rather stiffly.

I put my hand on his arm. "Don't be like that. You spoke as a friend and I do appreciate it, but I don't want to hear the rest of it."

"No." His voice was a lot warmer.

The sound of returning aircraft came through the open window, and we both got up and went outside.

"Let's hope they're all back," I said. "We've lost too many already today."

They were.

"Thank God for that," said Fellmann. "It would have been a bit much."

I forced myself to eat some dinner, and left the mess early. But I couldn't stand the sight of our room, and I went back to my office and sat in the twilight, staring at the wall and smoking.

There was a burble of conversation from the mess, and then I heard Weiss say, quite clearly, "Well, if you ask me they're a couple of poufs. Who knows what they got up to?"

"We didn't ask you," Lehmann said.

"You want to wind your fucking neck in," said Sobek.

"Yes," Sandberg said. "Frankly, I don't give a shit what their relationship was. The Old Man does a bloody good job, really looks after everyone, and he's fucking shit-hot in the air. And Leussow was shit-hot as well, and a really nice bloke."

"Yes, he was," said Buckow.

"You would think that," Weiss said. "You're Brandenburg mafia as well."

"That's got nothing—" Buckow began.

"Sandberg's right," said Herzog. "Leussow was bloody good to me when I got here, taught me a hell of a lot and didn't mind how many stupid questions I asked."

"Same here," Schlenz agreed. "I'd be dead but for some of the advice he gave me."

"He saved my neck more than once," Lehmann said.

"And he was really kind to me when I came back," said Zeitler. "I was really scared before my first patrol after I got back, because I knew what could happen, and he just put his hand on my shoulder and said, 'Don't worry – everyone's scared. You'll be fine once the fight starts.' And I was."

"And who gives a shit what other people do in bed, anyway?" asked Lehmann. "It's not our business."

"Anyway, Weiss, you can't talk," said Sobek. "Not after what one of Blanche's girls told me about you."

There was a brief silence, and then Weiss said, very uncomfortably, "Well, I'm off to bed."

He passed my office door without looking in. I couldn't help smiling to myself. *I wonder what she said...*

"So what did she say?" asked Herzog.

Sobek laughed. "Oh, I made that up! I reckon most chaps have some bedroom secret or other!"

There was a burst of laughter, and then Schlenz said, "He'll think we all know about it now!"

"Serve him right," said Buckow.

"It must be hitting the Old Man really hard, though," said Sandberg. "It's bad enough losing a friend."

"We'll all have to keep an eye on him," Sobek said. "Maybe we can take some of the load off for the next few days."

You all know, then – but it must have been obvious.

I crept quietly out of the building and went back to our – to my room. Karl's sweater was still lying on his bed, and the shirt and underwear that he'd worn on the early flight were draped over the back of a chair. I'd completely forgotten them when I packed his things.

The shirt smelled of him, and I put it on and got into bed, just as I had the summer before when he'd been shot down – but this time there was no hope. I curled up, wretched beyond words, and tried to sleep.

It was impossible. Every time I closed my eyes I saw the wreck of Karl's D.VII, and held his blood-soaked body in my arms.

It was a relief when Zeitler knocked on the door, and said, "Sir, we're due in the hangar in fifteen minutes."

"Thank you."

I put the gongs back on my best tunic. *This is going to be a real pain. I'll have to get another for best and use this one for everyday.*

This time there was something very strange about standing in the hangar in the small hours. I'd done it for more men than I could count, but never with a strong feeling that the dead man was standing right next to me. If it had been anyone but Karl, it would have been eerie and unsettling, but his presence was comforting.

'You'll never be alone, Franz – I shall always be by your side...'

I went to the mess with the others at the end of our hour, and had a very large brandy in the hope that I would sleep.

"It's hardly worth going to bed," said Buckow.

"What time is it?" I asked.

"Three, sir," said Zeitler, with a very kind tone.

"Well, half an hour's better than nothing," I said, and left them.

I wished I hadn't bothered. It was a warm night, and even with the windows open I was hot under the blanket.

And then I did fall asleep, and dreamt that I'd been shot in the stomach, like poor Kleber. The nurse was changing the dressings, and I was screaming as she pulled the gauze out—

I woke with a yell and lay sweating and shaking. *I don't mind being killed, but not mutilated...*

Schiffer knocked with the shaving water.

I'd better move the chair – oh. Why isn't it against the door? Karl's dead, you stupid bastard.

Black, unbearable emptiness engulfed me. *How am I going to go on without you?*

I dragged myself out of bed, feeling bloody awful.

"Schiffer, move the other bed out of here, would you?"

"Very good, sir."

Karl must have felt dreadful, up at seven thousand metres with a fucked lung and a failing heart. If he could fly and fight like that, then I can keep going too. Until the end comes.

I didn't want to look in the mirror as I shaved. When I got to the mess, the others looked at me with concern. *There's no need to worry about me. Whatever happens, I'll be all right.*

Zaffke came over to me as we suited up. "Sergeant Braun did tell me, sir," he said. "It was a good way to go."

"Yes, it was."

That reminded me that I wanted to tell the others why and how Karl had died, but that would have to wait until after the patrol.

Leave everything on the ground, I thought as I lined up into the light breeze. *Just concentrate on what you're doing.*

Nine aircraft climbed into the dawn sky. In the East the horizon was apricot, shading to pale blue that darkened overhead, the last stars visible in the West. The vastness of it brought me a small measure of peace.

And as soon as we engaged the Tommies, nothing existed except the fight. We had three inconclusive scraps – Lehmann winged one, but he didn't go down – and had to break off our pursuit of our foes after the last one, because the fuel state demanded that we go home.

The squadron formed up on me, and I looked round to see where Karl was.

In his coffin in Hangar One. Where the fuck else would he be?

As we flew home I felt worse than ever. On top of the usual post-fight reaction there was the utter desolation of knowing that later we would put Karl in the ground, and that somehow I had to live on.

Well, I won't have to do it for long.

After the debrief I went to find Zaffke. He was in Hangar Two, finishing Karl's cross, and seeing his name and the dates carved on it was almost too much for me.

"That's really beautiful, Zaffke," I said, with some difficulty.

"Thank you, sir. The boys have made a wreath of oak leaves, with a ribbon saying, 'With God for King and Fatherland.'"

"Good... Black and white?"

"Of course, sir."

"Zaffke – I wanted to tell you this first. Leutnant von Leussow left me a letter." I took a deep drag on my cigarette and tried to steady my voice. "He was dying. You remember how badly injured he was last year... Well, it wrecked his heart. They said he might have five years if he did nothing."

"I can't imagine Herr Leutnant doing nothing," Zaffke said with a smile. "Far better to go out in battle."

"Yes, I agree. I'd have done the same."

"He's with all our comrades, now, sir – all the men who fell at Verdun, and here, and everywhere else. In the Great Army."

"Do you believe that?"

He looked at me. "It's not really a matter of belief, sir – he's with them whether they're in Heaven, or Hell, or nowhere."

"You're right, of course. Well, I won't hold you up. Please tell the others."

"Of course, sir."

After second breakfast I stood up and rapped on the table, and told the pilots about Karl's heart.

"And Braun told me he'd been hit four times, from four different angles," I said.

They looked at each other.

"He never even tried to break off," said Lehmann.

"Jesus," said Sobek.

"I'm glad you told me, sir," said Buckow, "because I was just going to help him out when I saw him spinning, and I was blaming myself for not getting there quicker."

"So he came back here to die," Sandberg said.

"And never showed any sign of it," added Herzog.

Weiss was very quiet. He poured himself another coffee and added schnapps to it, then put in a spoonful of sugar and gave it a good stir.

"He was a bloody brave man," he said finally. "Thinking you want to die is one thing, but actually fighting on like that, taking hit after hit and not even trying to disengage, is quite another."

The others gave him a long stare. *If I hadn't overheard the conversation last night I'd wonder what that was about.* I didn't hold what I'd heard against Weiss – he was entitled to his opinion. I did wonder what he thought of Fellmann, though I wasn't about to ask him.

I went to my office, very pleased that Lehmann was leading the next flight. I just had time to get some work done, before standing in the hangar for the last time.

And I can have a bit of shut-eye in here, while the others are flying.

After about ten minutes there was a knock, and Sobek and Lehmann came in, closing the door behind them.

"Have a seat."

"Thank you, sir."

They looked at each other and then at me, as if not knowing where to start.

"What can I do for you, gentlemen?" I asked.

They both spoke at once, and then stopped, and then Sobek said, rather awkwardly, "Sir, we were thinking – we could lead more patrols, if you like."

You what? What the fuck – do you think I can't do my job?

That's a stupid reaction. They want to help, that's all. 'We'll have to try to take some of the load off the Old Man,' Sobek said. Maybe I should take them up on their offer... but if I start to reduce the amount I fly then my nerves could get even worse.

"Thank you for the suggestion," I said, in what I hoped was a kind tone. "I'll give it some thought, once we're back up to strength."

"We could lead while you train the new boys," Lehmann said.

Don't push it – and then I understood, and a genuine smile spread across my face. *You're trying to stop me getting killed.* It had never occurred to me that they might value me.

"That's a very good idea, Lehmann," I said. "We can share that out. I'll have more idea once they get here – I'm hoping we can get someone with experience."

Sobek sighed. "That would make a real difference." He looked at his watch, and turned to Lehmann. "You're due on patrol and I'm due in the hangar," he said.

"Thank you, gentlemen," I said. "I appreciate it."

As I stood in the hangar for the last time, I thought, *I just want to get this over with now.* I was dreading the funeral. Apart from the sheer awfulness of having to bury Karl, I was afraid I'd break down in front of everyone, especially when he was lowered into the grave, and we had to sing that song.

I can't do it – but I have to.

How many times in this war have you thought, I can't do that, but then you did it? Get a grip, Franz. It won't kill you.

The funeral was at 2pm, and the atmosphere over lunch was very subdued. I couldn't eat anything, and no one had much appetite. Fortunately, everyone had come back from the late morning flight.

After lunch I shaved again. I didn't really need to, but I had to be immaculate for Karl.

Ten minutes later, I was ready. Even my reflection looked strange. Franz Becker the law student had gone for ever. In his place was an officer in spotless field-grey, with the Pour le Mérite, the Iron Cross First Class and a row of medals. The face went with the uniform: it was pale and lined, the expression unreadable.

The gun carriage was waiting outside the hangar, the black horses gleaming in the sun. The band was there, and I was astonished by the crowd. Schutte himself had come, accompanied by half his staff, and there were quite a few pilots. *No Horstmann, though*, I noted sadly, and hoped he was all right.

In the hangar the pall-bearers and the guard of honour stood by the simple pine coffin.

So hard. So hard for you to lie on. We'll bump you as we take you to the cemetery. The road's so bad. My eyes filled suddenly with tears, tears I mustn't shed. *If it were me lying there, you wouldn't cry. I mustn't let you down.*

How young you look. You'll always be twenty-three, Karl. I may grow old one day, but you never will.

I remembered how he'd suffered in hospital the year before. *Dear God, why were we born, to suffer like that and then to die, with all the promise of our lives wasted?* I looked at his hands, and once again I sat in the concert hall while he played the Emperor Concerto.

Such glorious talent, extinguished – for what?

This is the last time I shall see your face. This is the last light that will ever touch it. Rest in peace, my love, until we meet again.

I nodded and Braun closed the coffin, shutting the light from Karl's face. Each blow of the hammer rang through my heart. I picked up the wreath and placed it on top of the coffin. Braun handed me Karl's flying helmet and I placed it with the wreath.

I rested the cushion on my arms, led the way out of the hangar and took my place at the head of the procession. The drums rolled, the band began to play the funeral march from Beethoven's 'Eroica', and we moved off. I was beginning to feel numb and detached, as if I were an actor in a play.

At the end, when the curtain comes down, we'll all go home. Karl isn't really in that coffin, he's in the audience, watching, and afterwards we'll drink champagne—

'I share Bismarck's ambition – to drink five thousand bottles of champagne before I die!'

I started and almost broke step, because for a moment I thought I'd actually heard his voice – and then it hit me again that he was dead. *You never did drink your five thousand bottles. Your life was far too short for that.*

The padre was waiting for us at the cemetery gates. I knew the Lutheran service off by heart, just as I did the Catholic one. The sonorous German phrases rolled through the summer air, sombre and appropriate. *Karl isn't really in that box, he's somewhere else now...* My mind kept wandering, no matter how hard I tried to concentrate. I felt completely numb, and the feeling of unreality was growing.

Karl is dead, my mind repeated endlessly. *Karl is dead, Karl is dead...* I was detached from the scene, watching from a distance. I could even see myself standing by the grave, the black velvet cushion resting on my hands, Karl's awards glinting in the sun.

The band began to play, and the effort of singing dragged me abruptly back.

"Now thank we all our God, With hearts and hands and voices..." The majestic old tune sounded magnificent, the brass band backing our voices.

The padre had finished speaking. *Oh, Christ, now we have to sing that song.*

"I had a Comrade, A better one you won't find..." My voice cracked and I almost lost control of myself.

Karl sang it at Johnny's funeral, without faltering. If he could do it, so can I. Just keep singing…

Oh, God. How am I going to manage the next lines?

"He lies at my feet, As though a part of me…"

The words pierced my heart, the pain appalling. *It's not 'as though' at all – part of me really is in that coffin.* For a moment I thought I would pass out. Finally the last notes of the song died away, and for a moment we all stood in silence.

The volleys cracked sharply over the open grave. It was over. Thank God, it was over.

As we left the cemetery, the band struck up the 'Prince Friedrich Karl March' – and suddenly I saw Karl's regiment as it had been before Verdun: the elite of the finest army in Europe, perfectly turned out on parade, with their blood-red colours flying.

Magnificent. My heart started to lift, just a little, as the music celebrated Karl's life, next with the 'Hohenfriedberger' for all his victories in the air, and finally with 'The Glory of Prussia'.

Men like you are the glory of their nation…

Fellmann had organised a reception in the mess, for everyone. He'd put a desk against one wall, with a photograph of Karl on it. I put the cushion next to the portrait, almost unable to tear my eyes from his.

"Thank you, Fellmann," I said. "You did a lovely job, as always."

Fellmann had given all the orders, as usual, with the crispness of the old pre-war Army.

"Thank you, sir. I have to say I'm glad it's over, though."

"So am I… I'd better talk to our guests."

Fellmann pulled a face. "Rather you than me."

Schutte and his staff were in a small group, at the other end of the mess from the ground crew, who looked uncomfortable at having a general there. The pilots didn't look much happier.

You can have the wake later, for Stoll as well as Karl.

"Thank you very much for coming, Your Excellency," I said.

"Not at all."

He wasn't the old fossil that I always expected a general to be, but probably about fifty-five or so. His hair was just greying, and his eyes were bright and alert, and I think I looked older than he did.

"We're losing our old aces at quite a rate," he went on. "My sincere condolences to you all."

"Thank you, Your Excellency."

There was a pause, and then he said, "Would you show me your aircraft, please?"

"Of course, Your Excellency." I hesitated. "We weren't expecting an inspection."

He laughed. "Good God, don't worry about that! It'll be a change to see a place that hasn't been tarted up."

I hadn't thought of that.

As we left the mess he said, "You want to keep an eye on that technical fellow of yours – he's a bloody Greek."

Greek? Fellmann's Prussian, I almost said.

"I'm sorry, Your Excellency – I don't quite follow."

"He engaged in Greek practices with one of my staff – had to send the fellow away. Can't have that sort of thing."

Greek practices? What – oh, I see. I felt my face going scarlet.

"I can only apologise for any offence, Your Excellency."

"Hardly your fault – and to be honest I don't have any proof. That is, no one *saw* anything, thank God."

What would you think if you knew about Karl and me? Hopefully you'll put my red face down to embarrassment at such an unsavoury subject.

My D.VII sat beside Sobek's and Sandberg's on the flight line, looking up at the sky.

"Would Your Excellency like to sit in the cockpit?"

"Yes, thank you. I've often looked up at you fellows and wondered what it's like."

"It's a shame we lost our two-seater, Your Excellency, or we could have gone for a quick flight."

I fetched a set of steps, and he climbed into the cockpit.

"I didn't realise how little you can see."

"Oh, it's a different matter once the tail's up."

I explained the instruments and controls, and he listened with great interest.

"D'you know, I think I'll learn to fly after the war."

After the war… You said that as if it really exists, but then for you it probably does.

"What's in the hangars?"

"This one has the workshop in it…"

I gave him a guided tour, and as we entered the workshop I realised that of course the ground crew's pin-ups were still on the wooden walls. *Oh, shit.*

"I do apologies for the pictures, Your Excellency."

"No need, no need…" He put his monocle in and studied them. "Hm. Very nice…"

Suddenly I wanted to laugh, and I had to bite the inside of my cheek hard. *Karl will really laugh when I tell him—*

The numb unreality vanished abruptly, and I felt as if I were falling into a vast black pit.

Get a grip, Franz. For fuck's sake don't break down in front of the General. God knows what he'd think.

He turned away from the girls and saw my expression.

"Time we were getting back, I think… How long had you known Leutnant von Leussow?"

"We were at Heidelberg before the war, and then we volunteered together, Your Excellency," I said, my voice seeming to come from some way off.

"Ah, yes… it is hard…"

What would you know about that? It's us young men who get killed.

We went back out into the bright afternoon. *How can the sun shine like this when he's dead? It should be black night out here.*

"There was a little group of us when I was a Leutnant," the General went on. "Bit of a wild crowd, to be honest – girls and cards, that sort of thing. One of them reformed and married my sister. His career went pretty well in step with mine. He fell at the Somme – always wanted to see for himself how things were going, d'you see?"

"Yes, Your Excellency, I do." *That shuts me up.* "My condolences."

We were back at the mess. Suddenly he stopped and turned to me.

"What do you need most here?" he asked.

"Well, Your Excellency, more Fokker D.VIIs. They're far superior to the Triplanes, and we'd be far more effective if we didn't have to put up mixed patrols."

"I'll see what I can do... Thank you for your hospitality – it's been most interesting."

He and his staff left shortly after, much to everyone's relief.

"Thank God he's gone," said Fellmann. "Stuffy old bastard."

"What did he want?" asked Sobek.

"To sit in a Fokker D.VII," I replied. "And he said he'll try to get us some more."

"I'll believe that when I see it," Sandberg said.

"So what did he think of it?" Buckow asked.

"Said he might learn to fly – mind you, he was more interested in the ground crew's pin-ups!"

"Crikey – at his age!" exclaimed Herzog.

"God – he must be nearly sixty!" Lehmann said. "You'd think he'd be well past it."

"Well now," said Sobek. "Annette did tell me something about him—"

"Don't believe you!" said the others in unison.

Weiss looked at Sobek. "You bastard! You made it up, didn't you? No one said anything about me!"

They started laughing, and I found myself joining in. And for a moment I actually felt better, until I turned and saw Karl's eyes gazing at me.

He wouldn't want me to be miserable.

And it's time to go flying.

I rapped on the table. "We take off in half an hour."

The mess emptied in five seconds flat – the ground crew to prepare the aircraft, and all of us to change.

I was last to leave the room, and I met Karl's eyes one more time. *See you in Valhalla, my love. The best way I can honour your memory is by trying to live up to your example. You didn't flinch, and neither shall I.*

The feeling of unreality had come back. I lit a cigarette, and found to my astonishment that my hands were completely steady.

I walked to the flight line, feeling as if I were in some strange dream.

"Sir," said Uhlig, "are you sure you want to wear that?"

"What? Oh." I still had my best tunic on, with the gongs. "No. Thanks."

I took it off and handed it to him.

Get your brain in gear, Franz. The others are relying on you.

The flight was a total blur. I knew we'd engaged the Tommies and that everyone had come back, but that was all. It might as well have happened to someone else.

This is not good, I thought, taxiing in, *but it's been a bad couple of days. I'll probably feel better in the morning.*

And now I have to debrief.

"Sobek, would you like to do the debrief?"

"Certainly, sir."

He went through the whole patrol, in some detail. *Well, I thought, surprised and impressed, you see a lot more than I'd realised. I'll get Lehmann to do it after the dawn flight.*

Apparently I'd fought as I usually did, which was a relief. *Have a few drinks and get some rest, Franz – you'll be fine in the morning.*

The wake began after dinner. Fellmann had put a picture of Stoll on the small table next to Karl.

I raised my champagne glass. "To our fallen comrades, Leutnant von Leussow and Pilot Stoll." I managed to get Karl's name out without faltering.

At about eleven I left the others to their boozing. I'd had quite a lot and I was afraid of losing control in front of them.

The room looked very strange, and for a moment I wondered why.

Karl's bed had gone.

Good, I thought as I undressed and put his shirt on. *I can pretend he's in Brandenburg, until I join him.*

I dreamed that I was in the shell-hole with Kurt, the rain pouring down on us as his blood ran into the water, and then it was Karl's body that I was holding, and I woke with a howl.

It was just a bad dream, Franz. In a moment he'll come to your bed and hold you—

No, he won't. Never again.

Grief overwhelmed me, and I couldn't stop myself crying.

I must have fallen asleep, because Schiffer knocked with the shaving water. In the first seconds after waking, I thought that Karl was asleep in his bed, and that it was time to wake him – and then black reality swung in.

Someone had removed the pictures and the cushion from the mess, and it looked normal. *It really doesn't matter now what happens to me.*

I wasn't thinking that an hour later, as we desperately fended off about twenty Tommies. We were fighting for our lives, and it was very grim until the olive-green Jasta came to our rescue.

Fucking hell, that was bad. Suddenly I understood exactly what Weiss had meant about Karl – thinking you want to die is one thing, but actually getting yourself killed is another matter. *I might think I don't care but I'm nowhere near where Karl was. Not yet.*

Lehmann made a very good job of the debrief. *Good – I've got two patrol leaders now, and Weiss should be capable very soon. Maybe I can give myself a few easier days, just until I get over the shock.*

After second breakfast I went to my office – and there on my desk was the cushion, with Karl's decorations on it, and it hit me again that he was gone for ever.

Take them off it, pack them up, and get everything in the post.

I was shaky and exhausted, and it was too much effort to move. I lit another fag and stared blankly across the room.

After some time I got up, and took Karl's awards from the cushion. I went back to my room and put them on the table, next to his gold ring. I picked the ring up and sat on my bed, looking at it, running my finger over the deeply engraved device.

It's so old, I thought, looking at the scratches and the scuffed places. *It's been worn for... what? Twelve generations? No one will wear it now. There are no more Leussows.*

I put Karl's medals carefully back in their cases. *They belong to Elisabeth now, and so does the ring. She might want to wear it, or one of her sons might, even if it is against family tradition.*

But how on earth am I going to get them to her? They'll have to go to Henning, or to Karl's lawyer, but they're far too valuable to put in the post.

I thought for a while.

If I use the official post to Berlin, to Hoeppner's office, they might be less likely to be stolen, and someone from the office can take them to the lawyer. I'd better do it now, before something happens to me as well.

I took Karl's awards and his ring to my office, wrapped them carefully, together with his silver cigarette case and lighter, wrote a covering letter, and packaged the whole lot up. I addressed the parcel to the Commanding General of the Air Service, and went to Fellmann.

"Could you see that this goes to Berlin?"

"Of course."

"It's Karl's valuables. I don't want them stolen in the post."

He hesitated. I could see what he was thinking – that even sending them to Hoeppner didn't guarantee their arrival. Things were so desperate in Germany that anything that might be worth stealing would probably disappear.

"If you remember, sir, I'm going on leave next week," he said. "I could deliver them, if you like. I have to change trains in Berlin."

"Thank you, Fellmann. I'd really appreciate that. Could you take them to Karl's lawyer instead? It's Feinstein and Co."

"Yes, I know – you gave me his letter for them."

"Oh, yes, so I did."

I went back to my office and looked at the pile of paperwork. For a moment I wondered what it was doing there, and what it had to do with me. I had no idea how I was going to get through the day. I lit yet another cigarette, and tried to force myself to concentrate.

Thank God Sobek's leading the next flight.

Black misery swirled over me and I lost all track of time, until the sound of aircraft engines ripped me from my trance.

Come on, Franz. Karl wouldn't go to pieces. You have to write to Elisabeth... but I couldn't face it.

"Here's your post, sir," said Fellmann.

"Thanks."

He hesitated. "What did Schutte have to say?"

"Nothing important."

"I was a bit concerned that he might not want to help us. I mean—"

"Oh, don't worry about that... Have you heard from the Moustache?"

He shook his head. "It was just a bit of fun, that was all."

He didn't sound convincing.

"Ah, well. Maybe 'after the war.'"

"Who knows?" he said, and went back to the Ops Office.

Poor Fellmann, always falling for someone who doesn't love him back – was that what Karl thought? That I didn't love him back?

Don't torture yourself, Franz. It's too late.

On top of the pile was an official envelope from Berlin. I sat turning it over in my hands. *If this is the result of Karl's medical report it couldn't be more irrelevant.* I was tempted not to open it.

That won't do. It might be something important. I knew we were building up for another offensive in Flanders, and there were rumours that something else was going to happen further south.

I tore open the envelope.

The letter was from Hoeppner. I sat up straighter, quite involuntarily, as if I should sit to attention while reading it. *Why in God's name is the big boss writing to me?*

I leaned back in my chair and rested my ankles on the corner of the desk, just as Karl had once done.

'With regard to your request for the medical report on Leutnant der Reserve Karl von Leussow, I am sure you will appreciate that this information is confidential. However, as his Commanding Officer, you are, I think, entitled to the facts.

You probably know that Ltn v Leussow suffered a severe chest wound last July. This injury and its complications affected his heart, and the prognosis is poor. The medical examination on 10th May 1918 found him to be unfit for service in any capacity, and he was recommended for a medical discharge and a disability pension.

Ltn v Leussow wrote to me, requesting that I allow him to return to the Front. He was fully aware of his state of health, but expressed a desire to continue to serve for as long as he was able. In view of his previous excellent record, I granted his request.

In retrospect I should perhaps have written to you sooner. You are best placed to assess Ltn v Leussow's ability to carry out his duties, and accordingly the decision as to whether he remains in your Staffel rests with you.'

No, it bloody doesn't. Not any more.

I lit another fag, staring into space. 'I should have written to you sooner'! *You wouldn't have written at all if I hadn't, you old bastard. You knew what Karl was asking for, and you let him come back here to die. And what about the rest of us? He could have endangered the rest of the Jasta, and you didn't give a shit. But then, we're all expendable.*

If only this had come in time. I'd have shown Karl the letter, sent him home at once, and written to Hoeppner that he was most definitely not fit for active service. As it is, the bloody thing just tells me what I already knew – except for the date of the medical, which was earlier than I expected.

I wonder if any of them noticed that it was his twenty-third birthday.

I sighed. I would only have condemned him to dragging through life until his heart finally gave out. As it was, he'd died quickly, and for Prussia – and to a Leussow that meant a great deal.

'That's what we're for' – *you spoke those words with bitterness in January, but that was the way you chose. And I would have done the same.*

You got the death you wanted. Rest in peace – no, that's not you. Bash the crap out of the Frenchies and the Tommies in Valhalla. Or go carousing with Johnny and the others. And keep a place for me.

I went to the window and looked out, seeing nothing except Karl's serene blue eyes staring at the sky.

Now I must go alone the way we should have gone together…

I was beginning, just beginning, to understand what losing Karl was going to mean.

It doesn't matter. It won't be for long.

There was a knock at the door.

"Sir, they want an escort for a two-seater that's got to take some photographs," Sandberg said.

"Yes, I'm coming."

Oh, Jesus, how am I going to do it? I had a horrendous fit of shaking, and could barely light my fag.

If you could fight in that condition, then I can do my duty until I join you. King and Fatherland – that was how you saw it, and that has to be how I see it. There has to be a purpose.

I remembered his father's letter telling him that Friedrich was dead. At the time I'd found it so callous, with its stark emphasis on Friedrich's death 'in the service of Prussia and the Empire', but now it made perfect sense. That was probably the only way the Major could bear it.

I must stop thinking about you, just long enough to fly.

We made the rendezvous with the two-seater, and watched over them while they took their pictures. We were well over Tommy-side and it made me very nervous. My right foot danced perpetually on the rudder bar, and I couldn't even pretend to myself that I was cold.

I felt sick with apprehension. *Something's going to go wrong. I can feel it. You get an instinct for these things.* I kept my head twisting, unable to believe that we were being left alone…

We were not alone. There was a patrol of SE5s east of us and above, waiting for us to make a move for home.

I don't like that. When we turn for home we won't have fuel for a long fight. At some point we'll have to disengage, and that'll be very dodgy. We'll have to hope they're lower on fuel than us. They're over our side of the lines, and they've been loitering for a while.

Don't focus on them, Franz. They won't be the only Tommies in the sky. They might even be a decoy for a larger group – but there was no one else that I could see.

The two-seater crew had finished and the observer waved us off. I rocked my wings and pointed to the SE5s, and we all turned for home together.

I'd been right about the Tommies. They were waiting for us. My heart pounded as if it would jump right out of my chest, and the tremor in my right foot spread to my whole body. Sweat ran down me. I was completely terrified. I hoped and prayed that the fear would go once the fight started, that I would be cold as I usually was…

The SE5s were diving down and my stomach was churning. It was all I could do not to be sick.

It's not whether you're afraid, it's how you behave when you're afraid. The others are relying on you. God help them.

The sky was full of aircraft, turning madly. One tried to get behind me. *I'm not having that*, I thought, suddenly calm, and threw my aircraft onto her wingtips and got away from him. An SE5 spun down out of the fight, and a couple of minutes later his colleagues broke off and headed west.

The two-seater crew was still with us, and they waved their thanks as we neared their base. And then reaction set in, worse than it had ever been before. I flew home soaked in sweat, shaking from head to foot.

Uhlig put the chocks in and I sat in the cockpit, trying to find the strength to get out. I could hardly take off my helmet.

"Are you all right, sir?" Uhlig had brought the steps and climbed up to me.

"Yes."

But he can see I'm not. The sweat on my face must be obvious, never mind the trembling.

He lit a fag for me.

"Thanks," I said, and took a long, shaky drag.

I'll have to get out. They're all watching me. I took a few more puffs of my cigarette and felt a little steadier.

"Will you take the steps away, please, Uhlig?"

Steps were only used for getting into aircraft. I slid down the fuselage and found that my legs would carry me.

"One more to you, Sandberg, I think?" I said.

"Yes, sir!"

Someone's happy, anyway. I might be falling apart but Sandberg's happy...

I kept my hands locked behind my back during the debrief, and hoped my voice wouldn't shake. At least this time I could remember the fight.

I went to my office with a large brandy. After a few more cigarettes and another drink, I felt a bit steadier.

I hope to God I'm not going to feel like that every time. I'll end up like Widemayer in no time if it does. I should take leave. I need it. But if I go, who'll look after the boys? And if there is about to be another big offensive, I can't go home just as it starts. I have to stay.

If I crack up, so be it. All my old friends have given their lives. I can give my sanity. It's not much in comparison. If I go mad they'll have to send me home, and I won't be maimed. It won't hurt.

Or will it? What happens when you go mad? What if I have some hideous, unending delusion that I'm at the Front? That would be worse than the reality. Or maybe I'd be in some happy dreamland in which Karl would be alive and well, and I'd sleep in his arms every night...

Fellmann knocked on the door. "Sir, I've just heard from the Alerting Service – Sandberg's victim's only about five kilometres away. He got off with a few bruises."

"I reckon lunch is on us, then," I said. "Why don't you and Braun take the truck and a salvage team – oh, and take Sandberg with you. He can keep the Tommy company on the way back."

They came back about an hour later, Sandberg clutching the number from the English aeroplane.

I scraped together my schoolboy English to welcome our visitor. *Oh, if only Karl were here, with his beautiful English!* But his body lay in the grave in the cemetery.

"You are hungry?" I asked the Tommy.

"Well, yes, it's a while since breakfast."

We talked about this and that, carefully avoiding the subject of the war. It would have been indecent to ask him questions about it, and I didn't want him to think I was doing so. Towards the end of the meal, I had an idea.

"I have a problem," I said, "and I... would like to ask for your help."

"Well, if I can," he replied.

"My good friend was killed and I want to write to his sister."

"I'm sorry to hear that," he said, his voice very neutral. I could see him wondering what on earth that had to do with him.

"She is married with an Englishman and she lives in England and I want to write in English. I don't want that someone thinks that..."

Oh, God, how do I say, 'I don't want anyone to think she's spying' in English?

"Yes, I see what you mean."

"And as you hear, I speak some English, but I can't write it good."

"Yes, I see. Well, I'll be more than happy to help."

I fetched the next-of-kin book from the operations room and we went into my office. I gathered up all the papers on my desk and put them face down, seated him at the desk and gave him a fresh sheet of paper. *They make bandages out of paper now, not paper like this, but crêpe...*

The entry in the book for Karl was in his writing. My eyes blurred.

"It is a very hard letter for the lady," I managed to say, "because all her brothers are dead now, and her parents."

The Tommy looked at me. "This is her last brother who's been killed?"

"Yes."

"What about her husband?"

"I don't know."

"Poor woman," he said quietly. "What... er... how was her brother killed?"

"Shot down."

He paused. "Look, old chap, I know I said I'd write this for you, but I'd have the devil's own job to write to *my* best friend's sister in circumstances like these. I didn't even know your friend, after all. I'm sorry, but I think you'd better write in German. I mean, your friend must have written in German."

"No, he wrote in English. Her husband is their cousin."

"Oh, I see. But there must be things you want to say to her about her brother."

"Yes, there are. Thank you."

We went back into the mess. Shortly afterwards the escort arrived, and the Tommy thanked us for our hospitality, and departed fairly cheerfully for prison. I wasn't sure if I envied him or not.

I forced myself to write to Elisabeth. I couldn't delay it any longer. She had more right than anyone else to know how her brother had died. The sight of the words in black and white was too much for me, and I fought hard for self-control.

It was no use. I couldn't stop myself crying as I wrote. *This is terrible. I'm not a child, I'm a grown man. I can't sit here like this, with tears running down my face. Suppose someone needs to talk to me?*

It's my nerves. They're completely shot. It was a horrible realisation. *I can't do any more. I'm finished – but I can't stop. I have to go on. How, in God's name?*

I wanted to write to Alfred, but there wasn't time before flying.

Once again I shook like an autumn leaf as we got ready, and could only hope that no one had noticed. Not that most of them were any better. Weiss's aircraft was next to mine, and he dropped his helmet and his gloves, and Schiffer picked them up and helped him put them on.

The sick fear as we climbed up and headed west was almost unbearable, and for the first time I actually thought of turning back and saying that the engine had been running rough – but I couldn't do it.

If I do that once I'll never be able to face it again, and I can't abandon the others. I'll just have to keep going.

This time we had the advantage, over a flight of Camels, and again the dread only stopped at the actual moment of engagement. I managed to shoot one of them down, God knows how, and felt only guilt and nausea. And then the shaking set in as we flew home.

I hope I join Karl before this gets any worse, I thought as I put on a fresh shirt.

The boys had a party for Sandberg's and my victories, and I drank steadily through the evening. *I should go to bed…* I was so tired that my eyes were almost closing, but I couldn't face the empty room.

The piano stood silent in the corner. Lehmann and Zeitler put on one record after another.

"Ten thousand men, Set off upon manoeuvres…"

Karl played this for us to sing, only a few days ago. I stared at the floor, seeing his face and hearing his laughter.

Fellmann joined me on the sofa and we sat for a while in silence.

"They know," I said quietly, my voice covered by the singing.

"Yes, but the only one with a problem is…" He hesitated.

"Weiss."

"Yes."

Weiss was playing skat with Sobek and Buckow.

"Not that I give a shit," I said. "And the others told him to shut up."

I told him about the conversation I'd overheard, and he burst out laughing at 'what one of Blanche's girls said about you'. I laughed as well, more than was healthy.

"I suppose I'd better go to bed," I said when we'd calmed down.

Much good it'll do, I thought, and I was right – I had another of those horrible nights when I dozed and dreamed, and woke and thought, and there was no separation between the two states.

I held Karl's lifeless, blood-soaked body again and again. He coughed blood in his garden in Brandenburg, lay grey-faced and still in hospital, and then he was playing the piano for us, for all the old crowd. The Chief was there, and Johnny, Geschke,

Buchholz, Lensch, Westermann... But Karl was a skeleton, and I realised the others were too.

I woke with a yell, put the light on and lit a fag. It was half past two, and I knew further sleep was impossible.

How I wish Karl were here... I looked across the room, to the space where his bed had been, and told myself that he was safe at home, and that one day, 'after the war', I'd go and live with him.

I almost managed to believe it, but then I saw him lying in the coffin, the light filtering onto his still, white face, and it was all I could do not to cry.

The old man with the scythe will come for me soon. It's asking for trouble to fight in the state I'm in.

Part of me felt he couldn't come soon enough. I'd had enough of the whole business.

The dawn flight went just as I expected it to – ghastly sick fear apart from the actual fights, when I had too much to think about to be afraid.

I couldn't face second breakfast, but went to my office with a brandy, and smoked and smoked in a vain effort to calm my nerves. Part of me seemed almost to be detached, watching my disintegration with something like amusement.

At about nine there was a knock on the door.

"Come in!"

The Chief calling out those words when he'd had the General with him, who'd come to tell Karl that his father was dead... Karl's eyes staring at the sky. *Oh, God, must I see that all the time?*

What would you rather see? Anton by the light of the flare? Kurt's blood running into the puddle in the mud? Otto's burning Triplane?

Dead, all four of them.

Horstmann came in, and for a moment I wondered why he was alive.

"Horstmann! What brings you here?"

"I – I've come to say goodbye. We've been ordered south." His eye was twitching madly, and the tic was spreading into his cheek.

"I see."

"And I wanted to – say goodbye, and I wanted to see… Becker, I'm really sorry about Karl. I know how close you two were…"

I wonder if you do.

"Would you like to see the grave?" I asked.

"Yes, if you've the time."

"Yes, of course. More wreaths have come, so we'll take those."

Horstmann and I walked down the road to the cemetery, retracing the route of the procession. *Was it really the day before yesterday?* It seemed as if Karl had been killed months ago, and yet as if it had never happened. The feeling of unreality came back as we walked in through the gates.

The fresh earth of Karl's grave showed clearly, from some distance away. I knelt and placed the wreaths beside the cross, being careful not to tread on the grave. It would have felt like disturbing him.

I knew that was rubbish, that nothing could ever disturb him. *Beneath the earth, his body has begun to decay…* I tried not to think about it, but I'd seen too many rotting corpses and I couldn't pretend to myself that it didn't happen.

Horstmann was standing silent, his head bowed, and I got to my feet and stood beside him. My eyes filled with tears. I couldn't cry in front of Horstmann – that was unthinkable.

I'll never love anyone else the way I love Karl. Not if I live to be a thousand. And I was so fucking blind.

We saluted his grave and turned to leave. As we walked back into the road I stopped, unable to take another step because I was shaking from head to foot. I had to lean on the cemetery wall for support.

This is worse than crying. If I'd cried, Horstmann would have understood. But this!

He stared at his feet, and then said quietly, "Becker, if you don't take a rest you'll be next to him in no time."

"I'm all right." My voice shook.

"You are not all right. Take some leave or become an instructor."

"I can't."

"You've done more than enough. If you go on like this you'll get killed."

"I'm all right, I tell you. It's just Karl – I'm finding it hard to cope with."

"Because you were… because you didn't send him home?" he asked softly.

I pushed myself away from the wall, and we began walking back towards the airfield. "No. I'm glad I didn't."

He looked at me in blank astonishment.

I took a deep breath, hoping to get the words out without breaking down. "His heart was failing. The doctors put him down as unfit, but he got Hoeppner's permission to come back here. He… he was going to die anyway."

"Oh, God… No wonder he was going grey. I thought it was just because he'd had such a plateful."

"You noticed as well. I didn't. I overheard some of the others talking about him. And then I saw, in the sunlight."

Horstmann was silent for a couple of minutes. "It was a good way to die," he said finally.

"Yes. Better than sitting at home, getting worse and worse."

"And you, Becker? What do you want?"

"I don't know. But I do know I can't take leave now. Hardly any of them have any experience. And I can't go when things are about to hot up again."

"Well, break your neck and legs, then!"

"You too. Write, won't you?"

"Of course."

He couldn't stay for lunch. I watched him go, and wondered if we would ever see each other again.

The day was hot and quiet, and I joined the others lying in the sun. *I'll look like an African soon, never mind an Indian.* In the lazy warmth I almost began to relax. *I could almost fall asleep now…*

"Sir. *Sir.*"

"What?"

"Sorry, sir, but it's half an hour to the patrol," said Herzog.

"Thanks."

I pulled on my overalls, and went to the mess for a coffee and a fag or two. *Here we go again*, I thought as I climbed the steps and settled myself in the cockpit of my D.VII. *I've lost count of the number of times I've flown off to fight. At first it was very, very frightening. Then experience and success brought me confidence, and I even used to enjoy it. Now I'm more afraid than I'd ever imagined a man could be.*

It has to end soon. I cannot continue like this.

We found an English two-seater and its escort, and then a flight of Camels joined in. And in the whirling, deadly dance, I found myself on the tail of a Camel. He was a good pilot and he was getting the best out of his machine. I couldn't quite get my guns to bear on him, as we went round and round and round…

Just a little tighter, that'll do it—

I tightened the turn, my cheeks sagging, the engine roaring at full throttle. I was gaining on him, gaining, he was nearly in my sights – bullets cracked past my ears and I heard the rattle behind me. I pulled the turn tighter still, hot and cold, sick with sudden terror. *Fucking idiot, Franz, not watching your tail.*

Jesus, he's close! – the buffet began and I eased the back pressure as little as I dared. There was a tug at my sleeve and something slammed into my right knee. The windscreen shattered, and suddenly there was thick smoke and a vivid burst of flame.

Jesus fucking Christ!

Get out! – but if I move I'll be riddled. I will be anyway.

So this is the end. Well then, kill me and get it over with.

Terror disappeared, replaced by apathetic calm. *It's over. All of it.*

He'd stopped firing. He'd gone. I was still alive. I couldn't believe it.

Get out, Franz, for fuck's sake get out!

Terror returned as I struggled to unfasten my harness, my hands shaking and fumbling. I could hardly breathe in the smoke, and the heat was increasing, the flames taking hold of the fuselage. I was starting to panic. I got the straps undone, but I couldn't move my right leg. I took hold of it with both hands and pulled my foot off the rudder bar, tried to heave myself out of the cockpit and failed.

Oh, Christ, I can't get out! I'm going to burn, just like Otto, just like so many of my victims.

The top wing caught fire, blazing fiercely. I tried to roll the D.VII inverted, but she wouldn't respond. I made a desperate effort, and pulled myself up with all my strength. I managed to get my shoulders over the side of the cockpit, pulled myself further out, my leg trailing behind me, and fell.

The parachute opened with a hell of a jerk. *Thank God. Oh, thank God.*

I'd escaped. I was alive.

I was suddenly frozen, shaking violently, my teeth chattering. My D.VII was plummeting, ablaze from nose to tail. I'd only just got out in time. My eyes followed her all the way down and I saw her crash, far below.

If this had been last year I would have burned with her, unless I'd jumped like Johnny.

I wished I hadn't looked down. The legs of my flying suit were soaked with blood, so much that I thought I must have been hit again and not felt it. My right lower leg seemed to be moving.

It can't be. It's an illusion. I must keep my right foot clear when I land – but I felt dizzy and faint, and my leg was completely numb and I couldn't move it.

I didn't realise how low I was, and suddenly the ground came up at me and I hit it hard, unprepared. My knee exploded in agony and I screamed.

I was lying on my back, half awake and half dreaming, in a sort of comfortable lethargy. *I wonder where I am* – but it was too much effort to open my eyes.

There was a curious swaying feeling.

Where the fuck am I, and what's happening?

Someone groaned, and a man said, "It's all right, mate. Not much further now."

It didn't make sense. No sense at all.

I tried to sit up. A black wave broke over me, dragging me down and down.

IX

I was half asleep, lying in the open air under the warm July sun, the soft breeze on my face. *We'll have to go flying soon* – but I was too tired and lethargic to move. *I'll have a cigarette and lie here for a while...*

Something was odd. I wasn't lying flat.

I opened my eyes and looked round in disbelief. Instead of lying naked on the grass with my pilots, I was wearing my flying overalls and covered with a blanket. All around me was a sea of stretchers and blankets, and I was reclining quite comfortably against the raised top end of my stretcher.

What the fuck am I doing here?

Slowly I remembered the fight, and the fire, and the parachute jump. My leg didn't hurt, but I knew that wounds often didn't hurt at first and I wondered almost idly when the pain would start.

It was just like the burning dream. That made my hair stand on end. I tried to rationalise it, but failed and gave up. I was too tired and groggy to think.

Karl is dead. I saw his eyes gazing at the sky, saw myself standing beside his grave, his awards gleaming against the black velvet.

I'll never see you again, never...

He told me I'd come through all right. *That's strange as well – but it's too soon to tell. I expect I'll be going back.*

The air was cool and I shivered, glad of my clothes and the blanket. *That's not right – it's a hot day. We were sunbathing, and the sun's still high in the sky. It can't be getting cold.*

An orderly was giving one of the other fellows a drink, and I realised how thirsty I was.

"Orderly!" It came out cracked and feeble. I tried again.

He looked round, trying to work out who'd called him. "Yes, mate?"

I raised a hand, and when he'd finished he came over to me.

"Could I have some water, please?"

"Not hit in the stomach, are you?"

"No." *At least, I don't think so...*

"Here you are, then."

He handed me an enamel mug full and I drained it, and three more. I began to feel a little better.

"Fancy a smoke?" he said.

"Christ, yes, thanks."

It was rough tobacco, but that didn't matter. I took a long drag and started to revive a little.

"Just don't set fire to yourself, or there'll be hell to pay."

I wonder how long I'll have to wait – there's a hell of a crowd of us. Oh, well, at least I'm not in pain, not yet, anyway. I had no idea what state my leg might be in, and the only thought I could manage was that I was out of it, for several weeks at least.

I can have a rest. I can stop. And by the time I've healed up, the war might be over. I could have cried with relief.

I closed my eyes for a moment. Suddenly I was back in my D.VII, the English pilot close behind me. Bullets flew round me, and I cried out in terror and then in pain as my knee was hit. I woke with a yell and a jolt.

The pain was real. It was tearing my knee apart. *I hope it's not going to get worse. I hope I don't have to wait much longer. I don't want to lie here like this for hours.*

I must have been asleep for some time, because the sun had moved across the sky. It was beating down on my head, and I was horribly thirsty. My knee was stabbing me, the pain sickening. I gritted my teeth, trying not to cry out again.

A Sergeant came and sat on the ground beside me. "No identification on you. I'd better get the details now."

Stupid of me, not wearing my tag – but with my aircraft being so distinctive I'd got out of the habit.

"Can I have some water?" My voice was so strained and hoarse that I don't know how he understood me.

"Zimmermann! Water! Name?"

"Becker."

"Rank?"

"Oberleutnant." I gulped the water down and held out the mug for a refill.

"Regiment, sir?"

I gave the Jasta number.

"Ah, a fighter pilot! You wouldn't get me up in one of those bloody things. Been at it long, sir?"

"Eighteen months or so."

"Bit more than the average, isn't it?"

"Yes, a bit. Luck ran... ran out, though."

Pain bored red-hot through my knee and into my thigh, and the world reeled in a vortex of giddiness and nausea. I shivered, cold and sweating, and suddenly afraid.

He looked at me closely. "Are you all right, sir?"

"No," I heard myself say. "No, I'm not."

He folded back the blanket, and I saw that someone had cut off the right leg of my overalls and my flying boot, and had splinted my knee and bound it up. The bandages were sodden with blood, and it had soaked into the stretcher as well.

I stared at it, terrified. *Jesus Christ, I'm bleeding to death!*

The Sergeant frowned, put the blanket back over me, and said, "I'll get you taken in next. Fischer! Rössler! Over here!"

They picked my stretcher up and carried me into a corridor. One of them bent over me, and started unfastening the buttons of my overalls. I tried to help, but my fingers were sticking out stiff and useless, and he moved my hands gently aside.

"It's all right, mate. I'll do that. You just relax... Bloody hell, didn't realise you blokes wore nothing under these!"

"We were sunbathing." My face was numb, and it was difficult to speak.

"Yes, you are nice and brown."

His hands almost caressed my skin as he pushed the overalls off my shoulders. The sudden longing for Karl, for his touch, was unbearable.

"I'll have to cut them off from here on down – but don't worry, I'll be careful where I cut!"

I couldn't help laughing. *You should be on the stage.* It wasn't only what he said. It was the camp delivery.

"Why did your Sergeant want me taken next?"

"You're bleeding. Sarge don't like that. 'S not good for you... This might hurt."

He moved my legs, and the pain was so vicious that I cried out before I could stop myself.

He tucked the blanket round me carefully. "All done now, mate. Next thing'll be they'll get you on the table, and then they'll knock you out and you won't feel a thing." He glanced at the label the Sergeant had tied to my wrist. "Oberleutnant. And I've been calling you mate." He shook his head. "Sorry, sir. You just can't get the staff."

"Doesn't matter." The pain had diminished a little but the nausea was worse, and I felt faint and frightened. My voice sounded strange and far away. "Am I going to be all right?"

"Oh, Lord, yes. You just relax, you'll be sorted out in no time."

'The sort of platitudinous crap I hope I'll never have to say to you.'

Karl? Oh, God, now I'm becoming delirious. I swear I heard his voice. I wish he were here. I've never felt so alone.

Some time later I was carried into the operating room. It stank of blood and chloroform. There was a flash of blinding pain as I was lifted onto the table, then the feeling of wood against my back.

I stared at the ceiling, sick and afraid, wondering how much it was going to hurt.

Someone cut the bandages off my leg, the scissors cold against my skin. The doctor bent over my knee, and white-hot agony seared through me.

I heard myself scream.

The doctor put his instruments down. "Where's Pfundt?" he demanded.

"Nipped out, sir."

"Well, get him back in here. This fellow needs chloroform."

I was whimpering. I couldn't stop myself. The pain was shattering.

The doctor went to the door. "Pfundt! Where the hell are you?"

"All right, Künzel, I'm coming. Keep your hair on."

"I can't operate with him in that state."

Pfundt ignored him. "Hurts a bit, does it? Don't worry, I'll soon stop that."

He put the mask on my face, suffocating, frightening. I cried out and struggled against the waves of smothering blackness, and Pfundt's distant voice said, "Keep still, now. You'll be…"

The tearing pain in my leg got rapidly worse. I was soaked in sweat, and starting to feel very sick.

I was in a large, rectangular room, full of beds, all occupied. There was a nurse not far away.

"Sister!"

"What is it?"

"I'm going to be sick."

"One moment."

It felt like eternity before she came back with a basin. I only just managed to hold on. I was sick again and again until I felt like a wrung-out rag. And I banged my knee against the cage which kept the blanket off it, and for a moment the world spun, dark, before my eyes.

The nurse was very kind and did her best to make me comfortable, but she couldn't stay with me long. I lay feeling utterly miserable, my leg throbbing. She'd left a bucket by my bed, and I hoped I wouldn't need it. *If I have to lean over, I'll bang my knee again...*

I closed my eyes and tried to think about something other than pain – and then I thought of Karl lying in hospital, and for the first time I understood what had happened to me.

The pain was appalling. *How can anything hurt this much?*

"Sister!" *Oh, God, she'll get fed up with me always wanting something.* "Sister, my leg hurts."

"You'll just have to be brave, I'm afraid."

Oh, Christ. Just like Karl. Terror seized me. *This won't stop, I can't get out of it, it's just going to go on and on, whether I can stand it or not.* I could see Karl's agonised grey face, hear him groaning, and I wanted to run away. *Run? With that knee? And what good would it do?*

Time dragged. My leg was torture and I gritted my teeth, trying not to cry out. Most of the others were suffering, and the ward was filled with groans and cries.

"Sister – the pain – *help me – please...*" *Oh, God, that's not my voice, begging like that?*

"I'm sorry."

"Oh, God!"

A while later I lapsed into restless semi-consciousness, white-hot pain tearing through me. Someone was moaning, and

I wished he would shut up. His cries grew louder and sharper as my pain got worse. At first I didn't understand, and when I did I wished I were deaf.

All I wanted was for the pain and the noise to stop, but they wouldn't. After an agonised eternity I felt my arm taken in a firm grip, and the needle hard and cold in the vein.

The pain began to ease and then disappeared. I was floating in soft warmth, drifting in sleepy contentment…

I woke to sharp, searing pain. It was night, and the ward was dark apart from a lamp at the far end, where the nurse was sitting. I lay trying not to think about the pain, knowing they wouldn't do anything about it until it became completely unbearable.

I shifted, trying to find a comfortable position, but there wasn't one and moving made my leg hurt more. The night was hot, and I was sweaty and sick from the heat and the pain, the blanket sticking to my skin.

My feeling of relief at being out of it had evaporated. *I'd be quite willing to be back at the airfield in one piece*, I thought, and then remembered how terrified I'd been on my last flights, and wondered where I was better off.

Karl is dead. My love is dead. I realised I was crying. The pain of losing him seemed to merge with the pain in my leg, and I felt completely wretched.

The night dragged endlessly, my leg throbbing, torturing me. Towards morning the nurse took pity on me, and gave me an injection for which I was pathetically grateful.

Karl and I walked hand in hand through his garden in Brandenburg. The roses were in full bloom, their petals glowing in the sunlight, their sweet fragrance filling the air. We sat down together and he stroked my hair, his blue eyes gazing into mine, and I said, 'I love you', and our lips met so tenderly…

For the first seconds when I woke, I thought I really had been with him – then I remembered that he was dead, and that I was in hospital. *I wish I could stay in that short time after waking, when I forget what's happened.*

He's dead and I'm lying here, with my leg on fire.

The pain and fever got worse as the day went on. *This is the price for being out of the fighting*, I thought in a brief moment of lucidity. *You didn't think you could get out for free, did you?*

And you deserve it, after what you've been doing. You deserve to lose Karl as well – how many women lost their husbands and their sweethearts by your hand?

You had no choice, I told myself.

They gave me some soup, but I couldn't keep it down.

I was in the trenches. I could hear men in No Man's Land, crying out and calling for help, and I wanted to go and fetch them, but Alfred held my shoulders against the side of the trench and stopped me—

I was trying to get up, and one of the orderlies was holding me down.

"Lie still, now, sir," he said. "You need to rest."

"But I have to – you can hear – they—"

"You're in hospital," he said patiently.

"Oh. Yes." *They must get this all the time...*

I was walking through a jungle, a tiger stalking me. I started to run but it caught me and bit into my leg, and chewed it and chewed it, and I was screaming and writhing but I couldn't get away...

The pain faded. Warmth ran through me, enveloped me.

Someone took hold of my hand.

"Karl?"

"Sorry, sir – it's only Fellmann."

Fellmann was sitting on my bed. His face swam into and out of focus, his cornflower-blue eyes looking at me with concern and affection.

"How are you?"

It was too much effort to answer. All I said was, "Franz, please."

I'm not your CO any more.

He squeezed my hand. "Paul, then."

"Karl flying?"

"The boys are very busy."

Of course – they must be. Karl will come when he can.

Paul carried on talking, but I couldn't make any of it out. It didn't matter. I knew where I was, and why, and that didn't matter either. *You're a good friend, Paul.*

Suddenly I felt completely safe. I hadn't felt safe for four years, and at first I didn't know what the feeling was. *I don't have to fight any more – I can just lie here with Paul holding my hand, and that's far more comforting than I'd ever imagined...*

When I woke it was evening and he'd gone, and I wondered whether he'd really been there.

The man in the next bed whimpered and then gave a series of horrible, shrill cries – I looked across and then quickly away, because the nurse was changing his dressings.

His bed was between mine and the door, and I realised with a stab of fear that it was probably my turn next. *I hope I don't make a fuss. I hope she doesn't hurt me as much as that.*

The trolley rattled as she pushed it to my bed.

I closed my eyes, sick with pain and apprehension, and because I didn't want to know what sort of mangled mess my knee was.

"Now, you're going to be brave for me, aren't you?" she said.

"Depends," I said, with a failed attempt at levity.

I wasn't 'brave'. God knows I tried to be, but I howled and felt ashamed – until I heard the others.

Quite a while later, I turned my head towards the fellow on my left.

"Is it always like that?" I managed to ask.

He gave a feeble smile. "'Fraid so. What happened to you?"

"Got shot down – bullet in my knee. How about you?"

"English shell – collected a couple of splinters. Name's Nehring."

"Becker."

Neither of us felt like saying any more. The orderlies came round with stew, and I tried to force myself to eat, but it was almost impossible.

And then I realised I needed a crap. Telling the nurse would have been horribly embarrassing, but luckily one of the orderlies was collecting the plates.

"Just a minute, sir – I'll get one of the others to bring a bedpan."

They had to lift me onto it, and the pain as they moved my leg was so all-obliterating that I almost forgot why I'd wanted the bloody thing in the first place.

Afterwards I curled up as far as I could, shrunk into myself in misery. *I can't do this – it hurts too much and I feel so weak and useless, and Karl's dead so what's the point in going on?*

Sobek came to see me the next day, or the day after, I can't remember which. It was kind of him, but I didn't really feel up to talking to him.

He stood beside my bed, looking nervous and awkward.

"Hello, Sobek. Sit down."

He sat down gingerly on the left side of my bed, obviously afraid of hurting me. He looked from my face to the bulge of the blanket over the cage, and back again.

"How are you, sir?"

"Not too bad, thanks."

That was a lie. My knee was dreadfully painful and it was a huge effort not to show it.

Karl sat in the trench for twelve hours with a broken leg, and didn't complain once. I didn't realise until now just how tough he was.

"I saw him going for you," Sobek said, "but by the time I got there you were already on fire. I went for him all the same."

"Did you get him?" My voice sounded strained.

"No, he got away."

"Was that why he broke off?"

"Yes."

"Thank you."

"I was so relieved when I saw your parachute open," he continued. "And then we heard you'd been brought here."

"Who's in charge now?"

"I'm acting."

"Good." I was starting to feel sick again, and I could hardly think. "Have you got pencil and paper?"

"I've got a small notebook," he said. "I carry it in case I get ideas for stories and so on."

"I didn't know you wrote."

I put my left foot flat on the bed and rested the notebook on my thigh. I wrote that Sobek had come to my aid, forcing the English pilot to break off his attack and enabling me to bale out of my burning aircraft, and I recommended him for command of the Jasta. My writing was spidery, but I hoped it would be legible. I signed it and handed it back to him.

"You write in the address and the date," I said.

He read what I'd written and blushed. "Thank you, sir."

"Don't mention it. I hope you get it."

And I wish you'd leave. This is getting too much for me.

"I'd better go," he said. "Oh, I almost forgot – Fellmann said to ask what you want us to do with your mail. There's rather a lot of it."

"Oh, just open it all – I only want the personal letters."

And no one's going to write anything that I want kept private, not now... Grief ambushed me again, and I had to fight for self-control.

"Thank you for coming – and break a leg," I managed to say.

He hesitated, then wished me a good recovery and left.

Thank God he's gone. I feel fucking awful. The dizziness and nausea were almost as bad as when I'd been lying outside, waiting to be treated.

I'm bleeding, I thought, and tried to feel if the bandages were wet. I couldn't reach. I raised myself with difficulty on my left elbow, and slid my right hand under the cage, down my thigh.

The bandages were higher up than I'd expected – and then there was nothing. *No. Please, God, no. There can't be nothing there.*

My hand felt cautiously, unbelievingly, over the bandaged stump of my right leg. My head reeled and I tried to scream, but the sound died in my throat. I fell back onto the bed.

I'll wake up in a moment. They can't have taken my leg off. My knee hurts. It can't not be there, it can't. How can it hurt when it's not there?

Cripple, said my brain. *Cripple. You'll be on crutches, and then they'll give you an artificial leg and it'll squeak, and in a few years' time no one will remember that you lost your leg in the war.*

No one's going to want you now. What girl wants a stump against her leg?

Karl would have wanted me. He wouldn't have minded – he'd just have made a joke about it and we'd both have laughed…

Sobek must have known. That's why he was so embarrassed, why he kept looking at the blanket, why he didn't know what to say when I said, 'Break a leg'. They'd told him, but they hadn't told me.

"Sister!"

"Yes – what is it?"

"My leg. You've taken my leg off."

"We had to. Your knee was – we couldn't do anything else."

"You didn't tell me."

"We were waiting until you were stronger."

"You should have told me!"

"Calm down."

"I want to see the doctor! Now!"

She came back with a tall, thin doctor.

"My leg. You've cut my leg off!"

"Your knee was smashed. It would have turned gangrenous. All we could do was amputate."

"You didn't tell me! You told my visitor, but not me!"

The doctor sighed. "You're not the only man here who's had his leg amputated. There are far worse cases than you. Now be quiet."

"*Don't tell me to shut up!*"

"Be quiet! You're disturbing everyone."

I raved and shouted, and he said something to the nurse. She went away, and when she came back I was still screaming and sobbing, half out of my mind, and two orderlies held me down so she could get the needle into my arm.

When I woke I thought it had all been a ghastly dream, but I felt under the cage again and knew it was reality.

I can't do this. And I made a real exhibition of myself. I should be ashamed...

Nehring was looking at me, with more sympathy than I felt I deserved.

"I've lost my foot," he said. "And my reaction was much the same as yours. Ullmann over there hasn't spoken since they took his arm off."

Ullmann was sitting up, staring at the foot of his bed, his face blank.

"Won't eat, either," Nehring went on. "Mind you, some fellows are more than happy to be out of it for good."

"Are you?"

He shrugged. "Haven't made up my mind yet. All I wanted was a nice Heimatschuss. The old thing about being careful what you wish for!"

The night was horrible. Sister Helga fetched the doctor, and they looked at my stump and I yelled as he examined it. By morning I had a high fever, and pain was boring up my leg.

There followed days and nights of fever, delirium and tearing, sickening pain, and the humiliation of being unable to endure it and begging, literally begging them for morphine, my voice plaintive, agonised.

Karl came and sat on my bed and held my hand, just as I'd held his the year before, but then I woke and remembered that he was dead and I cried. I held his bloodied body again and again, and Otto burned and I woke screaming. Skeletons danced round me, the men I'd killed stood laughing at me. Anton died by the light of the flare, I was with Kurt in the mud, Johnny fell blazing through the sky…

They put me on a stretcher and carried me outside, and loaded us into motor ambulances as fast as they could. I thought I heard someone say the English were coming.

The driver moved off as if the Devil had escaped from Hell. It was black night, and we lurched along the bad road and then hit a pothole with a hell of a crash, and we all screamed. They carried me into a room and put me down among countless other blanketed men on stretchers…

Slowly the pain and fever started to diminish and my mind began to clear, and I found I no longer cared about anything. I was completely numb.

The ward wasn't as crowded as the one in the field hospital, but all the beds were occupied. Each held the broken body of a once-young man. We were the debris of the war, shattered by it and thrown aside. I knew how the ward must smell, and I could hear the pain. I was aware of the pity of it but I was detached, as if I were watching from a distance. I was no longer capable of emotion.

Even my grief for Karl was blunted into black hopelessness.

Life went on from day to day, in an endless round of meals and dressings and bedpans, and nights that were either sleepless or full of bad dreams. My stump oozed blood and streamed with pus, and the crêpe-paper bandages disintegrated in no time. They washed the stump with antiseptic each time they changed the dressings, and each time I tried in vain not to cry out.

I passed the point where I could take no more. I thought of Karl, in Brandenburg after he'd left hospital, remembered the look in his eyes, and I understood.

The food wasn't bad, but I'd lost interest in eating. The nurses scolded me and I didn't care. What was the point in living? And I was frightened of needing a bedpan, because it meant someone handling what remained of my right leg, and I had become very afraid of being hurt.

My knee still hurt. Some days it hurt worse than the stump. It annoyed the hell out of me. How can something hurt which isn't even there? It mocked me, and I hated it.

I got a letter from Paul Fellmann. He asked after my health, and went on, 'I've got a couple of letters for you, from Alfred Friedemann and your family. I brought them to the field hospital but you were pretty well out of it, so I've got them here. Let me know if you'd like me to send them to you.'

The rest of it was squadron news, and I hadn't the energy or the desire to read it.

When Assistant Doctor Heuberger came on his rounds, I asked him how much longer I was likely to be there.

"Good question. I'll have to ask Staff Doctor Boldt. Getting homesick?"

"Just wondering whether people should write to me here."

"They could do. We can always send the letters on."

Or lose them – but they shouldn't take long to get here.

I wrote back, asking Paul to send the letters to me. The package arrived a couple of days later, accompanied by a rather touching letter from him.

'I'm so glad to have a letter from you. I was really worried last time I visited you, and I hope you're improving now.'

That's nice of him. It hadn't occurred to me that anyone at the Jasta would be concerned about me – it was usually out of sight, out of mind – but then he had more time to think than the others.

Alfred said he was back at Döberitz, healed up, but not fit for the front line yet.

Don't push it, Alfred. Just do what they say. I'd like to have one old friend left – and you've done more than enough.

'I'm so sorry about Karl,' he continued. 'You must be feeling dreadful. I saw it in the paper, with a photograph of the funeral.'

'Now thank we all our God...' The ward disappeared, and I was standing beside Karl's grave. Black misery swung in.
"Sir. *Sir.*"
Go away. Don't interrupt.
"Sir, it's lunchtime," said Hoffmann. "Nice stew – chef's finest."
"I don't want anything."
"Doctor's orders!" Hoffmann insisted cheerfully. He looked at me sympathetically. "Bad news?"
"No."
I'm being unkind, and he's always so kind to me. All the orderlies are. Some of the nurses are another matter, and as for the doctors – but the orderlies are good blokes. And they take a good firm grip and don't drop you, not like that Sister Agatha. That fucking hurt.

"Let's get you sat up a bit, sir," he said. "And please try to eat or I'll be in trouble."

"All right."

I forced some of it down, and went back to Alfred's letter.

'This is really rather pointless now, but it sounds as if Karl had a heart problem. It wouldn't be surprising – the passage of the bullet through the chest cavity, severe loss of blood, infection so near the heart – all those things would impose quite a strain and could cause permanent damage.'

Full marks, Alfred. Go to the top of the class. Some time I'll have to tell you the whole story, but I can't face it now.

All I wanted was to be with Karl. Nothing mattered. Part of me had been buried with him, and I had no desire to go on.

Hoffmann chided me gently for not eating much, and Staff Doctor Boldt gave me a real rocket, but they were wasting their breath.

"Aren't you going to read your letters?" asked Sister Hedwig later, and I realised I'd forgotten the ones from my family.

Schutte had cabled them personally, bless him, and told them I'd been shot down and wounded, but was expected to make a good recovery. I had to smile – I'd written that more times than I could remember. And Sobek had written to tell them about my leg.

They didn't know what to say about that, but their relief was clear.

'Thank God you're safe,' Mama wrote.

I almost laughed at that. Every other day someone was taken out of my ward to the dying room – some of them had been doing well until infection or gangrene took hold.

They were 'sorry' about Karl, and Papa made some stupid remark about how smart I'd looked at the funeral. *What you really mean is that he won't be a bad influence any more.*

Johanna will want all the details about my leg – but she wrote with real sympathy about Karl.

'Franz, I'm so very sorry – he was such a good friend and you must miss him so much.'

They wanted to come and see me. *Shit – I'll have to put a stop to that idea. But the letter's already over a week old. They might already be on their way.*

I'll have to stop them. I can't face them, not now.

Assistant Doctor Schilke had come to look at one of the others who was deteriorating badly, and as he passed me on his way out I called out to him.

There was definite apprehension in his face as he turned to me. "Becker – not feeling bad, I hope?"

"No, no – is it possible to get a cable to my parents, to tell them not to come here?"

His face cleared. "Yes. But won't a letter do?"

"They wrote over a week ago – I've only just got it."

"They'd have to get passes," he said, "and that takes a while, so we should be in time. I wouldn't want my parents to see me in here, either. I'll send one of the orderlies and you can dictate it to him."

"Thanks."

The telegram sounded horribly curt.

"Why not put 'on train soon'?" Menz suggested. "And 'letter follows'."

"Because then I'll have to write a blasted letter."

He looked at me. "You're lucky they care."

That took me aback – not just his words, but his matter-of-fact tone. It hadn't occurred to me that some parents didn't care.

"We can write it together," he added. "I'll take this to the office and come back."

"Won't they worry if it's dictated?"

He smiled. "You just say it's awkward to write lying down, so it might be hard to read. You can always put a paragraph at the end to prove the point – though if your writing's really bad, that just worries them more."

We got the letter written. Half of it was his words rather than mine, but he was good at putting a nice sentence together, and it saved me having to think.

"You write very well," I said.

"Thanks – I am a writer, by profession. Don't believe in killing people, so I volunteered for this instead."

"Oh."

I've never met anyone who said that before. What must you think of us?

I had to ask him.

That's a pointless question, Franz – you really think he's going to tell you?

He smiled. "It's not my business – it's between you and your conscience, isn't it? I'll get this posted."

Thank God that's done with. I sank back into apathy. I was so weak, and everything was such a bloody effort. *If I hadn't had a parachute I'd be dead – and maybe that would be better. It wouldn't hurt and I wouldn't miss Karl. We might even be together somewhere.*

The sudden longing for his voice and his touch was too much, and I curled up and pulled the blanket over my head, so no one would see me crying.

The orderly's words came back to me later. *Between you and your conscience...* The one thing a soldier can't afford to have, until he stops.

I'm paying for what I did – but what if everyone thought like

Menz? No one would fight for anything he believed in. Rubbish world that would be.

There was no point thinking about it, and I lay staring listlessly across the ward.

One day they took a lot of us to the station, where we lay on the platform for hours waiting for the hospital train. I was going home, and I couldn't have cared less.

The orderlies had to lift me from the stretcher into the bunk in the train. They were very careful with my leg, but I was having a bad day and it hurt like fire.

The carriage filled up and the platform emptied, and eventually we started to move. The journey was very slow, and at times the Belgian landscape barely seemed to move.

I could get out and run faster than this.

Crap, Franz. Complete crap. You'll never run anywhere again.

After a couple of hours we stopped, and sat stationary for God knows how long.

"What's going on?" asked a fellow across the aisle.

There was a series of jolting crashes. Half the others screamed, and I gritted my teeth as my leg was jarred.

"We're being shunted," the man below me said.

More jarring crashes, more screams.

"Why?" asked the first voice.

"Because the trains to the Front have to go past. They're putting us in the sidings."

"Jesus fucking Christ," said the first man, his voice very strained. "Do they have to bang us about like that?"

"They did last time I came this way."

Let's hope it's a one-off, but I don't suppose it will be.

As if on cue, a doctor appeared.

"Gentlemen, that was the train being shunted. I realise it's not pleasant, but there's nothing we can do about it."

Bloody Army doctors…

My leg was throbbing, and when we moved off I felt every join in the rails – and, of course, we were shunted again.

I wish they'd left me in the hospital. This is truly horrible.

It got dark, and I stared at the lights in the carriage. I was feverish again, and they danced in front of my eyes.

Karl, I want Karl... I knew he was dead, or at the airfield, or somewhere, and that I was on the train, but I wanted him to sit by me and I heard myself calling his name, over and over.

A nurse was standing beside me and she laid her hand gently on my face, and I thought of the orderly doing the same to Karl, and I was almost crying in despair because he wasn't there.

She called the doctor over.

"You've got quite a high fever," he said. "It would be best to put you off at the next station."

No. I've had enough of fucking Belgium. Suddenly I wanted, desperately, to see my homeland, just once more.

"*No.* Germany – please – take me to Germany – *please—*"

"All right, all right. We'll take you home," he said. "I'm going to give you an injection—"

"No!" *You'll put me off the train while I'm asleep, I know you will.*

"I give you my word, we'll take you home," he said, "but you need to rest. You'll feel much better when you wake up."

As they turned away, the nurse said something to him. The only word I caught was 'dangerous'.

"Yes, I know," he said, "but I'll take the risk. He deserves to go home – they all do."

When I woke, we were passing through a town. *I wonder where we are? Probably Liège or somewhere – but at least I'm still on the train.*

We pulled slowly into a station and stopped, and I craned my neck as far as I could, looking for a sign.

Aachen. My throat tightened, and my eyes were suddenly damp.

Aachen. Germany.

The doctor came into the carriage with two orderlies, and pointed out two men who were to be offloaded.

"Ah – you're awake," he said to me. "How are you feeling?"

"Not too bad." I gestured at the station. "Thank you."

That was all I could say.

"Not at all… They don't want any more here, so you can stay on a bit longer."

I had to blink hard, because I was getting quite absurdly emotional. He squeezed my shoulder and left the carriage.

A troop train pulled up alongside. One of the soldiers glanced across, met my eyes and looked quickly away. I stared at them, and suddenly it was '14 again, and I was looking from the outside at the train in which we all sat laughing and singing, on our way to war and adventure.

Nearly all the men in that train are dead, and their replacements, and theirs… How many millions have died?

All four of my friends remain in the war, for ever. I could hear our strong young voices ringing out, and my tears ran into the pillow.

Karl, oh, God, Karl – how am I going to go on?

Some time later I fell asleep, or passed out, and I woke up in a comfortable bed, in a private room. The sun came in through a chink in the curtains, and the room was silent. No one groaned, or called for the nurse. I closed my eyes again, weary beyond words.

I was woken by a nurse bringing breakfast. She looked rather lovely. *Perhaps I'm starting to get better.*

"I haven't been asleep since yesterday, have I?"

She smiled. "Yes, you have. It's probably done you a lot of good. Would you like to read the paper?"

"Yes, please."

I looked at the date with disbelief. It was 15th August. *Karl was killed on 11th July, and I was shot down three days later. It's over a month ago.*

I leafed idly through the paper, unable to concentrate. *I don't know why I'm bothering to look at this. It's all rubbish.*

Then a headline caught my eye.

'Germany's highest-scoring living ace!' it read. Beneath it was a photograph of Oberleutnant Erich Löwenhardt, forty-eight victories. I'd been overtaken, which was hardly surprising.

I was still fifth overall, but that wouldn't last much longer. Leutnant Ernst Udet had forty victories, only three behind me, and there were two pilots with thirty-nine each. I lay back against the pillows, and for the first time I was truly glad to be out of it.

My war is over. I will never have to fight again. They can carry on and shoot down as many aeroplanes as they like, and I shall lie here and relax, a much-decorated, wounded hero, permanently hors de combat.

The feeling didn't last long. Having a room to myself was quiet and peaceful at first, but after a few days I felt lonely, and the solitude became very depressing. All I could think about was the war. I might be out of it, but I couldn't relax and enjoy my freedom, because I had none.

I still belonged to the war. It went round and round in my head, the same images repeating themselves endlessly, like a film with only one reel shown over and over. Karl was dead, my friends were dead, and I was crippled. Most of the time I lay staring blankly across the room, haunted by the ghosts. Sometimes I even saw them.

The nurses brought me books and the papers, but I couldn't concentrate long enough for anything to make much sense. I read that our armies were retreating. It was dressed up, of course, but I knew what it meant.

We're losing. They all died for nothing.

Every night the war took full possession of me. Some nights I put the light back on, because it seemed to keep the demons away when I was too frightened to sleep. On really bad nights the men I'd killed surrounded me, rotting and stinking, and closed in further and further until I woke screaming, the stench choking me. And then all I wanted was Karl's arms round me, and his voice in my ear…

I still couldn't eat much – not that there was much to eat. All the staff were as thin as rails, and the reason was obvious.

Sister Erika came to take my lunch tray. "You haven't finished," she said.

"I'm not hungry."

"You're not doing yourself any good, you know." She sighed. "You've got visitors, so let's make you a bit more presentable."

'Don't look at him now,' Fellmann said. 'Wait till Braun's made him presentable.'

Karl's in that box, just two metres behind me. Oh, my love, my love – why didn't I realise I love you?

'You know now, Franz,' he said softly, 'and that's all that matters.'

"Oberleutnant Becker," Sister Erika said firmly. "That's the third time I've called you."

"Sorry – I was miles away."

"Try to look a bit more cheerful," she said.

"I could do with a shave. I must look like a tramp."

"You shaved this morning."

"Did I?"

I ran a hand over my face. She was right, but I couldn't remember – there was just something about Geschke…

"Can I get out of bed?"

"Not yet. Let's get you into this."

'This' was a blue and white striped jacket, part of the standard hospital clothing which I'd seen on some of the better cases in the base hospital.

She held a mirror for me to comb my hair, which was in dire need of cutting. I tried not to look at my face – it was gaunt and lined and pallid, and the hurt and despair in my eyes were all too apparent.

Not looking good for twenty-three. Karl will always be twenty-three. For one stupid moment, I thought he'd come to see me.

It was my parents and Johanna. They came into the room and stopped dead, their smiles fading abruptly. Then they plastered them back onto their faces, which was even worse.

I tried to smile, but I seemed to have forgotten how.

Karl sat on my bed and put his arm round my shoulders. 'I'm here, Franz – you'll never be alone. Be kind to them.'

"Hello, Mama, Papa, Johanna – thanks for coming."

"How could we do anything else?" Papa said.

Mama started crying, and then she sat on my bed and held me as if she would never let me go. "Oh, Franz – I've been worried sick!"

"No need, was there?" I said, as gently as I could. "I'm alive, and I won't be going back."

"How are you?" Johanna asked. "Is it healing all right?"

"So they say."

"You didn't want us to come to Belgium," Papa said, rather reproachfully.

And see that hospital full of human wreckage?

"This is much nicer," I said.

Mama took hold of my shoulders. "You're so thin."

So are all of you. I nearly said it.

"So what happened?" asked Johanna.

"Got shot down."

"Yes, but how?" Papa asked. "You're so experienced."

How in God's name can I explain? There must be words... But I was so ruined, in both mind and body, and so tired, and there was such a chasm between my world and theirs.

I shrugged. "Got it wrong – everyone does in the end."

"Are they looking after you properly?" Mama asked.

"Yes, fine."

"Can we bring you anything?" asked Papa.

"No." I remembered my manners. "Thanks."

"We had such a kind letter from Leutnant Fellmann," Mama said. "He sounds like such a nice young man."

"Yes, he is."

Make more effort, Franz, for fuck's sake – but I hadn't the energy.

"Knows a lot about aeroplanes," I managed to add.

"And Leutnant Sobek wrote as well, and sent your things," Mama went on. "Do you want us to unpack them?"

Unpack – no! You'll read Karl's letters and probably burn the erotica he left me – and those things are all I have left of him.

"No. Thanks. Just put the bags in my room." It came out very abrupt, but it was all I could say.

My parents looked at each other. They seemed to be upset, or fed up, or something.

"Franz, we've made quite an effort to get here," Papa said. "It's two changes of train and a long wait."

"I said thanks for coming."

"You've said almost nothing," he went on.

"When will you be coming home?" Mama cut him off.

Home? I can't get out of fucking bed, not even for a crap.

"I don't know."

Please go. This is too much – I'm exhausted.

Johanna gave our parents a stern look, which rather surprised me.

"You must be getting tired," she said to me. Then she put her hand on mine. "I'll write to you."

She turned to them. "I think Franz needs to rest," she said, with some authority in her voice.

Good for you, Sis. Where did you get that?

"We'll come again next week," Mama said.

"You don't... why not wait—"

"That's a very good idea," said Johanna. "We'll come again in a couple of weeks, when you're a bit stronger, so we don't wear you out."

"Thanks."

They wished me a good recovery, and hugged me.

As they turned to leave, I said, "Sis – would you stay a moment?"

"Of course."

She closed the door behind them, and came and sat on my bed.

"They didn't mean to wear you out," she said. "I said we shouldn't come yet, to wait until you asked us to, but they wouldn't listen."

"I know. Can you tell them... oh, find some words. I can't."

"Yes, I will. Don't worry about us – just get well."

What for? I almost said.

She ruffled my hair and kissed my cheek, and the tenderness of the gestures was almost too much.

"Door open or closed?"

"Open. Thanks, Sis."

Thank God that's over. Why can't they just be glad I'm alive, and not expect me to talk, and be as I was? Jesus, I can't even remember how I used to be.

They should just be glad I'm alive – they're better off than millions of families in Europe. Oh, God, poor Elisabeth! She must have my letter by now, and Karl's death must have been all over the English papers. I didn't want to think about her, didn't want to imagine what it must be like to lose your entire family.

Later, Sister Ursula came to change my dressing. She was the one I'd thought pretty, and she had lovely clear hazel eyes. I liked her, because she had a very professional manner and because she hurt me less than the others did. The dressings were still very painful, and I still didn't look. I didn't want to see it.

"Are you sleeping better now?" she asked, as she started to remove the bandages.

"A bit."

"You were calling Karl again last night."

"He's dead." I was sweating and my voice was very tight.

"Who was he?"

"My friend."

That felt like a pathetic lie, but it was all I could say. I certainly couldn't tell her the truth.

"I'm sorry… You're doing very well now. You should be able to get up soon. There's a day room downstairs. It would be good for you to meet some of the others."

I wasn't sure if I wanted to meet anyone, but at least they'd be mutilated like me. I was afraid of the outside world, of people staring at me. I was scared of girls. I didn't know how they'd react to me, but I could guess.

What was it Karl said?

'I can't stand the thought of girls feeling sorry for me.' His voice was as clear as if he'd been in the room, and I almost jumped.

And then there's the other thing he said: that girls only want healthy men.

"Sister, can I ask you something?"

"Of course."

"If you'd had, well, a friend – and he'd come home like… like this – would you still have wanted him?"

Her eyes filled with tears and she turned away. *Oh, Christ, I've really put my foot in it.* After a moment she turned back, her eyes brilliant.

"I would have been happy to have my fiancé back in any condition," she said quietly.

"I'm sorry. I didn't think."

"Are you worried about your girlfriend?"

"No, I don't have one. It was more whether… well, how the future might be."

I can't imagine loving anyone else ever again – but it would be nice to have a girlfriend to go to bed with. The thought of only fucking tarts for the rest of my life was too depressing.

She looked at me. "Anyone who's worth your time and trouble should be able to see you for yourself. Losing a leg doesn't change who you are."

I wasn't sure she was right. It had changed the way I thought of myself – and even if she was right, the war had altered my mind.

What girl would want someone who has nights like mine, who sees the dead and thinks they talk to him?

A couple of weeks later, I was allowed to get out of bed for a few hours during the day. I sat in a wheelchair by the window, wearing a striped suit and a dressing gown, and wrapped in a blanket like an old man.

I tried to read but I couldn't concentrate, so I sat and watched the people in the street. They walked purposefully about their business: old men and children, and women, some of them young and pretty.

The girls must like dancing. Once, I could dance. I remembered dancing with Maria, the feel of her in my arms and her beautiful blue eyes looking up at me, remembered making love to her in the afternoon in the hotel, the sunlight in her auburn hair, on her pale, clear skin.

I've got bugger all chance of that happening again. No woman's going to want to look at my pale, lined face, let alone go to bed with me. Not when there are healthy men.

Karl would understand, without either of us saying a word. I wanted, so much, to be with him, sitting together by the fire in the library. *It would be so peaceful, and I wouldn't have to be afraid of what he would think of me. And then we could go up to bed and my stump wouldn't matter.*

The papers said the Allies were advancing in the South, not in Flanders. I was relieved. I didn't want the shells to dig him up and scatter his bones.

That's stupid. He's safe. Nothing can hurt him now – but it was important to me that he should be left in peace.

I got another letter from Alfred, who was back at the Front. *That'll be the end of you, maybe has been already. God alone knows how you've lasted this long.*

'Dear Franz,

Sorry this has taken me a while to write, but I'm up to my eyeballs again. I got out of sodding Döberitz and am back in business against the Frenchies. I read in the paper that you'd been shot down and I hope you're recovering well. The newspaper reports didn't give any details about your injuries, so I hope they're not bad.

I hope you got my letter about Karl. I'm so sorry, Franz – he was really special, one in a million, and I was really looking forward to seeing him again after the war. You have my sincere sympathy – you must miss him a great deal.'

You're not wrong there, Alfred.

I couldn't remember whether I'd answered his previous letter or not. *I'd better write back now, tell him the full story about Karl's death.*

Framing the words in my mind wasn't too bad, but when I saw them in black and white on the paper, tears ran down my face and wouldn't stop.

Bloody weak bastard. Fucking cry-baby. Get a bloody grip, Franz…

That night Karl got into my bed and held me tight. His arms were strong, as they'd been before he was injured, and his voice and touch were so gentle… I fell asleep in his arms, my head on his shoulder.

I woke with a beautifully hard cock.

"Come here, you."

I reached out for him – and reality killed desire instantly.

He wasn't here. He's dead.

But at least I woke up with a stiffie – and that hasn't happened since I was shot down. I was starting to think it would never happen again. I must be getting better.

I turned over, onto a damp patch. *Shit – I've wet the bed!* Then I realised what it was. *That hasn't happened since I was shot down, either. Definitely improving.*

How embarrassing – but the nurses must see spunk stains all the time, and there are far worse things.

I had a vague memory of shitting myself in the field hospital, during the time when I was half conscious and tormented by pain and fever, and the orderly saying, 'Don't worry, sir – happens to everyone', as he cleaned me up. The incongruity of calling someone 'Herr Oberleutnant' as you wipe the shit off his backside struck me, even through the haze of semi-delirium.

'I blame the food, sir,' I'd heard him say later to a fellow sufferer. 'It's not much better than ours, and at least we can leg it to the bog!'

And never mind the poor bastards who'd been hit in the abdomen, and who leaked crap all the time. Or the fellows with gangrene who stank as if they were already dead.

Best not thought about.

Fortunately Sister Ursula came in with her lovely smile and a breakfast tray. I wasn't bothered about the food, but I was very pleased to have the distraction.

After lunch, Sister Angelika came in and said brightly, "You can go down to the day room today."

She was always far too bloody cheerful, and it annoyed the fuck out of me. It was like fingernails down a blackboard.

"I don't feel well enough." *I can't face them.*

"You can't sit up here feeling sorry for yourself."

"I'm not. I just don't feel well."

"Well, you've no choice in the matter. This room needs a good airing and it's not warm enough for you to be in here while we do it. We don't want you getting pneumonia."

Why the bloody hell not? I thought as she wheeled me down the corridor to the lift. *A good go of pneumonia would solve all my problems. Why, oh, God, why am I still alive, to drag out my life like this, crippled and useless? Is this my punishment for killing?*

The day room was on a corner of the building, on the ground floor. It was large and comfortably furnished, and sunlight streamed in through the windows. About a dozen men sat in wheelchairs or in the big armchairs, some in dressing gowns, others in uniform or hospital clothing. A small group was playing cards, and most of the others were reading, or chatting to each other.

They looked up as I was wheeled in, said, "Good day", and went back to what they were doing.

"Now, where would you like to sit?" said Sister Angelika cheerfully.

"Anywhere except in this bloody chair."

"No choice in that, I'm afraid. You're not strong enough for crutches yet!"

One of the men looked up from his newspaper and caught my eye, his eyes bright with suppressed laughter.

What's so bloody funny?

"By the window, then," I said, "next to the little table."

There was no one sitting at the table, and I wouldn't have to talk.

She parked me where I could see out, into the garden. The trees were tinged with autumn colour. *Four years ago, we were in the training camp. This time last year, Karl was in hospital, and I was flying.* I picked up a magazine and started leafing through it, but my attention kept wandering and I kept looking out of the window.

"May I join you?"

Oh, shit.

"Of course," I said, my tone ungracious.

"Nagel, Artillery." It was the man who'd caught my eye earlier, a thin fellow leaning on a stick.

"Becker, Air Service."

Nagel sat down carefully, and we shook hands. *You look just like me* – except that his left sleeve was pinned up, and his face was even more deeply lined than mine.

"You're surviving the attentions of our dear Sister Angelika," he said with a smile.

"It's that relentless bloody cheerfulness," I said. "It drives me mad."

"I know. It's frightful – especially at four in the morning. Just now, when she brought you in, I thought, *There's another poor fellow gritting his teeth.* Been here long?"

"Four weeks or so. You?"

"About the same. Where'd you get yours?"

"At about three thousand metres, somewhere near Ypres. You?"

"On the Marne. Well, not quite on the Marne. Some distance back, but that'll do as a description. We were moving the battery and the buggers shelled us. My arm was blown to shreds. I got splinters in my chest and hip as well. One of my chaps put a tourniquet on what was left of my arm, and they tell me he saved my life. So it's all over for me. And you?"

"Bullet in my right knee – or through it, I don't know which. The aircraft was on fire so I jumped – parachuted. You know how it is – they amputated."

Of course they amputated. I should have realised they would. I'd known that I was hit in the knee, that the joint must have been smashed, but my mind had convinced itself that everything would be all right.

"Yes, I do. Bastard, isn't it?"

Do I have to sit here and listen to your chatter? I picked up my magazine and tried to read, hoping he'd take the hint. He started reading as well, and after a while the silence felt almost companionable.

We're all in the same mess. It's almost like being at the Front again, but without anyone trying to kill us.

My attention drifted again and I gazed out of the window. A few clouds drifted past, the sky pale blue. *Westerly wind, good visibility. Good flying weather… but not for me. I'll never fly again, never leave the earth behind and rise into the sky. I'm shackled to the ground, for ever.*

Up there, the wind rushes round the wings, round my ears, and the ground far below is another world, distant and unreal, a world I can tilt and turn right over as I please. The sunlight glints on the wings and the wires, and a short distance away fly my comrades, close enough to see, but too distant to touch across the void that separates us…

It's over. There's no point thinking about it. I looked away from the sky, dragged my mind back to the hospital.

"Do they let us go out?" I asked Nagel.

"Yes, on warm days."

"It's hard to believe how long it's been going on… Are you a Regular?"

"No. War volunteer. More bloody fool me. What were you doing before the war?"

"I was at university. I volunteered. With my friends…" I couldn't finish the sentence.

"I was in Vienna. At the music academy."

I looked at him, at his empty sleeve. Singer or musician? I wanted to ask, but from the look in his eyes I had the feeling I knew the answer.

"My best friend was a pianist," I said. "He gave a couple of concerts when we were at university – played the Emperor Concerto. He was bloody good."

"Dead?"

"Yes. In July."

"I'm sorry."

I felt I should say something, but I had no idea what. *Music was so important to Karl, and it must be the same for Nagel.*

"It's all shit," I said.

"Isn't it."

My leg was becoming painful, and I shifted in the chair. *I wonder if I could go back to my room yet?*

"Is there a bell or something, to call the nurse?" I asked.

"Yes, I'll ring. You all right?"

"Leg's a bit uncomfortable, that's all."

He nodded in understanding and hobbled to the bell. A few minutes later, Sister Angelika came and took me back upstairs.

There was nothing to be scared of after all. They're all just like me.

X

I went to the day room every day after that, even if only for a short time. Some days sitting in my chair was almost unbearable – my stump started hurting, and my bones seemed to poke through my scrawny backside. Sister Ursula found me a pillow to sit on, which made it far more comfortable and saved me from spending too much time alone in my room.

The garden was quite large, and I longed for fresh air and the breeze on my face, but I wasn't allowed outside – too cold for my fragile health, apparently, which was hardly encouraging.

Jesus – I'm only twenty-three, and until a couple of months ago I was in the sky over the Front every day. And now I'm some sort of invalid.

Part of me knew they were right. I was still horribly weak. I'd thought it would be simple to get out of bed and into my wheelchair, but I couldn't do it without a lot of help. Balancing was ferociously difficult, and my muscles had wasted away. I was so thin I didn't want to look at myself. And I felt the cold terribly – my body seemed unable to heat itself, and the slightest draught had me shivering.

What a fucking wreck, I thought as Sister Ursula wrapped me up 'nice and warm'.

There was a large conservatory opening off the southern side of the day room. The glass magnified the heat of the sun beautifully, and on fine afternoons I lay in one of the reclining chairs, soaking in the warmth and remembering how we used to sunbathe on the airfield.

The summer's gone, and taken the last of my youth with it. I thought of Karl lying naked on the grass, and the kids staring at his scars... It was another age, vanished and irretrievable.

I became friendly with Nagel, and we often played cards with Wolffheim, Krug or Riege. Wolffheim was the only one of our little group who was ever likely to be fit for active service again and, what was more, the only one who wanted to be. He'd had both legs broken by a French shell, and had spent weeks in traction, but they said he was healing well. He reminded me of Alfred – he meant it when he said he wanted to go back. You can always tell.

Krug had a silver plate in his head, and his jaw had been wired back together. He wasn't quite right – sometimes he just wasn't with us, and would forget completely when it was his turn to play. Sometimes he stared across the room and muttered to himself, and now and then he got very agitated, and we had to ring for someone to take him back upstairs. It made him an uncomfortable companion, but the rest of us weren't that much better.

"Poor fellow," Nagel said one day, after Krug had been taken away.

That was the end of the card game, and we made our slow way to the window.

"Yes... Do I do that?" I asked.

"Do what?"

"Stare into space and talk to myself."

I was well aware that I often had to be reminded to play, and that people kept saying they'd been talking to me. It was just that the war intruded, so vividly that it was all I could see and hear.

Nagel gave me a very straight look. "I'll tell you honestly if you tell me."

I hesitated. *Maybe I'd prefer not to know...* "All right."

"Yes, you do stare into space, but no, you don't talk to yourself. Me?"

"Same."

"Thank God for that – I mean, you just can't tell, can you?"

"No."

Most of us existed in the same listless state, trying in vain to occupy ourselves. My concentration was so poor that I couldn't read an entire newspaper article. I would get to the end of a paragraph, and forget how it had begun and have to start again, and I hadn't the energy to persevere.

We were the lucky ones. In the rooms upstairs were men who were hideously disfigured, or paralysed, or who lay with sandbags stretching out their mangled limbs. We knew they were there, just as we knew about the mental wing, but we closed our minds to them.

Paul Fellmann wrote to me again.

'Things are getting quite tough here. Fuel is rationed now, so we tow the aircraft out to the take-off position and start the engines there, and then shut down straight after landing. Doing the spares order is almost pointless – we only get half the supplies we request, if that. There are no replacement tyres to be had, so we put wooden covers over the wheels for towing, to cut down the wear.'

Jesus. There's only one way this is heading.

'Sobek's doing the best job he can, but it's the first time we've had a CO with so little experience, and it shows. You were right to recommend him – we wouldn't have got anyone better – but the old days are truly gone.'

Paul was taking a bit of a chance writing all this – it could get him into real trouble.

We're finished. We're running out of men and materiel, and the time when we could have won the war is long past. And however much the papers dress up every backward movement as 'tactical withdrawal to a stronger position', they still mean 'retreating'. At this rate we'll soon be back to the German border.

I didn't even want to think about that – it was far too depressing.

If they do reach the border I'll fight, I thought with sudden resolve. *I can still fire a rifle.*

'I miss the old days more than I can say,' Paul went on, 'and think often of the comrades we've lost. I photograph all the new arrivals for the album, but the poor children don't last five minutes.'

We'll be running out of teenage boys next.
My poor country.

'Karl-Heinz (the fellow you called "the Moustache") fell last week. We'd become good friends in the short time I knew him, and… well, I'll leave you to fill that in.'

That's rotten luck after losing Johnny. Schutte was a right bastard sending the Moustache to the front line, just on his suspicion that they were up to 'Greek practices' – what harm were they doing, anyway?

I wonder what actually counts as being 'Greek' – do you have to fuck, or do Karl and I qualify? I'll write to Karl and ask him… The blade twisted in my heart again, and I closed my eyes. *Fuck. Fuck, fuck, fuck – why do I keep doing that? Why do I keep imagining he's still alive? I buried him, for fuck's sake.*

'I had a Comrade, a better one you won't find…' we sang, the band backing our voices.

That was the last thing I wanted to hear, but it went round and round in my head.

"Anyone else fancy some music?" I asked, wheeling myself over to the gramophone.

"Go ahead," said Fischer.

"As long as it's something cheerful," added Grünbeck.

I made sure it was.

Later I wrote to Paul with my condolences, knowing all too well how thin words are.

Grünbeck and Wiesbauer left us, the former to return to his regiment and the latter to make the long journey home to East Prussia. Most of him was going home, that is – he'd lost his left hand and eye.

We had a farewell party for them. Landauer, who was allowed out, managed to get a bottle of schnapps, and brought it back hidden in his coat pocket.

"You won't believe what the bastard charged me for it," he said, producing it with a triumphal flourish.

"Was the collection enough?" asked Wolffheim.

"Just about. I put in a couple of marks extra, but we won't worry about that."

"Bloody hell – that should have been loads," Nagel said.

"That's what I thought, but I had to get it under the counter."

"You'd have thought he'd have charged you less," said Hammer.

One side of Landauer's face was covered in a maze of fresh scars, and his left arm was in a sling. Being Landauer, it was a grey silk sling – even in uniform he was one of the most elegant men I'd ever seen.

"You are joking," he said. "He just wanted to screw as much money out of me as he could."

"Landauer looks too prosperous in that nice tailored uniform," said Fischer. "And as for that poncy sling! Maybe we should have sent someone in hospital clothing!"

"Yes," Riege agreed. "God knows how he managed in the trenches!"

"Oh, I was as filthy as everyone else, which is why I make a point of looking decent now," Landauer said. "And it wouldn't have made any difference – the bastard was only interested in his wallet."

Hammer looked at the bottle. "Is that going to be enough?" he asked doubtfully.

Nagel laughed. "Oh, most of us get pissed on a thimbleful these days."

"Speak for yourself!" Wolffheim retorted.

"How do you know, anyway?" asked Riege. "Where'd you get it?"

"I have my sources!" Nagel replied cheerfully.

"You didn't share it with us," Wolffheim said with mock reproach.

"Yes, he did," said Schieffer. "You weren't here. That was the day your wife came to see you."

"Ah, yes…"

"And I'll bet you didn't get out of bed all day, you lucky bastard! Or the day after!"

A slow smile spread itself across Wolffheim's face. "I'll leave everything to your fertile imaginations!"

"What I don't understand," said Nagel, "is why you're so keen to get back fighting when you've got such a lovely creature at home."

"Well, I've only ever wanted to be a soldier, ever since I was very small, and it's all I know how to do. I wouldn't know what to do with myself if I went home."

Schieffer grinned at him. "Oh yes you would!"

"For a few weeks, yes – but after that? I'd get bored."

"Each to his own," Riege said with a shrug. "Come on, let's get the party going. I'm thirsty!"

We shared the booze into cups and glasses, and wished Grünbeck luck and Wiesbauer a good recovery. It was a pleasant party, but very restrained compared to the ones we were all used to. The joke was that Wolffheim got half pissed on one finger of schnapps, while the rest of us were just nicely mellow.

Haven't had a drink since before I was shot down, I thought, wishing there were more.

"Shame the bottle's empty," said Riege. "I'm just getting into my stride."

"Told you it wasn't enough," said Hammer.

"Look," said Nagel, "if we get really pissed we'll all be confined to barracks—"

"Not that we give a shit," Krug interrupted.

"…and then there won't be another party till God knows when," Nagel finished.

There was a hell of a bang right outside the day room. We all jumped out of our skins. Riege and Landauer hit the floor. Krug dived under the nearest table, knocking it over, and then got behind it.

"Sound the alarm!" Fischer shouted.

Wiesbauer was on his feet, in the middle of the room. "All right, gentlemen," he said with calm authority. "It's all right. We're in Germany. We're safe."

Krug was shaking from head to foot, staring into space and muttering, and I was careful not to listen. My own hands were trembling, just as they had in my last days at the Jasta.

Riege sat up cautiously, and looked round. "Jesus. What the fuck was that?"

Nagel laughed nervously. "God knows. Could have done without it, though."

Doctor Holz came into the day room. "I do apologise, gentlemen – the laundry woman knocked the entire bin over."

"Tell the stupid bitch to be more careful!" Wolffheim burst out.

"Don't worry, I already have... Is everyone all – ah." He looked at Krug. "Oh, dear." He rang the bell and approached Krug slowly. "Leutnant Krug."

Krug's eyes were wild. "Sir – we – my company – forty men – the Frenchies—"

We all looked away. Nagel's eyes met mine, and I had the feeling we were both thinking, *When will that be me?*

Sister Angelika came in, accompanied by two burly orderlies. As they approached Krug, he picked up a chair and brandished it.

"Over here, boys! *The fucking Frenchies are here!*"

Holz gestured to the orderlies and they moved to the doorway, where Krug couldn't see them.

"Well done, Krug," said Holz. "That's seen them off. Now, you go to Battalion and make your report. I'll take over here."

Krug got to his feet at once. "Very good, sir."

"These two chaps will take you back," Holz said.

The orderlies stepped forward.

"Right," Krug said to them, "you'd better show me the way."

"We'll take this route, sir," said one of the orderlies. "It's safer."

The three of them left the room.

"We'd better make sure he gets to his room," Holz said to Sister Angelika, and they followed.

There was a long pause. None of us wanted to say anything. *I didn't need that.*

"Well, that's sobered me up," Grünbeck said.

"Poor bastard," said Riege.

"Could someone give me a hand up?" asked Landauer.

Grünbeck helped him to his feet. "Makes you think, doesn't it?"

Nagel laughed. "Frankly, I don't want to."

"You forget," Wiesbauer said slowly, "that we're only in hospital because someone tried to kill us, and failed."

"You know, I'd never thought of that," said Riege. "But you're right."

Yes, he is. You don't try to injure someone, not usually. You want him to go down and stay down.

"Everyone was jumpy as hell in the field hospital," said Hammer. "And it makes sense when you think of it like that."

"Yes," Nagel said slowly. "I noticed that as well."

I couldn't remember anything of the sort, but then my time in the field hospital was very hazy.

Doctor Holz came back half an hour later. "Are the rest of you all right?"

There was a subdued chorus of "Yes, thank you."

"How... er... how's Krug?" asked Landauer.

"We've managed to persuade him that he's gone into rest," Holz said with a sigh. "I'm hoping he'll be back with us after a good night's sleep."

It was two days before Krug came back into the day room, and then he told us some hair-raising story about the French getting into the trench, and having to counter-attack to throw them out again, and how his company had been down to forty men with him in command.

Oh dear, poor fellow. I could see the others thinking much the same. *He thinks it was real...*

"And that was last year, on the Chemin des Dames when the bastards attacked," he said. "And the other day, that loud bang sent me right back there."

We looked at him in surprise.

"I'm not as bonkers as you all think," he said quietly. "Just bonkers enough to really frighten myself."

"We're not much better," I said. "It all comes back to me as well."

"And me," said Nagel.

"I think," Landauer said softly, "that there comes a point when you've had too much, and the mind can't deal with it any more."

"Speak for yourself," said Wolffheim.

"Oh, I was… I'm sticking with it, though – I think everyone reaches that point in the end, but it's in different places for each of us."

There was a quiet murmur of agreement.

"Yes," said Riege. "I had a Sergeant – bloody good bloke, brave as a lion, until one day he broke down completely. Just sat in the trench shaking, couldn't move. Had to get him taken back."

"My best friend was at Verdun," I said, "and he told me that one fellow tore his uniform off, and ran about in No Man's Land stark naked and screaming, until a shell got him."

"You wonder if anyone who survives this will be really sane," said Schieffer.

"No one who was at Verdun is sane, not really," Riege said, and then added tactfully to me, "Well, maybe with the exception of your friend."

"No, he wasn't really," I said. "It left him pretty disturbed. He couldn't talk about it."

I could see Riege registering the past tense.

"I made a real idiot of myself," Krug said.

"No, you didn't," said Landauer. "Riege and I hit the floor as well, and Fischer shouted for the alarm to be sounded."

"Oh."

"You're among friends here," Landauer said, and put an arm round his shoulders. "Nobody minds."

"Thanks… that's one thing that really scares me, though – what happens when I leave? Everyone's going to think I'm crazy, and I'm really scared they'll lock me up."

"Don't worry about that," Nagel said. "It won't be as bad as you think – look, waiting to go in's always far worse than actually fighting, isn't it?"

A faint smile appeared on Krug's face. "That's for sure. Waiting lasts for ever, and you have to stop yourself thinking about all the things that could happen to you – but once you get going you're fine."

Unless it all goes horribly wrong, of course – but that's better left unsaid.

"And this will be the same," Nagel said. "Nothing like as bad as you imagine."

Everyone had the sense to keep his mouth shut. We could all see that Nagel was trying to convince himself as much as Krug.

"Like stage fright, really, isn't it?" Krug said.

Nagel gave a very sad smile. "You know, I really used to suffer from that before the war – used to actually shake before every performance – and now I wonder why. Even if you get all the notes wrong, you don't get taken out and shot… You'll be fine. Don't worry."

I hope you're right, because I'm worried about how I'm going to cope as well. I looked round the room, and saw the same thought in the others' eyes. Nearly all of us had obvious injuries, and we were all afraid of how people would react to us.

Maybe that's one reason Wolffheim wants to go back to the Front – so he doesn't have to deal with civilians.

Just how difficult that was going to be was brought home to me a week or so later, when my family came to see me again.

They arrived a bit after eleven. I was in the day room, and Sister Frieda showed them in.

"Hello, Mama, Papa, Johanna."

"Hello, Franz," said Papa. "How are you?"

"It's good to see you up and about," Mama said, as she bent down and embraced me.

"Getting better, they tell me."

I noticed their eyes wandering round the room, noticed too the hungry way my fellow patients were looking at Johanna.

Yes, she is lovely – but she's my sister, so keep your dirty thoughts locked up.

My parents were obviously uncomfortable, and it took me a moment to realise why. I was so used to the others' mutilations that I hadn't thought how they would look to outsiders.

Best get the parents out of here, before anyone gets upset.

Johanna was looking at Landauer with frank interest.

He smiled. "Becker, aren't you going to introduce us all?"

Wind your bloody neck in. It's your injuries she's interested in, not you, if I know her.

"Yes, of course."

Two seconds after he'd bowed over her hand, Johanna said, "May I ask what happened to you?"

"Sis, leave the poor fellow alone!" I turned to Landauer. "Do excuse her – she wants to be a surgeon."

"I've been accepted by Professor Goldfarb as soon as the war's over," she said.

"Oh – in Berlin?" Landauer asked.

"Yes, that's right."

"He's a friend of my uncle. Really nice fellow. Look, once you start your studies you must come and have lunch with us – with my family, that is."

She gave him the most beautiful smile, and I saw his eyes light helplessly.

"Thank you," she said.

"Johanna," said Papa, rather severely, "we've come to see Franz, not to further your career."

"Sorry."

"We've brought you some clothes," Mama said to me. "Would you like to get dressed, and we'll take you out for lunch?"

Lunch? That'll cost a fortune, and anyway— "I'm not allowed out yet."

"Oh. But it's such a lovely day."

It was the most beautiful crisp autumn day, but it had started with a frost which still lingered in the shadows.

"It's too cold for me," I explained reluctantly.

"Even if you wrap up nice and warm?" Papa asked.

That bloody phrase again.

"Why don't we go into the conservatory?" I said.

I managed to wheel myself most of the way there, which was an improvement. Johanna noticed I was tiring, and took over – and suddenly I was reminded of pushing Stefan Reddemann, back when I'd had two legs and been strong…

Karl was strong before he got that bullet through his chest, and now—

And now he's dead. Get a grip, for fuck's sake.

There were only a couple of fellows in the conservatory, and we sat at the table at the other end.

"This is very pleasant," Mama said.

"Yes – lovely and warm in the afternoon," I replied.

There was an awkward pause.

"Look what we've brought," Mama said, opening the suitcase Papa had been carrying. "I hope it all fits."

It won't. Can't you see how thin I am?

Then I saw the worry in her eyes, and realised that she could.

They'd brought underpants, socks, trousers, a couple of shirts and sweaters, a warm jacket – and a left shoe. I looked at it and suddenly I had to fight for self-control.

That fucking shoe just sums it up.

"Would you like to get dressed?" Mama said.

"No. Thanks."

It's far too much effort. We'd have to go upstairs, and you've no idea how much help I need…

"I dressed you when you were a little boy," Mama said. "I'm sure I can manage now."

"I'm a bit bigger and heavier," I said.

"Franz *is* dressed," said Johanna at the same time.

My parents looked at my blue and white striped suit, and the checked blanket over my knees – knee, that is.

"It's the latest fashion," I said, trying to smile.

"He can wear these tomorrow," Johanna said firmly. "How's your stump?"

"Healing, I suppose. Haven't seen it."

She looked at me. "No – I don't suppose you want to."

There was a long pause while I tried to think of something to say. My knee was hurting ferociously. *Bloody thing.*

"And how are you in yourself?" Mama asked.

I couldn't begin to answer that. I waved a hand at the day room. "Like everyone else." As I spoke I realised how curt it sounded, but I had no way of explaining.

You live in a different world, one where violence and death and serious injury are rare and unfortunate. Papa had once defended a man accused of murdering his wife. I had no idea how many men I'd killed, how many I'd seen die. My entire youth had been spent in murder.

"Franz, we've made a big effort to come and see you," Papa said. "You could make more effort yourself."

I'm making a fucking full-power effort. Can't you hear it?

Johanna looked at me and rolled her eyes.

"How long are you going to have to stay here?" asked Mama.

"I don't know."

"Would they move you nearer home? It would be so much more convenient."

Move me? Another bloody horrible train journey, being jolted over the rails? The thought had me sweating. *And I'm used to the fellows here. If they move me I'll have to start all over again with strangers.*

"I don't want to be moved." I was starting to feel very tired.

"What time do you have lunch?" Johanna asked.

"Twelve... 12:30 – I don't really know."

Papa looked at me in disbelief. "What do you mean, you don't know?"

"I don't have a watch."

And it doesn't matter, anyway. They feed us when they feed us. This is getting really wearing. I just want to be left alone now. I wish my fucking knee would shut up. It doesn't fucking exist...

Johanna looked at her watch. "It's almost lunchtime, then," she said, with that authority in her voice again. "Why don't we go and get something to eat, and come back for a short time after Franz has had his? We can ask the staff what the schedule is."

"That's a good idea, Sis," I said with relief.

"Why don't you go and find out?" she said to our parents.

To my astonishment, they got up and left.

"How did you do that?" I asked her, impressed.

She took hold of my hand. "For the first time ever, I know more than they do. I've read everything I can find about amputations and so on, and I've been explaining it to them – in layman's language, that is. At long last they've realised I've got a brain, and they've really accepted that I'm going to medical school."

"Sis, I'm so pleased for you." And I was, genuinely so.

"I've also been trying to explain about – please don't be cross..."

"About what?"

"About – about what the war's done to some men's minds."

"Oh. You mean we're all bonkers."

"Not all of you, stupid – but I'm trying to make them understand that it changes men, that it's going to be a big readjustment, going back to a normal life – whatever that is. One where you don't have to fight, anyway. There's some fascinating literature about it."

I gave a short laugh. "Maybe you can explain it all to me."

She smiled and kissed my cheek. "See you later – do you want to go back in?"

"No, thanks. They'll fetch me from here."

Fortunately, the visit after lunch was a short one.

Papa was fuming. "How that wretched man could charge us that much for whatever that stew was! Never mind the 'wine.'"

"At least we've got money," Johanna said. "We're not starving."

"All the same – it's a disgrace."

"Josef, I'm sure Franz doesn't want to hear about it," Mama said. She turned to me. "I hope they feed you better."

"They do their best."

"What did you have for lunch?" she asked.

"Can't remember. Have you got any cigarettes?"

"You can't remember?" Papa looked at me with concern. "But it's only half an hour ago."

It was just food, and Krug went a bit funny again and we thought he was going to have a full-blown attack, but then he calmed down.

"Papa, give Franz some cigarettes, for Heaven's sake," said Johanna.

He lit one for me and I almost choked. It was absolutely vile.

"What's in this?"

He pulled a face. "I've run out of those English ones you sent home... I suppose you did all right at the Front?"

Did all right at the – what the fuck do you think...?

"Oh, yes, we *did all right.*"

He flushed, and I could see him realising he'd put his foot right in it.

"I didn't mean it like that," he said. "You fellows deserve the best of everything."

"Paul Fellmann – our technical officer – could get us most things," I said, in as light a tone as I could manage.

Papa didn't know what to say, and I almost felt sorry for him.

"Is that the Leutnant Fellmann who wrote to us?" Mama asked.

"Yes, that's him."

'Fellow's a bloody Greek,' said Schutte. 'Had to send the other fellow away.'

Karl came and sat on the spare chair at the table.

Does what we do count as Greek? I asked him.

He smiled. 'Oh, most definitely! No hope for either of us!'

"Franz. *Franz*." Papa was looking at me with concern, mixed with irritation.

"What?"

Why's my father here? Where's Karl gone? And Schutte – I'm sure he was here.

"You were staring into space. We've been talking to you."

Oh, shit. "What did I say?"

"Nothing," he said. "You just stared straight through us."

"Sorry – I just wandered off a bit. We all do it."

Johanna looked at me thoughtfully, and I could almost see her running through a mental list of symptoms. She turned to our parents.

"Franz needs to rest," she said. "We're tiring him out."

Thanks, Sis. I wish you could come by yourself, but I don't suppose they'd let you.

"Yes, of course," Mama said gently. She held my hand tightly. "Please forgive us if we say the wrong thing. We can't imagine what you've been through."

"It's all right, Mama. Sorry if I'm a bit…" I didn't know how to describe it.

"No need," Papa said, quite unexpectedly. "Everyone talks about heroes, but – well, there's a price for everything, isn't there?"

Bloody hell. What has Johanna been saying to you?

"I suppose there is," I said.

They stood up, and I envied them being able to do that.

"Shall we leave you here?" Mama asked.

"No – er, Sis, can you push me to the lavatory?"

"Yes, of course."

"It's on the way to the front door."

"Do you need help?" asked Papa.

"No, thanks – one of the orderlies will do it."

"Are you sure?"

"Yes – I don't want you to put your back out."

We said goodbye, somewhat incongruously, at the loo door.

"Shall we leave it a couple of weeks?" Papa asked.

"Yes, do."

My parents embraced me, and Johanna ruffled my hair and kissed my cheek again.

"Thanks, Sis," I muttered into her ear, and she gave me one of her stunning smiles.

Bloody hell, Sis – you'll be bending men round your little finger.

"Wow, who's the dish?" Fischer asked when I went back into the day room.

"Who do you mean?" I had to tease him a bit.

"That lovely girl who gave you a kiss and a five-kilowatt smile."

"You know, Fischer, if you hadn't told me you were in the Pioneers I'd just have guessed. Five kilowatts!"

"If you'd had to wire an entire trench system for light and telephones instead of throwing some crate about the sky, you'd know what I'm talking about!"

"Hard luck," Wolffheim said. "She's his sister."

"Hey, that's even better!" said Fischer. "I thought she was his squeeze – now I'm in with a chance!"

"Except that Landauer's already asked her to lunch," Nagel said.

"He what? Christ, he's quick on the draw."

"Don't worry," said Wolffheim. "It was for some time 'after the war' and we'll all be dead by then."

"You might be," Hammer said, "but most of us won't be fighting again."

"That's right," said Riege. "No more war for me! Only compensation for being smashed up."

"Where's your fighting spirit, man?" Wolffheim demanded.

Riege pretended to think. "Probably in the mud at the Somme…"

Johanna was right about tiring me out. I was far too tired to listen to them, and I got Sister Ursula to help me onto one of the day beds in the conservatory, where I fell asleep in the warm sunshine.

"How did it go with your family?" Nagel asked me later.

I thought for a moment. "Mostly pretty hard work – but they are trying to understand, I'll give them that."

"Mine feel sorry for me. I can't stand it. Sympathy's the one thing I can't deal with. I manage by giving myself a bloody good kick in the arse several times a day, and then they're nice to me and it undoes half my good work."

He picked up an illustrated magazine, leafed through it, and folded it back on itself. "I've been meaning to ask you for a while," he said. "Is this you?"

He handed me the magazine. There was a studio portrait of a confident young man with the Pour le Mérite and a row of ribbons. 'Oberleutnant Franz Becker, wounded on 14th July,' it said underneath.

"Yes."

How did I manage to look so confident, when my nerves were already beginning to go? That was taken in January, during the aircraft trials, just after I'd left Karl's house.

I thought of the face I saw in the mirror now. *Nine months. Nine months ago I was still young.*

I opened the magazine out. On the facing page was a portrait of Karl, the same as the one I'd bought. His clear eyes gazed calmly at me – *the last time I saw your eyes was to close them. The last time I saw your face was as Braun closed the coffin.* Everything inside me was ripped out again, and I felt myself falling into the void.

My eyes filled with tears. I dropped the magazine and tried to turn my chair quickly so that my back was to Nagel, but I couldn't find the brake. I turned my head away from him. I couldn't stop myself crying. I was still so bloody weak, and it was just too much.

"'Leutnant Karl von Leussow, fallen on 11th July,'" Nagel read out. "Your friend the pianist?"

I nodded.

"I'm sorry," he said quietly, then squeezed my shoulder – and, bless him, he turned my chair so that my back was to the room, and left me.

All I wanted was what I could never have: Karl's embrace and his beloved voice in my ear. All I could see ahead of me was black emptiness.

And now I've cried in public, and God know what the others will think. I gazed out of the window at the darkening sky. *I wish I were dead.*

Some time later a hand appeared in front of me, holding a glass with water in the bottom. *That's a bit meagre.*

"Thanks."

I took a large gulp – and coughed and spluttered as the spirit hit the back of my throat. My eyes watered.

"That'll teach you to drink schnapps like water!" Riege said. He put his hand on my shoulder. "Stop being such an antisocial bastard, and come and play cards."

I was about to say that I didn't want to – but he was already turning me round and pushing me towards the card table.

"Usual stakes?" Nagel asked.

"All right, then."

Neither of them said a word about my breaking down, and nor did anyone else. Everyone behaved as if it hadn't happened, and after a couple of hours I realised no one minded, just as we didn't mind about Krug's funny turns.

I'm far from being the only man who's lost his best friend, and I wonder if any of you lost a lover as well… You just can't tell – I'd never have guessed about Karl if he hadn't fallen for me. I wonder when it happened.

"Becker – it's your turn to play."

"Sorry. Miles away."

"Don't we all wish we were!" said Nagel, and we laughed.

A couple of days later I got a letter from Horstmann, who was back in Flanders.

'The filthy Belgian weather has set in again, so I've got time to write. Sorry it's taken so long, but things have been rather hot.'

He wrote so vividly about flying and fighting that I was back in my D.VII, with the wind singing in the wires and a flight of Camels coming into view… And suddenly I missed it far more than I'd ever imagined I would. Three months away from the Front had diluted the fear – yes, I still had nightmares and lost track of reality, but my hands didn't shake any more.

I'd be happy to go back, if only I had two legs.

Is that so, Franz? Or do you only think that because you know you can't go back?

That was unanswerable.

Maybe I could get a job with Technical and Testing. Now that would be really interesting.

I put the letter down and stared out at the clouds. *I've just been thinking about having a future.* That was such an extraordinary thought that I ran it through my mind a few more times. *But I'd be leaving Karl in the past.*

'No, you won't, Franz,' he said, his presence so real that I expected him to touch me. 'You'll never be alone. I shall always be with you.'

The rain battered against the window in a sudden gust and he vanished, but the feeling of companionship remained. *I can do it, if you're really beside me.*

I carried on reading Horstmann's letter. He was rather more discreet than Paul and I had to read between the lines, but it was only too plain that we were nearing the end.

By the time I get out of here the war will be over. Let's just hope we can have an honourable peace... But we made the French pay in 1870. And we've made the Russians pay now. What can we expect the Allies to do to us? We should have made peace in '15 or '16, when we were in a position of strength.

"Christ," said Nagel, "you look as if you're *thinking!*"

I laughed. "You're right – and it's just as bad an idea as it ever was!"

A few days later, I heard from Alfred. He was also very careful what he said.

'My fighting is probably over,' he wrote, which was a good way of saying how near the end was. 'We were about to go over the top on a counter-attack, to take back a trench some Saxon bastards had been careless enough to lose, and a shell landed just behind us.

Fortunately the sandbags took most of it, but I got a splinter in my left arm (broken radius and ulna – forearm to you!), and another went through my steel helmet and into my scalp. It left quite a nasty gash which bled rather a lot. I was bloody lucky, really – if it had been going a bit faster it would have gone right into my skull, and I'd be with the Great Army. Proves the steel helmet does the job, though.

I was bloody lucky in another way, too – instead of going over, I put Rosenbach in command and went back to the Aid Post, and no one from my company has come back. Not one. I suspect most will have been taken prisoner – we've been losing quite a lot that way of late, though so far not from the storm troops.'

No – the elite will always be more reliable than the ordinary men.

'At least, I hope they're prisoners. Anyway, I'm in hospital and expect to be on the train tomorrow.'

And you obviously think the war will be over by the time you've healed up. Six weeks for broken bones, plus a bit extra to get the strength in your arm back, maybe another spell at Döberitz... If there were a God, I'd pray for your survival. As it is, I'll just hope.

Beyond the windows, the autumn advanced and the leaves changed colour. I was slowly getting stronger, and Doctor Holz said my stump was healing well. I still didn't want to see the bloody thing. I was still too weak to use crutches, and had to be wheeled around in that fucking chair.

I could, though, have a piss unaided, which was a small shred of independence.

It was a rather complicated manoeuvre, with huge potential for making a mess: park chair facing lavatory bowl, remembering to apply the brake. Put blanket over arm of chair. Unbutton trousers and get cock out, reflecting sadly that no one else is likely to touch it again, except for tarts – which is a bit much at twenty-three. Take hold of rails with both hands and pull self up. Lean forearms on rails and maintain firm grip with hands, balance being impossible. Check cock dangles over bowl with no clothing in between. Piss. Shake a bit. Lower self back into chair and reverse the initial steps.

By the time I'd done all that I was fucking exhausted. And I still couldn't get out of the chair and onto the loo without help. I was a long way from being fit enough to be discharged.

And the one thing that really pissed me off was the almost constant pain in my right knee. Some days it bored right up my thigh, as if my leg were on fire.

I asked Doctor Holz about it one morning.

"It's a very common problem," he said, "and no one knows what causes it. It could be something to do with the brain remembering the injury, and not accepting that the limb has gone."

"Is that a polite way of saying that it's all in my mind?"

He smiled. "Only in the sense that all perception is in the brain."

"Can you give me something for it?"

"No – and even if I could, I wouldn't." He gave me a very serious look. "When the war's finished and things are back to normal, you'll be able to buy whatever you want – but I advise very strongly against. Morphine or cocaine may help at first, but your body will get used to them and you'll need ever greater doses, and then you won't be able to do without. Believe me, addiction is very unpleasant and not easy to break out of. I've seen it destroy people."

I thought of Karl's Uncle Heinrich, and of poor old Winkler. "Like booze, you mean."

"Exactly. The drug takes over."

"So what do you suggest?"

"You'll have to learn to live with it. Find something to occupy yourself… Talking of which, you can start your physical therapy today. But be warned, it won't be easy."

Sister Ursula wheeled me to the gym, where a wiry Sergeant was waiting for us. He must have been about fifty, but looked a good bit younger. In fact, he looked younger than me, but that wasn't difficult.

"Good morning, sir," he said. "I'm Kahrstedt, and it's my job to get you moving again."

"Just tell me what to do and I'll do it," I said. "I'm sick to death of this fucking chair."

"You'll be sick to death of me soon, sir. Now, there are two things we have to do – get you strong enough to use crutches, and get you used to balancing."

He started taking me through the exercises, and after about ten minutes I was completely whacked. *Jesus – a few months ago I'd have thought nothing of any of this. These weights are tiny, and I can only lift them a few times.*

"Well done, sir," he said. "Now you're going to do them all again."

Again? Fucking hell, that's impossible!

The harder you work, the faster you'll progress, I told myself. I was beginning to understand how far down I'd gone.

My arms and shoulders felt like jelly.

"Right, this afternoon we'll get your leg working and get you balancing," he said. "Give your arms a bit of a rest – you'll need them for that."

The afternoon session was awful. Kahrstedt wheeled me to a pair of parallel rails.

"Take hold of them and pull yourself out of the chair, sir."

I could do that – but of course it was only the start.

"Now slide your hands along, take your weight on them again – good, now swing your leg forward… That's it, good."

I did that twice more and then collapsed into my chair, which he was pushing behind me. Once I'd recovered I had to get up again, and then try to let go of the bars without falling over.

It was impossible. I wanted to cry with frustration.

"And have a seat, sir. You've done very well indeed."

"You're joking – that was pathetic."

I'll never do it.

A couple of men I didn't know were using the weights, and another amputee was practising on his crutches. He reached the end of the room and turned round neatly.

Kahrstedt leaned close to me. "You see the gentleman on crutches? Well, he was much worse than you when he started with me – and look at him now. He'll be discharged soon."

"How long did that take?"

He smiled. "There's no point my telling you that, sir. Everyone's different. You just keep working, twice a day – I'll write out your programme so you can do it when I'm busy – and see how it goes."

"Thank you."

I ached all over the next day, and even worse the day after that, but I made myself work. Kahrstedt was a hard taskmaster, but he was just what I needed. Every time I thought I couldn't do any more, he'd say, "Just once more, sir", and I'd manage it somehow.

"What were you doing before this?" I asked him.

"Oh, I've been in the Army all my life, sir. I was training recruits until the war began, and then I got interested in physical therapy, and they sent me on a course. I've been here ever since."

"Well, you've got a job for life," I said.

"I'll be retiring soon, sir – I'm sixty next year."

"You're *what?!*"

He grinned. "I was born in '59 – too young for 1870."

I looked at him, trying to see a sixty-year-old man and failing completely. "I look older than you."

"Well, you have had a bit of a knock, sir."

"Doesn't it get depressing, seeing so many bashed-up young men?"

"Not when I can help," he said quietly. "And I don't, really – not the way you must have done... Anyway, I'd better get on – my next gentleman's due in five minutes."

A week or so later, I lifted my hands off the bars and *didn't fall over*. For a whole five seconds. And then the next day I couldn't balance at all.

"That's how it goes, sir," Kahrstedt said. "It'll come back."

"Like learning to land," I said. "One day you get it, the next it's gone again, but after a bit it falls into place."

He looked at me with interest. "What did you fly, sir?"

"Two-seaters for a few months, then fighters."

"May I ask – are you Oberleutnant *Franz* Becker?"

"Yes, that's right."

"Well! Could I have your autograph, please, for my grandson? He's mad keen on aeroplanes."

"Yes, of course."

The next day he turned up with a postcard of me, which I was glad to sign. If anyone could get me mobile again, Kahrstedt could.

I might be able to do better than a postcard. I wrote to Paul, asking if he still had any copies of the last portrait he'd taken of me.

A couple of days later it was 23rd October, the anniversary of Langemarck. I got my exercises done early and wheeled myself into the conservatory.

I sat gazing at the trees, not seeing them. *Four years ago today we walked forward, singing, against the English. Four years ago Anton died, his guts spilling onto the ground in the light of the flare...*

That day went round and round in my head. *Karl saved my*

life. If it hadn't been for his quick reactions, I'd have been filled full of lead. And the four years since have been full of blood, more blood than anyone could have imagined being shed. Kurt, Otto, and then Karl, among the millions of men slaughtered – for what? I wish I knew.

Nagel came and joined me. I wanted to be left alone with my memories, and I was less than polite. He tried several times to start a conversation, but each time I answered curtly.

"You're in a filthy mood today," he said.

"So what?"

"Becker, we've all lost friends. They're better off than we are, the dead. They'll always be young. They can't suffer any more, aren't in pain the way we are. Your friend Leussow is infinitely better off than I am. I was a violinist. It was my life. I had my dreams… Your friend doesn't have to live as I have to."

"What are you going to do?"

"I can still compose… Some days, if I could find that bastard who saved my life, I'd gladly shoot him."

He got up and left. I sat staring blankly out, aware only of loss. *Maybe it would have been better to die that day. What have these four years brought me?*

'Is what we shared so little, then?' Karl asked.

No. It was worth it, just for the times I lay in your arms with that wonderful feeling of love and contentment. I just wish I'd recognised love for what it was.

'You know now, and that's all that matters.'

The next day I got a letter from Elisabeth, which had taken weeks to reach me.

'Dear Oberleutnant Becker, thank you so much for your kind letter about Karl, and for the photograph of his funeral. It's so hard for me to believe, and I still haven't really been able to take it in.'

I'll bet. Your husband's people have killed all three of your brothers, and your father's death resulted from losing two of his sons. How does anyone cope with that?

'My three brothers were so different,' she went on, 'and I loved each of them for what he was. But there was something special about Karl – maybe it was his talent, or that he was the youngest and so I was a bit older when he was born.

Last year, when I heard how badly wounded he'd been, I thought that at least he would be spared – and then in July it was in the newspapers here that he'd been shot down and killed, and I couldn't understand how that had happened until I got your letter.

I wish so much that he'd taken the doctors' advice, and I still don't really understand why he insisted on going back. Surely it would have been better to have what life he could – but I fear he'd heard too many of our family stories.

The same paper said that you'd been shot down and wounded, and I hope you're recovering well. Karl was fortunate to have such a good friend, and I hope that we shall be able to meet after the war.

With very best wishes,
Elisabeth Bartlett.'

I hope your husband makes it to the end safely, I thought, and had to smile at myself for wishing a Tommy well.

Poor Elisabeth. Losing your whole family doesn't bear thinking about, and I expect she has to keep it to herself. No doubt all she hears is how evil the Germans are – and especially the Prussians – and how the war is our fault. Mourning dead Prussians wouldn't go down well at all in the enemy's land, and that's understandable when you think how many Tommies have fallen.

Paul wrote back a few days later and sent me the photo I'd requested. *I didn't look too bad even then, and that is quite a decent row of gongs. Buggered if I recognise myself now, though.*

I wrote, 'To Sergeant Kahrstedt, with heartfelt thanks' and signed it. When I went for my afternoon session I said, "I've got something for your grandson", and handed him the picture.

He was speechless.

"It's a bit more up to date than the postcard," I said. "Leutnant Fellmann, our technical officer, took it not long before I was shot down."

"Thank you so much, sir," he said. "He'll love it."

"Just don't tell him what a wreck I am now!"

My knee was playing up again. I worked hard on my exercises, hoping the burn in my muscles might blot out the pain. It didn't, but it was a distraction.

"You're doing very well today, sir," Kahrstedt said. "If you carry on like that I'll be putting your weights up."

"Maybe I'd better back off a bit, then!" I replied, and we both laughed.

I was glad I had something to concentrate on, other than the desperate situation outside. In early November, rumours reached us of widespread, serious unrest, and it sounded as if Berlin and Hamburg were close to outright revolution.

"Send the troops in, get the buggers back under control," Wolffheim said.

"And then who'll fight the enemy?" asked Landauer wearily. "The people have had enough. My uncle in Berlin says—"

"He's probably a leftie like them," Wolffheim burst out. "After all, he is a Jew, isn't he?"

"That's quite enough of that," I said, and Riege and Nagel both echoed me.

"They've never pulled their weight in the war," Wolffheim said.

"Bollocks," said Schieffer. "Just look at how many Jewish graves there are in the cemeteries behind the Front."

"Quite," I said. "All my Jewish comrades fought like everyone else – and what does it matter what religion someone follows? They're just as German as we are."

"And how many of us believe in any god anyway?" asked Riege. "I certainly don't."

"Yes, but it's not only religion, is it?" Wolffheim went on.

"Oh, do shut up," Fischer said. "We all have to stick together now – we can't afford divisions."

"But that's the whole point," Wolffheim said. "They've all got relatives in enemy countries – how can we trust any of them?"

"In case you hadn't noticed," Schieffer said, "the Kaiser's mother was English, and both the Tsar and the King of England are his cousins."

"And my best mate was part English as well," I added, "and it didn't stop him being a patriotic Prussian. He and his brothers have all fallen."

"And the Bavarian royal family's descended from the Stuarts," said Riege.

"Who was the surgeon who fixed your legs, again?" asked Nagel.

Wolffheim went scarlet. "Er… it was Doctor Stern."

"Stern?" asked Fischer. "Not – *Jewish* – by any chance?"

We laughed.

Wolffheim retreated behind his newspaper, and left the room about ten minutes later.

Hammer had sat saying nothing, and he left as well.

"Thanks, chaps," Landauer said.

"Don't be daft," said Riege. "None of us wants to hear shit like that."

"You want to speak up for yourself more," said Krug.

Landauer shrugged. "Believe me, there's no point."

"So who is this uncle of yours?" asked Fischer.

"Anyway, what did your uncle say?" Schieffer asked, almost simultaneously.

"Colonel of a Home Defence regiment," Landauer replied, "and he's sent his family to the country – the Reds are out on the street, and he's afraid it's going to be like Russia."

"Not a leftie himself, then?" Nagel asked with a smile.

Landauer laughed. "More in favour of shooting them than supporting them."

"What's happened in Russia's terrifying," said Riege.

"Oh, it won't come to that here," Fischer said.

"Let's hope not." Schieffer looked very serious.

"The trouble is," I said, "we're in our own little world here. We don't really know what's going on outside."

"What was it like last time you were out?" Nagel asked Landauer.

"Do you know, I didn't like it at all," he said slowly. "I got some very funny looks from people."

"Probably thought you were a pansy!" Riege said. "That sling'll get you into trouble!"

"I think you're right—" Landauer began.

"See – Becker's sister's safe with him!" Riege said. "I've got a chance after all!"

We all laughed, and after a moment Landauer continued, "…about getting into trouble, that is. There was quite a lot of hostility, not only to me but to a couple of other officers as well. One of them gave a private a rocket for not saluting—"

"What?" demanded Schieffer indignantly.

"Quite," said Landauer. "Unthinkable, isn't it? And what was even worse was that the fellow answered back."

"Bloody hell," said Fischer. "Was he drunk?"

"No. Not obviously so, anyway… His mate made him see sense, but – well, it wasn't a good atmosphere. I'm not sure what would have happened if it had been just the two of them in a quiet street. It rather gave me pause for thought, being as I can't defend myself easily."

We all looked at each other. *We'd better hope there's no revolution, or we'll all be stuffed.*

The next morning, 10th November, Doctor Holz came into the day room and rapped on the table.

'Right, gentlemen,' said the Chief. 'We're to rendezvous with the two-seater—'

There was a sudden uproar, and I couldn't work out why the pilots were all shouting.

Suddenly I was in the day room. My fellow patients were all talking over each other.

"What did he say?" I asked Nagel.

"The Kaiser's abdicated."

"We're a fucking Red republic!" Wolffheim burst out. "The fuckers have taken over!"

"Weren't you listening?" Fischer asked me.

"I'd drifted off," I said. I turned to Nagel. "Say that again."

"The Kaiser abdicated – yesterday – and he's gone to Holland."

"And there's a Socialist government in Berlin," said Schieffer.

"That's an oxymoron," said Wolffheim. "You can't have a Socialist government. They're a fucking rabble."

"So – who – I mean, how can we be a republic?" I was bewildered. "I mean, the Frenchies have a republic, and the Americans, but it's just not German, is it? What about our King?"

"The Kings have all gone," said Landauer. "Bavaria, Württemberg, Saxony – all abdicated."

"But…" *How can our King have gone? And the Kaiser?*

"What happens to us all now?" asked Schieffer.

"I'm buggered if I'm fighting for the fucking Reds," said Wolffheim.

Landauer looked at him. "The Fatherland still exists, and needs us more than ever."

Wolffheim snorted.

"For your information," Landauer said icily, "my family are all strongly conservative and have always had links to Court. The last thing any of us wants is a Bolshevik government – because we'd be put straight against the nearest wall, along with the Junkers."

"Oh."

"And if I hear much more crap from you, I'll want satisfaction," Landauer finished.

Good for you.

"And the war will be over soon, so you wouldn't have long to wait for it," Fischer said.

'It is, surely, superfluous for us to start killing each other,' Levy said, putting himself between Schalich and me.

Why was I calling Schalich out? Oh, yes – he thought Karl and I were a couple of poufs. Well, he wasn't wrong, as it turned out...

"Do you know Max Levy?" I asked Landauer.

He looked at me in astonishment. "No – that is, I know of him, but we don't mix in quite the same circles... We've always been scientists and doctors – they're related to the Rothschilds, absolutely loaded."

"Oh – that explains a lot. He always played cards for frightening stakes – frightening to me, that is."

Landauer laughed. "That's what I meant about different circles! How do you know him?"

"We were in the same squadron, a couple of years ago. Last thing I heard he was a PoW in Tommy-land."

"Well, if he's got any sense he'll stay there until Berlin's settled down, or they'll put him against the wall as well."

Wolffheim snorted, but kept his mouth shut.

"So what the fuck happens now?" asked Riege.

We found out the following morning.

Doctor Holz came into the day room and rapped to get our attention. This time I managed not to drift off.

"Gentlemen, may I have your attention, please? I… I have to tell you that…" He paused, seemingly lost for words. "That an armistice was signed this morning between the Central and the Allied Powers. Hostilities will cease at midday."

This time, no one talked. The silence was total, shocked.

Doctor Holz cleared his throat. "And I… I've been asked to tell you all that you are now released from your oaths of allegiance."

He looked as if he were about to say something more, then turned and left the room.

XI

So it's over. I stared at the floor. I didn't want to look at the others, didn't want to see their faces. *I should have known it was coming. It was plain from the newspapers and from the letters – but I didn't want to think about it. And now the bastards will impose whatever terms they like on us.*

The silence held. Finally, I looked round. Nagel was staring at his hand. *What are you going to do now with your shattered dreams?*

If we'd won, we could tell ourselves that the sacrifice of our friends' lives and of our health were for something…

Krug stared straight ahead through the wall, his mouth twitching. The dismal grey light crept in through the windows and lit our hopeless faces.

"Those damned Communists!" Wolffheim burst out. "Those filthy arseholes! They've sold us all down the river. This is the first thing they've done, as soon as they're in power! It's a dishonourable peace, made by scoundrels! The enemy's nowhere near Germany. We could fight on for months more!"

"For God's sake, don't you understand? The Army's finished."

The voice was weary and unfamiliar, and I turned to see who it was. I couldn't put a name to the face at first – he'd only arrived a few days earlier… *Bredt, that's it. Oberleutnant Bredt.*

"Finished? What d'you mean, finished?" demanded Wolffheim.

"They've no fight left."

"Won't fight? Never heard such bloody nonsense! What the hell are you talking about?"

"I was at the Front until three weeks ago. You can't expect men to fight when they haven't enough to eat."

"The bloody Reds have rotted them as well. All they need is some good old-fashioned discipline," Wolffheim declared emphatically.

"When did you get yours?" Bredt asked in the same flat tone. "It must have been months ago."

"What the hell's that got to do with it?"

"Everything. You obviously haven't seen the state things have got into. They've been sending us schoolboys whose uniforms don't fit, who haven't had a decent meal for years. They do their best but it's not enough."

"Well, why've we sued for peace now? We're still in the enemy's territory. They're not in Germany yet! And as for being released from my oath – I've never heard anything like it!"

"What does it mean, anyway?" I asked.

"We're not in the Army any more," said Krug. "We've all been discharged. Just like that. Thrown out, like – like rubbish."

"I swore that oath very solemnly," said Wolffheim.

God, you sound pompous – but then I suppose that's the end of your career. I couldn't care less whether I'm still in the bloody Army or not. I'm never going to fight again, so it hardly matters.

I suppose I'm plain Herr Becker now. It sounded very strange. I'd got used to having a rank.

"They won't pay us now," said Fischer. "In fact, they're not responsible for us any more. They don't even have to look after us."

"Of course the government has to look after us," said Nagel. "We got our injuries fighting for the Fatherland. They'll have to pay our pensions and give us our artificial limbs and so on. They can't just wash their hands of us."

"There isn't a bloody government," said Wolffheim. "There's just a bloody Bolshevik rabble with no honour and no decency. You think they're going to look after disabled officers? They don't give a shit about us."

"That's right," said Riege. "They'll say we didn't fight for them, we fought for the Imperial government, for the ex-Kaiser."

"You know, you may be right," Schieffer said thoughtfully.

"We'll just have to hope they don't bloody well shoot us," Wolffheim went on. "Frankly, I'd rather die in action than be murdered by some fucking rabble."

"Hardly matters, does it?" asked Landauer. "You're just as dead either way."

I'd had enough. I wheeled myself to the bell.

Sister Ursula came, looking as if the sky had fallen in on her. "Who called?" she asked quietly.

"I did," I said. "I'd like to go to my room, please."

We were silent in the lift. *It's all been for nothing. All for absolutely nothing. I've lost Karl, she's lost her fiancé, and we can't even think that their deaths helped to bring victory.*

"Would you like to sit by the window?"

"No. I'd like to get into bed."

And die, and join my friends. There's absolutely no point in going on. Everything's finished, and I wish I'd died the day I was shot down.

"Would you close the curtains, please?"

"Are you feeling unwell?"

"No. My leg hurts, that's all." My voice echoed Karl's, that day in my office: 'My chest hurts, that's all…'

It wasn't all, though, was it, Karl?

And my leg wasn't all either. It did hurt, it always bloody hurt, but it wasn't hurting any worse than usual. The feeling of black hopelessness was far worse than the pain.

This is the end of everything.

She closed the door, and I lay staring at the ceiling.

We have peace again. I tried to remember how life had been before the war, in that vanished time of innocence.

It was impossible.

I've forgotten what peace is. I don't know how to do anything except kill.

Karl said something once, about how there was no way back because we'd changed so much... That was it: 'The man I was then has gone for ever, and I can never go back to find him.' Suddenly I saw him lying in the pine coffin, the light filtering through the canvas hangar onto his still, white face.

My throat tightened until it began to choke me, but I couldn't cry. The tears wouldn't come. *For nothing. For defeat. If he had to die, why couldn't it have been in a victorious war – or at least in a war that needed to be fought?*

In the beginning, it had all been so clear. Germany was at war, so we volunteered. I never asked what it was about, just believed what was in the papers, that we were surrounded by enemies and had to fight for our survival – but then I saw what war was, and wondered what could justify such slaughter.

My lover and my friends were dead, and I was crippled, and I didn't know what for.

Oh, Karl, Karl, my love. Grief pierced me right through. *Oh, God, why?*

'Because we were at war,' Karl said. 'What else could we do? It doesn't matter what the reason was. And I would do it all again – and so would you.'

"Karl—"

I reached out my hand, but the room was empty.

Yes, it was simple for you. In the end you couldn't escape what you were, and you died like so many of your family. The Leussows are all gone now.

I saw his face so clearly, saw him marching beside me on our way to war. He came back into the trench in his cape, soaking wet, walked across the airfield with me, his hand in mine, held me and banished my nightmares…

How entwined your life was with mine – and now I'm alone.

The war filled my mind, filled the room. Kurt died in agony in the mud, the rain pouring down as his blood ran into the water. Schürmann stood beside me, firing a dead man's rifle, his broken wrist forgotten, Burkhardt died as I held his hand… and all the others, in a long, long procession.

So many fine men, dead for nothing.

The light changed beyond the curtains, and again, and I lost all track of time. I didn't eat. I couldn't. It was pointless.

Karl couldn't eat, when I was staying with him in Brandenburg… Schubert's 'Litany for All Souls' Day' came into my head, and we sat together by the fire, trying in vain to console ourselves for what we'd done.

I sat in the concert hall, spellbound as he played the Emperor Concerto, heard the applause. *Those hands will be bones now in the Flanders earth, those clear grey-blue eyes long gone… oh, God, why?*

The room disappeared, and all I could see was the Front: Anton by the light of the flare, Otto burning, Johnny falling on fire through the sky, Patschke crashing on take-off, the English boy dying in my arms, the Frenchmen in the rain, Krypke bleeding to death just too far away…

The men I'd killed danced round me, jeering, laughing from their dead, empty throats. 'We've got our revenge now,' they said, closing in. 'You've lost everything.'

Karl stood shoulder to shoulder with me in a blaze of light, and they disappeared.

'It's all right, Franz, I'm here.'

I fell asleep in his arms, but all too soon I was awake again and the loneliness was overwhelming.

I can't go on. There's no point and it's too difficult. I haven't the strength. I'll just stay here until I die, and then I can be with Karl.

Sister Frieda had grey-blue eyes, almost exactly like his. She came to take away another untouched tray, and as I looked at her eyes they became Karl's, staring at the sky. I wanted to cry, but still I couldn't.

"Your temperature's normal," Sister Ursula said, "and there's no sign of infection."

What on earth is she doing in the trench?

"You really should get up."

"I don't feel well enough," I said, and she left us alone.

I was sitting on the fire step with Karl, Kurt and Alfred. We'd taken our shirts off and turned them inside out, and we were digging the lice out of the seams and cracking them between our thumbnails.

'My parents sent me some insect powder,' I said, 'but it doesn't seem to work.'

'Nothing works except wholesale slaughter,' Karl said. 'If there's one thing I hate it's these bloody things – and the fact that this is my blood on my fingers. I'm a walking bloody dinner table for this lot.'

Doctor Holz stood by my bed. I stared at him, wondering what he was doing in the front line and how he'd stayed so clean.

"Oberleutnant Becker, if you do not eat this meal we shall force-feed you. If you wish to kill yourself, you are at liberty to do so once you have left this hospital. Until then you are my responsibility, and I intend to ensure that you make as full a recovery as possible. I shall come back in two hours, and if that tray is untouched you will be fed by tube."

"You can't do that to me. I'm not in the Army any more. I don't have to take orders from anyone."

He sighed. "I'm still in charge of this hospital, and you're still one of my patients. If you don't wish to be treated here you're free to leave."

I couldn't leave, and he knew I couldn't. The misery in my face must have been apparent because the tone of his voice softened considerably, but he didn't budge from his position. He went on to explain, step by disgusting step, exactly how it would be done.

I was listening, but there was a corpse standing behind him, sightless eyes staring at me from a black face. Behind it stretched No Man's Land, desolate and empty of anything living.

Doctor Holz turned and walked straight through the dead man, and suddenly my room in the hospital was clear and sharp.

I looked at the tray. I didn't want it, but neither did I want to be held down whilst a rubber tube was shoved into my stomach.

All right. I'll play your game. I'll do as you suggest. I'll kill myself after I leave here. It won't be difficult – the Reds will be quite happy to shoot me.

I forced myself to eat. When Doctor Holz came back he seemed pleased, and I realised he hadn't actually wanted to force-feed me at all. He was just worried about me.

It can't be easy dealing with us, especially now.

"Sister Ulrike will take you to the day room," he said. "You can't stay in here brooding. You'll end up in the mental wing."

I didn't want to go to the day room. Wolffheim would be going on about the bloody Communists again and I couldn't stand listening to him.

I scratched my face and couldn't understand why I had so much stubble, then realised I hadn't shaved for, what – two days? Three?

When Sister Frieda comes I'll ask her for some hot water. If I've got to go to the day room I'd like to look halfway decent.

I reached over and opened the drawer of the bedside table. My razor had gone, and so had my mirror.

That's odd – I'm sure I put everything back in that drawer the other day. I wonder where they can be.

I couldn't get out of bed to look for them. I was stuck.

Sister Frieda came in about fifteen minutes later.

"Where are my razor and my mirror?"

She hesitated. "We took them for safekeeping," she said awkwardly.

"Well, can I have them now, please? And some hot water?"

She hesitated again, and suddenly I understood. No mirror, no razor – nothing I could use to harm myself.

"It's all right," I said. "I won't do anything stupid."

"I'm sorry," she said. "But Doctor Holz said you weren't to have anything like that."

"Well, I'm not going to the day room looking like a bloody gorilla. Look, can you fetch him? Then at least the two of us can discuss it."

It was a good hour before she came back with the doctor.

"Sister Frieda tells me you've asked for your razor," he said.

"Yes. Would you want to be seen looking like this? I look like a bloody scarecrow at the best of times. I won't do anything stupid, I promise."

"I suppose no one's told you," he said slowly. "I've already had one suicide, and, having regard to your depressed state, I'm concerned that you might… well, I don't want to lose another patient."

"Doctor, I promise you on my honour that I won't try to kill myself in your hospital. All I want is to shave. Now can I please have my razor?"

If you say no then I won't go to that bloody day room again, and I won't eat another thing, either. You can do what the fuck you like.

"Yes, you can. But we'll keep it for you and a nurse will have to be with you whenever you use it."

"Do you think I won't keep my word?" I was starting to get angry.

"No, I don't think anything of the kind," he said gently. "What concerns me is that you might forget that you gave it."

I couldn't be bothered to argue any more. "Oh, forget it. I'll grow a beard."

He sighed. "I said you may have your razor. Sister Frieda will stay with you while you shave."

"I'm not mad," I said to her when she brought my razor.

She smiled sweetly and put the mirror on my table.

Oh, Jesus, do I really look like that? The face looking back at me was even more haggard than usual, and the stubble made me look like some sort of desperado.

I looked into my eyes, and understood why they were being so careful with me. *If I saw someone looking like this, I'd think he was mad. Perhaps I am and I just don't know it. I have been seeing things, after all. Perhaps that's how it starts – or perhaps it started while I was still at the Front and it's been getting worse ever since.*

I must make an effort or I will end up in the mental wing, just as Doctor Holz said. But what sort of effort do I have to make to stay sane?

I washed and shaved, trying not to think about it. Sister Ulrike helped me to dress in the blue and white hospital uniform, and settled me in my wheelchair.

She took me to the day room and put me next to the window, where I'd sat the first time I'd gone in there. Nagel joined me. He looked terrible, his face deeply lined, his eyes despairing. I don't think he'd slept for days.

"How are you?" he asked.

"Bloody awful. You?"

"About the same."

I looked round. "Where's Krug?"

He didn't want to answer, I could see that.

"Had another funny turn," he said slowly. "Thought he was in the front line again, ducked behind a chair and kept shouting, 'Fire!' It was pretty horrible. They took him away and we haven't seen him since."

I thought of the things I'd seen in my room, and shuddered. *How close am I to breaking down completely?*

"I went to see you," Nagel continued, "but you told me to bugger off."

"Sorry. Didn't realise it was you. Sister Angelika said she'd send the chaplain to see me." The last thing I'd wanted was someone banging on at me about 'God', and I hadn't recognised Nagel's voice through the door. "You should have said it was you."

"Oh, not to worry."

"Who killed himself?" I asked.

"It was one of the fellows with a wrecked face – cut his throat, apparently. Can't say I blame him."

"No…"

We sat in silence. After about half an hour, Wolffheim came in, picked up a newspaper, read for a minute or so and then threw the paper down angrily.

"Those bloody Bolsheviks!" he exclaimed.

Oh, God, he's off again. I can't stand listening to him. If he doesn't shut up I'm going back upstairs.

"The Army should march on Berlin and sort them out. Shoot a few of the bastards, that's the only answer."

"I blame the Prussians," said Schieffer. "They started it."

"No, we bloody didn't," replied Riege. "We're all in this together."

"Your bloody generals directed the shambles," said Schieffer.

"If we had a proper government we'd still be fighting," said Wolffheim. "Shoot a few of the buggers and send the rest into exile in Russia, that's the only answer, otherwise we'll have a blasted Soviet republic of—"

"Hey, Wolffheim, pipe down a minute," said Nagel.

"Why, what's your bloody problem?"

I'd heard something as well. "Shut up and listen!"

He shut up, very sulkily, and we all strained our ears. I could hear what sounded like shouting and banging doors. Nagel looked at me as if to ask what was going on.

There was a commotion right outside the day room. The door flew open, and six soldiers wearing red armbands burst in. Matron followed, with a face like thunder.

We all drew a sharp breath, clearly audible in the sudden silence. The soldiers were armed, and we were defenceless.

Shit – we're all going to be shot. What a fucking stupid way to die.

They didn't move but stood in silence, staring at us.

Someone had better say something, ease the tension a bit.

I wheeled myself towards them. "Good afternoon," I said, as pleasantly as I could. "Can I help you?"

"This is an officers' hospital, isn't it?" demanded one of them.

"Yes, it is."

"We've come from the Soldiers' and Workers' Council. This is a den of privilege—"

"Privilege?" I said. "You think we're privileged?"

"Course you are. We've come to—"

"Have a look round this room. Look at us. We're all mutilated. You can start with me." I wheeled myself to the window. "Have a look," I said, moving the blanket aside. "A really good look."

He studied my face. I knew how pale and emaciated I was, how hollow and empty my eyes were. His gaze travelled down and stopped at my right trouser leg, which was neatly folded and pinned.

"You call this privilege?" I said. "You've got two legs. You can walk. Have a look at the others. And when you've finished in here, Matron will take you upstairs and show you the privileged officers who are paralysed, or who have no faces."

He was staring at me.

"Yes, I'm an officer," I said. "I volunteered in '14 as a private, and I fought till last July when I got this." I gestured at my stump. "Is it a crime to have been promoted? Do you think we're a different species? Do you think our blood's a different colour to yours, that we don't feel pain the way you do, that we don't grieve just the same when our friends get killed? What do you think we are, for God's sake?"

The room was utterly silent. One of his companions put a hand on his shoulder.

"Come on, Jürgen," he said. "Leave the poor bastard alone. He's had a bad time."

That was too much for me.

"*Don't feel sorry for me!*" I screamed, and burst into tears. I buried my face in my hands and sat there sobbing.

I shouldn't have said that. They'll probably start shooting. I don't care.

No one spoke, or even seemed to breathe.

"We… er… we didn't realise you was all so bad," said Jürgen. "We… er… we'll put a notice on the door, tell… er… tell the others to leave you all alone."

Boots clumped on the wooden floor, and the front door banged shut.

"Well done, Becker!" said Nagel, and thumped me on the shoulder.

There was a chorus of "Well done!", but I couldn't stop crying. I was furious with the soldiers, and furious with myself for breaking down.

I felt myself being wheeled out of the day room, into the lift, and to my room. I was hysterical, sobbing and cursing, beside myself with rage and grief. Sister Ursula helped me to undress and get into bed, and a minute or two later I felt the needle in my arm.

Karl lay beside me, and wrapped his strong arms round me. I buried my face against him, and he stroked my hair.

It's curious, I said, *but when I stayed with you last January, I was strong and you felt so fragile, and now it's the other way round.*

His embrace tightened. 'You'll be strong again, my love,' he murmured.

And there was the familiar, soft smell of his sweat mingled with mine, and nothing else mattered...

I drowsed in the early twilight, still surrounded by that comforting scent – but as I woke fully I remembered that he was dead, and I realised I'd been dreaming. It was like losing him all over again, and I lay alone and miserable – and yet somehow my bed really did smell of him, as if he'd just got up and left.

Imagination, Franz. Pure imagination.

The previous day came back to me, only too vividly, and I felt bitterly ashamed of breaking down in front of everyone. I didn't want to face them. Sister Angelika persuaded me to get out of bed and into my chair, and I sat looking out of the window, completely wretched.

About halfway through the morning, there was a knock on my door.

"It's Nagel. May I come in?"

"All right."

He sat on my bed. "Aren't you coming down today?"

"No."

"Becker, everyone wants to see you. You were the hero of the hour yesterday."

"Don't be ridiculous."

"Oh, I'm not. You started speaking before Wolffheim could open his mouth. If he'd got going they'd have shot us for sure. You got them to go away, and with a bit of luck they won't come back."

"I don't want to come down."

"I wouldn't have been able to say all that without breaking down," he said. "None of us would. You said everything we wanted to say, and you said it well. Come on. Please. We all want you to."

I couldn't believe what he was saying, but he seemed sincere enough.

"All right, then."

I wheeled myself down the corridor to the lift, Nagel walking beside me. He opened the door of the day room, and as I entered everyone began to applaud. Even Wolffheim came and shook my hand. It was all horribly embarrassing, but it was far better to be embarrassed by their goodwill than by my crying fit.

After lunch, Sister Ursula came to take me to the gym. I didn't see the point in that, or in anything else.

Kahrstedt looked at me with sympathy, mingled with reproach. "I heard you weren't well, sir – I hope you're feeling better."

"It was just… the news about the Armistice rather got me down… I lost – a lot of… good friends…" I broke off, not trusting my voice.

He nodded. "Yes. It's hard to understand how we find ourselves here, isn't it? Still, best to keep yourself occupied, sir, so let's get started."

I had the feeling that he wanted to occupy his mind as well.

You mentioned a grandson, and your son would be of military age but you haven't spoken about him… I didn't like to ask. It felt too much like intruding, especially in the circumstances.

The exercises were a shock. I'd guessed I would have lost some ground, but it was frightening how far back I'd slid in just those few days. *Not eating didn't help, either – I must have lost even more weight.*

"You really need to work every day, sir," Kahrstedt said. "No one knows how much longer you'll all be able to stay here, or what you'll have to deal with when you leave."

"Don't worry," I said. "I'll work."

And I did, until my muscles burned with the effort.

A couple of days later, Krug came back into the day room, looking very uneasy. Nagel and I went and sat with him.

"How are you?" Nagel asked.

"I don't know," Krug said slowly. "That was really horrible – I was stuck at the Front, and I don't know when it's going to happen again. It's really frightening – it's all I can see and hear… I don't think I can go home – I just…"

Nagel and I looked at each other. *Poor sod.*

"It'll get better in time," I said, hoping I sounded convincing. "It's all still so raw – I think our minds have to heal as well as our bodies."

Krug looked at me. "You have problems as well?"

"Oh, yes – I see things. The Front, men I knew, that sort of thing. And like you say, it's completely real."

"What about you?" he asked Nagel.

"Sometimes, yes…"

I realised Landauer and Fischer were listening.

"I'm all right until something sets me off," Fischer said.

"My friend Karl was like that after Verdun," I said, surprised that I could talk about him. "He said it was usually something someone said."

Landauer nodded. "And it all comes back."

"If you ask me, you're all fucking well bonkers," Wolffheim said.

Nagel shrugged.

Fischer just grinned. "Probably accurate, but I don't give a stuff."

"I've seen you staring into space," I said to Wolffheim.

"Just thinking," he replied, but there was a defensive note in his voice that none of us missed.

"I'm scared I'll hurt someone," Krug said. "Suppose I think my dad's a Frenchie? What happens then?"

Nagel put his hand on Krug's shoulder. "Didn't you learn not to worry?"

Krug gave a weak smile. "Yes – must have forgotten."

"What are you going to do now?" I asked Wolffheim. I wanted to change the subject.

"God knows. We'll still have an army, so they'll need officers. I suppose I'll just have to hope there's a place for me – I mean, with there being so many fit young chaps coming through."

Bredt looked at him. "Oh, I wouldn't worry about them. Half are dead, and the rest in prison or hospital."

"That's if the Allies let us have an army," Hammer said.

"What the hell are you talking about?" Wolffheim demanded. "Whoever heard of a country without an army? And Prussia without an army is unthinkable."

"We didn't have much of one after Napoleon had finished with us," Riege reminded him.

"Yes, but we were defeated and occupied then – as it is, we're still in the enemy's territory."

The arrival of the post broke up the argument, to my relief. It was all pointless speculation.

Nagel opened his letter with some difficulty, started reading it, and then crumpled it up and threw it on the floor. He got up and left the room, leaning very heavily on his stick, his shoulders sagging.

Landauer picked up the ball of paper, and put it on one of the tables.

Through the window I saw Nagel slump onto one of the chairs in the conservatory. Whatever he'd read had obviously hit him hard. *Best leave him alone.*

When I got back after my exercises it was dark, and he was sitting in the day room, staring into the empty grate. *Pity we can't have a fire. This room's bloody chilly, and it's not even winter yet.*

I wheeled myself alongside him. "Bad news?" I asked quietly.

"The bitch has thrown me over," he said bitterly. "Doesn't want a man with one arm and no prospects."

"Did she say that?" Fischer asked, appalled.

"Not in so many words," Nagel replied. "But that's the sense of it."

No one knew what to say. We all looked at each other, at the parts that were missing, at the disfigured faces.

After a long pause, Hammer said, "Don't know where the silly cow thinks she's going to find another fellow", in as flippant a tone as he could manage.

"Quite," said Wolffheim.

"Oh, she's got one already," Nagel said. "Some bastard in a reserved occupation."

"That fucking stinks," said Schieffer.

"Well, she's welcome to him," I said. "What sort of man is that?"

"One with two arms," Nagel replied.

"And no guts," said Wolffheim, "or he'd have volunteered."

I suddenly remembered the Prof, pissed off to buggery about having to leave the Jasta and go back to his laboratory. *He wasn't short of guts.* But I kept my mouth shut.

"Fancy a game of cards?" Nagel said to Krug and me.

He played very badly and lost five hundred marks.

"Will you take an IOU?" he asked.

"Don't be stupid," I said. "You know no one has to pay up until he leaves."

He just smiled and wrote it out.

After dinner, I cornered Doctor Holz.

"I don't like talking about men behind their backs," I said, "but Nagel's girlfriend's just broken up with him, and he's taking it very hard – and he insisted on giving me an IOU for his losses at cards."

The doctor raised his eyebrows. "Did he? Thank you, Becker. Thank you very much. I'll make sure we keep an eye on him."

Nagel didn't come down for a couple of days. In the meantime we were joined by a new patient, who sat motionless in his wheelchair, staring at the floor.

Landauer went over and introduced himself, but there was no response. None at all. He didn't eat anything at lunch, just sat in exactly the same position with the same blank expression.

He had both arms, legs and eyes – but as we all knew, injuries to the body can be far worse. We couldn't tell if his morose silence was due to physical problems or mental ones.

"Shouldn't he be in the mental wing?" Landauer asked me in the conservatory.

"Presumably not," I said. "But I'm buggered if I know what's wrong with him." I'd tried to speak to him as well, but with as little success.

"I expect we'll find out," Landauer said, but the next day the man was just the same.

Nagel rejoined us, looking somewhat brighter than I'd expected.

"I've decided she's not worth getting pissed off about," he said.

"That's the spirit," said Hammer.

"After all, there are far more women than men in Germany," Nagel continued.

"True," said Fischer, "but I don't feel like a prime catch. I mean, you should see the scars." He too was missing a hand, and had collected half a dozen shell splinters.

"You don't have to be, these days," Landauer said. "I'm cautiously optimistic."

"Yes, but you're not mutilated," I said. "Who's going to want a fellow with one leg? I mean, she'll have a stump against her leg in bed..." I broke off, shaken by what I'd just said.

"And how can we give her an arm when we're on crutches?" asked Schieffer.

"At least you've got a knee," I said. "You'll be able to walk fine on an artificial leg."

"It's the same problem in bed, though," he said. "What girl's going to want that?"

"Lucky fucking bastards."

The voice was unfamiliar. We looked round the room.

The silent man was staring at us, his eyes so full of anguish that I could hardly look at them.

"You don't know how fucking lucky you all are." His voice matched his eyes.

We looked at each other.

"Sorry," said Landauer. "We seem to have offended you."

He gave a bitter laugh. "Offended me? No."

He stared at the floor again, and I thought he wasn't going to say any more, but then he continued, so quietly that I could hardly hear him.

"I'd change places with any of you – women are over for me because – because... I can't... I... I've lost my... my... *everything's gone*."

Jesus fucking Christ. My stomach turned over.

None of us could look at him. We exchanged horrified glances. There was absolutely nothing that anyone could say.

He had fallen silent again, and it was a long time before we started talking, very quietly, to each other.

Sister Angelika took him back upstairs straight after dinner.

"I shall never complain about anything ever again," Fischer said.

"I'll hold you to that," said Schieffer, and we all laughed far too hard and far too long.

Nagel, Wolffheim and I sat down to play cards, and Hammer put a succession of records on the gramophone. None of us wanted to talk about the poor sod, or even to think about him.

I was just about to go to bed when there was a lot of noise outside.

Shit! Those Red bastards have come back—

Doctor Holz came into the day room, looking very uncomfortable.

What the fuck has happened?

"Gentlemen, I'm very sorry to have to tell you that Leutnant Bartz has committed suicide. He threw himself out of a top-floor window and landed outside the kitchen."

Bartz?

"Do we know him?" Landauer asked cautiously.

"He was with you the last two days – we thought a bit of company might help as he was very low. We were watching him, but he slipped out of his room."

Oh – that was Bartz. Who wants to live like that?

"I'd have done the same," said Fischer, and there was a chorus of agreement.

"Ah," said Doctor Holz. "He told you, then?"

We all nodded.

"Well, I'll leave you to your pastimes," he said. "I thought it was best you knew what the noise was about."

"Thank you," said Nagel.

"Jesus," Landauer said. "It doesn't bear thinking about."

"There was a fellow in my company got hit like that, back in '15," I said.

"What happened to him?" asked Fischer.

"Don't know. He was unconscious when they took him away, and he'd lost a lot of blood, so we hoped he wouldn't make it. Karl and I promised to shoot each other if it happened to us."

"You served together back then?" Nagel asked me, clearly keen to change the subject.

"Yes – we shared a flat in Heidelberg just before the war. We all volunteered when it began, all the law students."

"Just like my class," said Schieffer. "I was studying geography in Berlin – we all went to the recruiting office together."

"I wasn't old enough until mid '16," said Nagel.

"I was at Lichterfelde when it started," Wolffheim said, "and they commissioned a lot of us early, to be officers in the new regiments." He gave a short laugh. "Buggered if I know how I survived that Langemarck business. Right fucking mess, that was."

I wished he hadn't mentioned Langemarck.

"It's all been a right fucking mess," Fischer said.

"And the biggest mess of all is the one we're in now," said Hammer.

No one felt like going to bed, and we stayed up until Sister Ursula came and told us off.

"This room's far too cold for you all," she said sternly. "You should be in your nice warm beds."

"Yes, Sister," Nagel said, with a wink at the rest of us.

"I'll be back in ten minutes and I don't want to see any of you," she added, and left the room.

Nagel sighed. "What I couldn't do with her!"

We all laughed.

"I know, I know," he said. "Use my imagination!"

That's all any of us is likely to get, I thought as I curled up, pretending the pillow was Karl's shoulder. *You wouldn't have cared, would you, about the stump?*

'Of course not. You didn't mind about my scars, did you, or my bones sticking out?'

A few days later, Sobek arrived, looking awkward in a cheap brown suit which didn't quite fit. I'd only ever seen him in uniform, and at first I didn't recognise him.

His expression was different, too. He'd been a confident, cheerful young fellow, but his face was lined and his eyes were shadowed with worry and uncertainty, as if he'd lost his way and didn't know what to do next.

We looked at each other for a moment, and then stared at the floor, neither of us knowing what to say.

"How… er…" He cleared his throat. "How are you getting on, sir?"

"Not too bad, thanks. What… er… what's happened… what have they done with the Jasta?"

"Broken up. We managed to fly as far as Cologne, then we couldn't get any more fuel. The Soldiers' and Workers' Council wouldn't let us have any. I said goodbye to the others there. We're all making our own way home. We could have fought on, but the last order we got was to return to Germany. Then there weren't any more orders, and we were told we'd been released from our oaths."

"What about Fellmann and the ground crew?"

"They got the train. We destroyed all the stores, then I made sure they got away first, then we swung the propellers for each other. I hope they got back all right."

We were both silent.

"I'm sorry about your leg, sir," he said. "They told me not to say anything – before, in the field hospital."

"Yes, I know… Sobek, why in God's name are you calling me 'sir'? We're not in the Army any more."

"Sorry. Force of habit, I suppose."

"'Du' would be better."

He smiled. "Have they said when you can go home?"

"Not yet."

Home. How in God's name am I going to cope at home, with all those civilians?

"They don't know when I'll be able to have an artificial leg," I added. "With all the trouble."

Sobek sighed. "Everything's upside down. It's not safe outside in uniform. The Soldiers' Council threatened to shoot us. They surrounded us after we got out of the aircraft, all armed. They even had a machine gun. I think they meant it at first, but then they changed their minds and let us go. We officers all kept our flying jackets on to hide our epaulettes, and then I got this suit in exchange for my best boots.

"And yesterday I saw a poor old Major get beaten half senseless. I wanted to go and rescue him, but there were five of them. If I'd still had my pistol – but the Soldiers' Council took our weapons. After they'd gone I went to help him. I was so ashamed of myself."

"There wasn't anything you could have done. You'd just have got beaten up yourself."

"I should have tried," he said.

What a bloody world. We fought for these people – or thought we did. And this is what we get.

"The Soldiers' Council came bursting in here, all armed as well," I said. "They made some remark about it being a den of privilege, or some other stupid expression. We wondered if they were going to shoot us."

"For God's sake! The filthy cowards!"

"Exactly. Anyway, they went away. I think they realised they'd got it wrong… You haven't come out of your way to see me, have you?"

"No, I was passing through. It's a long story. I won't bore you with it… I – I thought you might like these." He opened his battered case and handed me the squadron photograph albums.

"Thank you," I said. I could hardly speak, and for a second I thought I might break down again.

"You see, you're the... our longest serving pilot who's still alive, and they'll mean more to you than to anyone else. I've got plenty of souvenirs of my own."

"It's... I appreciate this more than I can tell you. Thank you again."

I daren't open the albums. I would have to do that in private.

"Well, I... er – I'd better be going. I've still got a long journey ahead of me."

"Where are you going?"

"Breslau. Home. It's a long story. There was a girl, a nurse. I hoped – but she... anyway, I'll be off. I hope you... I mean, that you..."

"Oh, I'll be fine. Break a leg."

"Goodbye, then."

We shook hands. *I don't suppose I'll ever see you again*, I thought as Sobek left the room.

I held the albums in my hands. *Some time, not today, I shall open them. There will be Karl and Otto and the Chief, Johnny, Widemayer, Patschke, Buchholz, Geschke, Lentzke... all of them. Photographs of young men dead far too soon, photographs of aeroplanes, of parties, of funerals. All the life of the Jasta is in these books, and therefore most of my life too.*

When I can face it, some time, I shall sit in my room and turn the pages slowly, one by one, remembering. And I shall mourn their memory.

I put it off for the best part of a week. It turned out to be even worse than I'd expected, and I couldn't do it in one go.

The first few pages weren't too bad because they were before my time, but Otto was there, of course, and seeing the Chief's face reminded me vividly of him. Then I reached the first photograph in which all the faces were familiar.

All of them were dead. Johnny's scarred face brought back the image of him falling blazing through the sky... My dreams that night were awful, and I woke sweating and screaming and afraid to go back to sleep.

I used to smoke on bad nights. I was dying for a real cigarette. Beech leaf 'tobacco' was no bloody use at all and I'd given it up.

I lay wide awake, but whether my eyes were open or closed made no difference to the horrible visions. I was hot and cold and sweating like a pig, my leg – especially my missing knee – hurting like fire. The pain spread all over my body and then concentrated itself in my head. I ached as if I'd been beaten from head to foot, and even the slightest movement was unbearable.

We were having a party in the mess. Karl was playing the piano and we were all singing – but the others were skeletons and I was in a wheelchair. I was drenched in sweat, the songs going round and round in my head until I couldn't distinguish waking from dreaming.

Morning came eventually. Sister Ulrike took one look at me, took my temperature, and fetched Doctor Holz.

"What's wrong with me?" I managed to ask.

"You have influenza."

I was too relieved that my dreams had a physical cause to worry about the illness.

A short while later I was too ill to care about anything. I fell into the same horrible delirium that I'd suffered from in Belgium. I was occasionally aware of the hospital, of the nurses coming in and out, but the rest of the time I was at the Front. I sat by Karl's bed, hearing him gasping for breath – then I was lying there suffocating, the air gurgling in my lungs...

I woke in terror, fighting to breathe, drowning.

After an eternity of torment the fever broke, leaving me dreadfully weak and with a horrible cough.

Sister Ursula smiled at me, her hazel eyes warm. "We thought we were going to lose you as well," she said.

"Who's died, then?"

"Ten so far. And three of the staff."

"Good God. Anyone – anyone I know?"

The war's still killing us. It's just using a different weapon. How can our weakened bodies fight a disease like this? It's killed three of the staff, and they're all healthy.

She hesitated. "No."

That was a lie, of course. A fortnight later, when I was strong enough to go down to the day room, I found out that Nagel and Krug were dead. The flu had completed what the war had begun.

Nagel's life was in ruins anyway, and Krug was never going to be right in his head again. And as Nagel said, the dead are better off. Neither of them has to suffer any more, or worry about the outside world.

I looked around the drab day room, at the hollow-eyed, thin faces, and the place made me shudder. *I have to get out of here. I have to get out of this bloody chair and learn to walk again, and get out.*

I managed to wheel myself to the gym. It was fucking hard work and I had to pause twice. *I hope Kahrstedt's still alive.*

Of course he was. Kahrstedt was indestructible.

"Hello, sir," he said with a smile. "How are you?"

I shrugged. "I've come to find out... You've escaped the flu, then?"

"It's a funny thing, sir, but it seems to be taking the young people and not us old bastards."

That is odd. You'd think the older people would be weaker. Must ask Alfred about it – assuming it hasn't got him.

"I heard you were very ill, sir," Kahrstedt said, "so you're going to have to be patient."

After ten minutes I wanted to scream with frustration and anger. All my hard work had been wiped out, as if I'd done nothing at all.

"I might as well not have bothered," I said bitterly.

He shook his head. "Think where you'd be if you hadn't done all that work, sir. You'd quite possibly be dead."

I might as well be – I'm never going to get out of this sodding place.

"You can do it, sir," he said. "We'll work at it together, bit by bit."

"Thanks." *Good bloke, Kahrstedt, just what I need…*

What a wretched state I'm in, I thought as I had to pause on the way back to the day room. *I'm twenty-three, it still isn't six months since I buried Karl, and now I'm so wasted that I've got no strength at all.* I thought of us in his garden, walking slowly along the avenue of limes, and understood how wrecked he must have felt.

God, that's nearly a year ago. One whole year, and yet only one. Even those days are another world.

My longing for him was so sharp and sudden that it was a physical pain. *All I want is to see your face, hear your voice, and feel your touch, just one more time. Somehow I have to go on without you…*

It was almost Christmas and the days were short and dark. There was still no proper government, and so no fuel and not much food. The hospital was so cold that our breath clouded, and we all sat wrapped in blankets. The only time I felt warm was when I was doing my exercises.

I was fed up with being frozen and I wrote to my parents, asking them to send me a shawl or a sweater or something. They replied that they daren't send anything through the post.

Papa complained about the anarchy that he said was ruining the country.

It's what you wanted. You wanted Socialism and now you've got it.

"Going to be a dull Christmas, this," said Fischer. "My family say they're not sending me anything."

Wolffheim snorted. "Not that there's anything to send."

"And as for the peace negotiations…" Landauer said with a sigh. "I don't understand why the Allies think the Kaiser's a criminal."

"Nor do I," I agreed. "I'd be happy to have him back."

"Yes," said Bredt. "We'd have stability then."

"They can't blame him for starting it," said Landauer. "If you ask me, it was the Serbs' fault. If they hadn't shot the Archduke, none of it would have happened."

"We shouldn't have got involved anyway," Bredt said. "What was it Bismarck said?"

"'The Balkans aren't worth the bones of a healthy Pomeranian grenadier,'" said Fischer.

Well, he was right. I don't think they're worth the leg of a healthy Württemberg fighter pilot either, or the bones of a Brandenburg Junker – but that won't do me much good. They caused the trouble and we suffer for it.

Fischer was right about Christmas being dull. No one felt like celebrating, and there wasn't much to eat or drink. A couple of the orderlies went and got us a Christmas tree, and we lit the candles and sang all the old carols, but there weren't any presents.

"Not quite how I imagined Christmas in the homeland," said Bredt.

That's for sure. Sitting mutilated in a cold, bare hospital hadn't figured in any of our dreams.

Last year we had a bloody good feast and a piss-up in the mess – oh, yes, and the Tommies raided us. And it's four years since we had that astonishing Christmas truce, laughing and playing football with the Tommies.

We should have put an end to the war then, just refused to fight any more. If we'd all done that, our governments wouldn't have been able to do anything about it.

But it hadn't occurred to us, and even if it had, there were plenty of men who would have continued fighting.

Europe was determined to destroy itself, and I wonder if anyone will ever understand why.

And this Christmas we've got nothing. I don't even have letters from my family.

That turned out to be unfair – their letters arrived the next day, having taken two weeks to reach me.

'I do hope you're getting over that dreadful flu,' Mama wrote. 'Almost everyone here has had it, and a lot of people have died – mostly young people, which does seem rather strange. Fortunately, Johanna only had a slight go of it. I'm so sorry we couldn't come and see you again – we were so worried about you, but it's too dangerous to travel.'

Dangerous? You don't know what dangerous is. Dangerous is being shelled, or a flight of Camels coming at you out of the sun. If you really cared, you'd have come. I could have died of the flu. It would have served you right. You can't even manage to come and see me.

That's unfair, too. It really is dangerous out there. People are getting killed, and I don't want my family out in that sort of trouble. I'm getting by all right here, and I'm starting to get stronger again, thanks to Kahrstedt.

Alfred wrote that he was in Berlin, based at the Guards barracks.

'You wouldn't believe the state of the place. I've healed up enough to be able to fight, and it won't be long before I have to.

The last thing I want is civil war, but we can't let the bastards take over or we'll be in the same crap as the Russians. There are so many rival groups that you hardly know who's who.

To add to the mess, half my fellows have come down with that sodding flu and three of them have died so far. At least it's hitting the Commies just the same.'

Paul Fellmann sent me his best wishes. He'd made it back to Frankfurt an der Oder, but said he was off to Berlin to join the fight against the Reds. I was suddenly aware that he'd never actually fought anyone, for all that he'd learned the theory.

I should put him and Alfred in touch – if anyone can teach him the reality of fighting, it's Alfred. I hope it's not too late.

It was suddenly very important to keep Paul safe – he and Alfred were the only two friends I had left apart from Horstmann, and I didn't know if he was still alive.

I wheeled myself to the admin office, and asked if I could send a couple of cables.

"Yes – but you must realise that the system's not working as it should."

"I'll take a chance on that. Thanks."

A couple of days later I got a letter from Horstmann, saying he was back in Potsdam. He was very angry about the outcome of the war, of course, but said that he and Susanne hoped to marry in the summer, if things had settled down.

'You must come to the wedding. You'll be out of hospital by then, and you're more than welcome to come and stay with us.'

I'd love to – and then I realised it would mean socialising with strangers, either on crutches or in a wheelchair, and how was I going to get to Potsdam?

Don't be so fucking pathetic, Franz. Susanne's family are all soldiers, like Karl's, and they won't give a shit about the leg. And you'll have to learn to manage. You can't be a hermit.

New Year's Eve was even worse than Christmas. None of us wanted to contemplate the bleak year that lay ahead of us. *This time last year I didn't know how much longer I would survive. I was looking forward to my January leave and wondering if I'd be alive to go on it...*

And now it's 1919, I thought on New Year's Day. *I've survived the war, but I've no idea how I'm going to live.*

Karl was right. I have come through, but for what? What on earth am I going to do?

Some days later, the calendar caught my eye as I went into the day room. It was exactly a year since I'd made the journey through the snow to Karl's house, a year since we'd had that week together. I hid behind a newspaper, hoping no one would talk to me.

This time last year there was love, and tenderness in your eyes, and your soft skin against mine. That week you really belonged to me, and I to you. It was the happiest week of my life.

Never again. I'll never lie in anyone's arms like that again.

Is it ever going to get easier, being without you?

All I could think about was the year before. Part of me wanted to stop, because I was torturing myself, but thinking about Karl seemed to bring him closer. More than once I had the strange experience of waking with my bed smelling of him, and a strong feeling that he really had been with me, and I was never able to explain it away.

There has to be a rational explanation – but at the same time, I didn't really want one. *It's like his house – there's definitely something there.* 'You'll loiter in the house with all the other relatives,' Johnny had said to him – but instead it felt as though he were loitering with me, and it was immensely comforting.

Does it matter whether it's real or not, if it makes me feel better? And it's far better than seeing the Front, or dead men...

The others noticed that I was in a bit of a strange mood, but no one said anything. Everyone had his memories.

Maybe they thought I was worried about the situation outside – Berlin had descended into civil war, the Freikorps and the Communists were fighting openly with machine guns and flamethrowers, and the rest of the country was a hair's breadth away from following. I had no idea whether Alfred and Fellmann were still alive, or whether Horstmann was also fighting, or whether my family was safe.

"Come and have a drink," said Fischer. "It's Wolffheim's last night."

"What, already?" I'd forgotten that he was going to be discharged.

Landauer poured a finger of schnapps into our coffee mugs.

"Where did you get this?" Bredt asked.

"Ask no questions!" Landauer replied.

"Shut up and drink your schnapps!" said Fischer at the same time.

"What are you going to do?" I asked Wolffheim.

"Go and give those fucking Commie bastards something to think about," he replied.

"I've got a friend in Berlin doing just that," I said. "Oberleutnant Alfred Friedemann – at least, I hope he's still with us. He was a storm troop officer, bloody mad bugger – just the sort of fellow you want beside you."

Wolffheim's face lit up. "Where can I find him?"

"Last thing I heard, they were in the Guards' barracks."

"Thanks, Becker – we have to stop the rot or we'll be a fucking Soviet republic."

"I'll come and help once they let me out," said Landauer.

"So will I," Riege said.

Schieffer, Fischer and I looked at each other, at our missing limbs. *None of us would be any bloody use.*

"Got any more schnapps?" I asked Landauer.

He shook his head.

Pity. I could do with getting pissed.

Landauer was discharged a few days after Wolffheim, with the same destination in mind.

"Never thought I'd be fighting on the streets of Berlin," he said on the day he left, "but it has to be done."

"Someone please tell me how we got into this mess," said Fischer.

"It was the Serbs," Landauer said again.

"I think we'd had peace for so long that everyone forgot what war really is," said Schieffer. "And Austria and Russia had rattled the sabre before over the Balkans, and nothing happened, and they thought nothing would happen this time, either."

"No, that's not it at all," Hammer said. "The bloody Frenchies wanted to get their own back for 1870, and the Tommies got pissed off with us for wanting a navy—"

"And what use was the bloody Navy anyway?" Bredt demanded. "All that money, that we could have spent on the Army – if we'd had all those extra divisions we'd have won the war. Instead, we got a load of ships that only got used once."

"Does it matter?" I asked wearily. "All I know is it wasn't my fault and I'm stuck paying for it. I couldn't give a shit what bastard started it."

"I just want to know why my brother and cousins died," Fischer said.

"None of it makes any sense," Riege said. "You think, *We're over here in field grey, and you're over there in khaki or horizon blue, and we're all the same really, but our governments have fallen out and so we have to kill each other.* God knows what that's supposed to solve."

"Indeed," said Landauer. "All it ever does is give people a reason for another war."

"There can't be another war after this one," Fischer said.

'That's probably what the cavemen said after they'd slaughtered their neighbours,' Karl said.

"Let's just wish Landauer success and good fortune," said Schieffer, "and hope we can all go home soon."

We all drank to that, but 'soon' wasn't likely. Not for me, anyway. I was still making up the ground I'd lost to the flu.

"You were very lucky," Sister Ursula told me as she helped me to dress. "Don't tell the others, but we lost most of the spinal injury cases and about a third of the facial patients. And we won't talk about the chest wounds – nearly all of them are dead."

"Jesus."

"And some of the survivors are far worse than you are… We've lost quite a few colleagues as well. Sister Angelika, for one, and four orderlies – but they were all on the mental wards, so you won't know them."

So that's why I haven't seen Sister Angelika. I felt rather guilty – I'd been so relieved at her absence that I hadn't wondered about the reason for it. *She was just trying to cheer us all up – I don't suppose she had any idea how bloody irritating she was, and now she's dead.*

I want to get out of here. It's getting very depressing being surrounded by mutilation and death. The harder I work, the sooner I'll be home – but at the same time I was afraid of leaving the hospital, where everyone was maimed and everyone was haunted by the war.

The days were getting longer, but my spirits refused to lift. My progress was frustratingly slow, and some days I couldn't balance at all.

"You're getting there, sir," Kahrstedt said encouragingly.

"Bollocks. You're just saying that."

He smiled, and pointed to the weights I was working with. "Two weeks ago you wouldn't have been able to lift those."

"All right, then – can I try crutches?"

Schieffer was practising on his, making it look so easy.

"Yes." Kahrstedt saw where I was looking. "Leutnant Schieffer's had quite a bit of practice. You have to be patient."

Just getting out of my chair and onto the crutches was almost impossible. I hadn't realised just how solid the rails were, and at first I couldn't get any leverage.

Then suddenly it worked, and I was upright, gasping for breath from the sheer effort. *God, if just getting up's that hard, how in God's name am I going to move forward?*

"Now balance on your foot and one crutch, lift the other, place it half a pace forwards, same with the other – good. Now take your weight on both crutches and swing your leg forwards, just like you did on the rails – very good! And again."

It was exhausting. I managed to swing my leg forward twice and had to collapse back into my chair, and as I did so I banged my stump and the pain was so appalling that I was almost sick. I barely registered Kahrstedt saying, "Well done, sir."

"How the fuck do you do it?" I asked Schieffer later.

"It did feel fucking impossible at first – but you'll get the hang of it."

What he didn't tell me was how truly fucking impossible it was to get up when you fell over. The first couple of times, Kahrstedt helped me up, but then he said, "You have to learn how to do it by yourself, sir", and, being Kahrstedt, he didn't budge from that.

You could give me a hand, you bastard, I thought as my crutches slipped yet again and I landed on my arse – and then I realised that he was giving me the best hand he could, that helping me too much wouldn't help me at all.

"Do it again, sir," he said for the thousandth time.

"Kahrstedt, you can – stick your 'again' – up your arse," I gasped.

"You'll thank me later, sir," he said cheerfully. "Come on, now. Up you get."

It's like being a fucking recruit again, except I haven't got a monkey on my back and I'm not getting covered in mud.

I managed, somehow, to get up.

"Well done, sir. Keep going like that and you'll soon be fully mobile."

How soon is 'soon'? I'd like to get home for my birthday…

At the beginning of February, I got a letter from Johanna. She was itching to start her medical studies,

'but I can't go to Berlin until the trouble is over. Honestly, you'd think everyone would have had enough of war, but instead they want to fight each other. Though I don't want to see a Soviet republic – they'd take everything we've got. I think Papa's realising that their Socialism isn't quite the same as his!'

The next part was rather peculiar.

'The Hertels have come back, but without Maria. Apparently she's staying with her grandmother in Stuttgart. God knows why – it's much more peaceful here, but they won't explain. The politics is just as bad as ever – he won't talk to Papa at the club, but I think it's Frau H. who's the real problem. They won't have anything to do with us, anyway – and that's no great loss.'

Now, that is curious. Suppose Maria had my child – that would be a good reason for her not going home. In a large city you can put on a wedding ring and tell everyone you're a widow, and no one will know any different.

But they'd want us to get married, surely? Whatever they think of Papa's politics, it would legitimise their grandchild, and make their daughter a respectable woman again – but maybe they don't want her to marry a one-legged veteran with no qualifications.

A half-mad, one-legged veteran, I thought in the early hours after yet another ghastly nightmare about the Front. *And what woman wants to marry a man who sees things and thinks the dead talk to him?*

That was really worrying me. I wasn't as bad as Krug had been, but I kept having what I could only call 'episodes' when the war intruded and reality disappeared, and I would find myself staring into space, having lost all sense of where I was. I wanted to ask Doctor Holz about them, but I was too scared of being taken to the mental wing.

Landauer and some of the other fellows have the same problem, I reminded myself. *And most of the time I do know exactly where I am.*

What sort of a father would someone like me make, anyway?

That really was getting two and two to make twenty-two. I was assuming that there was a child, and that it was mine.

There are all sorts of reasons why a young woman would want to live in the city. Maybe she wants a career, like Johanna.

Even if she does have my child, maybe Karl was right about not marrying her. I don't really know her, Johanna doesn't want her as a sister-in-law, my parents won't want the marriage and nor will hers. It's not the best start to the rest of my life.

No point worrying about any of that now. It's all hypothetical.

XII

Fischer left a week after Schieffer. Every man who was discharged was replaced by another wreck, but I didn't want to get to know any of them. I was determined to get out as soon as winter was over.

"What's up with Bredt?" Riege asked one cold February day.

Bredt was sitting in the conservatory, staring blankly at the snow-covered garden.

"Verdun, I expect," said Hammer. "It's the 21st."

I remembered Karl sitting sleepless and haunted, gazing out of our hut at the airfield, lost in memory.

"Ah," I said. "He was there at the beginning, then?"

"I should think so, wouldn't you?" Hammer said.

Bredt didn't come down the next day, or the one after that, and when he did he looked like a man who'd spent the whole time surrounded by ghosts.

"Come and play cards with Becker and me," Riege said to him.

"What?" he asked vaguely.

"Cards," Riege said. "Usual stakes."

Bredt just stared at us, or rather through us. After a moment he shook his head. "Sorry, I… er…" His eyes wandered round the room, as if he were wondering what he was doing there. "Yes, of course. Be glad to have something else to think about."

He was obviously very preoccupied, and kept losing track of the game.

"Sorry, chaps," he said after twenty minutes or so. "I'm just spoiling it for you."

"Don't worry about it," I said. "My friend Karl was at Verdun, and he was – well, he never really… it left its mark, let's just say that."

"It did on me too, in more ways than one," Bredt said slowly. "We lost so many bloody good blokes it broke your heart, and it was nearly the end for me too… We were supposed to take the village of Beaumont, but it was on a hill and the Frenchies had built their trenches like terraces all the way up, and we had over a kilometre to go across open ground to get there, almost no cover at all, and as if that wasn't enough, we got flanking fire from both sides. The air was practically solid.

"Some of us actually got halfway up the hill, God knows how, but we couldn't dig in because the ground was too stony, so we were just lying there in the open. It must have been like fucking target practice for the Frenchies – I don't know how they didn't get us all.

"I got hit after about an hour, and I had to wait till it got dark to be taken back. A lot of fellows died waiting, and I thought I would too. The Frenchies kept on shelling all night – one of my stretcher-bearers got killed and I had to wait for another, just lying there in the open with the shells crashing in all around. Those stretcher-bearers were fucking heroes, I can tell you – anyway, really it saved my bacon, because I was out of it for months after that, and then at Döberitz till halfway through '17."

There was a long pause, and then he added, quietly, "I didn't find out until I was back in Germany that my best mate fell the day after I was hit. We'd been friends since our first term at cadet school… It was my wife who told me, she's his cousin. Anyway, it's time I shut up."

We were all silent for several minutes. *What idiot ordered an attack like that?* The very idea of it made my blood run cold.

"Time for my exercises," I said, and went to the gym. I'd had enough of hearing about the war, and I needed to work.

The next morning, to my utter joy, I managed to get onto and off the lavatory by myself. I got Bloch to wait outside, just in case I needed his help, but made it without ending up on the floor.

Hoo-fucking-ray. Franz Becker, at the age of twenty-three, can have a shit without assistance – though that's a fucking sight more than some of the poor bastards in this hospital will ever manage.

"Thank you," I said to Kahrstedt later.

He raised an eyebrow in inquiry.

"For another bit of independence," I said. "This may sound trivial, but this morning I had a crap unaided, for the first time since last July."

"That's not trivial at all, sir – it's a major step towards going home. There's a list of things you have to be able to do before Doctor Holz will discharge you, and that's on it. And it's a big morale boost."

"You're not wrong there. And now I want to start on stairs."

His eyebrows went up again. "All right – but it's going to be harder than you think. You'll start by going up and down on your bottom."

"You are joking."

"Not at all, sir. If you use your crutches then you have to hop – I'll get you doing that on the rails later – and there's a much higher risk of falling. It's easier and safer on your backside."

I hadn't thought of that.

We went to the main staircase. About ten metres away from the bottom of it, Kahrstedt said, "Get onto your crutches now, sir, go to the stairs and sit on whichever step is easiest... Right, now put the crutches on the step beside you, and use your hands and leg to push yourself up onto the next step. Good. And again – and remember to take the crutches with you."

I managed about ten treads before needing a rest.

"Well done, sir. Now come back down."

It wasn't that bad – I kept catching my lower back on the edge of the steps, which was irritating, but apart from that it went quite well.

"I'm going to see how far back I can get on my crutches," I said.

"That's the spirit, sir," he said with a smile.

The answer was about halfway, which was less than I'd hoped. *I wonder if I can get Riege to push my chair while I practise.*

I was a bit reluctant to ask him, but to my surprise he jumped at it.

"Course I will – I need to walk more as well, and leaning on your chair will make it much easier." He laughed. "I'll be like my little son pushing the pushchair!"

I laughed as well. "Just don't expect 'Papa' to pick you up if you fall over!"

Kahrstedt kept his promise to get me hopping between the rails.

"Think how high a tread is, sir," he said. "That's how high you have to manage. Rail in one hand, crutches in the other – now push down and jump as high as you can."

I barely left the floor.

"Again, sir."

And on it went, Kahrstedt and his bloody 'again' until I wanted to strangle him.

Riege was lifting weights across the other side of the gym, and he caught my eye. "Jump, Becker, you lazy sod!" he called out.

"Shut the – fuck up!" I gasped, and when I'd got my breath back I added, "Do twenty squats, why don't you?"

"Oh, piss off!" he retorted cheerfully.

At the end of my session he hobbled over to me. "Right, Long John Silver," he said, "let's go and read the paper before dinner."

"Bloody hell, is it that time already?"

"Certainly is, sir," Kahrstedt said. "I'll see you gentlemen in the morning."

"Do you think they'll have seeds for your parrot?" Riege asked as we left the gym.

"Shut up and push the bloody chair!"

We made it most of the way to the day room.

"Hang on a minute," he said. "I need to sit down."

"*You* need to sit down? It's my fucking chair!"

"It's this bloody hip," he said, limping to one of the chairs in the corridor.

I had a breather as well, in my own chair. I needed it more than I'd realised.

"Fucking hell," Riege said after a while, his face pale.

You've overdone it, and I don't feel too good either. It's been a bloody hard day.

"Let's rest for a bit," I said. "I'm knackered as well."

A few minutes later he said, "That's better – bloody thing does start grumbling."

We continued on our slow way to the day room, where he lowered himself painfully into one of the armchairs.

"You never did say what happened," I said.

"Oh, it was a grenade. Lindau – my Sergeant – took most of it. Killed the poor sod, but I got a fine collection of bits in my hip and thigh. I was bloody lucky I was sideways on to the bang, or I'd have ended up like poor Bartz."

"You wouldn't wish that on anyone."

"No – but then we probably did."

That wasn't something I wanted to think about.

"Didn't have much choice, did we?" was all I said.

"No… Who's got the paper?" Riege asked.

"Here," said Geinitz, one of the more recent arrivals. "Right load of crap, it is – fit for one purpose only."

I picked up an old magazine and started leafing through it.

Come on, Becker! Krypke was shaking my shoulder.

Watch out, sir! I shouted, but too late.

The Tommy slammed the club into his head, and blood and brains showered everywhere—

Bredt was holding my shoulders. "It's all right, Becker. Sorry – my fault for shaking you."

"What the...?" *Where the fuck – oh, in the day room.*

"It's dinner time. You'd nodded off."

Which means I won't sleep later. But I was so tired from the exercises that I went out the moment my head hit the pillow, and I actually stayed asleep until about three.

I spent the rest of the early hours in a haunted half-doze. I was trying to find my way back to the front line, through a maze of comms and second-line trenches. The Tommies were shelling intermittently, and one stretch of comms trench was commanded by one of their bastard snipers, and every time I got lost I found myself in it again, bent double, convinced I was about to be shot at any moment...

I woke with yet another jolt, sweating, my heart pounding. *If only Karl were here!* I stared into the blackness of my room, my longing for him unbearable.

Eventually it got light. Sister Frieda brought my breakfast, looked at me with some concern, and took my temperature.

"You're to stay in bed today," she said. "You must have really overdone things yesterday."

"Can't I just go to the day room? I don't want to be stuck in here by myself."

"I'll ask Doctor Holz."

Fortunately he said yes, but with a strict prohibition on going to the gym.

"And I'll be telling Sergeant Kahrstedt not to expect you," he said. "He must have worked you too hard."

"It wasn't his fault," I said. "I did too much the rest of the time."

"That's all right, then – but you're to take it easy today."

"Boring," Riege said when I told him. "He said the same to me… Look, why don't we see how we feel after lunch, and maybe go for a bit of a walk?"

"Well, maybe," I replied cautiously. "I don't want to set myself back."

"We don't have to go far."

"I'll let you know."

I did feel a bit better by the afternoon, and we set off for a slow amble along the corridor. We were heading towards the gym, but with no intention of actually going there.

"I don't want to get Kahrstedt into trouble," I said, and Riege agreed with me.

We were doing pretty well until he got it wrong. Suddenly my chair flew away from him and he fell heavily, and of course he landed on his bad hip and let out a loud yell.

"Riege, are you all right?"

"Fine, fine," he lied, obviously in a lot of pain.

"Can I help?" I asked, and, like a fool, I leaned over.

In a split second I went over too far and landed half on top of him, and of course I banged my stump and it was my turn to yell.

A moment later, we heard running footsteps.

"I might have known," Doctor Holz said wearily. "What am I going to do with you two?"

"Help us off the floor?" Riege suggested, his voice strained.

"No – you can sort yourselves out," he said. "Bloch, Kreuser, the gentlemen can manage without you."

And they left the two of us lying there in a crumpled heap. It was some minutes before either of us felt like moving, but gradually the cold started to overcome the pain.

"Miserable bastard," Riege said.

"He's right, though," I said. "Kahrstedt wouldn't have helped us either."

"True."

"I'm getting cold."

"Me too. You go first, then."

After about three attempts I was upright. Riege crawled on his hands and knees to my chair, put the brake on and pulled himself up.

"Just like my little boy," he said. "The number of times I saw him crawl along and pull himself up."

"How old is he?"

"Hans is six now, and little Erika's two. I'll show you their pictures some time – I'm dying to get home and see them and Trudi again. It's been so long and I've missed so much of their childhood. I've only seen Erika once."

By the time we were about halfway back, he was obviously struggling.

"Becker, mind if I sit in your chair?"

"No, go ahead – let's stop at those chairs, though." I was starting to ache all over.

"Good idea."

"What's it like, being a father?" I asked him after a minute or so.

He thought for a moment. "I'm probably not the best man to ask – with the war and that. But I'd say my kids are the best thing that ever happened to me, after my wife, that is, or probably alongside my wife... Why d'you ask, anyway? Got one on the way?"

"I don't know... There might be one already."

He gave me a puzzled look. "You don't know?"

"No, not yet anyway. I'll probably be able to sort it all out when I get home."

"You're not in touch with the girl, then?"

I shook my head. "It's a bit complicated. Forget I spoke."

"No problem… You know what I could do with?"

"What?"

"A few stiff brandies."

'I thought you'd like a stiff one,' I said, and Karl smiled.

'You know me too well,' he said, his eyes warm—

"Becker. Stop staring into space."

"Sorry. Let's get going."

The next morning I was covered in bruises, and could hardly move. Riege didn't come down until after lunch, and seemed to be worse than me.

"What's up with you two?" Bredt asked.

"Fell over," said Riege. "And, no, we weren't pissed."

"Would've been better," I said. "Wouldn't have hurt."

"What's the chance of getting pissed in here?" asked Hammer. "We haven't even got Landauer's mysterious source any more."

"Ah well," said Geinitz, "I may be able to help there."

We looked at him.

"My old man owns a distillery, not too far from here," he went on. "And it's just possible that he might come to visit me."

"That would be bloody marvellous," said Bredt, echoed by the rest of us.

I'll believe it when I see it, I thought, and a good two weeks passed before Geinitz's father turned up – but when he did, he brought bottles of his best brandy for Doctor Holz and the staff, and for his son and us as well.

"Medicinal," he said with a wink. "You chaps all look like you need a pick-me-up."

"Quite literally!" I said.

"This is more likely to have us falling over," said Riege happily. "It's the best I've had for months."

"Thank you," said Geinitz Senior, "though I'm not sure what the competition was!"

He was a friendly, jolly sort of fellow, and he sat and chatted with us for a couple of hours, taking no notice whatever of our various mutilations.

"Weren't you taking a bit of a chance travelling?" Bredt asked him.

"Oh, Pa's probably armed and dangerous," Geinitz said.

His father smiled.

"Pa's a crack shot," said Geinitz. "Leading light in the shooting society, with rifle and pistol."

"Well, I'm sure you're all far better than me," said his father. "I've never had to do it for real – it must be quite different, especially when they're shooting back."

"Nice bloke, your pa," Hammer said after he'd gone. "And this is bloody good brandy."

"Hope he gets home all right," said Riege.

"Oh, he will," Geinitz said. "Pa's indestructible. A few years back a barrel got dropped on his foot and broke it, and it got infected and bloody near killed him. We all thought he'd had it, but before you could say 'coffin' he was up and limping about. Joachim – my older brother – said, 'Well, that's the end of our inheriting – we'll probably go before him.' And that was true for him, and nearly so for me."

"Mercenary bastards!" said Bredt. "You're lucky to have a father like that."

"What's yours like, then?" Geinitz asked.

"Dead. He was a Hussar colonel, got killed in the East in '14 – and as for inheritance, there wasn't any. He'd gambled everything away, left a mountain of debts."

"It takes hold of some men, just like booze does," I said. "I once met an Austro-Hungarian officer with the same problem."

"But you play cards," Hammer said to Bredt. "Aren't you worried it could happen to you?"

Bredt smiled. "I don't expect to win. I used up all my good luck in the war – so I set a limit each time as to how much I'm prepared to lose, and when I hit it I stop."

"This is very pleasant," Riege said, stretching. "I can't feel anything!"

And indeed, we were all nicely mellow.

"Better ration it," Geinitz said. "We don't know when the reinforcements will arrive."

That turned out to be a very good point – the unrest flared up again, to such a pitch that even Geinitz Senior stayed at home. Our evenings were much more convivial while the brandy lasted, though.

Having a small drink, and actually enjoying it, made me realise how much I'd been putting away at the Front, especially towards the end – but then it had been almost the only form of relaxation.

By that time it was nearly the end of March. Daffodils were out in the hospital garden and the trees were budding. I could get up and down a whole flight of stairs and right round the ground floor, and at last the weather was warm enough to go outside.

I made my way carefully down the step from the conservatory into the garden and stood in the sun, feeling the breeze on my face for the first time in months. I looked up at the sky automatically – good visibility, a few small cumulus drifting past on a light south-westerly breeze. *Beautiful flying weather, but not for me. Not any more.*

'Wouldn't it be lovely, Franz, to fly and just look at the sky and the clouds?' Karl said.

'In that mythical land called "after the war",' I replied.

I set off along the path. *I've made it to 'after the war', unlike how many million men, but what in God's name am I going to do now I'm here? How can I find my way back to a normal life?*

There was a dead man lying in front of me, both legs blown off, and I was going to have to step over him.

'There is no way back,' he said. 'You're still in the war, just as we are, and you always will be.'

He disappeared, and I made my way to a bench and sat down. Karl sat beside me and put his arm round my shoulders, the feeling of companionship strong.

How lovely and warm the sun is. How brightly it lights the flowers. I am alive when God knows how many are dead, and I should be happy.

If only it were that easy.

Riege joined me. "You're looking very thoughtful," he said.

I laughed. "Should know better than to think!"

"Maybe we have to start thinking again."

"Yes, maybe we do."

"They've said I can go home," he said.

That just leaves me and Bredt. Hammer had been discharged a week earlier, and I didn't really know Geinitz or any of the others well.

"Congratulations," I said. "What's the journey going to be like?"

He sighed. "God knows. I've been told to avoid Berlin, which would be the usual route, but there it is. I'll make it eventually… If I were in better shape I'd have a bash at the Reds, but there's no way I'm up to it."

Fighting had broken out in Berlin again, and many other cities were in a state of anarchy. Bavaria was a Soviet republic, but that wasn't likely to last. It was a moot point just how much peace there was.

"And they call this peace," Riege said, echoing my thoughts.

"The Allies must be really happy to see us on our knees," I said.

"If they are then they're fucking stupid. It's in everyone's best interests to have a stable Germany – if the Red rot spreads to us then who'll be next? The Bolsheviks shot the Tsar – what'll they do to the King of England?"

"Oh, they'll be all right on their island," I said. "They always are."

"Words and ideas don't have borders – oh, bugger it, who cares? I just want to see my wife and kids, and everything else can hang itself."

The next morning I wished him a safe journey, and then went to Doctor Holz's office.

"I'd like to go home tomorrow," I said.

"You mean you want to discharge yourself?"

"Yes."

He took off his glasses and rubbed his eyes. "Well, I suppose I can't stop you. You're not in the Army any more, and I doubt the Soldiers' and Workers' Council wants to keep officers in hospital any longer than absolutely necessary… I don't know what sort of journey you'll have, though."

"No one's going to take any notice of me. I'll just be another cripple."

"How are you planning to get home?"

"By train."

I really didn't want to travel by train. The thought of jolting over the joins in the rails turned my stomach, but I couldn't think of a better way of getting home. I had thought of hitching, but I didn't know how much traffic there would be. Hitching would be exhausting, anyway – far too much waiting around in the cold – and I didn't want to have to talk to anyone. That could be very dangerous. The train would be easiest and probably safest, and I'd just have to grit my teeth and put up with it.

He looked at me. "I don't think you realise – there's no reason why you should, after all, you've been in here – but it's not as simple as that. There's no proper timetable. You might have to wait until one goes in the right direction."

"What do you suggest?"

"That you stay here for a few more weeks until things have stabilised."

I shook my head. "I want to get home. I… look, I don't want to sound rude or ungrateful, but I've had enough of being in hospital."

He smiled. "Yes, of course you have. I'd feel the same in your position. I'm advising everyone to go to the station and talk to whoever's running it – one of those Council fellows, no doubt" – his distaste showed – "and tell him you've just been discharged from hospital and you need to get home. I'm sure you know what to leave out."

"Yes, I think so."

"We'll send your things on after you. You wouldn't find it easy to manage a bag, and there's always the risk of being robbed."

"Thank you. How do I get to the station?"

I had no idea exactly where in the town the hospital was. I'd almost forgotten that there was an outside world, a world of whole people who went to work, came home, made love… I was so used to the hospital, and the company of my fellow cripples, that the thought of the world outside was suddenly alarming.

It'll be strange to sit in a normal carriage again. I hope it won't hurt. My knee was aching, as always, and I could only hope it would be bearable.

"Sorry, could you say that again, please? I was thinking about something else."

"The vegetable man comes tomorrow. I'll ask him to give you a lift. Now, you'll need some papers. What would you like to be called?"

"What? What's wrong with Franz Becker?"

"You're forgetting how famous you were. Those bastards won't help Oberleutnant Franz Becker, Pour le Mérite, et cetera, et cetera. Quite an imposing list of decorations, if I may say so – but they won't see it that way."

"I'm hardly the only Franz Becker in Germany, and no one could possibly recognise me from those photographs – not now. I can't even recognise myself."

"Just in case. Make it something easy to remember."

You must have issued a lot of false papers, I thought suddenly. *You suggested it in such a matter-of-fact way.*

I thought for a moment. "Ludwig Vogel."

Ludwig's my middle name, and I used, once upon a time, to fly like a bird...

"Have you got any clothes?"

"Yes – but I could do with a coat, in case I have to wait around. My parents gave me a bit of money and I've got my winnings at cards—"

"Hold on to that. We can get you a coat – I'll send Kreuser to the second-hand shop this afternoon."

"Thank you."

I went to the day room and gave them the news.

"You as well?" Bredt asked, rather sadly.

For a moment I felt as if I were abandoning him. He was nowhere near being well enough to leave.

"Oh, you won't have much longer to wait," I lied, as cheerfully as I could.

"Just sick of hospital, that's all – it is the fourth time. Still, I'm better off than some of the fellows, so I'd better not complain."

I had one more game of cards with him and Geinitz, and won a few more marks.

"Settle up in the morning?" Geinitz asked.

"Yes, fine."

I wrote to Alfred, and Horstmann, and Paul Fellmann, told them I was going home and gave them the address. *I hope you're all still alive – I've had enough of losing my friends.*

This is my last night in hospital, I thought as I went to bed – and I was suddenly very afraid. I lay there sweating and trembling, my pulse racing, almost as much as it had at the Front.

I'll have to leave here and face the outside world, and people will stare at me.

For fuck's sake, Franz – you fought through nearly four years of the worst war in history, you nearly lost your life more times than you can count, and you're scared of being stared at? What harm can that do? If you're going to be scared of something, then how about Reds with guns?

If they do shoot me then I'll be with Karl, and anyway, that risk's only temporary. What's happened to me in body and mind is a life sentence.

I wish I could go and live with him…

The next morning, I put on the clothes my parents had brought. They hung off me.

Christ, I look like a bloody scarecrow, I thought as I looked in the mirror – and then I saw myself in spotless field grey, with all my decorations, the day of Karl's funeral.

Grief hit me in the stomach and I had to sit down.

'I'm not dead, Franz. There is more, far more, than you realise.'

"Karl—" But he'd gone.

I packed my things, and straight after breakfast I wished the others a good recovery and went to Doctor Holz's office.

"It's not too late to change your mind, you know," he said.

"I'll be all right," I said, with more confidence than I felt. "Could you take special care with these, please?" I handed him the squadron photograph albums.

"Yes, of course – I might have to hold on to them for a few weeks." He gave me my papers. "You'd better have some more money. It might take you days to get home."

He unlocked his desk drawer, and handed me a small wad of banknotes.

"They're low denomination. You'll find them easier to use. It's better not to look rich these days – talking of which, I hope this fits."

'This' was a rather shabby coat, very worn at the elbows.

"It's perfect. Thank you." I hesitated for a moment.

"Send me a cheque when you get home."

"Thank you very much," I said, and heaved myself up. "Well, goodbye, Doctor, and thank you for everything you've done – I really do appreciate it."

"Don't mention it. I hope your journey goes smoothly, and that you continue your good progress. Make sure you keep doing your exercises."

I went to the gym to say goodbye to Kahrstedt.

"I can't thank you enough," I said. "I'd lost hope and you've given it back to me."

"Just my job, sir," he said warmly. "You'll be fine now. Just keep doing your exercises."

I waited at the back door for the vegetable man, enjoying the breeze on my face. It was a lovely clear spring day.

Beautiful flying weather. In a minute I'll get into my D.VII and in no time we'll be up in that crystal sky, flying towards the Front in the limitless expanse of blue—

"Look, mate, do you want a lift or not?" asked an impatient voice.

"What?"

An old man was standing over me. *What's he doing at the airfield?*

"I've been asking you where you want to go," he said, leaning on his cart.

Oh. You're the vegetable man.

"Sorry – miles away. The station, please."

"Get in the back, then."

The cart was solid wood and looked very uncomfortable. I almost asked if I could sit with him, but the fewer people I talked to, the better.

It took me three attempts to get in, and the bastard didn't even try to help me. I made a bit of a seat among the meagre sacks, with my back to him and his scrawny horse. It was up to pulling the cart, anyway, and trotted off more briskly than I'd expected.

Shouldn't have called it scrawny – it's in better shape than I am.

I had to hold on tight. The wood was very hard and there was no suspension to speak of, and my leg soon started hurting. *Christ, I hope it's not far or I won't be able to move when we get there.*

The town was very quiet, the streets empty. Everyone seemed to be staying inside.

I wonder how long it's going to take me to get home – suddenly I was frightened of the empty space around me. I wanted to turn round and go back to the hospital, to where it was safe, where everyone was crippled, where no one would stare at me.

Doctor Holz didn't want me to leave, he doesn't think I'm well enough yet. Perhaps I should go back, just for a few weeks more…

The cart stopped. The vegetable man looked round.

"Station," was all he said.

I struggled off the cart and almost fell headlong. *You could help me, you bastard*, I thought, but he was already driving away.

It was too late to change my mind, and I went into the station.

It was utterly desolate. There were no civilians in sight. The ticket windows were broken and deserted, and there was rubbish strewn everywhere. The departure board was blank.

A few soldiers with red armbands lounged on a bench, smoking and staring at the ground. They looked bored to death. *No one to beat up and no trouble to cause. I hope they don't see me as a suitable diversion.*

I made my way slowly across the empty concourse to their bench. They looked up at the sound of my crutches, but there was no sympathy in their faces, just a sort of idle curiosity. Men with missing limbs were hardly rare.

I hope to Christ none of them recognises me or I'll be finished. My mouth was dry and my heart racing. *Get a grip, Franz. You don't look anything like those photos now – and how many people paid that much attention to them anyway, or to the film?*

"Where've you come from, then?" asked one.

"Hospital. I've just been discharged. Can you tell me where I can get a ticket, please?"

They stared at me.

My bloody voice. I don't sound like a worker.

"Try the stationmaster," said another, sarcastically.

"Where's his office?"

"Over there." He waved his hand at a broken window in the corner of the station.

As I turned away, they began imitating my accent. *Ignorant Northern slum-dwellers. If I were stronger I'd wipe the smirks off your faces.*

I was still far weaker than I wanted to admit to myself, and by the time I reached the office door I was almost at the end of my strength. I paused for a moment to get my breath back and then knocked.

"Come in!"

I opened the door and went in. The office was filled with cigarette smoke, and considerably warmer than the concourse. I realised to my astonishment that the smoke was from real cigarettes.

Looted from somewhere, no doubt. The country's run by vagabonds these days.

The 'stationmaster' was yet another dirty soldier with the inevitable red armband. He looked me up and down as if I'd crawled out from under a stone.

This is what Papa wanted. This is Socialism.

I wonder if you were ever at the Front, I thought, trying to keep the distaste out of my face. *That won't do, Franz. Play for sympathy, ask nicely.*

"I hope you can help me," I began. "I've just left hospital and I'm trying to get home."

"Where's 'ome, then?"

"Near Stuttgart."

He took his cap off and scratched his head.

My muscles were trembling and my armpits were aching. "Could I sit down, please?"

His small, hard eyes softened slightly. "Yeh, all right then… Smoke?"

"Yes, please!"

I took one of his cigarettes and he lit it for me. I drew the smoke deep into my lungs. *Oh, that's bloody wonderful! I'd forgotten how good tobacco is. I wonder if he'd sell me a packet or two?*

I was about to ask him when he produced a bottle from a drawer, uncorked it and passed it across the desk.

"Thanks."

It was some kind of rough schnapps, and it settled in my stomach with a warm glow that revived me a little. *Not a patch on Geinitz's brandy, but who cares?*

"Where'd you lose yer leg?"

"Ypres."

"When?"

"July."

"You talk like an officer."

"We talk like this down South," I said, hoping he hadn't met too many of my countrymen.

He gave me a sideways look. *Oh, fuck, he knows I'm a rich Württemberger and not a poor one. How could I have thought—?*

"Let's see yer 'ands."

I held out my hands, callused from digging trenches, and more recently from the gym and the crutches. He looked at them with evident satisfaction. *Karl's hands were the same. You'd have put a nobleman down as a worker with that stupid test of yours.*

"I need to get home," I said, and recited my prepared story. "My girlfriend's pregnant and she doesn't know about – about the leg. At least, I don't think she does. I mean, she knows I've been injured, but I haven't told her everything – but she's stopped writing so maybe someone else told her and she… I don't know. I need to see her."

It was all true, or mostly true, just not in quite the right order.

He took a swig out of his bottle and passed it to me again. I took a long time taking a small sip. It was months since I'd been a hardened drinker, and I daren't get drunk.

"What's yer name?"

"Vogel, Ludwig."

"Papers?"

I handed them over. He studied them for a moment and then gave them back.

"Well, Comrade Vogel, there's no timetable. You'll 'ave to wait for the next train south. Might be today, might be tomorrow."

I sagged in the chair. "Where do I wait?"

"In 'ere."

I must have looked surprised. He pulled the glove off his right hand. It was metal.

"Marne, '14," he said. "I was a toolmaker. Wot the fuck am I supposed to do now? Fucking capitalists' war. Fucked me up for good, they 'ave. And wot did they bloody give me? A miserly fuckin' pension. Well, it's all going to change, cos now we're going to take everything they've got and give it to blokes like us wot deserves it… Wot was you, then?"

"Builder. Digging foundations, that sort of thing." *Foundations for dugouts…*

"You don't sound like a builder," he said suspiciously.

Careful, Franz. You've got to make it stick, or God knows what will happen to you. Remember what Sobek said about that Major getting beaten up? And suppose someone recognises you?

They won't, I thought again. *I wouldn't recognise myself. Those photographs are all months old. They were all taken before I lost my leg, almost before I started cracking up. The man in those pictures doesn't exist any more.*

"You get all sorts," I said. "Men who are in trouble, need somewhere to hide, that kind of thing."

We all needed somewhere to hide, especially when they shelled us.

"Was you in trouble, then?"

I shrugged. "Not really. I just had a lot of rows with my dad and left home."

I was beginning to enjoy myself. Every word I'd said was true. It was just slanted.

"Well, don't worry, Comrade Vogel, the Party'll look after you now. You a member?"

Oh, fuck.

"Not yet," I admitted.

"Now's yer chance. I'm Membership Secretary for this district," he said self-importantly.

There was no way out of it. If I refused to join I wouldn't get home. And so I became a member of the Communist Party.

"Thanks," I said, putting the card in my wallet.

This will either get me home safely or get me shot. At least it's not in my real name.

"You know wot really pisses me off?" he demanded.

"No."

"My fuckin' 'and. 'Urts like fuck, it does. Drives me mad. It's fuckin' gone and it still fuckin' 'urts. Dunno 'ow the fuck it does it."

"What happened?"

"Shell splinter."

"Some people would say you were well off out of it. I knew plenty who'd've been happy to lose a hand if it got them out of the trenches."

"Yeh, well I missed all that. 'Ow'd you get yours?"

"Bullet in the knee, during that business the Tommies started at Ypres last year."

"Does yer knee 'urt, then?"

"All the bloody time," I said, with perfect truth.

My stump hadn't recovered from the cart and was throbbing nastily – but the pain in my missing knee was almost constant. Sometimes I noticed it wasn't hurting, which just brought home that it usually did.

He passed me the bottle again, and I took another cautious swig. *I could do with a lot more of that, but if I get drunk and start babbling about what really happened, they'll put me up against the station wall.*

"We're better off than my brother, any rate," he said. "Poor bugger got shot dead by a sniper. I dunno 'ow they can do that, just shoot men in cold blood like that. I mean, it's one thing if they're comin' to kill you, but wot those buggers do's another matter. Fuckin' murder, 'fyou ask me."

Karl stood motionless at the loophole, staring through his telescopic sight, waiting...

"My best mate was a sniper," I said, and edited the truth again. "But they got him in the end. It's a dangerous life."

"Yeh, well, maybe."

Karl fired, and the shot was so sudden and unexpected that I started, and almost dropped the periscope.

'Well done, Leussow,' said Hafner.

'It might be a bit soon for congratulations—'

"You all right, mate?"

"What? Er... yes, yes, fine."

I looked round the office, wondering what I was doing there. *Karl is dead, and the war's over...*

"You was miles away."

"I was thinking about my friend. He was a bloody good shot." *That was the day he got that Tommy sniper.*

"Well 'e must of been. Wouldn't of been a sniper otherwise, would 'e?"

"He took some awful risks, though," I said, remembering Karl pulling Taschner out of the shell-hole.

I wanted to stop talking. The pain was vicious and I was getting very tired. It was becoming hard to concentrate, and I was afraid of making a mistake.

"Look, is there anywhere I can get a bit of sleep? I don't feel too good."

"There's only the benches outside. I'll wake you 'f a train comes."

"Thanks."

There was a chilly breeze blowing through the station and the bench was rock-hard. I wrapped the coat round me but it didn't help much, and being cold seemed to make the pain worse.

I hope a train comes today. I don't want to have to stay here until tomorrow. If it's a really long wait then I'll go back to the hospital. At least it's relatively warm there, and I'll have food and a comfortable bed.

That's running away, Franz. You're here now, so just bloody get on with it.

I turned over and nearly fell off the bench, then settled myself a little more comfortably.

I could see Karl so clearly. *Whenever I think of you or dream about you, you're so vivid that it's as if you were still alive. When will I ever get used to your being dead? It's over six months now and I still can't get it into my head that you're dead. I buried you and I still can't believe it.*

Why didn't you take your pension and accept those few years? We could have lived together and been happy. You got what you wanted, my love, but part of me is in the grave with you.

Thinking about Karl was too painful. *I should have brought a book. God knows how long I'm going to have to wait.*

Karl was so good at waiting – how did he manage all those hours by himself in No Man's Land, with only his thoughts for company? Staying alert must have been really difficult – so easy to make one mistake, and that would have been the end of him, like Dietz and Spots...

The cold was starting to make me feel ill. The clear spring day wasn't as warm as I'd thought.

Try to get some sleep, Franz. You'll feel better if you do.

I couldn't find a comfortable position. I only dozed, and the brief snatches of sleep were filled with dreams. I was sitting in a dugout with Kurt, and Karl came in, dripping wet. They began to shell us. The explosions got louder and the roof of the dugout caved in, and I cried out in terror and woke drenched in sweat.

The soldiers were looking at me oddly. I turned over with my back to them and tried again to sleep. I was horribly tired, but the sweat chilled my body and I shivered. I closed my eyes and saw Karl's eyes staring sightlessly at the sky, saw the light filtering through the canvas hangar onto his lifeless face, and I woke to bleak emptiness.

This is hopeless. I sat up.

There was a rat rooting about in some rubbish, its scaly tail twitching. *Horrible bloody thing.*

The rat looked at me from the top of the parapet. It was sleek and well fed, and it seemed to bare its teeth at me in anticipation.

'Fucking thing!' said Bauer. He threw a clod of earth at it, and it scampered off under the wire.

'I wonder how many rats there are here,' Tiny said.

'More than there are of us, I reckon,' said Kurt.

'Saw plenty on patrol last night,' I said.

I didn't elaborate. A star shell had lit the night to brilliance, and we'd dropped to the ground and lain motionless, hardly breathing. I'd found myself eye to empty socket with a dead Tommy. His skull was bare and his hand half eaten, and there was a rat sitting on his chest, staring at me in the ghostly light as if I were next on its menu. I wanted to grab it and choke the life out of its nasty little throat.

They were bold bastards, and bloody hard to catch. They came into the trenches, and stole our food and ran over our faces while we slept.

Kurt woke with a yell and lashed out.

'Hey, watch out!' said Alfred. 'You nearly hit me.'

'That fucking hurt,' Kurt said, inspecting his hand. 'The bastard could have waited till I was dead before trying to eat me.'

There was a bite mark, oozing blood...

The rats were still scavenging in the rubbish and I realised I'd been dreaming.

How much longer am I going to have to wait for this bloody train? I wish I'd stayed in the hospital.

I wonder what time it is? The watch I'd been wearing on my last flight had disappeared, no doubt into someone's pocket. *There must be a station clock... but maybe it's better not to know.*

I shivered, and tried to curl up to keep warm.

'Franz, wake up!' Karl was shaking me. 'Wake up! The French are coming!'

I started awake, reaching for my rifle—

"Comrade Vogel, there's a train to Stuttgart!"

"What?" I rubbed my eyes and forehead stupidly.

"You wanted a train south. There's one for Stuttgart. That wot you want?"

"Christ, yes!"

I leapt off the bench in panic, afraid of missing the train, and fell headlong. I just managed to keep my stump from hitting the ground, but I landed heavily on my left arm and the shock jarred right through me. *Stupid fucking bastard! How can you forget you've only one leg?*

The stationmaster helped me up, and handed me my crutches. "'Sall right, it won't go without you. Take it easy."

He accompanied me along the platform and helped me into a first-class compartment.

"You can travel in style," he said, "being as you're a Party member."

"I don't have a ticket."

"You've paid yer fare," he said, pointing at the air below my right thigh. "I'll 'ave a word with the guard, sort it out."

"Thanks very much."

"Don't mention it, Comrade."

The heating was on, and the padded seats felt very soft after the wooden bench. I lay down across them and fell asleep.

I woke in the hospital train, my leg throbbing, every join in the rails jolting me. I opened my eyes, and couldn't work out why I was lying in a compartment instead of a bunk. My left arm felt bruised from shoulder to wrist, and I ached all over.

The pain and the swaying of the train were beginning to make me feel sick. I sat up with an effort and looked out of the window – and stared.

We were rolling along beside the Rhine. The river sparkled in the sunlight, and the steep slopes were vivid green with the spring. I hadn't seen anything so lovely for a very long time.

'Fast stands and true the Watch, The Watch on the Rhine...'

I shall never be able to see the river again without hearing that in my mind, without seeing us all going off to war.

This is what I fought and bled for – my beautiful, beloved homeland. This is what my friends died for.

Was it worth the sacrifice of our lives and our health?

Karl sat next to me, his arm round my shoulders. 'Wrong way round, Franz – the question is whether we were worthy of our country, whether what we gave was enough.'

You gave everything.

'And still it wasn't enough.' There was a pause, and then he said, 'I never told you, or anyone else, come to that, but every time, in those last minutes before the attack, I always thought of home. For me, it was always for Brandenburg, for Prussia.'

I think I knew that, without your saying it.

We sat together in companionable silence, looking at the beauty beyond the window. The sun sank behind the hills and the train moved into the shadows, and I was alone. And yet... and yet I knew that I would never be alone, that Karl would always be by my side.

You really are bonkers, Franz, imagining that the dead keep you company.

But does that matter, if it makes me feel better?

Just don't talk to him out loud, or they'll take you to the nuthouse, and you'll spend the rest of your days with the Krugs...

It was getting dark, and I lay down again. I was so bloody tired.

I must have fallen asleep, because I was woken by the guard opening the door.

"You'll have to get out, Comrade," he said. "The train stops here."

"Are we in Stuttgart?"

He shook his head, embarrassed. "Er, no, not exactly."

"What do you mean, 'not exactly'? Where are we, then?"

He named some small town I'd never heard of.

"I thought this train was going to Stuttgart."

"Well, it was, only it isn't. It's stopping here. You see, it's the driver's wife's birthday, and he's missed all her birthdays since '14, and he says he's not going any further until he's been home."

Bloody marvellous.

"So what do you suggest?" I had to make a huge effort not to be sarcastic. "I mean, can't I stay here until he comes back?"

"Well, no – you see, the thing is, it might go anywhere."

"Oh, all right."

I was so sore and stiff I could hardly move. I needed his help to get down onto the platform, and my left arm was horribly painful. *At least it blots out the pain in my knee...*

Another fucking station bench. I might as well be a tramp. I suppose I could try to find a hotel, but I've no idea how far I'd have to go, and if I leave the station I'll probably miss the only train south.

I lay down, shivering. *I'd love a cup of nice hot coffee, even if it is fake, or a cigarette. I never did get round to asking that 'stationmaster' if he'd sell me a few fags.*

I was bloody hungry, but there didn't seem to be anywhere to get something to eat. *I should have stayed in the hospital*, I thought again, imagining the others sitting down to dinner and then going up to their warm beds.

The night dragged interminably. Every time I tried to turn over on the bench, I almost fell off it, and once I woke with a cry of pain because I was lying on my bruised arm.

At least this time I wasn't the only one waiting. By morning there were about twenty other people, all hoping for a train that would carry them a bit nearer to their destination.

Some enterprising soul opened up a kiosk selling soup and other bits and pieces. My stomach rumbled and I realised how hungry I was.

I could really do with some soup, but there's no way I can carry it. I'll have to ask someone to buy some for me – but that means going up to a stranger and asking them for help, and I'm not sure I can do that. They'll stare at me, and asking for help means admitting that I need it.

A middle-aged man sat down at the other end of my bench, holding a cup of steaming soup and a roll. The soup smelled wonderful, and my stomach rumbled again, loudly.

Go on, ask him. What can he do to you?

"Excuse me," I said, rather nervously.

He ignored me, staring straight ahead.

I tried again. "I wonder if you would be so kind—"

"No. Sorry." He got up and walked briskly to another bench.

Thanks a million, bastard. You thought I was begging – and what if I was? Would it be too much to buy me a mug of soup? I got maimed fighting for people like you. All I wanted you to do was take my money and go to the kiosk for me.

I'll try one more person, and if they say no then I'll just have to go hungry.

I made my way slowly to the kiosk and stood beside it, waiting. A young woman came up to it, and I was struck by how lovely she looked. She barely even glanced at me.

I used to get piles of letters from women all over Germany, women I'd never even met. Maybe I should have kept some of them…

Success and decorations are attractive. A one-legged man isn't. I don't suppose any girl will ever look at me again. I just don't exist for them.

The girl took her soup and turned to go. I watched her walk away, watched her hips swinging gently. *It's eight months since I was last in bed with a woman.* A sudden longing swept over me, not lust so much as desire for the soft warmth of a girl's body, for her arms around me, for a bit of tenderness.

'Jesus, Franz, it's been months since anyone else touched me like that,' Karl murmured in my ear.

Now I know just how you felt…

You can forget it, I told myself. *Love isn't for you, not any more. You'll have to pay for the rest of your life, and even the tarts won't want you. They'll take your money, but they won't really want to know.*

"Can I help you, sir?"

The kiosk owner was looking at me expectantly. She looked middle-aged, her grey hair scraped back untidily from a pale, weary face.

"I'd like some soup and a roll," I said, "but I can't carry them."

"Come round the back and come in," she said. "I've got a little seat in here. You can sit on that."

"Thank you very much." *Bless you.*

"Not at all," she said briskly. "Least I can do."

I sat down and she handed me a steaming mug. I wrapped my hands round it, feeling the warmth flow into them.

"It's only cabbage."

"Cabbage is fine. How much is that?"

She shook her head. "I won't take your money."

I was embarrassed. "But you've your living to make—"

"You've paid," she said firmly.

"Thank you," I said. "I really appreciate this. It's very kind of you."

I think she'd have been happy for me to sit there for the rest of the day, but as I told her, I had to stay near the platforms, because I didn't know when the train would come and I was so slow.

Fortunately I didn't have to wait much longer, and I swear the train was the same one.

After much stopping and starting, we finally arrived in Stuttgart at about five the following morning, and I had to wait six hours for a connection.

Gradually the station got busier, and finally the buffet opened. I sat down awkwardly at one of the tables and waited to be served.

And waited, and waited. Others who'd come in after me had their orders taken, but the staff ignored my attempts to catch their eye.

Eventually, a waiter came to my table. *At last.* The man at the next table had grey bread and margarine, but it looked bloody good to me.

The waiter looked at me with obvious disdain. "We don't serve 'gentlemen of the road'," he said sniffily.

Gentlemen of the...?

"I'm not a tramp," I said. "I left hospital a couple of days ago, and with all the chaos it's taking me a while to get home."

"Of course, sir," he said. "If you would kindly leave—"

"I can pay."

People were starting to stare. Not that I gave a shit.

"You're disturbing our other customers, sir," he said. "I really must ask you to leave."

"Fetch the manager."

"He isn't in yet. If you don't leave I'll call the police."

"Go on, then. Call them. I'm sure they'll be pleased to hear you've thrown a one-legged veteran out."

The man at the next table looked across.

You can fuck off too.

"Would you care to join me?" he asked.

That shuts me up. "Thank you – it's most kind of you."

"Not at all."

The waiter looked most put out. "The gentleman is just leaving," he insisted.

"No, he isn't," the man said firmly. "He's my guest – and if you don't serve him you'll be all over the newspaper."

The waiter hesitated.

"What would you like?" the man asked me.

"I'll have the same as you – I do have money, though."

He smiled. "'Guest' means just that."

As I moved to his table I caught sight of myself in the mirror – or rather, I caught sight of a thin, unshaven fellow in a shabby, rather dirty coat.

I laughed. "I have to say I see what he meant! I haven't been able to shave since I left hospital."

"Grumach," he said, holding out his hand.

"Beck— er, Vogel," I replied. *Careful, Franz.*

He smiled again. "Vogel it is, then."

"It's most kind of you to help," I said, wanting to change the subject. "Are you local or passing through?"

"Oh, I'm local," he said. "And I wasn't joking about putting this place in the paper – I'm on the editorial team, you see. Have to get into town a bit early these days, then I have breakfast here before I go to work."

Oh fuck, a bloody journalist. I wonder what sort of crap you published about the war. Better be very careful what I say.

"Whenever I see you fellows, I think of my son," Grumach said quietly. "He was wounded on the Chemin des Dames in '17 and died four weeks later."

Poor bastard.

"I'm very sorry," I said. "Did he make it back to Germany?"

He shook his head. "He wasn't well enough to travel. We had a very kind letter from the hospital chaplain, and my wife was happy to believe it."

But you don't.

The thought must have shown in my face, because he continued, "I know a nice piece of writing when I see one."

Of course you do.

There was a slightly longer pause, and then he said, "I'm not proud of some of the things we printed, but at the time it seemed the right thing to do – keep morale up, keep the people supporting the Army."

I don't have to be ashamed of anything I did, I thought suddenly. *Yes, I killed rather a lot of men, but they were all enemy soldiers and as Johnny said, it wasn't a tea party.*

"Thank you very much for your help and for the meal," I said. "I should head back towards the departures board – I'm a bit slow."

"Yes, of course. Very pleasant talking to you – I hope you get home soon."

About an hour later, I was sitting in what I hoped would be the last train. It was half full, as if normal life had resumed for some people. They were all on their way to work, and no one wanted to sit next to the scruffy tramp – which suited me, as it gave me room to stretch out a bit. I was getting very tired and I just wanted the journey to be over.

The names of the stations were all familiar now. *Nearly home...*

I dreamed of this for years, dreamed of the end of the war, of coming home. I never thought it would be like this. I imagined coming home in triumph after a few months, a conquering hero in a parade, girls showering us with flowers. I never pictured this solitary journey through a defeated, chaotic Germany, never thought that all of me might not come home.

Here it was, at long bloody last. I struggled off the train and into the street, wondering how I was going to get home. *I always used to walk to the station* – and now I stood leaning heavily on my crutches, my whole body aching. I couldn't even think of getting home by myself.

Papa's office was about half a kilometre away and it felt more like fifty. By the time I got there I was fit to drop, and I couldn't face the stairs.

I rang the bell. No one answered. I rang again, longer, and after a minute or so I heard footsteps on the stairs, and then Papa's voice said cautiously, "Who is it?"

"It's me, Franz."

He opened the door. "Franz!" He threw his arms around me. "Franz, my dear boy!"

His voice was thick, and to my amazement I found I couldn't speak.

He stepped back and stood looking at me, holding my shoulders as if he couldn't believe I was really there.

"You were lucky to catch me here," he said. "I work mostly at home these days. I just came to pick up some papers."

"Where's Schwaiger?" I croaked.

"At home in bed. The poor man's got influenza. Since he's not here I've closed the office up. Everything's upside down."

I was suddenly overwhelmed by pain and tiredness. "Can we go home?"

"Of course we can," he said quietly. "Sit on the steps. I'll go and get a cab."

You haven't asked me how I am, or how I got here, I thought as he walked away, *but I suppose I did give you a bit of a surprise.*

He asked me both questions in the cab.

"Oh, not too bad," I said, and hadn't the energy to say any more.

"So how was the journey?"

"I'll tell you all together."

I just want to go to bed. I'd love a hot drink, and then sleep and more sleep.

"Your things are in your room, waiting for you."

"Thanks." *I hope you didn't unpack anything – I don't want you seeing Karl's last letter, or his erotica.* "How are Mama and Johanna?"

He hesitated.

Oh, God, what's happened?

"They're fine."

There was obviously something he didn't want to tell me. Well, whatever it was, it could wait.

The cab stopped outside our house. *I didn't believe I'd see this again – in those last months at the Front I'd given up all hope of surviving.*

I suddenly realised how long the journey back from the other side was going to be, and wondered whether I had the strength to make it. *'You're still in the war,' the dead man said...*

Papa went into the house first, and I followed him slowly.

"Franz is here!" he called out.

Mama ran out into the hall. "Franz! Oh, Franz!"

She clung to me as if she would never let me go again, and I managed to free an arm to hold her. She was crying, her face against my shoulder.

"*Franz!*" Johanna came running out as well and threw her arms round me, almost knocking me over.

Fatigue and all the pent-up emotion of the past months hit me, and I had to shut my eyes tight.

I'm home. The war is over and I've made it home.

XIII

"Sorry," I said, "but I need to sit down."

"No, it's our fault," Mama said. "We shouldn't have kept you standing here. You must be worn out."

"And I'll bet you're hungry," said Johanna.

"I had some breakfast in Stuttgart, thanks."

I sat down, weary beyond words.

"Would you like coffee?" Papa asked. "I managed to get some."

"I'd love some. Thanks."

Mama looked at me with love and concern. "So how…"

Sunlight was pouring into the drawing room. *What – how did I get here?*

"Sleepyhead!" Johanna said.

"What?"

She laughed. "You've been sitting there snoring for the last two hours."

"Oh, God, how rude of me – I've hardly slept since I left hospital, oh, two days ago. I think it was two days ago, anyway."

"So tell us how you got here," Papa said.

"Why not tell us over lunch?" said Mama.

I suddenly realised how hungry I was, and to my surprise Klara produced a reasonable meal. Papa uncorked two of his better bottles and kept topping my glass up.

At least I don't have to worry about keeping my story correct any more, I thought as I told them about the journey home. I even showed them my Communist Party card.

"I'd burn that, if I were you," said Papa.

"I think I'll hang on to it for a while. It might come in useful again – don't worry, I won't boast about it. It's not even in my name, anyway."

"My brother the Red rabble-rouser!" Johanna said.

There was a sudden atmosphere that I didn't quite understand, as if our parents disapproved of her in some way. *I thought all the business about medical school was sorted out, so what's wrong? I expect she'll tell me later.*

After lunch I settled back into the chair by the fire, feeling rather drunk. Papa came towards me with his hands behind his back, and suddenly produced a box of cigars.

"Where on earth did you get those?"

"I saved them, for your homecoming." He lit one for me. "Would you like a brandy to go with that?"

"Yes, thank you." *You believed I'd come home – but then I suppose you had to.* "It's excellent, and so's the brandy."

"You've no idea how pleased we are to see you home," Mama said. "It was very brave of you to leave the hospital."

I stretched out in my chair, warm and content and lazy...

The strange aircraft *were* English. One of them was turning onto Karl's tail.

'*Karl, look out! Look out, for God's sake!*' But it was too late. His aircraft reared up and fell over into a spin—

"Franz, wake up!" Papa was shaking my shoulder.

"What? Oh... I... I must have been dreaming. Sorry."

They all looked at each other, and I realised I must have shouted in my sleep.

"You didn't bring any luggage," Mama said, obviously changing the subject.

"No, I couldn't manage it. The hospital's sending my things on, but I don't know when it'll all get here. Sobek – the fellow who took over the Jasta after I was shot down – he visited me on his way home and he brought me the photo albums. I hope they don't get lost."

"Those would be very interesting to see," said Papa.

Shit – I hadn't thought of that. I wished I hadn't mentioned the albums. I didn't want to have to take my family through them and answer their questions. It was too private, and I wasn't sure I could do it without breaking down.

"The portrait you sent from Berlin was lovely," Mama said. "We had it framed. Johanna, bring it and show Franz."

"Thanks, but I know what it's like." I didn't want to see that picture, didn't want to look at the confident young man I'd once been.

"There was one of your friend Karl in the same package," she continued. "We had that framed as well and it's in your room."

"Thank you."

Papa cleared his throat, as he always did when he had something awkward to say. "Franz, I know I didn't approve of your choice of friend – listen, please – but I want to say… well, I've never told you how sorry we are. It must have been a great shock for you. There were pictures of his funeral in the illustrated papers, and an obituary. We've kept them for you."

"Thank you."

'Now thank we all our God, With hearts and hands and voices…' The old tune rang out across the cemetery, the brass band backing our voices—

"The papers said he'd been shot down."

"That's right."

"How did it happen?"

Karl's coffin stood in the hangar, his face still… *Why did you have to ask me about that, of all things?* I stared at my hands.

"I liked him," Johanna said. "I'm sorry he's dead."

"He could have stayed at home," I said slowly. "They offered him a medical discharge and a pension, but he wouldn't take them. He might still have been alive…"

And I could have sent him home – to do what? To sit by the fire, getting sicker and sicker until he died?

I would have looked after him. We would have been together—

'You as my nurse, Franz?' he said. 'That wouldn't have done.'

We could have hired a proper nurse.

'It's better this way.'

Papa was saying something.

"Sorry, Papa – what did you say?"

"You've never told us how you came to be shot down."

"Oh, it was the classic mistake. I forgot to look behind. Next thing I knew I was being attacked, and of course he had the advantage."

"But how could you have made such a mistake, when you were so experienced?"

"I was tired, and it was just after Karl…" Why did I still find it so hard to say? "…just after Karl's funeral. The war – it wears you down… Look, can we talk about something else?"

My parents looked disappointed. No one seemed to be able to think of anything to say, and the silence grew embarrassingly long.

I sighed. I'd known it was going to be difficult, but I hadn't realised they'd be so eager to talk about the one subject I wanted to avoid.

It's all too raw. One day I might be able to talk about it, but not yet.

"Your things are in your room," Mama said. I must have looked blank, because she added, "Leutnant Sobek sent them to us, with a very nice letter."

"Oh yes, of course. I'd forgotten. You haven't unpacked them, have you?"

"No. You asked us not to."

Thank God for that. They won't have seen Karl's letters, or the erotica. I'll have to hide them in my desk.

"Well, I'd better do some work," Papa said. "Would you like the paper?"

"Thanks."

I couldn't concentrate on it. The war kept intruding.

Somehow I have to become a civilian again – and I haven't the faintest idea how. In hospital we were all soldiers, and the war lived on in our injuries and our minds – but here there's no one like me.

There must be a veterans' association in town. Perhaps I'll join. It might make things a little easier. Or maybe I should try to get away from it completely—

Johanna started laughing.

"What's so funny, Sis?"

"Gentleman of the road! Well, you do look like a tramp!"

"Cheers. I love you too!"

"At least you don't stink of booze and fags any more."

Mama gave her a stern look, and then said to me, "It would be a good idea to wash and shave before dinner, Franz."

"I'll give you a hand with the stairs," Johanna said.

"I can manage, thanks. We practised stairs in hospital."

She was looking at me as if she wanted to say something.

"But since I had so much wine, I could probably do with some help."

The stairs were harder work than I'd expected. They were steeper than the ones in hospital and quite awkward to get up, especially with my painful left arm.

I managed to hop as far as the half-landing, and was grateful for Johanna's support as I got my breath back.

"We'll put a chair here," she said, "so you can rest on the way up."

Karl could do with that—

You stupid bastard, Franz. He's dead. Can't you get that into your thick head? You buried him and you still forget, still think of writing to him, of going to visit him. Bloody idiot.

I made it the rest of the way on my arse, to my sister's amusement.

"You're all heart, Sis, you know that?"

That's what Burkhardt always used to say. Good bloke, he was – and it wasn't a bad way to die…

"Franz. You're staring into space."

"Sorry, Sis. My observer when I was on two-seaters, Burkhardt – he used to say that all the time. 'You're all heart.'"

She squeezed my arm. "Come on."

My bedroom hadn't changed. The last four years might not have happened.

Bollocks. I'm on crutches and there are two bags addressed to 'Oberleutnant Franz Becker' sitting under the window.

On my desk was the framed portrait of Karl, in his best uniform with the Pour le Mérite at his collar, gazing at me with calm dignity.

Oh, my love, my love… The pain in my heart stopped me breathing, and I sat down heavily on my bed, unable to tear my eyes from his, hoping I wouldn't cry in front of Johanna.

Oh, my love, why did you leave me?

"He was a fine man," she said.

"Do you think so, or are you just saying that?" My voice sounded strange and remote.

"No, I mean it… Papa doesn't mean to be tactless. He feels guilty because he was so nasty about Karl, and now he's dead. He wanted to say something to you, but he got it all wrong. They can't understand what's happened."

"Can you?"

I didn't want to tell her how Karl and I had really been, but at the same time, part of me hoped she would understand.

She closed the door and sat beside me. "Do you remember Georg Maurer?"

"Not very well."

His brother had been in my year at school. Georg would have been about two years younger than me.

"He was killed last year. Last November, two days before the Armistice." She was twisting her hands together. "He came home on leave in the summer, we saw each other quite a lot, and then when he went back we wrote to each other. Mama and Papa thought we were just friends, but we were going to get married after – after the war.

"Then when the Armistice was declared I was so happy, because he was going to be safe. And then a fortnight later he was in the casualty lists, and they sent me his letters back and the picture I'd given him, and I couldn't believe it. It was… it was just so cruel."

I put my arm round her shoulders. "Sis, I'm so sorry."

What shit timing.

"And Mama read the letters and showed them to Papa, and they called me all sorts of names."

"They did *what?!*" *Jesus Christ.*

"*Sh.* Not so loud. They were worried about my virtue, they said – but they needn't have been, because I didn't – he wanted me to – to go to bed with him and I wouldn't, and then when I read that he was dead I wished I had, because now it's too late." Her voice was quiet, desperate, but she wasn't crying. "I wanted to talk to you because I knew you'd understand, but I had to talk to you alone, and I couldn't, until now."

"Where was he killed?"

"Stenay."

"Where's that?"

"It's near Verdun – it was the Americans who killed him."

"When things have settled down, we'll go to France and Flanders," I said slowly. "We'll find his grave and I'll show you Karl's, and Otto's. It might help us."

"Do you think so?"

"I don't know."

I might be clutching at straws, trying desperately to find something which would give some meaning to the last four years. *Would it really help me to see Karl's grave again?* I couldn't imagine that it would, but it might help Johanna to see her boyfriend's grave. Assuming he had one.

"Please don't say anything to them," she said. "I don't want it brought up again. As soon as things are stable I'm going to Berlin, and I'm just going to concentrate on my studies."

"Good idea." *I wish I had something to concentrate on – though it's too soon for that.*

"I wanted to talk to you, because you know what it's like to lose someone you care about."

I looked at her sharply, but there was no hint in her face of any hidden meaning.

"I'll leave you to get washed and changed," she said.

I held her tight for a moment, and then she got up and left the room.

Poor Sis, just when she thought he was safe. And why in God's name was anyone still fighting when the war was as good as over? There should have been an immediate ceasefire as soon as the negotiations started, instead of that farce of waiting until 11am on 11th November. The time doesn't even work for us – it was twelve noon in Germany.

And what the fuck were our parents doing, reading Johanna's letters? I was so angry that I didn't know how I was going to be civil to them.

Better keep Karl's letters hidden, especially the last one.

I made my way to the bathroom. There weren't any rails, and the mirror was too high for me to shave sitting down.

This is going to be difficult – but I'll have to learn to manage.

I looked in the mirror and wished I hadn't. I'd forgotten what I looked like. It wasn't only my thin, pale, unshaven face – it was that bleak stare, of a man who'd seen and done far too much.

I wouldn't want anything to do with me.

I managed to soap my face and shave half of it before I had to sit down – and then I was so weary that it was a real struggle to get up again. Washing was very awkward, and there was no way I could carry my discarded clothes back to my room.

Is there anything more ridiculous than a naked man on crutches? Or rather, most of a naked man on crutches?

Unpacking can wait until after dinner. Better get dressed and downstairs before I fall asleep.

What my parents had done to Johanna made my blood boil, and it was very difficult not to show my anger. Papa finished working and joined us in the drawing room, and I had to bite my tongue hard.

"You're very quiet, Franz," Mama said over dinner.

"I'm tired."

Johanna kicked me under the table.

"I'll be fine after a good night's sleep." I tried to make my voice a bit warmer, for her sake. "Oh, Mama – I'm very sorry, but I had to leave my clothes on the bathroom floor."

She smiled. "It really doesn't matter."

"Any chance of another brandy?" I asked when we got back into the drawing room.

"Franz, I really don't think—" Papa began.

"Papa, for Heaven's sake, Franz isn't a student any more," Johanna said.

He frowned. "You know I don't like your using that expression."

"Josef, I'm sure Franz knows how much he can drink," said Mama.

"Last time he was here he drank far too much," Papa replied.

"*Last time I was here* I didn't expect to live much longer," I said. "I never expected to come home again. We all drank too much."

He looked at me in silence for a moment. "Yes, well… er… the last four and a half years can't have been easy for you."

You have no idea. You can have no idea.

He got up and poured me a brandy.

"Thanks."

I stared into the fire, adrift and without purpose in a strange world where nothing made any sense. *It was all so simple…*

We were sitting in the barn, and outside the rain poured down. One of Karl's aunts had sent him a pair of fine leather gloves, and he was carefully unpicking the seams of the underside of the right index finger. As we talked he kept working, unpicking until he reached the palm, securing the thread, and finally cutting off the loose leather.

It seemed so cold-blooded, but the weather was freezing, and I knew that when he was out in No Man's Land his life might depend on shooting first and accurately, and that neither cold fingers nor clumsy gloves would help.

'Your aunt would have a fit if she could see you mutilating her expensive gloves,' I said.

Especially if she knew why you do it.

'I'm sure she'd prefer me to be in one piece rather than the gloves,' he answered.

'Does it make that much difference?'

He shrugged. 'I think so.'

'You just want to beat my score,' Taschner said with a grin.

For a moment I couldn't understand how the barn had turned into my parents' drawing room. Mama was smiling at me, but I could still see Karl's hands, those broad, capable hands that had played the piano so superbly, working patiently away…

He's dead. When will I ever get used to him being dead?

"Franz, why don't you go to bed?" Mama said. "You'd be much more comfortable."

She was right. My leg was hurting. I couldn't imagine it ever stopping, and it was becoming bloody depressing. And my left arm was throbbing. *I hope I haven't broken anything. I'm sure it shouldn't be as sore as this.*

"Yes, I think I will. Good night."

I fell asleep the second my head hit the pillow, but five minutes later I was pressing myself into the mud as the shells rained down—

I woke with a yell, and that was the end of sleep.

So, what about Maria? I thought as I lay staring at the ceiling, waiting for the dawn. *I wonder if she'd still want me... All I want is a bit of intimacy with someone, just to lie in their arms and feel their skin against mine, just a bit of warmth and tenderness.*

I sighed. *No one's going to want you, Franz – and probably least of all a girl you had a fling with, when you were whole and famous.* I couldn't work out whether I had more chance with her than with a stranger, or less.

Only one way to find out – and I have to know if she has my child.

I asked Johanna about her after breakfast. Both parents were out, and Klara was in the kitchen.

"It's really strange," she said. "The Hertels won't talk to us at all, because of the politics – she's even worse than him – but Liese told me that Maria's in Stuttgart and won't be coming back. And that's all she'll say. I asked Lotte – Liese's friend and the biggest gossip I know – but of course Liese hadn't told her anything."

"So you don't know what she's doing there?"

She shook her head. "Why are you so interested?"

"I'm not."

She gave me a look. "Bollocks."

"Sis! You can't use that word!"

"Why not? You do."

"Like I said before, I'm a soldier and you're a young lady."

"If you don't want me using bad words you can tell me the truth! Though I think it goes something like this: Maria got you into bed in June '17, but she got more than she bargained for, because she got pregnant. So they all went away before it started to show, and now she's hiding in Stuttgart with your child."

I didn't want to believe her. "So why isn't Herr Hertel after me with a shotgun?"

"Because they'd rather have a bastard in their family than you."

"Cheers, Sis... What do you mean, *she* got *me* into bed?" *Wasn't it the other way round?*

"She was as smug as anything after you went back. Girls are more like men than you realise – some of them had been talking about you for weeks, saying how it would be the best thing in the world to lose their virginity to a famous hero. She didn't actually say anything, but she was all knowing every time sex got mentioned."

I laughed. "Oh, I do realise – I used to get letters from women all over Germany. Most of them just wanted me as a notch on the bedpost."

"And so did she. Please tell me I've got it all wrong."

"I don't know how much you've got right... Yes, I did go to bed with her, but I thought *I* was seducing *her*. And we wrote to each other, but then her letters stopped, and that would have been about the time they went away, so you may well be right about the rest of it."

"So what are you going to do?"

"If I do have a child, then I don't want it to be a bastard."

Johanna gave me a very serious look. "You can't marry her, Franz. She's an empty-headed, shallow little... she's stupid and self-centred and she won't make you happy. She wanted you and she had you, and the rest of it's her tough luck."

"You really are all heart! The thing is, Sis, it's the child who's going to suffer."

"How many bastards do you think there are in Germany now? No one's going to care."

"I'll care," I said. "Even if Maria and I live as strangers under one roof, I have to give my child my name and legitimacy – if there is a child. And I have to find out."

And I can't bear the thought of only fucking tarts for the rest of my life.

Johanna put her hand on my arm. "Franz, please think very carefully about this – you need to know her before you make your mind up." She sighed. "I admit I don't like her. I never have. So make your own mind up – but don't rush into marriage. Please."

"You sound just like Karl."

"Well, he was right, then. You'll be able to have your pick of girls – why not wait and choose the right one?" She gave me another very serious look. "Assuming marriage is what you want."

It was my turn to give her a serious look. "What's that supposed to mean?"

"Just wondered."

Oh, did you now?

"And what was that crap about having my pick of girls? I've only got one leg, in case you hadn't noticed."

"And a chest full of decorations."

"No one cares about those now."

"That's what you think – and even if they don't, how many millions of girls are there in Germany with no hope of ever finding a man? I've given up on that idea, I can tell you. It's medicine and only medicine for me."

"Sis, you're young and... well, I think you're beautiful, and so did the others at the hospital. Don't give up on love. Not yet."

She shook her head. "It makes it all much simpler. Having a career *and* a husband and children would be almost impossible. But now I can focus on what I'm passionate about, without distractions. I can always have affairs, if I want to."

"You'll be cutting your hair off and wearing trousers next!" I teased.

"And smoking cigars."

We were both laughing, and I felt better than I had in a long while.

"I'm going to see Herr Hertel," I said. "Someone has to start telling me the truth."

"Good luck," she said with a shrug.

I heaved myself back upstairs and got my best suit out of the wardrobe. The jacket was too short in the arms and too loose on the body, and looked ridiculous.

My best uniform was in one of the bags, but it was probably crumpled – and I wasn't sure whether it was safe to wear it. I would just have to go as I was. I looked a bit scruffy, but that was probably the least of the problems.

Maria's house was further away than I remembered. It was bloody hard work getting there, and I had to pause by the front door for several minutes to get my breath back.

It's so fucking depressing – now I understand why Karl was so low a year and a bit ago. That was only six months after he'd been wounded. It's eight months since I lost my leg, and I'm starting to despair of ever being right again.

I rang the bell. After a minute or so a maid opened the door.

"Could I see Herr Hertel, please?"

"Who shall I say is calling?"

"Oberleutnant Becker," I said automatically.

She looked at me rather sideways.

"Franz Becker," I corrected.

"Come in, sir."

I followed her into the hall.

"Wait here, please, sir." She looked at my right trouser leg and indicated a chair. "Please take a seat."

She came back after a couple of minutes, looking rather embarrassed. "I'm sorry, sir, but Herr Hertel isn't at home."

It was obviously a lie.

"When are you expecting him back?"

"I'm sorry, sir. I don't know."

"I see. What about Frau Hertel?"

"I'm very sorry, sir, but Frau Hertel is out as well."

The poor girl was scarlet, and I felt quite sorry for her. *They really should do their own dirty work, rather than hiding behind the maid.*

"Will you tell them I called and I'll be back tomorrow?"

And the next day, and the day after that, until the bastards tell me where their daughter is.

"Yes, sir."

He's there, I thought as I left. *I know he's there.* I turned back and looked at the house, and thought I saw a lace curtain move. *I'll be back, you bastards. You won't get rid of me that easily.*

The way home felt twice as long as the way there, and I wondered if I was going to make it.

What did you expect? You knew you'd be persona non grata. Maybe you should just leave it alone.

"How did you get on?" Johanna asked.

"He wouldn't see me – at least, the maid said he wasn't at home, but I'm sure he was. She wasn't there either, apparently."

"She's the one who calls the shots. Franz, why don't you just leave things as they are? If Maria wants you then she must know you're home, but she hasn't written, has she?"

"Like I say, Sis, it's not her, it's the child. I have to know whether I've got a child."

Maybe I should go in uniform next time. If they're so bloody patriotic then they can't refuse to help a veteran, can they? Especially a crippled one with a record like mine...

Better get my uniform unpacked and tidied up.

I couldn't face the stairs, and decided it could wait until after lunch – and then I just sat on my bed, looking at the bags. *I'll have to unpack them*, I thought, but I couldn't face that either.

Oh, get on with it, for God's sake, or the bags will sit there for months – or your parents will decide to unpack them, and then they'll read Karl's letters. And you don't want that, now, do you?

I sighed and opened the first bag. There was my best uniform, neatly folded.

The last time I wore this was for Karl's funeral, I thought sadly. *And where's my other one? Maybe it's at the bottom, or in the other bag—*

You stupid cunt. You threw it away, remember? Because it was covered in Karl's blood.

I don't think I can do this. There are too many memories in these bags.

Get on with it.

My sweaters, my shirts – and a grey silk shirt, rather bigger than my own. I buried my face in it, but there was no trace of Karl's scent. It had faded away completely.

The feeling of loss, of bleak emptiness, was unbearable. *I wish I'd died the day I was shot down. There is no point whatever in being alive.*

Turn your brain off and get on with it.

Two cases rested among the clothes. I picked up the larger one, turned it over in my hands and opened it.

I should be proud of these. When I went to war I never imagined I would acquire so many decorations, so much glory.

Just to win the Iron Cross was every young man's dream, never mind a collection like this. If only they hadn't been bought with other men's lives.

I don't suppose I'll ever wear them again. I'll put them in a drawer and make sure my children never see them. Glittering baubles to dazzle young minds...

The other case contained the Pour le Mérite. The blue enamel and the gold eagles shone against the velvet lining. *This was what every fighter pilot coveted: the highest military award of the Kingdom of Prussia, of a kingdom that no longer exists. Will they ever give these again, or will I be a curiosity one day?*

I will anyway. The world will turn, and our war and our suffering will fade into the past. One day all of us who survived will be dead. No one will remember standing in the trenches at dawn, or flying over the lines in a fragile machine made of wood and fabric. One day we will all be ghosts.

The old priest's words in the confessional in St Hedwig's came into my mind: 'Nothing of this world lasts for ever, my son. One day the war will be over, or you will be killed or wounded. All you have to do is endure until then.'

The war is over, and I have to learn to live again.

There was my identity tag, which of course I should have been wearing – but I knew the Alerting Service watched a lot of the combats and would recognise my white knight, so I didn't bother. *Stupid, really – once I'd parachuted out, no one knew who I was.*

Doesn't matter now.

My two thick sweaters were in the second bag. The first one was unexpectedly heavy, and there was something hard rolled up in it... My pistol, which I'd never used. It had been issued to me when I was commissioned, but as I didn't have any use for it in the Air Service I'd kept it in a drawer. Sobek obviously hadn't known whether it was Army issue or personal property.

Strictly speaking I should return it, but to whom? It might be useful if the unrest gets any worse, and I've got used to having a weapon. I don't suppose anyone will miss it.

Sobek, being a thoughtful fellow, had hidden a box of ammunition in the other sweater. I put that and the gun in my desk.

He'd wrapped Karl's erotica carefully in my flying underwear, no doubt with a smile. I leafed idly through one of the books. The images did nothing for me.

Jesus Christ – a few months ago they'd have had the intended effect, and now all I can think is that the men all have two legs, and that no girl is ever likely to want me.

I put them in the desk drawer next to the gun, and locked it. *Ridiculous, having to hide my choice of books from my parents. Bloody ridiculous. Still, I suppose it's their house.*

My cigarette lighter was in my socks. I turned it over in my hands, looking at my initials engraved into it. *The men who made this are probably all dead now. January '16 is a very long time ago.*

Beneath the socks were several bundles of letters. Like everyone, I'd kept all my personal letters in a drawer, in piles according to who they were from. Sobek had carefully tied up each stack with tape.

The sight of Karl's handwriting went right through me. *I didn't realise you'd written me so many. I shall keep these for ever.* On the top envelope it said, 'To be opened only in the event of my death.' *This is the most precious letter of all, the one that says what I should have known all along.* 'I love you, Franz. I love you with all my heart and all my soul...' *As I love you, Karl, and always will, until I die – and perhaps even after that.*

I locked the letters in the desk as well, and put the key in my pocket. *I mustn't lose that,* I thought suddenly, *and I don't want anyone finding it.* I put it on the same cord as my identity tag and hung them round my neck.

I looked at Karl's portrait, met his calm, level gaze once again. *You always did have such presence, and those eyes of yours saw so clearly, even when the rest of us were blinded by enthusiasm as we rushed to volunteer.*

'Anyone would think you were scared!' Kurt said, and Karl gave him the same answer he'd given me.

'Not yet, but we will be. Oh, we will be.'

I shook my head. The dead were with me in my room, as if they were still flesh and blood, as if I could touch them, could hear their voices.

No one had wanted to believe Karl that day.

How right you were. I was scared more times than I can count. I remembered how bad the fear had been in the last weeks before I'd been shot down, and it made me shiver.

No one should have to endure that. It's more than anyone can stand. It's a fucking miracle we didn't all end up like poor old Widemayer – but how sane am I, with my endless nightmares and my hallucinations?

And what in God's name was it all for? You died, and for what?

Karl's face blurred as tears filled my eyes and overflowed down my cheeks. *I'm a grown man, not a child* – but I couldn't stop myself crying. I lay on my bed, trying to control myself, trying at least to keep silent. I didn't want my family to hear me sobbing. My grief for Karl was too enormous and too private to share.

An hour or so later I forced myself to go downstairs, and tried to be 'normal', whatever that was.

The next morning I went to Maria's again. I felt rather frayed at the edges, but I couldn't let that bastard win.

I'd had a bad night. It had started with the usual insomnia, staring at the ceiling in the darkness, thinking about Karl. I dozed briefly, woke with my head full of the war, and lay wide awake, trying not to hear the chimes of the clock downstairs.

I felt like taking a hammer to the bloody thing as it measured out my sleepless hours, mocking me by chiming two and three o'clock in the morning, times when decent people with clear consciences were fast asleep.

In the end I dreamed vividly about Kurt in the grey mud, the rain plastering his blond hair to his head as his blood ran down into the water.

I woke to a feeling of sick terror, because I was going to have to get up soon and go flying – then I remembered that the war was over, that no one was going to try to kill me any more. And then I remembered that Karl, Kurt and the others were dead, and that my knee couldn't be hurting because it wasn't there.

I lay listening to that bloody clock until it got light.

The sky was grey and heavy as I made my way slowly to the Hertels' house. It began to rain just as I reached the gate. Grey sky, grey mud – suddenly I couldn't go any further. All I could see was Kurt. I had a dreadful attack of shaking, and it was all I could do to stay upright.

Oh, Christ, I thought this was over! I haven't had such a bad attack of nerves since I was shot down. My heart was pounding and I couldn't move.

"You all right?" The face was thin and haggard, the voice thin to match.

"Fine." My voice shook.

"Bad business, the war."

"I said I'm fine," I snapped.

His face soured and he turned away. *I didn't mean to be rude – but it was too late to explain. If he's a veteran he doesn't need an explanation, anyway.*

The shaking had diminished, and I opened the gate and went to the front door.

The previous day's pantomime was repeated. The maid told me, with considerable embarrassment, that Herr Hertel was not at home and that she didn't know when he would be back. I left the same message.

You'll have to see me eventually. You can't just keep fobbing me off like this.

I stopped at a bar on the way home, and sat alone in a corner with a couple of brandies. I didn't know anyone and I had no desire to talk. All I wanted was to get that bastard Hertel to tell me whether his daughter had had my child, and if so, where they were.

The men at the next table were speculating about the likely terms of the peace treaty, and I didn't want to listen.

They'll hammer us. It's as simple as that.

I could have done with another brandy, but I'd had enough of their conversation. It was far too depressing.

They all died for nothing, I thought as I left.

Papa had obviously been waiting for me. "Ah, Franz, there you are. Come into my study for a moment. We need to talk."

"What about?"

His manner was very serious. I never liked it when he was in one of those moods.

"Sit down."

He put me across the desk from him. I smiled to myself. *This is just what I used to do to anyone I wanted to feel uncomfortable – even to Karl.*

'Karl – I'd like a straight answer to this, please. What's wrong with you?'

He sat quite still, his face impassive, his eyes clear. 'I'm fine, Franz.'

"Franz, are you listening?" Papa sounded irritated.

"What? Oh, sorry – I was miles away."

"You could at least pay attention when we're discussing your future."

"My future?" Now that was a novel idea. "I… er… I hadn't really thought about it."

Because there wasn't one.

"Well, presumably you want to go back to Heidelberg and resume your studies."

"Back to *Heidelberg*?" What was he thinking? It was impossible. Heidelberg without Karl was unimaginable. "Papa, I don't think—"

"It doesn't have to be Heidelberg, of course," he said hastily. "It would probably be better for you to start again somewhere else. I don't know if your studies so far will be accepted, having regard to the long interruption, but we'll have to ask."

I felt a thousand years old. How could I go to university and join the children who were just leaving school? How could I study law when I'd devoted four years of my life to killing?

We are all beasts. Civilisation is only a millimetre thick.

"Papa, I can't. Not yet. I need more time."

"You're twenty-three. Next month you'll be twenty-four. You have no qualifications and no prospect of obtaining any. The young men leaving school will have several years' head start on you. You need to resume your studies as soon as possible. You have to think of your career."

"I can't. I need more time." *For fuck's sake, didn't you hear me the first time?*

"Will you listen to sense? The war's over and you can't keep dwelling on it."

I got up with a huge effort. The walk had tired me out.

"I'm not listening to any more," I said. "I don't know what I want to do. I don't want to be a lawyer. Not now. I need time to think."

"Franz—"

I was already closing the door behind me.

I went into the drawing room and sagged into one of the chairs by the fire. *Bugger my father! How can he expect me to act as if nothing's happened?*

"Is everything all right, Franz?" Mama asked.

"No."

"Has your father been talking to you about university?"

"Yes."

"You should think about it, you know. You have a lot of years ahead of you."

"I need more time," I said crossly. "Leave me alone, can't you?"

She looked so hurt that I felt thoroughly guilty. *All I know how to do is hurt people*, I thought, thinking suddenly of the young Englishman.

"Mama, I'm sorry, I shouldn't have snapped at you. It's just too soon, that's all."

"Don't take it out on us, Franz. It was your choice to go."

"If I hadn't volunteered, I'd have been conscripted later. The results would have been the same."

"There are three letters for you." She obviously wanted to change the subject.

"Thanks."

One was from Alfred, who was up to his eyeballs in the fighting in Berlin.

'Honestly, Franz, I never thought I'd be fighting like this in my own home town, but what can we do? The government needs us to stop the Bolsheviks taking over. Frankly, I hope it's over soon. I really have had enough.'

That's something I never thought I'd hear from Alfred.

'Your Paul Fellmann is a very handy fellow – bloody good shot, and a very cool customer. Not too keen on Wolffheim, though. Bit of an unpleasant piece of work – fights very well, but I don't care for his politics. I'm doing this to stop Germany turning into a Soviet republic and to restore the rule of law, but he's somewhere to the right of Attila the Hun, and if you ask me, far right is just the same as far left.'

I wonder what you'd say about my – or rather, Ludwig Vogel's – joining the Communist Party? I thought with a smile. *Have to tell you over a bottle of schnapps some time.*

The second letter was from Horstmann.

'What in God's name did we all achieve? But there's no point thinking about that – what's done is done, and we have to make the most of the future that we find we've got. Susanne and I are getting married in July, and we'd love you to come to the wedding.'

Sure enough, there was a formal wedding invitation, to the ceremony at the Garrison Church in Potsdam and the reception afterwards.

'I realise you'll have a few problems travelling, so I could come and meet you and give you a hand, if that's what you want. Just let me know nearer the time.'

I shall certainly go. Wild horses wouldn't keep me away.
The third letter was from Berlin, and was addressed in an unfamiliar but rather stylish hand. *Who on earth is this from?*
There was more of the stylish writing inside, on paper headed 'Feinstein and Company' with their very smart Berlin address.

'Dear Oberleutnant Becker,
Please forgive the delay in writing to you, but things are very disturbed here, as no doubt you are aware. I am the executor of

the late Leutnant Karl von Leussow, and he left you a bequest about which I need to speak to you in person. I realise that this may be difficult for you, and I cannot ask you to travel to Berlin for the foreseeable future, but I could not delay writing to you any longer. I look forward to meeting you at the earliest possible time.

Yours sincerely,
Jakob Feinstein.'

Good God. That's the last thing I was expecting.
Karl, what have you done that your lawyer has to speak to me instead of just carrying out your wishes? You didn't have to leave me anything.

'I know I didn't, you stupid bastard. But I wanted to.'
"Bad news?" Johanna asked.
"No. What makes you think that?"
"You look rather stunned."

I laughed. "My friend Horstmann's getting married in Potsdam in July, and I was wondering how I'm going to get there."

"That's very close to Berlin," Mama said. "Will it be safe?"
"If anywhere's safe it'll be Potsdam – it'll still be full of the Prussian Army."

Anyway, I don't care. I can go to Berlin at the same time, see Karl's lawyer.

"Alfred's written," I said, changing the subject and putting the lawyer's letter in my pocket.

"The Alfred I'm going to stay with?" Johanna asked, her face brightening up.

Lucky Sis, having a vocation. I wish I knew what I want to do.
"Well, let's hope so."

I gave her a look which said, *Shut up, I'll tell you later*, and fortunately she got the message.

"Let's sit in the garden," she said after lunch. "It's warm enough near the wall."

And indeed it was, beautifully warm.

"So what's Alfred up to?" she asked quietly.

"Fighting the Communists – has been since the end of the war."

She started laughing. "So is he one of those frothing-at-the-mouth 'shoot all the Reds' chaps?"

"No – but that's what the parents would think. Alfred would rather bring back the Kaiser, or preferably Frederick the Great."

"Oh, a Prussian patriot. Well, I think we should have all the Kings back. At least we had stability and prosperity, and we were on our way to full democracy." After a moment she asked, "Who was the other letter from?"

"Horstmann."

"Not that one – the third one, stupid."

"None of your business."

"Got a secret lover, have you?" she teased.

"You really think I'm going to answer that?"

"Man or woman?"

My jaw dropped and I stared at her.

"What sort of question is that?" I managed to croak.

She put her hand on mine. "Don't worry, I won't say a word to anyone."

"About what?"

"About anything you tell me. You know that, don't you?"

"Sis, I can assure you I don't have a lover, secret or otherwise."

Because Karl is dead, and I shall never love anyone else.

"One day, if you do have, remember you can trust me," she said, and got up and went inside.

Well, bugger me. What in God's name made her think I might have a male lover? And if she thinks that, who else does?

Too complicated. Let's get the business of my child sorted out. I'd put money that I've got one – why else would Maria's father refuse to see me?

The following morning saw the usual performance. The poor maid couldn't meet my eyes any more.

It really isn't fair. They shouldn't make her tell fibs.

"Where did you go?" Mama asked me over lunch.

"Oh, just for a walk," I replied casually.

"I hope you're not trying to see the Hertels," said Papa.

"Why would I do that?"

He gave me a very straight look. "I don't believe that needs answering."

And I don't believe it's your business – except that, of course, it was their business. I just didn't want to say anything to them until I knew the truth.

"Have you joined the veterans' association yet?" Papa asked.

"No – I'd forgotten all about it."

"It would be a good idea," he went on. "You'd have men like yourself to talk to."

"There is that," I conceded. "Though what I really need is a gym where I can do my exercises."

"There should be one at the hospital," Johanna said. "After all, there are a lot of men needing rehabilitation."

"Could you find out for me, please, Sis?"

"Of course."

I had to force myself to go to the Hertels' the next morning. It wasn't a good day for it – I wasn't feeling well and my leg was hurting more than usual. I'd had another bad night, and I felt so weary that all I really wanted to do was stay in bed.

There's no point going, I thought as I left the house. *He won't tell me anything, but I have to try. I have to know the truth.*

I was worn out by the time I got there, and my knee was throbbing.

The maid looked at me with sympathy and a great deal of embarrassment. *Poor girl.*

"Take a seat, please, sir. I'll just see if Herr Hertel is in."

I know what the answer will be – but to my amazement, when she came back she said, "Come this way, please."

I heaved myself out of the chair, and followed her along a corridor papered with some fussy floral pattern.

Very feminine, I thought, and then realised I'd seen no evidence of Frau Hertel. *She calls the shots, Johanna said, so presumably she stays in HQ and sends her husband out to do the dirty work.*

The maid opened a door. Hertel was seated behind his desk.

"Come in," he said coldly.

The maid closed the door behind me. Hertel sat looking at me with fishlike eyes. He didn't invite me to sit down, the bastard.

"What do I have to do to stop you coming to my house?"

"Tell me where Maria is."

"My daughter wants nothing to do with you. She left here to end a flirtation which she recognised had been a mistake. I certainly shall not tell you where she is – and you will leave my wife and myself in peace."

Or else what? I sat down.

"That's not enough," I said. "I need to see her. Just give me her address. If she really doesn't want anything to do with me, I promise I'll leave you all in peace. But I need to see her."

He was looking at me with distaste – no, it was stronger than that. I hesitated to put a name to it, because the only one I could find was 'hatred', and I couldn't understand why he would feel like that.

"If you think I would permit any liaison between you and my daughter—"

"Why not?"

"Your father and I have never agreed about politics. Before the war I could ignore his opinions, repugnant as I found them, but that has become impossible. Your father is a Socialist, one of the people who have ruined this country and delivered it to our enemies, I could almost say a traitor."

"I'm the one who wants to see Maria, not my father."

"You're even worse. You're a Communist. Everyone knows that."

How in God's name... Klara must have been listening, when I told my family about joining the Party, after I'd had a bit too much wine. Presumably it's all over town, no doubt without the rider that I'd had to do it in order to get home.

"I don't think you've heard the full story about that—"

"I'm not interested."

"It's up to Maria who she sees, anyway."

"That brings me to another problem. Maria... I'm very sorry to have to tell you this, but she... well, she's found a young man we find suitable."

It sounded false. "I don't believe you."

"For Heaven's sake, will you listen? After you went away—"

"Went back to the Front, you mean."

"...she was very upset. But then she met a very suitable young man—"

"Why wasn't he in the Army?"

"He was in a reserved occupation."

"Lucky bugger," I said sarcastically. "No doubt he's still in one piece."

"Well, yes, he is."

He looked at me with an expression that attempted to be sympathetic and failed completely. It was as false as his voice.

"I really didn't want to have to tell you this, but when Maria heard about your... er... disability, she – well, she's a healthy young woman. I'm sure you appreciate her feelings."

"No, I don't," I lied. *I knew no girl would want a stump against her leg.* "I don't believe you. I have to hear it from her. Please give me her address."

"It's quite out of the question. I promised her she wouldn't be disturbed."

"So is this fellow bringing up my child?" *Out of the sun, that was always the best way.*

"Child?"

That went home.

There was a brief pause while he collected himself, and then he said flatly, "There isn't one."

You're a very bad liar. Almost as bad as Karl.

He rang the bell. "It's time you left. If you come here again, I shall call the police."

"Oh, I shall be back," I said quietly. "I want to see my child, and I shall see him or her."

"I've already told you, there is no child."

I got up and left. There was no point wasting any more words.

As I headed home the sky darkened, and it began to rain. It was hard going in the mud on my crutches, and I tried to hurry because the Company was going to attack and I was going to be too late. The rain poured down and I was lost. I must have taken a wrong turning… but why was I going along a street?

I stopped and looked, astonished, at the undamaged buildings, and realised that I was at home. I was in a strange part of town and I had no idea how I'd got there.

There was a bar. It looked dingy and unwelcoming. I went in and sat by the window.

"Schnapps, please. Make it a large one."

What in God's name is happening to me?

Suddenly what Hertel had said hit me. *Yes, Maria does have my child but she's with some other bastard, and for all I know he's already been registered as the father and I've got no right even to see my own flesh and blood – and that's the most important thing in the world to me now. I've lost so much. I can't lose this as well.*

I drank the spirit straight down, and another.

The rain lashed against the window.

It was dark night, and the flares lit the rain to a silver curtain. The shells screamed and the explosions shattered my ears, hammered at my brain until it hung limp in my skull.

'The French are coming!' shouted Karl – and there they were, dark figures in the dancing light.

I shook my head and the image disappeared. The rain was still running down the window. It rained at the Chief's funeral, as if the sky were weeping for him. We were all soaked long before we got to the cemetery...

I carried on drinking. *You don't deserve to be happy after what you did. You don't even know how many men you killed. Even mass murderers know that. 'Even mass murderers'? What do you think you are, then? What about the young Englishman? And why only him? What about all the rest of them?*

Did you really think you could have a normal life after that? You'll always belong to the war, it'll never leave you. You can't even walk down the street without thinking you're at the Front.

I had lost track of reality completely, and it terrified me. When would it happen next?

Maybe Hertel can see how bonkers I am. Maybe that's why he wants to keep me away from his daughter and his grandchild.

A group of young men came in. They were happy and healthy. They all had two legs and two arms and two eyes, and they were talking at the tops of their voices.

"Shut the fuck up, can't you?" I growled.

They turned, astonished.

"Wot the fuck's it got to do with you?" said one of them.

"I just want a peaceful drink – just want a bit of peace."

"Yeah, well who's stopping you?"

"You are, you noisy bastards."

Healthy young bodies – none of you left a leg in Flanders. My son or daughter is saying, 'Papa' to someone like you.

"'Ere, listen to 'im! 'Oo the fuck d'you think you are?"

Oberleutnant Franz Becker, Pour le Mérite etc, etc.

"Just want a bit of peace. Been a bit rare the last few years."

He looked at my crutches. "Oh, Christ, another bloody veteran thinks 'e can tell the rest of us wot to do. Listen, mate, if we 'adn't of made the weapons you couldn't of used 'em. That right, boys?"

"Too bloody right!" chorused his friends.

Reserved occupation. Maria's new man's in a reserved occupation.

"So you're the bastards who stayed at home while the rest of us were in the trenches. You make me fucking sick, the lot of you."

The barman was looking worried. "I think you've had enough, sir," he said to me.

"You're right there. I've had enough, all right. Enough of bloody shirkers."

"Don't you call us shirkers—"

I threw my glass at him. He leapt at me, and as I levelled a crutch to fend him off, his mates grabbed him.

"'E's a cripple, Karl," said one. "You don't fight cripples."

Karl. *His name's Karl.* Blue eyes staring through me and Fellmann, his mouth and chin covered in blood – then I heard the rest of the sentence.

You don't fight cripples. They've taken my child and I'm not even worthy of fighting them.

"The gentleman was just leaving," said the barman.

The rain battered at the window. I looked at it, and saw a vast expanse of mud and desolation, bleak in the light of a dirty grey dawn, the shapeless long-dead corpses like bundles of grey washing.

I picked up my ashtray and flung it with all my strength. The world shattered into fragments and I collapsed, crying.

The cell was clean and dry, and vastly better than many of the places I'd slept in.

They treat criminals better than soldiers. And no one shells the criminals, or shoots at them. They don't have to fight. They just live in nice, comfortable places like this and stay dry and get fed, while honest fellows like me get turned into cripples and lunatics and corpses.

The policemen were not unkind. They reminded me of the older reservists who'd been in our company in '14. They even brought me a cup of 'coffee'. I drank it, wrapped myself in the blanket, curled up on the wooden bed and fell asleep.

Someone was shaking my shoulder. "Herr Oberleutnant!"

Schiffer's face came slowly into focus. *Oh, Christ, it must be time to go flying. That was a short night.*

"What time is it?" I asked.

"It's half past eight."

"Why did you let me sleep so late?"

It wasn't Schiffer. For a moment I couldn't work out who it was, then I saw the police uniform.

"Your father's here, sir."

"My father?" I said blankly.

What's he doing here? And why did the policeman call me 'Herr Oberleutnant'? I suppose I must have given my name and rank when I was arrested.

"He's come to take you home," said the policeman patiently. "Come on, sir. You go home and have a nice long sleep, and you'll be all right."

I won't. The one thing I'll never be is all right.

I struggled out of the blanket, and the policeman helped me to get up. *How in God's name did I get here?*

Suddenly I remembered Maria's father telling me that some other bastard had my child, and I didn't want to go home. I wanted to drink until I couldn't feel anything any more.

Papa was furious. "Get in the cab, Franz."

"All right, all right."

I could hardly manage my crutches, and he had to help me to get in.

"You're still drunk," he said with disgust.

"So bloody what?"

"I never thought I'd have to bail you out of a police station. What did you think you were doing?"

"I can't remember."

"You're a disgrace."

"That wasn't what you said when I came home with the Pour le Mérite."

"Then I had a son I could be proud of, not a drunk getting arrested in a fight in a bar."

"They go together… How did you find me, anyway?"

"Your mother was worried sick because you hadn't come home. She thought you might have had a fall. In the end I rang the police station. I couldn't believe my ears when they said you were there." He snorted. "What they *actually* said was that they had a one-legged drunk who claimed to be Oberleutnant Franz Becker. Oh, they know all about you. The Sergeant said he'd followed the war in the air with great interest, especially the career of our very own, very highly decorated fighter pilot. He thought you were a drunken liar, until I told him that you really are the famous ace.

"He'll tell the entire town that you were his guest, no doubt. Your poor mother will be mortified. And I shouldn't think you've any chance with the Hertels now."

"I haven't anyway. He told me she's with some bastard who was in a reserved occupation, some fucking coward who still has both legs."

"Franz, your language is appalling. Will you please try to remember that you're not in the field now."

"Oh, for fuck's sake, shut up." I turned away and looked out of the window into the darkness.

"Franz!" He went on lecturing, but I wasn't listening.

When we reached the house, I practically fell out of the cab. Papa opened the front door and I stumbled in.

Mama came out into the hall. "Franz, thank God you're all right!"

Why does everyone keep telling me I'm all right? I brushed past her into the drawing room.

Johanna got up from her chair. "Ah – the brother I know and love, stinking of booze and fags!"

"Get me a brandy, Sis."

I half-fell into a chair and she handed me a glass with a generous measure in it, bless her. I took a large swallow—

My parents came in.

"Franz, you've had quite enough already!" Papa was livid.

When I'd been a child, I'd been afraid of his anger. Now I could only look at him and wonder what he could do to me.

"No, I bloody haven't. Leave me alone, can't you?"

"Would you like something to eat?" Mama asked.

"No, I bloody wouldn't. Just leave me alone!" My voice broke on the words, and I threw the rest of the brandy down my throat.

Karl would have understood. Oh, if only I could live with him!

"Get me another," I said to Johanna.

"You will do no such thing!" Papa said.

"Oh, for Christ's sake!"

I heaved myself out of the chair and went towards the table. Papa barred my way, and I realised I hadn't the strength to push him aside.

I held Karl's wrist so easily in the garden, Karl who had been so strong...

"I'm going to bed," I said, with as much dignity as I could manage. "Will you give me a hand, Sis?"

We got up to my room, and I sat down heavily on my bed.

"He said she's with someone else," I said. "They're all dead and she doesn't want me because – because I'm a… because of my leg, and he said there isn't a child but he was lying and I don't know what to do. I'm going mad, Sis. I went… I thought—"

I wanted to tell her that I hadn't known where I was, that I'd thought I was back at the Front, but I couldn't get the words out. It was too frightening.

All I could say was, "Karl's dead, and I don't know what to do…"

She sat beside me and put her arms round me. "Maybe Hertel was telling the truth."

"He was lying. I could see it. Some other bastard's bringing up my child and I'll never see him or her."

"Why don't you get some sleep, and we'll talk about it in the morning?" she said gently. "I'm sure we can work something out. Look, I'd better go and try to calm the parents down."

She got up, and then reached down and ruffled my hair. "Good night, Oberleutnant Booze and Fags."

She closed the door behind her and I lay down, overwhelmed by a sudden longing for tenderness.

You can forget that. No one wants you now.

XIV

I must have passed out, because I woke up lying fully dressed on my bed, feeling sick and with a thumping head. My first thought was that I'd been drinking with Karl, and then I remembered he was dead.

I hate that moment, when the waking illusion disappears and cold reality comes back in.

The previous day was rather hazy, but bit by bit I remembered Maria's father telling me she had someone else, and then I remembered the bar, and smashing the window, and crying in public like some hysterical woman – and that some of the time I no longer knew where I was, or what was happening.

Memory and reality were blurring together, and I was losing the distinction between them.

How long before they take me away, and lock me up with the Widemayers and the Krugs?

I made a real exhibition of myself. I'll probably be prosecuted. That'll look good. No doubt they'll put a suitable photo in the paper, probably one of Fellmann's, with all my medals. 'Air ace in bar brawl' – that'll be a good headline.

So what. So bloody what.

Finally it got light. I had no desire to see anyone.

Mama knocked on the door. "Franz, dear, would you like some breakfast?"

"No thanks. I'm not hungry."

She knocked again some time later, and I heard Papa calling, "Leave him alone. He'll come to his senses at some point."

I wish I could.

I lay staring at the ceiling.

She doesn't want me. No one's going to want a one-legged wreck... I tried to close my mind to it but for a long time I couldn't, and then when I did the war went round and round in my head. I lay waiting for the next terrifying loss of reality, and I lost all track of time.

Mama put her head round the door. "Franz, lunch is ready. Won't you eat something? I'll bring a tray up here if you're not feeling well."

"I'm not hungry." Karl's words, Karl's voice, echoing in my head.

"What's the matter? Is your leg hurting?"

"Yes." Which was true, but which also made a good excuse.

An hour or so later, Johanna came in and sat on my bed. "Bet you've got a hangover."

"What would you know about hangovers?"

She laughed. "Lotte and I bought a bottle of wine and got tipsy at her place – we wanted to find out what it was like."

"What – you got drunk on half a bottle of wine?"

She laughed again. "We don't live on booze and fags, not like some people!" She lowered her voice. "Are you feeling any better?"

I shook my head. "Close the door, would you, Sis?" I asked quietly.

She sat down again and studied my face, waiting for me to speak. I wanted to tell her about my – *episodes*, when the war came back and blotted out reality, but I couldn't find the words.

"So what really happened in the bar?"

I looked at my hands. "Sis – you promise you won't tell anyone?"

"Of course."

"I... I – sometimes I see the war," I blurted out.

She nodded. "You're a long way from being alone in that, from what I've read. What were the others like, in the hospital? Did any of them have the same thing?"

"That's what really frightens me." I could hear my voice trembling. "There was one poor fellow, Krug – he'd been hit in the head and he had these – turns... where he thought he was in the trenches. And that... that..."

That's what happens to me, I wanted to say, but saying it out loud was too frightening.

"What happened to him?"

"Died of the flu, and I thought it was the best thing, because he was never going to be right again."

"So was he the only one?"

"Yes... No. No, he wasn't. Once there was a loud bang, right outside the day room, and quite a few of the fellows hit the floor, and afterwards one or two of them admitted they saw things. It's just – it..." my voice fell to a whisper "...takes over. And everything else disappears."

"Is that why you broke the window? To make it go away?"

"I suppose so."

She put her hand on my arm. "Lying here brooding isn't going to help – the best thing is to try to live as normally as you can. It'll fade with time."

"Do you think so?"

"Yes. Look, why not get up and come downstairs – I'm sure Klara's kept you some lunch – and then afterwards we can sit in the garden."

"I don't want to face anyone."

"Well, you can't stay up here for ever." She got up. "I could do with some company too, you know. They're still being funny with me over Georg."

Shit. I'd forgotten about that. Selfish bastard, Franz. Get a grip.

"I'll be down as soon as I can."

She gave me that stunning smile. "Thanks."

Fortunately, the parents were out. I remembered being very rude to Papa, and regretted it, but at the same time I wasn't ready to apologise.

I wasn't hungry, either, but I knew I couldn't afford to lose more weight, so I forced my lunch down.

"Papa's got some decent cigarettes now," Johanna said.

"Good – oh, bugger, I've left my lighter upstairs."

"Where is it?"

"On my desk."

I heard her feet running up and then down the stairs, and I was suddenly so jealous of her.

"Here you are – what's the matter?"

I tried to smile. "Just wishing I could still run up and down stairs."

"Oh... Yes, of course." She looked at the lighter. "It's beautiful – superb workmanship."

The metal was slightly scuffed in a couple of places, but my initials were still clear. *It was bloody good of my fellows to give me this.*

"What's it made from?" she asked.

"It's a cartridge case for a rifle bullet – you eject it after you fire, so sometimes there'd be quite a lot lying around. You have seen it before, Sis."

Her face changed slightly, as she realised what I'd said.

"Yes," she said neutrally, "but I've never had a good look at it. You didn't make it?"

I laughed. "No chance! No, it was a leaving present from my fellows, when I left the regiment to join the Air Service."

"They must have thought a lot of you to make that."

"It was a surprise… A lot of fellows made things to pass the time. Spots – one of the snipers – used to carve, made beautiful wooden animals. He gave Karl a hare…"

As I got out of bed I saw the hare on Karl's bedside table, so alive that it looked as if it were about to leap onto the floor and bound away—

"*Franz.*"

"What?"

"Was it the war again?"

"Sort of… Karl sometimes saw things as well, after Verdun." My throat closed and I had to stop speaking.

"Let's go into the garden," she said.

We sat in the sun by the wall.

This time last year, you were still alive and safe at home in Brandenburg, and I thought that you would survive the war and I would be killed…

"Sorry, Sis, what did you say?"

"I asked what Hertel said to you – you weren't very coherent yesterday evening."

"He said Maria's with someone they approve of, and she doesn't want anything to do with me because of my leg. And he swears there isn't a child, but he was lying."

"Let's take that one thing at a time. What exactly did he say about her? Can you remember?"

"She was very unhappy after I went back, and then she met someone, and then she heard – hang on, that doesn't make sense. He said she'd already met the fellow before she heard about my leg."

"So the leg can't have made any difference."

"Or he's making the whole thing up."

"Mm. And what about the child?"

"I just threw that in, without any lead-up, to try to catch him out. And it worked. He went as white as a sheet, then pulled himself together, and denied that there is one."

She looked at me very closely. "Franz – are you absolutely sure that's what you saw?"

"Oh, for God's sake, Sis – don't you believe me?"

I knew I shouldn't have told you about seeing things.

"What I mean is that – please just listen – you're so sure there is a child that you could be interpreting everything in that light."

"If you're going to come out with crap like that, you can fuck off and leave me in peace."

She shrugged, completely unoffended.

"You've been reading too much Freud or whoever," I said. "Just stick to bones."

"Stuttgart's not on the other side of the moon," she said. "She must be registered with the authorities."

"If that still happens these days – and under what name?"

"That is the problem… and how would we get the address?"

"I'll just have to keep badgering Hertel until the bastard tells me."

That got me another serious look. "Franz, do you think that's really a good idea? You're pinning an awful lot on there being a child, and we don't know that there is one."

"You think I'm bonkers?"

"No, stupid, of course I don't. But I am a bit concerned about you – you don't want to get obsessed with this."

"I'm not obsessed."

She sighed. "I didn't say you were, did I? But it might be better for you to get away for a couple of weeks, have a break from this."

"Oh, might it? And where do you suggest I go?"

"Why not go and stay with that friend of yours who's getting married?"

"Horstmann? I can't foist myself on him. I'd only be in the way."

There's only one person I want to go and stay with.

The sun had gone in and a sharp breeze had sprung up. I shivered.

"Let's go in," she said. "It's getting chilly."

"I'm not a bloody invalid!"

"I didn't say that, either. I'm getting cold."

She was wearing a summer dress, and there were goosebumps right up her arms.

"Sorry, Sis."

She put her arm round me. "It's all right, Franz. Come on, let's have some coffee."

My parents had come home.

"Mama, Papa, I'm really sorry about yesterday," I said.

Papa gave me a stern look. "You'd be well advised to avoid the Hertels', and you'll just have to hope you don't get prosecuted."

"If that happens I'll plead guilty, get it over with. I hope there isn't any publicity."

"So do I, Franz." *Because it would be very bad for my practice,* he didn't have to say.

"Are you feeling better?" Mama asked.

"A bit, thanks."

"You need something to occupy yourself," she said.

Oh no, not that again.

Klara knocked on the door. "There's a policeman to see you, sir," she said to me, very awkwardly.

"Oh." *Shit.*

"Grete, Johanna, would you go into the conservatory for a while, please? Franz, I think I should be with you when you talk to him."

I hadn't heard Papa taking charge like that for quite some time. *Nicely done.*

"Thanks, Papa," I said. "I'm so sorry about all this."

He looked at me. "Yes, I'm sure you are. Klara, show the policeman in, please."

It was the same Sergeant who'd woken me in the cell, and he greeted me again as 'Herr Oberleutnant'.

The habits of military service obviously die hard – but didn't Papa say the Sergeant had followed the war in the air?

"I went to see the owner of the bar," he said. "He's not a bad sort, and he said if you go and apologise and pay for the window, he won't press charges."

"Thank you very much indeed," I said. "What about the fellow I threw the glass at?"

"You didn't do him any damage. Strictly speaking it was assault, but he hasn't made a complaint." He looked at the carpet for a moment, and then said, rather awkwardly, "I'm sorry I didn't believe you, sir, when you said who you were when we arrested you."

"That's all right. I was pissed, and I don't look much like those photographs these days."

"No, well…" He looked at my leg, and I could hear him thinking, *That must have taken it out of him.* He cleared his throat. "May I ask a favour, sir?"

"Of course." *Why's he asking me for a favour? Surely I'm in his debt.*

"Would you be kind enough to autograph this for my grandson, please?"

He produced a postcard from his pocket and handed it to me. I smiled wryly as I recognised the portrait taken in Berlin.

"What's his name?"

"Kurt."

I flinched, and saw the look of dismayed embarrassment that flitted across his face. *Oh, damn. How do I explain?*

I wrote on the back, 'To Kurt, with best wishes' and signed it.

As I gave it back to him I said, "What a – what a coincidence. I had a friend called... Kurt. He – died..."

The rain poured down, plastering his hair to his head. I couldn't stop him bleeding, couldn't even get him to shelter. All I could do was hold him and listen to him—

I was sitting in a chair in my parents' drawing room. Papa was bending over me, looking very worried, and then he and the policeman exchanged glances.

How did I get here?

"Is this what happened in the bar?" asked the policeman quietly.

Oh, Christ. "Why? What did I say?"

"Nothing," he replied. "But you weren't here. You were looking straight through us. We were talking to you and you didn't seem to hear us."

"I... I..." My hands were shaking and I folded them together, hoping they wouldn't notice.

The policeman turned to Papa and said, "I'd go and see the owner of the bar before he changes his mind, sir. Though I don't think there'd be much point in a prosecution, in the circumstances."

What circumstances? Oh, because I'm bonkers, obviously.

He left and Papa turned to me. "Franz, are you all right?"

"Yes, of course. It's just... Kurt – he – he got hit and... there was nothing I could..." I couldn't finish the sentence.

Papa was looking very thoughtful. "I'll pay for the window, Franz," he said. "I know your pension hasn't come through yet, and I don't suppose you've got any money. I don't want you to be prosecuted – for your sake, not ours."

"Thanks very much, Papa, but I have still got my pay in the bank – there wasn't much to spend it on."

"No, you'd better keep that."

"Thanks, I do appreciate it. Look, I – I realise I'm being difficult, but..."

I didn't know what I wanted to say.

He shook his head. "No, you're not. Or, rather, yes, you are being very difficult, but you must be finding everything difficult yourself. It's easy to talk about heroes as the papers did during the war, and to give men medals, but, well, none of us can imagine what you actually had to do."

Be thankful you can't.

"And it must be a big readjustment. Do you feel up to going to see the barman today?"

I shook my head. "I'll go in the morning."

"Yes, you'll probably feel better after a good night's sleep."

I wonder what one of those is?

I wondered that again as I lay awake in the early hours, too frightened to go back to sleep in case the men I'd killed were still waiting for me. *If I stay awake they'll go away...*

If anything I felt even rougher than I had the day before, but I made myself as presentable as possible.

"I can take you there in a cab," Papa said. "I still can't get petrol for the car, I'm afraid."

"No – thanks, but I'll make my own way there. I need the exercise."

"I'll come with you," said Johanna.

"No, you won't, Sis – it's in the rough part of town."

"Are you sure you'll be all right?" Mama asked.

I looked at their faces, and realised they were worried about my going out on my own.

"I'll be fine," I lied.

I had no way of knowing whether I'd be fine or not, but I couldn't hide in my parents' house for the rest of my life. Yes, I was apprehensive about having another turn in public, but I just had to get on with it. It was hardly the most scared I'd ever been.

As Papa gave me the money for the window, he said again, "Are you sure you want to go by yourself?"

"Yes."

It's embarrassing enough on my own. I didn't want to face the barman again. I'd made a complete fool of myself and cried in front of him.

Hero? That was a joke.

The policeman had given Papa the address of the bar, which was just as well as I'd never have found it otherwise. The outside was distinctly grubby, and the boarded-up window made it look even dingier.

What on earth was I doing in a place like this?

I opened the door cautiously, and was relieved to see that it was empty. The barman turned as I entered.

"I've come to apologise for breaking the window," I said. "Can I pay for the damage?"

"Have a seat," he said.

"Thanks."

"I can't let you drink here – you're banned."

"Of course."

"Still, you gave me an excuse to ban those loudmouths as well."

"What?"

"They annoyed my other customers too. Where they get the money from I don't know. They're all out of work now, of course. Annoys me too, the wages they earned during the war. Must annoy you even more."

"I lost my girl to a bloke in a reserved occupation. I'd just heard about it when I came in here that day."

"Well, you'd obviously had a real plateful."

"You can say that again." I was embarrassed. He knew I'd had a real plateful because I'd had hysterics, and I didn't want to be reminded of that. "How much will it cost to replace the window?"

He told me, and I got Papa's money out of my wallet to pay him.

Maria's picture fell out and fluttered to the floor. *Why on earth am I still carrying that around? I don't love her and I never did, and I don't suppose she cares about me either – I just want to give my child a decent future, and to not be alone.*

He bent down and picked it up. "This your girl?"

"She was."

"Bad luck."

He handed me the picture, and I stuffed it back into my wallet without a glance.

"Thank you for being so… well, so…"

"It's only a bit of glass. I've had far worse fights than that in here, and mostly no one pays for the damage. Prosecution's all very well, but it don't pay the bills."

Makes sense, I thought as I went out into the bright sunshine. *In his shoes I'd rather have the money as well.*

There was a sharp breeze, but at least it wasn't raining. I tried to tell myself that the only problem I had with rain was that it was wet, but I knew that wasn't true.

I wonder if there's a list of things that will set it off, and whether I can avoid them. 'It's usually something someone says,' Karl said, and sometimes it is for me, too.

Maybe I need some sort of ritual, like the one he used to try to keep the Verdun demons in their box. I saw him again, putting a cigarette into the holder very slowly and carefully, and then lighting it with the same deliberate movements.

Didn't always work, though, did it? I thought, seeing the shadow creep out of his eyes and spread itself across his face.

And it shouldn't be forgotten, any of it. Never mind what it does to us, we who are left have to remember.

It was a long way home, and I hadn't the strength to do it all in one go. I'd made it to the bar without stopping, but that had half worn me out. I went into the park and sat on one of the benches, thinking about Karl.

I shall always love you. No one will ever understand me the way you did. I'll never have that closeness with anyone else…

The wind was cutting through my coat. *I'll make myself ill if I stay out here much longer – but does it matter? If I die then I'll be with Karl.*

'Go home, Franz,' he said gently. 'I'm here and I always shall be, but now you must go back to the living.'

I was exhausted by the time I got home, but also relieved because *it* hadn't happened again. My parents looked up as I went into the drawing room.

I sat down carefully, my leg aching viciously.

"How did it go?" Papa asked.

"All right, thanks. He was really nice about it. Oh – I've got the rest of your money here."

"Don't get up," he said, got up himself and then sat down again. "Keep it, Franz. This shambles of a government might sort out your pension one day."

"And a leg," I said.

"Yes, of course… You were gone a long time."

I felt a brief surge of resentment that they should know about my – 'episodes'.

"I'm all right. It was a long way, that's all. I'm a bit slow these days."

Karl's voice again – that was what he'd said to that Home Defence fellow who'd come to search his farm.

Karl stood by the window, humming 'The Glory of Prussia', his fingers drumming the rhythm on the frame. 'We went in singing that on the first day at Verdun.'

'I'd have thought Langemarck would have put you off singing.'

"Franz, it's lunchtime," Papa said.

My parents were looking at me with concern.

"You were staring into space," said Mama.

"I was thinking about Karl. Where's Johanna?"

"Out with a friend," Mama replied.

"Oh, I've been meaning to ask you," said Papa. "Would you like to have lunch at my club tomorrow?"

"Er..."

The last time I had lunch at your club I was in uniform with my new Pour le Mérite, and all the old buffers asked me stupid questions and seemed to think I was some sort of hero. And it feels like a century ago.

"I don't have anything smart enough to wear."

"Neither do most of us these days. The others keep asking after you – they'd very much like to meet you again."

"Can't think why... Papa, it's really kind of you, but they'd be very disappointed. I'm nothing like the fellow they met last time."

"Well, if you change your mind just let me know. Reddemann was asking after you – Stefan's home now."

"Oh, right – tell him to give me a ring, would you?"

Papa gave me a rather stern look. "So long as you don't get into more trouble."

"Did we get into trouble last time?" I asked with an air of innocence.

"You were seen in—" Papa broke off, obviously not wanting to mention the red-light district in Mama's presence.

"You don't want to believe everything you hear," I said.

"The police station a couple of days ago wasn't hearsay," he replied.

I bit my tongue, hard. *For fuck's sake. I'm twenty-three and until a few months ago I was the commander of a fighter squadron. I'm not a child.*

I had wanted to go to the Hertels' again, but I was far too tired. *It'll have to wait until tomorrow. Best not to be too predictable, anyway.*

"Don't do it," Johanna said as I was getting ready to leave the house the next morning.

"Do what?"

"Or at least let me come with you."

"You're joking."

"No, I'm not. They won't be expecting me, and I might be a better judge than you as to whether he's telling the truth."

"You know, you've got a point there. I'll buy you coffee afterwards."

"Thanks!"

The maid looked quite taken aback when she opened the door. *Yes, I've got reinforcements – and she's a damn sight more useful than you might think.*

No one was at home.

"Bollocks," Johanna said as we walked back down the path. She turned and looked at the house. "Don't look now, Franz, but we're being watched."

I turned round, with some difficulty. "Where?"

"You know, I think you want trouble," she said. "You're too late, anyway. It was the window just to the right of the front door. The lace curtain moved."

"That's the one I saw move before. Did you see anyone?"

"No."

"Pity."

"Come on," she said. "Let's have that coffee you bribed me with."

"*I* bribed *you*? It was your idea to come along."

We took a seat in the café, and to my dismay she got a cigarette case out of her handbag.

"Give me a light, Franz?"

'Give us a fag, Bruv.' Johnny flopped onto the small sofa between Karl and me.

"*Franz.*"

"What? Oh, sorry, Sis. Decent girls don't smoke, light your own – oh, sod it, all right then. Look like a tart if you want to."

She ignored that completely. "Where were you?"

I sighed. "Back at the squadron, with Karl and Johnny – Karl's brother… So what do you reckon?"

"They're hiding something, of course. That's obvious. I can't see why she won't tell you herself that you can't expect anything."

"Exactly."

"But I don't think badgering them is the right way to go about it. I think a bit of stealth would work better."

"No more frontal assaults," I said.

She blew out a cloud of smoke. "Well, they didn't work in the war, did they? No, what you want is intelligence, and then you can plan how to outflank them."

I laughed. "Sis, you sound like a staff officer! Where did you learn to talk like that?"

I regretted the words the second they left my mouth.

"Georg wanted a staff job," she said quietly. "He was really clever and very interested in strategy – he'd read so much: Frederick and Clausewitz and Napoleon. It was such a waste."

"It's all such a waste, Sis, believe me."

"But especially right at the end, like that—"

She broke off, and I squeezed her hand.

"And I can't talk about him at home," she went on a couple of minutes later.

"You can talk to me whenever you like – even if it's in the middle of the night. I'm often awake."

She gave me that glorious smile. "Thanks."

We got home just in time for lunch.

"Oh, Franz – your things have arrived from the hospital," Mama said.

There won't be much in the bag, just the squadron albums. I hoped my parents had forgotten about those. I had absolutely no desire to show them the photos – I wasn't sure I could do it without crying, or having an episode.

They hadn't forgotten. After lunch Papa said, "Franz, we'd like it very much if you'd show us some of those photographs."

"I – I'm sorry, I don't…"

"We're doing our best to try to understand. You'll have to help us."

I couldn't argue with that. "All right."

I sat on the sofa, my parents either side of me. Johanna pulled up a chair and sat next to Mama.

"Shall I start at the beginning?"

"Wherever you like," Mama said softly.

"This is before I joined the squadron," I said. "Here's the Chief – that's what we always called him. 'Oberleutnant Adalbert von Kralewski-Zentzytzki' was a bit of a mouthful."

"He's very famous," Papa said. "Almost as famous as Richthofen."

"Yes, that's right." I found the last formal portrait of him. "You think I've got medals. Look at that."

"Very impressive," Papa said.

The Chief looked at me from the page. He was so kind to Karl in the field hospital, and then I saw his beautiful Elise at the reception in Berlin, and the look of love in her face…

We could see the khaki figures clearly. Some ran, others dived for cover, some were firing at us. We followed the Chief as if we were glued to him – then his aircraft spun, hit the ground and burst into flames—

"What happened to him?" asked Mama.

"We were shooting up the English trenches. He got hit and spun in."

That poor woman, that awful letter I'd had to write, that coffin which probably contained bits of him, bits of his aircraft, and earth to make up the weight. I couldn't tell my family that.

I turned a few pages. "Here's Bruch. He shot himself."

"Why?" asked Papa, clearly shocked.

"His nerves were going and he was afraid of letting us down."

"But wouldn't they have sent him home?"

I shrugged. "Maybe. I don't think he was rational by then… Geschke got shot down in flames… Buchholz crashed and then died in hospital."

My family looked at each other, and I could see them wondering whether any of the men had survived.

Mama turned a couple of pages. There was a group of us standing by an Albatros.

"There's the Chief again, and Horstmann – he's still alive. I'm going to his wedding in July."

"That's Karl, isn't it?" asked Papa.

"Yes."

Karl was standing beside me, smiling, his black cigarette holder clamped between his teeth. I could hear his voice, his laughter. The photo was black and white, but I could see his light brown hair and those clear grey-blue eyes, the eyes I had closed. *Oh, my love…*

I found my voice. "It's his aircraft we're all leaning on – see the black and white stripes round the fuselage? That was always his personal marking."

"Of course," Papa said. "The Prussian colours."

"Exactly." I tore my eyes away from Karl's. "That's Patschke."

Don't climb so steeply, you bloody fool! Get your nose down! But it was too late—

"Is he still alive?" asked Johanna.

"No. He crashed on take-off. Our airfield was being attacked."

The young Englishman looked up at me, but couldn't speak through the blood pouring from his mouth. He died as we lifted him out of the wreckage. There was blood on my hands and my sleeves, and on the front of my tunic.

"Franz," said Mama softly.

"What? Oh, sorry. That – er – that's Widemayer. He – er… he cracked up. Went mad. That's Otto – Otto from university. He…"

Otto's Triplane caught fire properly, and he just sat there. *Get out, Otto, for God's sake, get out!* He didn't move, and the flames covered him…

Johnny was on the facing page, looking at the camera with his usual impudence.

"That's a lot of duelling scars!" Papa said, laughing. "Oh – he's Johann—"

"Johnny, Karl's older brother."

"Why do you call him Johnny?" asked Johanna.

The fire had taken hold right back to the Red Eagle, and Johnny jumped – but it was too late and he fell blazing like a meteorite—

"I'm sorry, I can't do any more of this." I was shaking, and I could hear the tremor in my voice. "I'm going outside."

I got up and the album fell to the floor. Mama picked it up.

"Franz, I'm sorry," she said. "We didn't realise—"

"I said I didn't want to, but you wouldn't bloody listen, would you?"

I went out into the garden and sat by the wall. I dropped my fags and then my lighter, and then it took me four attempts to get the thing lit, four flames that I tried not to look at.

The coffin contained a pitiful bundle, wrapped in a tent quarter.

'Don't bother with more earth,' Karl said. 'It's too late.'

They should have sent you to Technical and Testing after your father died, I said to him, *or given you a staff job. Then you'd be alive.*

'And I wouldn't be able to look in the mirror, Franz.'

The sun was well down and the air was chilly, and I realised that I'd lost all track of time, and that I needed a piss.

I went inside, and as I passed the drawing-room door I heard raised voices. I stopped and listened.

"He's impossible!" Papa said. "We keep trying to meet him halfway, but he's completely unreasonable."

"Josef, nearly all the men in those albums are dead. Their parents would all have been happy to have their sons back safely. We're very lucky."

"Yes, you're right, of course, but—"

"There is no 'but,'" Mama said firmly. "Think of all our friends whose sons fell."

"And think what it must be like to lose all your friends, to have men killed around you all the time, and to know you're likely to be next," said Johanna. "You heard him say that last time he was here he didn't expect to come home again, that he expected to die. How hard do you think it must be to come back from that? You think he can be the same man he was before the war?"

"I don't think any of us is the same," Mama said.

"You want someone who doesn't exist any more," Johanna went on. "You're treating him like a student. He was the commander of a fighter squadron, for God's sake. How do you think he got all those medals you're so proud of? Why did they write all those articles you kept? He shot down forty-three enemy aircraft. What do you think happened to the men in them?"

"That's something else that disturbs me," Papa replied. "I don't like thinking about what he did. Sometimes I look at his eyes and wish I hadn't."

Thanks, Papa. I really wanted to hear that.

"It's what soldiers have to do, isn't it?" Johanna said, exasperation in her voice. "Kill the enemy. Just be thankful they went down in flames and not him – and that all the young men went and fought and died and got mutilated to keep us safe, and that you didn't have to do it."

Well done, Sis, I thought, surprised and impressed. She was fighting my corner far better than I could have done.

I hope they've changed the subject by the time I join them, or I'm going to be horribly embarrassed.

As I came out of the loo, the phone rang.

"It's for you, sir," Klara said to me.

"Thanks." *I wonder who it is. Maybe Hertel's seen sense.*

"Reddemann here. Do I have the honour of addressing Oberleutnant Franz Becker, Pour le Mérite et cetera et cetera et bloody cetera, far more gongs than a man should have?" said a chirpy voice.

"Hello, Stefan, you piss-taking bastard!"

"Herr Hauptmann to you!"

"Christ, sir, they were scraping the bottom of the barrel."

He laughed. "That's for sure! Fancy a night on the town?"

"You bet I do."

"Finding Civvy Street a bit difficult?"

"That's about the size of it, yes… Tomorrow?"

"I'll call for you at seven."

I went back into the living room, feeling perkier than I had for quite a while.

"Who was that?" Papa asked.

"Stefan Reddemann – we're going out tomorrow night."

"Oh, good," said Johanna. "You'll stink of booze and fags like the brother I love!"

"Cheers, Sis."

Leave the Hertels out today, I thought in the morning, *or I'll be falling asleep later.*

Stefan arrived on the dot of seven.

I managed a bit of a bow. "Apologies for not greeting Herr Hauptmann correctly, but it's a bit awkward with only one leg!"

He studied me with mock concern. "Sure you can make it into town, crip?"

"Just watch me. Where are we going?"

"The Golden Lion, of course. At least this time I can walk there – well, hobble, anyway."

"More than I can do."

We set off, him leaning heavily on his stick – his right leg didn't work properly and he had to drag his foot along the ground – and me on my crutches.

I had to laugh. "What a pair of crocks!"

"At least we're alive."

The beer was cool and refreshing. I took a long swallow, and then another.

"Your operation worked, then," I said.

"Well enough."

"So what have you been doing?"

"Lecturing officer cadets about small-group tactics, giving them problems to solve, that sort of thing. Wasn't bad, really. Then they made me head of that section of training."

You must have got pretty senior to be promoted to Captain.

"I read about you in the paper," he went on. "Bloody careless of you to get shot down!"

I was feeling more relaxed than I had since leaving hospital. *Johanna was right about the veterans' association. I could do with more company like this.*

After a couple more beers and some food I was almost my old self.

"You know what you really need," Stefan said. "Come on, how long is it since you got your end away?"

"Bloody months…"

"My turn to take you to Rosenstraße! Let's go now, then we can get properly pissed afterwards."

"That's the best idea I've heard in a long time!" I said. *A German woman, a real live German woman – even if she is a tart.* "I haven't fucked a German woman since January last year."

"They tend to be a bit thin these days," he said, "but now the war's over they'll start plumping up again." He lowered his voice. "Truth to tell, I'm being a bit of a naughty boy – got a rather nice girl now, but she won't drop them till we're married. Sin and all that."

"What does she expect you to do?"

"Quite."

We went to the expensive whorehouse again. I still had the rest of the money Papa had given me for the window, and I reckoned it might as well go on a treat.

But when we got near the door I suddenly got cold feet. *She'll feel my stump against her leg. And I'll feel her leg against my stump, and I'm not sure I'll be able to do it.*

I stopped.

"Want to rest a bit?" Stefan asked.

"I'm not – I mean, I don't..."

"What's the problem?"

"My leg – I mean, my lack of a leg. My stump."

"Oh, Christ – she won't care about that!"

"No – but I might."

"Oh – yes, I know what you mean. Or rather, it wasn't quite that bad for me. I just had to ask the girl to go on top the first few times, until I was allowed to move my pelvis."

And if I do the same, then the stump won't touch her and I won't be able to see it either.

"Come on, then," I said.

The girl wasn't the hard-faced tart I'd been expecting, but a rather shy, sweet little thing, who reminded me of the girl Lensch had fallen for.

She got on top of me, and to my embarrassment it was all over in ten seconds flat. Well, it was my first fuck for God knows how long.

"I'm sorry," I said, wondering why I was apologising for giving her such an easy job.

"You've got the rest of the hour," she said, and then I wondered why she was being so nice to me.

"Turn the light off," I said as she moved. "I don't want to see my leg."

I know what I do want, but it'll sound a bit odd…

For fuck's sake, Franz, she must get asked for things that are really odd. And it's another easy job for her.

"Would you… I'm sorry if this sounds odd…" I felt her stiffen slightly. "Would you just lie next to me, in my arms, for a while?"

She relaxed and snuggled against me.

"You see, my love is… dead…" I couldn't say any more.

She laid her arm across my chest. No one had held me like that since Karl died, and the feeling of bare skin against mine reminded me so vividly of him. Grief welled up in my throat, and for one awful moment I thought I was going to cry.

A while later I was aware of her small breasts, and of the warm, female scent of her soft body…

By the time I went back downstairs I was feeling much happier. *I'll have to do this again. I actually feel human.*

'I feel human again!' Reinholz said.

There was a burst of laughter.

'You feel what?' demanded Schulz. 'Hey, chaps – Reinholz is claiming to be human!'

'No chance!' said Neumann. 'Gorilla, more like!'

'What he means is that he felt humans,' Winkler said.

'What, you mean they let him?!' said Magenau.

"Franz," Stefan said firmly.

"Sorry – I was thinking about some of the fellows in my two-seater squadron, back in summer '16."

"So many good men we knew… Still, we're alive so let's make the most of it!"

We went back to the Golden Lion, and sat smoking and drinking.

"So what happens to you now?" I asked him.

He shrugged. "Good question. I've been chucked out for now, like a lot of blokes, but presumably we'll still have an army and I'm hopeful of a training or staff job."

What if they don't want you? I just managed to stop myself saying it.

"But then there are plenty of capable fellows who can run and jump, and not just teach theory... I don't know what I'll do otherwise. Probably go into the family business – but that's going through a flat patch now the war's over."

No need to churn out uniforms now.

"Still, I'm just thankful I'm not paralysed... What about you? Back to the law?"

I shook my head. "I don't know yet. I've got a lot of readjusting to do."

"I'll bet you have. You had two years more than me. Look, there might be a training job for you in the new Air Service, or a technical post."

I hadn't thought of that.

"I'm not sure I'd want to be around aircraft and not be able to fly," I said. "Be a bit like being impotent in a brothel – and there are plenty of good fighter pilots who can still fly."

"Well, at least we're alive," he said again. He raised his glass. "To the fallen."

"To the fallen."

By the end of the evening I was feeling no pain at all.

"Closing time, gentlemen," the barman said. "Time to go to your nice warm beds!"

I started to get up.

"Franz, *stop!*" ordered Stefan.

Too late. I was already falling sideways. I grabbed the edge of the table with my left hand just as the barman caught me.

What – why—?

"I think you need these, sir," he said, handing me my crutches with his other hand.

Why do I...? "Oh, shit! So I do!"

Stefan burst out laughing and got up carefully. "Do 'scuse my friend," he said, surprisingly coherent. "Silly sod forgot he's only got one leg! Jus' think – he w's a fighter ace – dunno how he remembered to land!"

"Were you really, sir?" asked the barman.

"Yes. Franz Becker."

He looked at me in complete disbelief.

"No, he really is," Stefan insisted.

"Le's go home," I said. I was getting rather fed up with people not believing that I was me.

"Bloody hell," Stefan said as the night air hit us. "You've led me 'stray, you b'stard!"

"*I've* led *you*, *sir*?" I was finding my crutches absurdly difficult.

"Yes – bloody Air Service, loada pissheads! I think this stick's piss'd as well."

I started laughing. "So're my crutches!"

"Berra getta cab."

The cab driver looked quite sideways at the pair of us, and scowled at me when I got out. Perhaps our loud chorus of 'The Watch on the Rhine' had pissed him off, or was it that I'd started teaching Stefan the Liesl song? Either way, I didn't give a shit.

"Bes' evening 've had f'ra long time," I said to Stefan. "Do it 'gain soon."

My parents had left the porch and hall lights on, bless them, but no one was up. I made it up to bed on my arse, and passed out.

I woke with a horrible jolt, because daylight was coming through the curtains and Schiffer hadn't woken me. *That was a good party*, I thought, trying to remember the details. There was something about Johnny and Westermann jumping on the table and wrecking it yet again, and Karl playing the piano…

In Valhalla. And they're probably all flying over the lines now, looking for the Tommies.

Johnny turned in his seat and waved to me, the Red Eagle on the fuselage catching the sun. 'We'll keep a place for you,' he said.

I jolted awake. *Get up, you lazy bastard, before you fall asleep again and dream something worse.*

I had a lazy breakfast, then settled myself in the living room with a fag and the paper. Everyone else was out, and I felt better than I had in a very long time, in spite of my hangover. I actually had some small measure of peace, and at first I didn't realise what it was.

Could it be that I'm starting to get over it all?

Not over Karl, though. I don't think that will ever happen, and I don't think I want it to.

About ten minutes later, Klara knocked. "I'm sorry to disturb you, sir," she said, "but Frau Hertel is here."

Just then I heard voices: my parents' and Frau Hertel's.

"You'd better come into the drawing room," Mama said. "I'll see if I can find Franz – oh, there you are."

Frau Hertel had followed Mama, and was looking at me with marked distaste. Papa came in next, and his expression suggested that I stank of booze and fags.

"Do sit down, please," Mama said. "Klara, would you bring us some coffee?"

"I don't intend to stay in this house a minute longer than necessary," said Frau Hertel. "It was all I could do to force myself to come here at all."

We looked at each other.

"In that case you can leave now," Mama said.

"Not before I say this." Frau Hertel turned to me and gave me what she imagined was a basilisk stare. *Wasting your effort.*

"You are to leave us alone. My daughter wants nothing to do with you, and we do not want a Communist in our family."

"You'd rather your grandchild was a bastard?" I asked in a very level tone.

"I don't know where you get that absurd idea. And, to be frank, we wouldn't want any child of yours in our family anyway. You may have been a hero in the war, but you're a drunken Red lout."

"That is quite enough," Papa said. "Get out."

Frau Hertel turned, and as she flounced out of the room I burst out laughing.

"Silly cow!"

She heard me and half-turned, then slammed the living room door behind her. A moment later she gave the front door the same treatment.

I laughed harder.

"Well!" said Mama indignantly. "Who does she think she is?"

Papa sat down and looked at me. "Franz, what was that about a child?"

"Oh, I just wanted to piss her off even more." It didn't sound convincing.

"Are you saying we have a grandchild?" Mama asked.

"I don't know. You heard what she said. He says the same thing."

"So you went to bed with the Hertel girl," said Papa wearily. "What in Heaven's name possessed you?"

"The thought that I wouldn't come home again. Though I'm not sure which of us seduced the other."

"I hope you went to confession after that," Mama said.

I lit another cigarette instead of replying.

"So that's why you keep going to their house," said Papa.

"Yes. I just want to know the truth – and if she does have my child then I don't want it to be a bastard."

"Franz, you can't marry Maria Hertel," Mama said. "She'll turn into her mother one day."

"No," agreed Papa. "Quite impossible, not to mention their appalling politics... And you didn't say you *want* to marry her."

I sighed. "I don't. I don't want to marry anyone."

Johanna came in just as I said that.

"Look," Papa said, "why don't you wait until they approach you?"

You and Mama are taking the whole thing so calmly – I expected you to be livid.

"I agree," said Johanna.

"I suppose you know all about this," Mama said to her in an unkind tone.

"Yes, I do," she replied.

"Why didn't you come to us, son?" asked Papa.

"About what? I've only got a suspicion, nothing more – and they keep denying it."

"I think we all need coffee after that," Mama said. "The nerve of the woman!"

"What happened?" asked Johanna.

I told her, and she laughed.

"If I were you, I'd just be happy they don't want you!" she said to me.

"Johanna's right," Papa said. "Forget the whole business and start rebuilding your life."

Far easier said than done... One leg, half bonkers, no prospects that I can see, probably no child – or perhaps one that no one wants me to be a father to. Not much going for me at all, really.

You're alive, Franz. That's got to be worth something.

I stayed in for the next few days, not wanting to face the world outside, until Stefan called and reminded me that we were going out again.

We went to the same knocking shop, and I was hoping for the same girl but she was busy.

"You can wait for her if you like," said the madam.

'I never like it when the girl's just had someone else,' said Westermann.

I shook my head and her face came back into focus. "No, that's all right," I said. "One of the others will be just fine."

And I made exactly the same request, and she lay in my arms in the darkness, and for a few minutes I could imagine that someone wanted me.

As I left I had the most profound feeling of depression. *That's all I'm going to get for the rest of my life – a bit of bought warmth.*

"What's with the long face?" Stefan asked, back in the pub. "Wasn't she any good?"

"She was fine – it's just the thought that I'm always going to have to pay."

"Bollocks. There are thousands of single girls in Germany – one of them's got to be desperate enough to take you!"

"Cheers, bastard!"

"Things'll get back to normal before long. The war hasn't been over a year yet."

"I suppose so."

"Drink up, and be happy you're not in the mud in Flanders or somewhere." His face darkened.

Verdun. God knows how many of your men are in the mud there.

"Now who's got a long face?!" I said. "You're thinking."

He laughed and bought another round of beer and schnapps.

The depression returned when I woke the next morning, when black reality hit me as it always did. *Karl is dead. I shall never see him again. There will be no more nights of love, no more waking in his arms to see his blue eyes gazing at me with tenderness…*

Who else is going to want someone who wakes up screaming, who sees things and doesn't always know where he is? What sort of life would that be for a young girl, married to a wreck like me? Maria's family is right to keep me away from her.

I don't think I'll go to the house of joy again, I thought as I dragged myself out of bed. *I got used to doing that in the war, because there wasn't an alternative and I'd lost all hope of surviving, but now it just feels empty and grubby. I won't go again unless I'm completely desperate.*

After breakfast the parents went out, leaving Johanna and me alone in the drawing room.

"I've got something for you," she said. "I picked it up yesterday – early birthday present."

She handed me a package. I'd completely forgotten that my birthday was approaching. *Last year the squadron threw that surprise party for me… and who's still alive? Horstmann, Fellmann hopefully, Bretti, Sobek, Kleber if he survived being shot in the stomach…*

"Aren't you going to open it?"

"Sorry, Sis – thanks."

The package contained a frame. I turned it over, and almost dropped it.

Karl and I stood by his aircraft, his arm round my shoulders and mine round his waist.

You can see it so clearly, that we love each other. It must have been obvious to everyone who knew us – to everyone except me. How could I have been so fucking stupid?

I couldn't speak.

"You sent that home, do you remember? And the parents didn't like it, of course, so they put it in a drawer. I found it the other day, and I thought you'd like it for your room."

"Thank you," I croaked.

She put her hand on mine. "Love is just the same, whoever the lovers are."

I looked at her, trying to find something to say.

"I'll take it upstairs for you," she said.

"Thanks, Sis." I leaned forward and kissed her cheek.

She ruffled my hair and left me.

Karl took her place. *All I want is to be with you*, I said.

'It isn't time yet, Franz. But remember, I'm always here.'

It's not enough. I want your lips, your body against mine. I want to see you and hear your voice, I want you to hold me tight and murmur into my ear. I'm dying for the lack of you.

"Oh, here you are," Mama said.

I started violently and Karl vanished, the spell shattered with almost physical force.

When I got up to bed that night, I saw that Johanna had put the picture on my bedside table, so it would be the last thing I saw when I put the light out.

I wonder when she realised.

I curled up, imagining as always that I lay in Karl's arms with my head on his shoulder. *One day we'll be together again. We can loiter round your house with your ancestors, or get pissed in Valhalla…*

I don't think I can do this, I thought when I woke. *I can't go on without you. I can't stand this blackness every morning, when it hits me again that you've gone. I have neither the strength nor the desire to live without you.*

What am I going to do?

I made myself get up and go downstairs.

Over breakfast, Mama said, "Oh, I've got tickets for a concert this evening – I thought it would be nice to get out of the house."

I didn't want to go to a concert. I didn't want to do anything, but I was aware how difficult I'd been. *Better make an effort, especially after they were so reasonable about the Maria business.*

They'd taken a box, and it was a massive effort to get up the stairs. I sat down with relief, which was short-lived as the edge of the seat was hard and too close to my stump. *That's going to bloody hurt after a bit.*

There was a piano on the platform. *I really don't want to hear piano music. Maybe I should leave now* – but the conductor was already making his way to the podium.

They played the Egmont Overture, and the effects of the war on the orchestra were only too plain. It was nothing like as good as it had been.

The soloist appeared, bowed and took his place rather theatrically. The first chords from the orchestra and the swelling arpeggios from the piano went right through me. *I should have looked at the programme. I would never in a thousand years have come to hear the Emperor Concerto.*

I closed my eyes and the years vanished. I was in Heidelberg, before the war. Karl sat at the piano, his hair bright under the lights, and the same glorious music filled the hall.

You played a bloody sight better than him, my love. The pain of losing him turned to rage that such talent had been destroyed for absolutely nothing, and then to bitter grief, so strong that it was a physical pain in my heart.

My leg was really hurting, and I almost enjoyed it. I wanted to bang my head on the floor until it bled, until I could feel nothing.

I have to get out before the slow movement. That poignant, tender music will be too much. The last time I heard it was in Brandenburg, when Karl played it for me with such feeling…

I found my crutches, struggled to my feet and left the box. The music dimmed as the door closed behind me, and I found I was shaking.

The steps were smooth, and I was in such a hurry to get out of there that I almost slipped several times. It should have been frightening but I didn't care.

If I fall and crack my head open like Karl's pa, then it'll all be over.

Outside it was drizzling and the cool air hit my face. *The rain will be falling on Karl's grave – oh, God, why didn't they bury me in Flanders as well?*

There was a bar. I desperately wanted a drink, but I didn't want another incident.

Who cares?

"Schnapps, please. A large one."

My hands shook as I paid. *He probably thinks I'm an alcoholic. So fucking what.*

I had three more large ones, but they did nothing to dim the pain.

There's another way. A permanent one. My family won't be home for another hour or so.

But they were home, and Papa was livid.

"God knows, Franz, how hard we're trying to make allowances for you – but you've just ruined the evening completely. We had no idea where you'd gone, or why, so we came home and you weren't here, and now you stink of drink again…"

He went on, but I didn't hear a word.

I was at the airfield, suiting up to fly. Karl's aircraft was next to mine, and there was the Chief, and Johnny, and Geschke… all of them, the whole squadron.

I looked at Karl. *Wait for me, my love.*

"Have you anything to say for yourself?" Papa demanded.

"No," I replied calmly. "I'm going to bed. Good night."

They'll hear the shot, but it'll be too late. A tremendous feeling of peace filled me as I climbed the stairs. *It's almost over. In a few minutes I'll be where I belong.*

'Break your neck and legs!' the Chief shouted, and one after another we took up the cry.

Uhlig took hold of my propeller.

Last flight. I won't be coming back from this one.

I unlocked my desk drawer, got my pistol out and loaded it. As I raised it to my head, I met Karl's eyes gazing at me from the portrait on my desk.

'Don't do that, you stupid bastard. *Get a fucking grip.*'

There was real anger in his voice, as if he had hold of my shoulders and was shaking me.

'We died so you could live. Not for you to sit at home and shoot yourself, like some pathetic cunt.'

I put the gun on the desk.

'That's better. Now pull yourself together and get on with living,' he said, with contempt as well as anger, and I was suddenly deeply ashamed.

You wouldn't have done it, I thought as I looked at him. *But when you wanted to die the Tommies were there to oblige.*

'Come to bed, Franz,' he said gently, and put his arms round me.

Maybe it was the alcohol, but I fell asleep almost at once.

Karl and I sat on the terrace, watching the sun set across the lake. The evening was beautifully warm, the wall of the house holding the heat, and the soft air was filled with birdsong. Overhead the sky was paling, while in the west it flamed red and gold, and the still water reflected the colours back to Heaven.

He took hold of my hand and we sat there in silence, in the most profound feeling of love and peace. *I could sit here with you for ever...*

The light had almost gone. Without a word we got up, and went inside and up to bed.

When I woke it was as if he were still there, and my bed seemed to smell of him. *It was only a dream*, I thought as I became fully conscious. *He's dead – the house in Brandenburg is empty. And yet...*

I don't know what I'm going to do. I can't kill myself but I don't know how I'm going to go on. There is nothing left for me.

I have to stop feeling sorry for myself. I'm alive, and somehow I have to try to make a life.

There was a definite atmosphere when I went down to breakfast.

"Sorry about last night," I said.

Papa looked at me and sighed. "I just wish you'd said something. We were worried about you."

"My leg was hurting, and I didn't want to interrupt when you were listening."

"Is that why you got drunk? Because of the pain?"

I shrugged. "Partly."

"Well, I'm off to work," Papa said.

I lit a fag and poured myself another cup of coffee. *Go on living – but how?*

That bastard Hertel claims to be such a patriot. If I do go there in uniform then he can't refuse to help, can he?

As soon as I'd finished breakfast I dragged myself back upstairs and got my best uniform out of the wardrobe. I fastened my ribbons, Iron Cross First Class and pilot's badge onto the tunic, and thought for half a second about adding the wound badge.

No point, I thought – I shared Karl's opinion of them, and it was only restating the glaringly bloody obvious. I rolled up the trouser leg and pinned it, and got changed.

The Pour le Mérite was in its case in my desk, and I put it over my head and eased the ribbon under my collar.

I looked in the mirror. Franz Becker the law student had gone for ever, and in his place was an officer in spotless grey.

I walked to the hangar. Outside it, the band and the gun carriage were waiting. In the hangar Karl's coffin lay on the trestle table, the light filtering through the canvas onto his still face.

'I had a Comrade, a better one you won't find...'

A part of me really did die with you.

My bedroom came back into focus.

I'd better take my pistol, just in case of trouble. Hopefully the ungodly will see the holster and think twice, and I won't have to use it.

Mama came out of the drawing room, just as I reached the bottom of the stairs.

"Franz, you can't go out like that!" she exclaimed. "It's not safe!"

"I'll be fine. Don't fuss."

I got one or two sideways looks as I made my way to the Hertels' house, not that I gave a shit.

This time I'm not leaving without her address. I'll stay until I get it, even if I'm still there at Christmas.

When the maid answered the door, I pushed past her into the hall.

"Where's Hertel?" I demanded.

"In his study, sir," she said.

I knew the way. I flung the door open and went in.

"What the devil—" he began.

"Tell me where she is."

"I've already told you. She's found someone else."

"I want her address."

"Get out of my house or I'll call the police."

"You think you're such a patriot. Our company commander at Langemarck was older than you, and he died a hero's death. You stayed at home and joined the Fatherland Party."

"My health—"

"Your health. I knew men who went back to the Front after being badly wounded, even though they weren't fit. Don't give me that shit."

I hadn't raised my voice. I didn't need to. I felt completely cold, the way I used to when I dived for the attack.

"You stayed here and let us do the fighting. You wouldn't even see me, and then you fed me a load of crap. Give me her address. Now, you bastard."

Hertel had gone a nasty shade of greenish white, and his eyes were fixed. "All – all right," he stammered. "All right. Just – just give me a moment to write it down."

His hand was shaking so much he could hardly hold the pen. He finished writing and held out the paper to me. My right hand moved forward to take it. He shrank back with a choked little sound – and I looked down and saw the pistol in my hand.

Oh, Jesus Christ, what the hell am I doing?

"Don't try to stop me leaving," I said, taking the paper in my left hand.

I folded it one-handed and put it in my pocket, put the gun away, and left as fast as I could, wanting to put some distance between me and the house, in case he did call the police.

I took a winding route and found myself in the park. I sat on one of the benches, shaking from head to foot.

Would I actually have shot him? I remembered what Karl had said about Sophie von Schönwald's husband, when he'd gone home on leave and shot her lover dead: 'Shooting people becomes normal.'

I've spent four years of my life shooting people. Am I tainted for ever? I tried to tell myself I wouldn't have pulled the trigger, but I couldn't make myself believe it. *I wasn't even aware of having the gun in my hand until I looked down, so how can I know what I'd have done?*

Better get home and lock the gun away before I do shoot someone. I suddenly realised how fucking stupid I'd been. *Half the time you don't know where you are or what's happening – no, worse than that, you think you're at the Front. And you're out with a gun. What happens if you think some passer-by is a Tommy dropping down into the trench?*

They'd lock me up in some ghastly institution, and throw the key away.

I hurried home and up the stairs to my room, locked the gun in my desk and sagged onto my bed, trembling with relief – and then sat bolt upright.

How do I know nothing happened?

I scrabbled to unlock the drawer, my hands shaking.

The magazine was full.

Thank fuck for that. I locked the desk drawer again. *Maybe I should drop the key down a drain somewhere…*

There was a knock at the door. For a moment the room swam before my eyes.

"Franz, are you coming down to lunch?" Mama asked.

"Yes, I… er… I'll just get changed."

Papa gave me a very straight look when I joined them. *Oh shit, Hertel called the police and they're on their way to arrest a dangerous armed lunatic…*

"Where did you go?" he asked. "Your mother said you went out in uniform."

"To the Hertels'. Has he said anything?"

The look got even graver. "Why would he?"

"Oh, I was… er… rather rude, that's all."

"How did you get on?" Johanna asked.

"Well, I got Maria's address." My tone was very neutral, because now that I had the address I didn't quite know what to do.

My family exchanged looks.

"You did? What are you going to do?" Johanna's voice matched mine.

"I thought you were going to wait for them to approach you," Papa said.

"Franz, think very carefully," said Mama. "If she wanted you, she'd have got in touch by now."

"I think I need to see her," I said. "I need to know what's really happened."

"Just don't rush into anything," Mama said. "Especially not marriage. You're young and there are plenty of nice girls."

None of whom is likely to want a half-mad cripple, I didn't feel like saying.

"If she has my child then I'll want to get married."

"If."

"Who was the King who said that?" Johanna asked. "Wasn't he Spartan?"

Nice change of subject, Sis, I thought as Papa chided her for forgetting.

After lunch, the two of us went into the garden.

"Got a light?" she asked.

"Sis, what if they see?"

She shrugged. "Franz, would you like me to come with you?"

"No. Thanks, but I need to go by myself."

"Well, for God's sake don't go in uniform."

I laughed, rather uneasily. "Don't worry, I shan't do any such thing."

There was a long pause, and then she said, "Don't you think you should give yourself a bit more time?"

After what? I almost said, but there was no point trying to pretend.

"It wouldn't make any difference," I said slowly. "I think I'll feel just the same in thirty years' time."

She squeezed my arm.

"I'm not queer, Sis, not like Alfred. I've never wanted any other man. Just Karl."

"He was really special," she said. "There was something about him."

"Yes, there was."

Maybe she's right, I thought later. *Maybe it is too soon.* I looked at the picture of Karl and me, just before putting the light out. *I won't be able to have that on the bedside table if I'm married.*

What should I do? I asked him.

'You know what I think. I told you in Brandenburg – support the child, but don't get married unless you really want to.'

Is there a child, then?

But there was no answer.

I did nothing for three days, partly because I still wasn't sure whether Hertel would call the police and report me. That bitch of a wife of his was more than likely to spur him on – but I couldn't imagine him having the courage to tell her what had happened.

"Aren't you going to go to Stuttgart?" Mama asked over breakfast.

"Yes, some time."

Better get it done. No point having cold feet – and what for, anyway? What's anyone going to do to me?

I made myself as presentable as I could and got a cab to the station. All the way there I tried not to think about what I might find, because I had no idea what I wanted.

No, that wasn't true. What I wanted was to be back in summer '14, and have the idiot politicians and generals avoid the fucking war. Karl and I would still have fallen in love at some point, and we would have been happy.

I fell into a reverie. Karl was a famous concert pianist and I was his manager, and we travelled the world together...

Shit – we're here already. I almost fell off the train, and made my way to the taxi rank.

The horse trotted slowly out into the suburbs, the cab swaying on its knackered suspension. I looked out of the window at the spring blossom, and tried to be glad that I was alive.

"Here we are, sir."

"What? Oh, yes, thanks."

I got out awkwardly, and found I was in front of a neat house with a pretty, well-kept garden. The roses were covered in buds, and my longing to be with Karl in the rose garden was so strong that my throat tightened.

Get a grip, Franz.

I opened the gate, more aware of my mutilation than ever, and had a sudden attack of shaking.

'They're coming!' shouted Peter.

I shook my head. *I mustn't have an episode now.*

After a moment the shaking eased. *Get on with it, Franz. No one's going to shoot you, are they?*

I rang the bell, and waited. And rang it again.

I was about to give up when the door opened.

A small, grey-haired woman stood there. Maria, grown fifty years older. "Yes?"

"Er – does Maria Hertel live here?"

"Who wants to know?"

"Franz Becker."

She studied me closely.

"I really am," I said. "I don't look much like those pictures any more."

"Yes, so you are. I can see that now. You'd better come in."

She led the way into the living room and rang the bell.

"Do have a seat. Would you like coffee?"

"Er, yes. Thank you."

"Maria's out, but she shouldn't be much longer."

There was a rather awkward silence, broken by the maid bringing coffee.

Where in God's name do I start?

"I'm Maria's grandmother, on her mother's side," the woman said, her tone not exactly friendly.

"I would have come before," I said, "but I didn't have the address."

She looked at me in frank disbelief, which turned to neutrality. "Oh. That doesn't entirely surprise me. My daughter... well, maybe that should wait."

"Maria's father told me she has a... that she met someone."

"Oh, did he? Well—"

The door opened and Maria came in, saw me, and stopped dead in astonishment. The small child on her hip gazed at me with brown eyes, just like my own.

The three of us stared at each other, Maria and I both speechless.

"I'll leave you to talk," said her grandmother, and left the room.

Maria put the child on the sofa and sat down. "How are you?" she asked.

She was thinner than I remembered, and her auburn hair was tied back in a rather severe bun. Her skin was just as lovely and clear, and her blue eyes looked at me with an expression that I couldn't quite read. She didn't seem pleased to see me, but she didn't seem annoyed either.

"Oh, fine, thanks. And you?"

"Yes. Fine... I'm so sorry about your leg."

The child was still staring at me. "Mama."

"Yes, darling?"

"Who's that?"

"That's your papa."

That's... your... papa.

"Maria, did you say...?"

She smiled for the first time. "Yes. Can't you see? His eyes are just like yours."

"What's his name?"

"Karl, after your friend. There was so much about you both in the papers."

"May I hold him?"

She picked him up and placed him carefully on my left leg, the sudden weight surprising for such a little fellow. His eyes grew huge and he reached towards her.

"Karl," I said softly, and a pair of warm brown eyes looked up at me. My heart contracted.

My son. This is my son. And whatever happens, he comes first, now and for the rest of my life.

"What I don't understand is why you've turned up now," Maria said.

"Your parents wouldn't tell me where you were."

She sighed.

"And you knew I was home," I added, "but you didn't contact me."

She sighed again. "You stopped writing."

"Only after you did. I think you'd better tell me the whole story."

"A couple of months after you went back to the Front, I realised I was pregnant. Mama and Papa were livid. They called me a – they said I'd brought disgrace on the family. Mama locked me in my bedroom – actually locked me up like a prisoner – and then they took me to Konstanz. They rented a villa outside the town, and told everyone my husband had been killed. I wrote to you, several times, to tell you I was expecting your child, but you never replied."

"I never got the letters. I wrote to you but you didn't answer, and I thought you'd lost interest in me."

"Mama told our housekeeper to forward all mail to her. And she didn't let me out on my own."

"So your letters to me never got posted."

"So it seems… Anyway, when Karl was born they wanted me to give him away, but I couldn't do that. Grannie had come to stay for my last three months, and she backed me up." She laughed.

"She pointed out that a war widow wouldn't give away her late husband's child, so they were caught out by their own lie. But they kept on, and I was afraid they'd take Karl away in the night, and tell everyone he'd died. Grannie said I could come and live here."

"You've had quite a time." *Brave girl*, I thought with sudden respect.

"It wasn't easy."

"But why didn't you write when you got here, and tell me?"

"Because you hadn't written for months, and I'd started to believe what they were saying – that you'd just been having fun with me."

I was, and you were having fun with me – but little Karl changes all that.

"And I had made up my mind to give him up, but every time I looked at him I just couldn't."

"I am so glad you didn't," I said, and suddenly I couldn't say another word.

I put my hand gently on Karl's head, felt the warm life beneath my palm as I stroked his hair, and then I took one tiny hand in mine.

I have taken more lives than I can count, and here is one, just one, to put in the balance...

"Tell me what happened to you," she said.

I managed to find my voice. "There's nothing to add to what you read in the papers. I got shot down and my knee was wrecked, so they amputated. I was in hospital for months and I got home a few weeks ago."

And that is all I can tell you. I'll never be able to say anything about how much I will always love Karl, or about the war.

The gulf between us was enormous, and there was no way of crossing it. At the same time I knew that, as Lentzke had once put it, I had to do right by little Karl, and by Maria. *No one is going to call my son a bastard.*

'Be careful, Franz,' Karl said. 'Acknowledge the boy, support them – but you don't have to marry her.'

But I do.

'Then break your neck and legs!'

Maria and I were on the train. Karl stood on the platform, his eyes grey and sad. The train started to move, and we waved to each other until I couldn't see him any more.

I sat down, and Maria smiled.

'You're all mine now, Franz,' she said.

I shivered. *That was that stupid dream I had in '17 – and now Maria and I are leaving Karl behind...*

'Of course you're not – I'll always be beside you. Do whatever you need to do.'

I shook my head. I was facing Maria, with my son on my knee.

"Maria, will you marry me?"

She smiled, and it lit her eyes. "Yes."

Whatever may happen, whether we're happy together or not, I have a son and a wife. Maybe in time she and I will come to care about each other, maybe not. It doesn't matter. I have already known the love of my life and I can't expect to feel that again, for anyone.

"Karl," I said, and his warm brown eyes looked up at me again.

I brushed the dark hair back from his forehead. *I wish there were a God, so I could pray for you to be safe.*

All I can do is hope, with all my heart, that my son will never go to war.

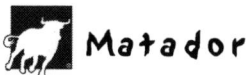

For exclusive discounts on Matador titles,
sign up to our occasional newsletter at
troubador.co.uk/bookshop